ABOUT THE AUTHOR

Hugh Cornwell is one of the UK's finest songwriting talents and accomplished live performers. As the original guitarist, singer and main songwriter in the British rock band **The Stranglers**, he's enjoyed massive success with ten hit albums and twenty-one Top 40 singles, etching himself into Europe and the USA's musical psyche with classic songs, including 'Peaches', 'No More Heroes', 'Golden Brown', 'Always the Sun' and 'Duchess'. His latest solo album *Totem & Taboo* was released to rave reviews. Cornwell's first novel *Window on the World* was published in 2011 and *Arnold Drive* is his second work of fiction.

ARNOLD DRIVE

ARNOLD DRIVE

Hugh Cornwell

unbound

This edition first published in 2014

Unbound
4–7 Manchester Street, Marylebone, London, W1U 2AE
www.unbound.co.uk

Typeset by Unbound

Cover design by Mecob

A CIP record for this book is available from the British Library

ISBN 978-1-78352-051-0 (limited edition)

ISBN 978-1-78352-052-7 (PB edition)

ISBN 978-1-78352-053-4 (ebook)

Printed by Printondemand-worldwide.com, UK

10 9 8 7 6 5 4 3 2

ACKNOWLEDGMENTS

With special thanks to the Pajaro Verde near Cadiz and the Posada del Mar on Isla Mujeres and all who sail in them, for providing the creative atmosphere without which *Arnold Drive* could never have been written. I'd also like to thank Caroline Michel of PFD and Rachael Kerr of Unbound for their unswerving support.

CHAPTER 1

Arnold sat down and closed his eyes. He waited, knowing it was the only way to deal with the situation. If he kept his eyes closed for long enough he knew he'd open them up again and be able to carry on. By that time the sun would have passed on in the sky and there would be no shadows cast by its rays hitting the window frame. Whenever the sun came out at this time of year, he was always unable to move around his living room. The criss-cross lines of the lattice-work's shadow fell across the plain buff carpet and he found it impossible to negotiate his way around the south-facing room without his feet landing on one or more of the bars. With any luck, a cloud or two would pass directly in front of the sun and he could feel the lower light intensity through his closed eyelids and be able to move across the room, either to his study or the kitchen, or, if not that far, to the hallway. He'd tried to do this a couple of times without opening his eyes but had bumped into the furniture on the way, leaving him even more distraught. It had made him feel relieved to see grey skies in the summer and when he thought about it, he couldn't remember when he'd started noticing the bars on the carpet.

It had all started when he was small and he'd been given a

proper bed to sleep in rather than a cot. He would get ready for bed and find it impossible to get in without disturbing the tucked in edges of the blankets. The top white sheet had been neatly folded over for him to rest his chin on once he was in, but he would have to go around the bed first making sure the blankets were properly tucked in between the mattress and the base. Once he was sure all was in place he would carefully ease himself in without disturbing anything so that, once in, he could look down and see the bed as it should be. Only then could he switch off the bedside lamp and go to sleep. In those days, he experienced a recurring dream. He was in bed in the middle of a vast empty room and would feel terribly small, bewildered and alone. Sometimes he still experienced this sensation before falling asleep and would have to switch on the light and get his eyes accustomed to the dimensions of the bedroom again before being able to sleep. He'd managed to get over that hurdle with time but other things began to preoccupy him over the years. When he'd tried to rationalise it all, the relative importance of these preoccupations had started to confuse him and he would have to stop, or risk becoming very muddled and disturbed about life in general. The only thing that helped was to think of God. In fact, the only place he really felt relaxed was in a church, safe within the stained glass, and it had seemed as good a reason as any to decide to become a priest.

He felt the light fade on his face but waited before opening his eyes as he was enjoying the sensation. When he did open them he saw a large bank of clouds moving in front of the sun which meant he could wander about his living room for a while. He decided to make a cup of tea and tidy up a few things before thinking about what he would wear for the last supper. The Indian restaurant was booked for 7.30 and he was looking forward to the occasion, although the reason that prompted it was regrettable. Despite a campaign lasting more than three years, the church authorities had decided to close St. Tobias's and sell it to a property developer. The dwindling numbers of his congregation had persuaded the Diocesan Advisory Committee and the Church Commissioners to consider the church's market value in such a prime location in the West Country. Arnold had made a study of estate agents' windows in Corsham and estimated the church and the acre and a half of surrounding land could be worth several million pounds. The insides of the church were to be knocked out and the building converted into luxury apartments, though thankfully the exterior would remain and the graves would be preserved because they lay within hallowed ground.

The final congregation had gathered the Sunday before and Mrs. Cartwright had suggested then that they have a little get-together. There would be just the four of them: Professor Hatswell, Mrs. Cartwright and her daughter Lucy, and Arnold. Lucy was down on vacation from Durham University for the summer and Arnold could see no reason to object to Hermione bringing her along. He vaguely recalled meeting her years before at a fete at St. Tobias's, but all he could remember was that she had blonde pigtails. Thankfully the grey clouds remained and Arnold was able to move about freely the whole afternoon. He'd noticed several wispy cobweb threads dangling from a light fitting in the hallway that morning and he was looking forward to removing them.

There were breaks in the cloud as he strode down Corsham High Street towards the Jaipur. He'd been there before several months earlier when the visiting bishop had taken him for lunch, to tell him the news about the church being sold. He'd enjoyed the food and was looking forward to reading through the menu again. Before he went in he saw Professor Hatswell through the window sitting next to the bar with a smug grin on his face, as always, obviously relishing the fact he'd got there first, and was in the position to monopolise the evening as he usually did.

'Arnold, old chap. Only a few minutes late. Not to worry. Everything's under control. Hermione will be late, of course.'

Arnold chose not to reply to this taunt and changed the subject:

'Hello, Trevor. Can I buy you a drink?'

'No, let me do the honours, as I was here first. Gin and tonic?'

Arnold noticed Trevor hadn't been there long enough to order himself a drink and took solace in that, as he nodded and sat down.

'Any news about your cottage yet? As I said before, you can always shack up with me if you get stuck, there's plenty of room.'

'No, none yet,' Arnold offered.

Now that the church had been sold off he was expecting something official in the post telling him to move out of his cottage, which also belonged to the Diocese. The bishop had explained he would receive something in lieu of his stipend, but unfortunately the cottage was to be sold as well, so he would have to find somewhere else to live.

'Look at it on the bright side, Arnold,' he'd told him. 'It's an opportunity for you to get out of this straitjacket. You've been in Corsham longer than I care to remember. You've still

4

got an active, curious mind. Here's your chance to exercise it. Jump, and a net will appear, as Our Lord tells us.' Arnold wasn't sure whether the Lord actually had said those words, but he recognised the window of opportunity the redundancy represented. It was whether he could jump or not that was more to the point. But he had no intention of taking Hatswell up on his offer. It was difficult putting up with the pompous fellow at the best of times and he couldn't imagine anything worse than having to deal with him on a daily basis. Lord, no. He would have to find some other solution.

The drinks arrived and they'd just clinked glasses when the door opened and in trotted Hermione Cartwright followed by her daughter Lucy.

'Hello, you two. Sorry we're late. Women's prerogative, I'm afraid. Something you two bachelors won't be used to. Arnold, you do remember my daughter Lucy? Grown up a bit since you last met her. Lucy, this is Trevor Hatswell.'

Arnold couldn't identify this Lucy as the one he'd met before. He did a quick calculation and realised it had been at least five years earlier, making her a young teenager at the time. She'd since grown into a younger version of her mother and had overtaken her in height.

Hatswell made a feeble attempt to be charming. He fawned over her, which made Arnold think of Terry-Thomas:

'What a delightful daughter you have, Hermione. You must be very proud of her. Obviously inherited your beauty, and hopefully with it your unquestionable ability to put all men at her mercy. How say you, Lucy?'

Lucy smiled politely, not bothering to hide how bored she was at this comment. Instead she turned to Arnold:

'Hello again. I remember meeting you once on my fifteenth birthday, at St. Tobias's. It was the Harvest Festival, and mum's pumpkin won first prize. Do you remember?'

Arnold's memory was failing him. He'd given away so many medallions for prize vegetables over the years. He had no idea which year she was referring to and muttered:

'Oh, yes, yes. I think I do recall the year,' and nodded, offering a faint smile.

Trevor ordered some drinks for the ladies and they all sat down and studied the menus. Lucy seemed to be an expert at Indian food, having travelled to India during her gap year, and she explained the names of several of the dishes to them. It gave her an opportunity to contribute to the evening as she'd assumed she would be the gooseberry, sitting there with two of her mother's admirers.

They were shown to their table, which was a booth for four, and Arnold made sure he wasn't hemmed in at the window by excusing himself before sitting down. In the toilet he washed his hands and was wiping them on a paper towel when he spotted a hole in the wooden panel under the sink in which, he presumed, he should place his used towel. Feeling curious he opened this hinged panel to find no basket there for the used towel to fall into. He felt one of his familiar panic moments coming on and stood there transfixed, not knowing what to do next. He must have stood there for several minutes, unable to move, and could think of no way out of the situation. The door opened and another diner came in so he quickly closed the panel door and stuffed the wet paper towel into his jacket pocket, and left to rejoin the others. He sat down and found himself sitting next to Hermione, opposite Lucy.

'There you are, Arnold,' Hatswell said, 'we were just wondering where you'd got to. Hermione tells me the church will stand empty for several months, before they begin the conversion. Have you been lucky enough to look over the architect's plans? Spill the beans.'

It was true the work wasn't due to start until the autumn at the earliest, which made the closure even harder for Arnold to bear.

'Not yet,' he replied. 'I'm expecting an invitation to the architect's office in Bath this week, as a matter of fact. I hope they don't mess around too much with the floor. Apparently they intend to move the brass to a new location, but it hasn't been decided yet where to put it.'

Lucy claimed to have rubbed the brass herself and still had the rubbing hanging on the wall of her bedroom,

'Took me a whole day to do that. I'll never get rid of it. It's one of the things I really like to see when I come back from uni.'

She told him her interest in brass rubbing may have helped her gain her place at Durham studying Philosophy. Apparently the tutor interviewing her had his own brass rubbings up on the walls of his rooms and it had obviously helped break the ice between them.

'I like to think maybe it kept me in his mind when they made their final choices for the course,' she said brightly. Arnold felt she was being unfair on herself. She looked striking enough to leave a lasting impression on anyone.

The food arrived and they all tucked into the various curries and Lucy became the guide to what she'd helped them order. It was clear Hatswell had decided to make a night of it, ordering gin and tonics throughout the meal for himself and anyone else who cared to join him. Arnold didn't drink that much and after the first two rounds he moved on to water. Hermione was determined to keep pace with Hatswell and the two of them chattered away about various local issues, sometimes completely forgetting Arnold and Lucy were sitting there with them. Arnold quietly enjoyed his food and listened to their conversation, occasionally adding weight to what one or the other was saying. Lucy was also kept on the sidelines and Arnold felt her staring at him once or twice, but he never looked back. Disappointingly, she fell into the role of being the representative of the younger generation and would be referred to by Hermione as if she wasn't even there, with expressions such as:

'How can they even begin to realise how lucky they are!' and 'How they can be so worldly, yet so young!'

At one such outburst Arnold looked across and saw Lucy raise her eyes to the heavens as if to say, 'Please spare me this, Mother!'

Everyone seemed to be very hungry and in no time they'd eaten their way through all the dishes and were ordering coffees. Hatswell insisted they have a brandy together and as they fell silent to digest the food Arnold could sense their minds were returning to the subject of St. Tobias's. Hermione turned to him and gently placed a hand on his wrist, squeezing it:

'Dear Arnold. What are you going to do with yourself? Have you even thought about it?'

All eyes were upon him and he opened his mouth as if to say something. He sensed they were expecting something of note to issue from his lips but nothing came to mind:

'No, not really ... It hasn't yet ... quite ... sunken in,' was all he could manage to say, and he nervously looked around to see if he could find any answers in their faces.

Hermione increased the pressure on his wrist and offered him a 'brave face' smile.

'Shall we get the bill?' he offered, to lighten the mood and to divert attention away from himself. He could feel the dampness of the paper towel as it had seeped through the pocket lining of his jacket during the meal. He'd inadvertently sat on it and now had a wet left buttock.

CHAPTER 2

As he walked home that night through lamplit streets, Arnold noticed how different Corsham looked to during the daytime. The true colour of the Bath stone seemed mute in the orange light and a uniformity he didn't care for enveloped the town. It looked like the streets of any number of English towns, with none of Corsham's charm and character. He found himself heading in the direction of St. Tobias's and didn't try to fight the impulse. Besides, the warm air was serving to dry out his trousers from the paper towel. He was still feeling irritated by Hatswell, who'd insisted on picking up the entire cost of the meal despite all their protests.

'Don't be silly, Arnold, we all fall on hard times. You may have to do the same for me one day,' he had thrown in, as he scooped up the wallet containing the bill the waiter delivered to the table.

What annoyed Arnold was the fact that he wasn't broke at all. The Diocese was still paying him full salary for another three months and after that he would be on a small monthly pension. But he'd certainly feel the pinch once he started to pay for his own accommodation. Rounding the next corner he saw St. Tobias's church, flanked by its mature yews, and stopped to admire the building. Even the ugly amber light from the street couldn't mask the beauty of the flying buttresses supporting the tower. His fingers moved around the key fob in his right trouser pocket and felt the large key that would open the church door. He walked up the flagstone path, placed the key in the lock, and heard the familiar sound of the old mechanism turning. He unlatched the twisted iron ring and slowly pushed the door open. His footsteps echoed in the chill space as he advanced into the vestibule. He needed no light to help him navigate his way around the body of the church, as he was familiar with every little unevenness in the flagstones beneath his feet. The only light available was thrown through the windows from the street lamps but he didn't mind it there within the church. All was as he'd left it the Sunday before and he was glad he'd decided to come by. He sat down in one of the pews midway to the nave, next to the central aisle, and closed his eyes for a few moments to pray. He was halfway through when he heard the front door moving on its hinges. He'd left it ajar when he came in, but was panicked at the thought of being discovered there alone at night. He stood up, stepped into the aisle, turned, and was immediately caught in the spotlight of a torch.

'Vicar! Relieved to see it's you, sir. Saw the door open and thought we had an intruder. Everything all right?'

'Yes, officer. Nothing to worry about.'

'Well then, I'll leave you to it. Goodnight, sir.'

The light went off and he was alone again in the darkness, blinded for a time. He heard the door pulled to, and the policeman mount his bicycle and pedal away. Arnold had felt his heartbeat quicken, and he sat back in the pew to let it slow down to normal speed. He recommenced the Lord's

Prayer and got all the way through this time without being disturbed.

In the post the next day was a letter from the architects in Bath inviting him to call by and take a look at the plans. He was curious to find out how they were intending to carve the space up into pieces and make each one into a self-contained unit. He assumed one apartment would benefit from having the bell tower and he wondered what would become of the bells. He made a note to bring the subject up with the architects.

It was a dry day outside, so after his boiled egg and soldiers he decided to take a cycle ride around the meadow behind Corsham Court. He enjoyed it there, as he was unlikely to bump into anyone he knew and be drawn into conversation away from his muddled thoughts. As the bishop had pointed out over lunch, there were many possibilities for him. Over the years he'd sometimes felt a wanderlust that he'd never had the time or the money to indulge. He certainly wouldn't be awash with cash, but a man with time on his hands is a rich man. Spain had always been a place that had fascinated him and although he'd never been there he'd read a lot about its turmoil throughout history. Perhaps he would go there for a visit.

People would be surprised to discover just how much time a church took to maintain and keep ticking over, even one with low attendances like St. Tobias's. Since the early seventies, when he'd arrived in Corsham, there had been a constant battle against the ravages of time and the plunderings of nature. He'd also been expected to take part in the local community and its activities, and most evenings of the week there were meetings and events to attend. He knew all the constabulary by their names. Well, he had done until they'd closed the local police station.

He approached the mere and got off his bike to sit for a while and look at the comings and goings of the birdlife along the banks. Yes, you could say he'd been nothing but a glorified caretaker for the past thirty years, who each Sunday was allowed to get up on his soapbox and reveal God's love amid the woes of modern society. These were some of the thoughts in his head that morning.

'Hello?' he heard from behind him. He turned to see who it was and Lucy Cartwright came striding towards him through the uncut grass.

'Good morning,' he replied. She came and perched herself on a tree stump a few feet away from where his bicycle lay on the bank.

'Hope you're feeling better than mum does this morning. She didn't get up till way past nine ... Oh, now, I don't think I should be telling you that sort of thing, should I?'

They both laughed and he told her not to worry. She took that as licence to continue:

'God, the way she and the professor were knocking it back ... Oh, sorry, I didn't mean to ...' she went quiet and blushed.

Arnold shook his head dismissively, saying, 'Now what sort of a man of the cloth would I be if I couldn't converse in the vernacular? Over the years I've known your mother I've discovered that nothing surprises me about her. But don't worry, she carries herself very well. I'm very glad we're friends.'

'Yes,' she said. 'So am I.'

They sat in silence for a minute or so. She got up and

wandered past him down to the bank and stood with her back to him, and he caught himself admiring her shape. He noticed she was wearing shorts.

'I like it here,' she said, 'it's one of the first places I come when I get back from uni. Ducks are my favourite animals. They're so funny. The way they waddle about.'

'How do you like studying Philosophy?' he asked her.

'Oh, it's quite interesting. After a while, though, you realise there are more questions than answers. Don't you find that with religion?'

After saying this, she felt she was being too forward and turned to see if she'd made him feel awkward, but Arnold was enjoying their conversation and paused to think of an answer for her.

'The trouble is,' he said, 'I'm not too sure what I understand about faith any more.'

He realised he was being far too frank with her and wished he hadn't been so honest, but he needn't have worried.

'That makes absolute sense considering what's happened to St. Tobias's,' she nodded.

She came back up to where he was sitting on the grass and said, 'Mum's terribly worried about you, Reverend Drive.'

He looked up and caught her eyes in his, and said 'Please call me Arnold.'

Arnold found himself marooned in various rooms at home over the next few days, due to the reappearance of the shadows on the living room carpet. He'd spent the whole of Wednesday morning stranded in his kitchen, and had filled the time scrupulously cleaning the sink and its surround. It was gleaming like new by the time the clouds came and the latticework of the windows disappeared from the floor. On Thursday, he missed lunch as he found himself stuck in the hallway when the sun came out. He'd just got in the doorway after arriving back from the bookshop, and was taking off his bicycle clips from around his trouser bottoms, looking forward to browsing through a book about the Spanish Inquisition. He was making his way to the kitchen to get something to eat when the bars reappeared.

'Blast!' he said to himself. He ended up sitting at the bottom of the stairs reading for several hours, and by the time the sun had gone it was past four o'clock and he was famished. The only way of dealing with these inconveniences was to keep the living room curtains drawn the whole day, but he'd tried that and it had made him feel depressed.

Friday arrived, the day he'd arranged to visit the architect's offices and have a look over the plans. Hermione had offered to give him a lift into Bath as she had some shopping to do, and at ten o'clock he heard the sound of her car horn outside.

'All set?' she asked as he got in next to her. He nodded and they pulled off from the kerb, heading towards Pickwick. They spent the first ten minutes in silence and Arnold discovered he was quite sad not to see Lucy in the car. He wanted to ask Hermione where she was, but Hermione was able to satisfy his curiosity as soon as they reached Box.

'Lucy's gone to some festival for the weekend, called the Big Chill, or something. Can't quite see what the attraction is, camping out in a field full of strangers, using those awful smelly Portaloo things, just to listen to some music. But it's supposed to be quite civilised, so she tells me.'

'Do you have any idea if she takes drugs at these things?' he asked, suddenly realising how blunt it must have sounded.

'Well, her boyfriend from Durham looks the type, but these days it's hard to tell. She seems the same as ever when you talk to her, so I presume if she is it's not something desperately dangerous, or harmful. He's meeting her there, apparently.'

Arnold felt a lump come into his throat, which he thought was strange, and swallowed. Perhaps it was the mention of the word 'boyfriend', but he considered the whole possibility of him feeling jealous too ludicrous to consider. He was glad Lucy was with someone Hermione knew and trusted.

'I'm sure there's nothing to worry about, she seems pretty level headed to me,' he said, and they drove on towards Bath in silence.

Hermione switched on the radio and they listened to *Woman's Hour* for the remainder of the journey. The sun was out and the city looked at its best as they drove in from the A46 roundabout past the rugby ground. Arnold rarely went to Bath unless for a specific reason, and because of this was always surprised how striking he found the architecture. The grand terraces stood to attention as they moved slowly along London Road in the queue of traffic. It took them a good fifteen minutes to get to the top of Milsom Street where she dropped him off. They arranged to meet in a couple of hours back at the same place, by which time Hermione thought she would have shopped herself out. Arnold entered an open front door on George Street and climbed the stairs to the first floor where a receptionist sat, who checked a list of names in front of her.

'Ah, yes. Reverend Drive. Here you are,' she said, finding his name. 'Please take a seat for a moment and Mr. Cubitt will be with you shortly.'

A few minutes later, a door opened and a bespectacled man in his shirtsleeves appeared and led him into an office.

'So glad you could make it in, Mr. Drive. We're all really excited about this project. I hope you'll find what we've come up with interesting.'

He took him towards a table by the window on which sat a remarkably accurate scale model of St. Tobias's. Next to it there were some large detailed sheets bearing the elevations and proposals. Cubitt pulled up a chair for him.

'Please take a seat and have a good look. May I offer you a cup of tea or coffee?'

Arnold asked for some water and turned his attention back to the plans. Cubitt left the room and Arnold tried to make sense of what he was looking at. It was unfamiliar to his eyes, and he was just recognising certain aspects of the building when Cubitt came back with a glass of water in his hand.

'It's going to be three marvellous apartments. The one on the top floor will inherit the bell tower, *sans* bells, of course, and the lower two will lie to the left and right of the stairway.'

'The Holy Trinity,' Arnold said.

'Sorry, I don't follow you?' Cubitt replied.

'Three apartments ... the Holy Trinity,' explained Arnold. 'I thought it may have been intentional. Perhaps not.'

'Oh, I see. Yes, quite. Well, as you can see we've made a point of making as few structural changes as possible to the layout of the church. That way each apartment becomes a unique piece of its history. Distinctly different, but linked? It should create an atmosphere of community amongst the owners. Well, that's the theory. Look, I'll leave you alone for a while. Take your time. I'll be next door if you need anything.'

He smiled and left Arnold to draw his own conclusions.

It became clear the architects had paid great attention to detail. Not only had they resisted the temptation to tamper with the basic structure of the church, they'd also tried to retain many of the internal features and incorporate them into their designs. This came as a pleasant surprise to Arnold, who recalled being told by someone in the building trade that the initials RIBA stand for Remember I'm the Bloody Architect. All the stained glass windows had been preserved in their entirety and the choir stalls had a footnote attached, allowing them to be kept in place if a prospective buyer so desired. This he was especially relieved to learn, as they bore some interestingly carved misericords. A tightly spiralled, wrought iron staircase ascended into the bell tower where there was a bench seat for viewing purposes. This would afford views across to the Almshouses and Corsham Court, a good half-mile away.

He spent half an hour studying the plans as he knew Hermione would quiz him when they met up later on. Drawing his chair back from the table, his eyes fell upon the scale model of St. Tobias's. He noticed a provision for underground parking but realised that in itself could be problematic. The last thing they wanted was to disturb any of the poor souls lying underground. Many of them had been victims of the Black Death. He picked up his glass of water and drained it. The door opened and Cubitt entered, and Arnold sensed his time was up.

'How's it going? Anything you'd like to ask?'

'There was just one thing. What will happen to the bells?' he ventured.

'Ah, the bells ... Well, I presume they'll remain the property of the Diocese. I suggest you take it up with them. They'll be stored, no doubt, until their final destination is determined. Anything else?'

Arnold couldn't think of anything, but did enquire as to what would become of the scale model, as he'd taken quite a fancy to it. Cubitt assured him he would be welcome to it after the project had been completed.

'Please accept it as a present. I'll make a note to that effect and attach it to the project file. All we'll need is an address, or phone number, to let you know when it can be collected.'

He took Arnold back to reception and down the stairs to the front door, adding, 'Yes, my wife was baptised at St. Tobias's, probably by your good self. Her parents used to live in Corsham in the seventies. In fact, that's where she was born.'

He didn't recognise the surname Cubitt mentioned, but was grateful for the promise of the miniature St. Tobias's to keep.

Strolling down George Street to Queen Square, he realised everybody he met cleverly avoided the subject of what would happen to him. It bemused him that he was never, ever seen as a normal human being, doing normal things, and subject to the vagaries of existence like most people in society. He supposed most would think he'd be sent to some other church somewhere in the country, rather like a supply teacher, or a member of the armed forces, going wherever he was needed, to the latest campaign somewhere. That's how they probably saw it, a constant battle between

Good and Evil, and he was the crusader, struggling to save the fallen souls from landing in the lap of the Devil. How out of touch they all were.

He'd been made redundant; it was as simple as that.

CHAPTER 3

By the time Hermione came to pick him up, Arnold was ready to leave Bath. He'd strolled up to Victoria Park and had a coffee in the cafeteria above the tennis courts. There were a couple of games in progress but he hadn't paid much attention to them. All that perforated his bubble on the veranda was the noise of the ball hitting the rackets and he spent his time trying to work out how many bars there were in the railings surrounding the courts. Then an argument broke out in one of the games, and he found himself being dragged out of his calculations into the real world of frustration and anger. He drained his coffee and got up to leave. His whole visit had taken about two hours, so he thought that by the time he reached George Street he should be just in time for his lift.

As he rounded the corner, he spotted Hermione's car next to the steps. The emergency lights were flashing and he hoped he hadn't kept her waiting. A traffic warden was taking an interest from across the street, so he quickened his pace. He got to the car, jumped in and they sped off, heading east towards the London Road.

'My word, you've been busy,' he declared when he saw what looked like bags from clothing shops piled high on the back seat.

'I know, it looks bad, doesn't it?' she agreed. 'But they're not all guilty pleasures, Arnold. Some of them are for Lucy. One of the advantages of having daughters. You can make guesses about styles and sizes for them. And if she doesn't like something, I can have it. How were the architects?'

'There was a lot to take in. On the whole, I like what they've done.'

'Tell you what, why don't you come and have lunch with me and give me the details?' she invited.

'Yes, I'd like that. Thank you.'

The thing he admired about Hermione was she always seemed to know what was needed at any given time. They'd become friends after her husband had left her for his secretary and she'd started helping him out at St. Tobias's. Lucy had been away at boarding school then, so she'd had plenty of time on her hands. From flower arranging to organising fetes, Hermione was able to turn her hand to just about anything and bring in results with a minimum of fuss, which was what particularly appealed to him. If there's one thing he abhorred in life it was fuss. If anything involved too much of it he could quite easily go without.

They pulled up outside her house and Arnold helped carry in the bags from the back seat.

'There, that's done. Now let's go to the kitchen and I'll make you something. Will an omelette do?'

Once he was seated at her pine kitchen table he was ready to tell her about what he'd seen. He liked sitting there, talking to her whilst she busied herself preparing food. They'd done it many times, especially when there were important things to discuss concerning St. Tobias's. He watched her as she moved about the room, knowing exactly where everything was, bending down or reaching on tiptoe to open a cupboard for something she needed, a whisk, or an ingredient. Whenever he did the same thing at home it would take him forever to remember where anything was, with the result that his cooking was a painfully slow process. But he'd got used to the pace of that aspect of his life and was accustomed to remaining hungry for long periods of time.

He told her all he could remember of what he'd seen, and finished by telling how he'd been promised the scale model. She noticed the pleasure with which he said this and stopped to look at him for a few seconds.

'Dear, dear Arnold. Bless you,' she announced before turning back to continue cooking.

After they'd eaten they sat and exchanged memories of some of their shared moments in the history of St. Tobias's. There were the awful storms in 1988 when a tall plane tree had missed the bell tower by a matter of inches, followed by the fund to raise money for the subsequent damage to the nave. Then the period in the mid-nineties when it became clear someone was pilfering lead from the roof under cover of darkness, and the arrest of the gang responsible after a raid by police on a remote country pub. Hermione even recalled the first time she'd met Arnold; at a Women's Institute talk by a local stone sculptor, in the library. He felt terribly ashamed to admit the details had slipped from his mind and she mockingly reprimanded him about it. He found himself accepting a glass of brandy from her and chinked glasses across the kitchen table. It was the first alcohol he'd drunk since their meal the week before at the Jaipur and it went straight to his head. Hermione put on some music and they started listening to Glenn Miller. She impulsively grabbed his hand and said:

'Come on, up you get, sir. The lady wishes to dance!'

She led him through some steps but he was finding it difficult to keep up. Then a less frenetic number began to play and their pace slowed. She clung to him and continued to lead, and he obediently followed her. It was the closest he'd ever been to her and he liked the way she smelt. It was comfortable and secure having her head resting there on his right collarbone. Then he felt her face turn towards his and she gently raised her mouth and kissed him on the lips. The music ended and they both stopped still in the silence. That brief period before the next number started was one of the longest passages of time Arnold had ever known. It wasn't unpleasant, but he had no idea what to do next. He began to feel embarrassed and drew away from her warmth, then instantly knew he'd done the wrong thing. He felt her body tense up and she looked unhappy, and all he could think of was to say,

'I'm sorry, Hermione. You must forgive me. I think I should be going home now.'

By the time he'd walked home the effect of the brandy had worn off. He turned the last corner and managed to walk on the paving stones without touching any of the edges, and this made him feel more his normal self. He didn't know what had come over him. He'd never, ever, thought about Hermione in a sexual way in all the time he'd known her, and he wondered if in some way he had accidentally given her the wrong impression. He spent the rest of that day going over and over the chain of events at lunch, trying to find some-thing he'd done that could have sparked her behaviour. In the end, he concluded he hadn't done anything wrong and she had kissed him, not the other way round. As dusk fell, he began his familiar little rituals around the house in the hope it would make him feel better. The telephone rang several times but he didn't answer. If it was something important they would ring back, but then it occurred to him it may have been Hermione.

He made himself a sandwich and a cup of cocoa, and sat in his favourite chair in the living room to eat. Yes, it may well have been Hermione trying to call him. She'd realised she'd upset him and wanted to apologise. It had been a strange sensation, kissing on the lips. He tried to recall the last time he'd done it. Slowly he trawled back through his life and settled upon the girlfriend he'd begun to see during his undergraduate days in Guildford in the late sixties.

He remembered drinking pints of beer and sitting down by the river with her in the summer months, and kissing then. They'd seen each other for several months before she had broken it off, without them ever becoming intimate. The kissing had been quite passionate at times, he recalled, but his shy nature had prevented him from letting go and allowing his hands to explore her body. He remembered enjoying the kissing. The girl had introduced him to French kissing, with the tongue, and he'd found it rather novel. He started to look back objectively, almost as if he were thinking not about himself, but about another person entirely, it had been that long ago. He wondered what had stopped him from becoming more adventurous with women. Carnal pleasures had never been directly condemned in his studies, just promiscuity. So he had to admit it was his own, introverted nature that was at fault. But the concept of blame was not helpful, as that suggested a wrongdoing, and more than just the outcome of his inaction. There was no wrong or right about it.

He wondered if he would ever get to spend a night with a woman, and what it would feel like. He finished his cocoa and went to bed.

Soon after nine o'clock the next day, which was a Saturday, there was a knocking at Arnold's front door. He'd just finished his bath and was getting dressed, so he went down to see who it was. Trevor Hatswell was standing on his doorstep.

'Morning, Arnold. Sleeping in at the weekend these days, are we? Tut, tut. Spoke with Hermione last night on the blower and she tells me you've been to see the plans at the architects'. Why don't you invite me in, old chap, and give me the gen? I wouldn't say no to a cup of tea if you were offering one.'

And with that he waltzed in past Arnold along the hallway. Arnold closed the front door and followed him into the kitchen.

Arnold had a love/hate relationship with Trevor, and always had done ever since they'd met. His first impression had been of a self-opinionated, conceited, thick-skinned, fanciful loudmouth bore and he'd learnt nothing about him in the intervening years to change that. His area of expertise was mathematics, and he'd retired from teaching at Bristol University a good fifteen years earlier. He'd bored his long-suffering wife to death in 1999, and Arnold had put her in the ground himself. They'd had no children and Trevor had taken it upon himself to dedicate his life to St. Tobias's, making Arnold's life insufferable in the process.

Over the years he'd given Trevor massive hints to find

something else to occupy his time, but they'd fallen on deaf ears. Arnold and Hermione had grown to put up with him, and he had become an integral part of St. Tobias's survival. He had impressive contacts from his time at Bristol and they had utilised these in procuring services and favours in all manner of fields to keep St. Tobias's functioning. There was a limited amount of funding available from the Diocese but it had never been enough to tend to the old age of the church. It reminded Arnold of an old boat well past its prime, always springing a new leak, with them – the crew – managing to forever find some way to keep it afloat. It didn't seem that long ago when they were celebrating the four hundredth anniversary of the founding in 1997, when Trevor and his wife had pulled out all the stops to make sure it had been a success.

But Arnold wasn't in the mood to entertain him that morning and pretended he was out of milk to avoid him prolonging his visit. He knew Trevor liked his tea in the morning, and if a cup wasn't readily available Arnold knew he'd be off visiting someone else in the neighbourhood to get one. Arnold gave him a truncated version of what he'd told Hermione the day before and sure enough Trevor started twitching and looking at his watch.

'Well, Arnold, it all seems tickety-boo. I've just recalled ... I promised to drop by a builder chappie's round the corner this morning to pick something up. So, must dash, I'm afraid. Suppose I'll see you tom– Ah, no, of course I won't, will I ...? Righto, then. Speak soon.'

And he beetled off to the front door, which Arnold held open for him, thanking him for the meal the week before, and Trevor scurried down the path to the front gate. Arnold closed the door on him with relief, and could still hear him jabbering on as he headed off down the road. Now he could enjoy his egg and soldiers in peace.

CHAPTER 4

In the post the next morning there was a crisp-looking envelope with the franked postmark that comes on all official mail from institutions, and he carried it into the kitchen and carefully put it above his place setting at table. The wait was over. He'd been expecting the letter and now it had arrived he was relieved. He prepared his egg, soldiers and coffee and solemnly ate his breakfast before opening it. Recognising the familiar seal of the Diocese, at the top of the single sheet of notepaper enclosed, he unfolded it to read:

Dear Mr. Drive,

As the finalisation of the sale of St. Tobias's has now been completed it will become necessary for you to vacate 3 The Cottages, Priory Street, by the end of the month, as the property has been placed in the hands of Hamptons for immediate sale. Please be kind enough to acknowledge receipt of this letter at your earliest convenience.

Yours sincerely,
Kenneth Finlay

Property Department

Diocesan Board of Finance

Succinct and dry, thought Arnold. It conveyed the information, nothing more and nothing less. He started to experience a strange feeling after he'd read it through, as if the cottage he'd been living in all this time had suddenly become nothing more than a tent, something flimsy and liable to fall down at any moment. Through its thin material he could now feel the chaos of the outside world pressing in, trying to reach him. He'd been there ever since arriving in Corsham, some thirty years earlier, and it was the longest he'd lived anywhere. He'd become part of the cottage and in a few weeks he would have to wrench himself away from it, never to return. It made him question what he'd achieved during all the time he'd spent there. He was forced to conclude he'd merely been God's servant, supplying the people of Corsham with a link to solace and an understanding of His nature. There was no need to question this conclusion, or evaluate it; his place was to accept it as his life's work. If he'd had some success, that was his achievement. The end of the month meant in three weeks' time. He tried to pray for support but it didn't seem to help him. He needed to hold on to somebody and the only person he could think of at that moment was Hermione. He felt driven as he washed up his breakfast things and placed them next to the sink to drain. He went to the hallway and put on his jacket and shoes, and placed his keys in his jacket pocket before opening and going out of the front door.

It didn't take more than a few minutes to walk the several streets to Hermione's house and as soon as it came into view he began to feel better. He strode up to her front door, rang the bell, and heard her approaching on the other side. No sooner was the door opened than he was close to her again, smelling her smell, and gaining comfort from the reality of a fellow human being. She said nothing and just allowed him to hold on to her. He felt he should say something, so he whispered,

'I got the letter today, telling me to leave the cottage.'

'Oh, Arnold. I'm terribly sorry,' she whispered back.

Then she was leading him carefully and gently, and he allowed her to take him up the stairs and along the passageway into a room. She made him sit down on the side of a bed and lifted his legs and turned them so that he was lying down on his side. He felt drenched in the concentrated essence of her smell and he wanted to close his eyes and fill his body with it. In his darkness he felt the bed give under her weight to his right, and she was there stroking his face and his hair, and it was the most beautiful thing he'd ever experienced. Her lips found his and this time he responded positively. He wanted to kiss the French way as he had done all those years before in Guildford. She helped him take off his clothes and it reminded him of when he was a small boy, when his mother would do the same and put him to bed. He still kept his eyes closed because he thought if he opened them he would wake up and find that none of these things were really happening. He allowed her to pull the blankets from under his body and felt their weight descend on top of him and he sensed her taking off her clothes. There was the warm glow of another body, her body, there in the bed beside him and he knew this was what he wanted more than anything. And when their bodies become one, all the anxieties that had built up within him over the last few months were dissipated in the space of a few seconds.

Arnold must have fallen into a deep sleep. When he opened his eyes he was curled up in the bed but she was gone. The curtains had been drawn halfway across the window to prevent the sunlight from directly hitting the bed, something she must have done when he was asleep. He thought somehow he should have felt shame at what had taken place, but he felt none. Had he abandoned God or his Faith? He felt he had done neither. What's more he didn't feel abandoned by God. The love he'd shared with Hermione hadn't been siphoned off from his love for God. On the contrary, it felt as if his love supply had been topped up. As he woke up he started to feel his cup really was overflowing with love. He checked the time on his wristwatch. It was half past two, so he must have been asleep for several hours. The bedroom door opened and Hermione appeared. She had put on a dressing gown and came over to sit on the bed.

'Hello, Arnold, did you have a nice sleep?'

He lay back on the pillows and looked up at her, and said,

'It's funny, yesterday I was wondering if I would ever spend the night with a woman. But I didn't expect it to happen during the day, if you see what I mean.'

She smiled at him and understood, saying,

'I thought it might have been the first time. I do hope it hasn't been too much of a shock.'

She took his hand and raised it to her lips to kiss. Then he said,

'No. Not at all. More of a surprise than a shock. Thank you. I'm glad it was with you. It was a wonderful experience.'

'You know, you're the first man I've been with since Tony left.'

It struck him then that if Lucy hadn't been away at her festival none of this would have happened.

They went downstairs and sat in the kitchen and talked across the big pine table. She prepared an early meal for them and they took it outside to eat in the garden. He allowed himself a glass or two of rosé wine with the food and found himself laughing with her at her little teases. The shadows began to lengthen and Arnold climbed the stairs to again take refuge in Hermione's warmth and spent his first night with a woman.

Lucy was due back from the festival the following day, and when they woke they agreed he should return home after a late breakfast. Hermione made him egg and soldiers as he was used to, and he found himself thinking as he strolled home what a different life he could have had if he'd got himself married off when he was younger. He could still have been a vicar but there would have been a different thread, one a family provides. He wondered if his understanding and interpretation of his faith would have been any different from the way it was. The appearance of sex in his life was a major development, and he found he was enjoying it. He'd made love to Hermione two more times, once before they had fallen asleep, and again in the morning as the first rays of dawn had brightened the room. He thought he was getting the hang of it and she had been very patient and encouraging. He had no idea of how they were going to proceed with their relationship, especially in light of the fact that Lucy was at home that summer and would no doubt remain there until mid-September at the earliest. Perhaps they would be forced to meet up clandestinely, the thought of which excited him somehow.

It was the first time he'd been away from the cottage overnight since he'd attended a forum in Edinburgh on Arminianism in 2001. He'd been away for three nights then and had rued agreeing to attend as soon as he'd got on the sleeper train taking him there, from Temple Meads in Bristol. He remembered Hermione driving him to the station. This time coming home he had no such regret, as he was finding it difficult to see it as his home any longer since he'd received the letter. He moved around the rooms sensing a growing impermanence, as if he were just a temporary visitor on the way to somewhere else. When he spotted the letter lying on the kitchen table it was just a piece of paper with some writing on it. He concluded the strength he'd gained was from the time he'd spent with Hermione and he was glad about what they'd done and what they had allowed to happen. He started to read his book on the Inquisition and was surprised to discover it was past five o'clock when he paused at the end of a chapter. He strolled into the kitchen to consider what he could prepare simply to eat for the evening and realised it was a Sunday, the first Sunday since St. Tobias's had closed. Ever since he'd heard about the impending closure all those months before, he'd wondered what it would be like on a Sunday, not going there and conducting the service as usual. Instead he had been sleeping with Hermione. He was filled with guilt. He fell on his knees on the kitchen floor to pray for forgiveness. At the precise moment he put his hands together he saw a bright flash of light, which he interpreted as a sign of God's anger. He started to pray,

'Heavenly Father. Forgive me, for I have sinned ...'

He heard a distant rumbling and realised a summer thunderstorm was approaching. The noise got louder and the flashes grew more frequent and before he'd finished praying he heard the sound of heavy rain striking the ground outside. There were dull thuds as the large raindrops hit the windowpanes around him. He heard the drops running together, forcing courses to open up along the uneven paving stones in the yard outside, as the water tried to seek lower level. He finished his prayer and got up from the hard flagstone floor feeling pain in his knees, and as soon as it had appeared the storm moved away towards the east, and left what sounded like a host of clocks ticking at different speeds outside.

CHAPTER 5

As soon as he woke up on Monday morning, he knew finding somewhere to live was at the top of his agenda. The day was bright, but he managed to get showered and have his breakfast before the sun had entered the living room windows to trap him in the kitchen. Another storm had passed through during the night leaving the streets damp and he wheeled his bicycle out from under the shelter of the front porch and headed off to the newsagents. He wanted to buy copies of the local newspapers and take them down to the mere, where he could sit undisturbed and search to see if people advertised houses and flats available to rent. He'd never had to do this sort of thing before as he'd gone straight from university lodgings in Guildford to some arranged accommodation to complete his training, and then had come directly to Corsham. But he guessed they did. He said hello to people he recognised from his congregation as he cycled through the streets towards Pickwick and wondered what they'd done the day before instead of going to St. Tobias's. He hoped they hadn't fallen by the wayside. Perhaps they'd attended service at nearby St. Bartholomew's? He'd never seen himself as ever being in competition with the other churches in Corsham, preferring to think they had a combined duty to help the people in their life struggles. He was on good terms with the other two vicars but couldn't say he'd become friends with either of them.

He put the papers in his front basket and headed past St. Bartholomew's onto the footpath that led to the mere. The grass was damp but he'd predicted this and brought along a folding seat, together with a thermos of coffee to help him concentrate. He wasn't sure where in the papers he'd find what he was looking for, and he had to slowly thumb through the pages of news until he got to the section carrying the ads. It was quite cleverly planned out, he thought, neatly sub-divided into Cars, Accommodation, Buy and Sell, and Personal. He didn't understand what Personal meant so he had a quick look, to discover lonely people wanting to meet others like themselves. He was surprised at how many of these there were, and couldn't understand why his congregations had been getting so small if there were that many lonely people out there. It didn't bode well for the future of the church. He realised he was getting sidetracked and headed back to Accommodation and the rental section.

There was about a quarter of a page of ads, most of them people looking for something rather than those who had somewhere to rent. There wasn't anything suitable in the first paper and he moved on to the next, only this time he didn't have to wade through all the pages and went straight to the ads. It was the same pattern, lots of personal ads and very few places to rent. By the time he had looked in all three papers he had nothing to show for his efforts, apart from a small house that was for rent in Trowbridge, but he didn't want to move all the way down there. He thought somewhere in the Corsham area, Bradford on Avon, or Box would suit him, as they were all relatively close to one another, and he wanted to be within easy reach of Hermione.

On his way home, he made a detour along the High Street in order to check the estate agents. He knew as well as buying and selling properties they also did a fair amount of renting, but he saw only houses suitable for families in the windows. By the time he got home he was feeling despondent, and it began to dawn on him how difficult it was going to be to find a place to live. His budget meant he could only afford to rent a small flat and prices were high in that part of the country. He'd heard of boarding houses where religious orders put retired members of their community, but the idea of sitting out the remainder of his life with others like himself didn't appeal. Hermione had told him there'd been a television comedy based on a similar sort of place, called *Father Ted*.

Arnold settled into the same routine each day that week. He woke up, got showered and dressed, and after his egg and soldiers cycled to the mere with a thermos and the papers. He thought he may bump into Lucy there, or even Hermione, but it added to his sombre mood when neither appeared. Saturday arrived and he discovered the papers had ballooned in size, and there was an increase in the number of ads. He found a few that sounded suitable and made up a list with their contact details, and when he got home he telephoned them. Most had already gone but there were three still available, and he arranged to go and see them that weekend. One was on the edge of Box village and the other two were in Colerne, which he thought he should go and see even though it was a fair distance, as he was starting to feel a little desperate. He decided he would use his bicycle to go that afternoon.

It would be quite a ride but he would try Box first and then make his way up the valley to Colerne. If the hills got too steep he could always get off and walk. He was poring over an Ordnance Survey map of the area to pinpoint the locations of the three places when the phone rang. It was Hermione. He was pleased to hear from her and apologised for his lack of communication since the weekend before.

'Not to worry. Since Lucy got back I've been rushed off my feet,' she told him. 'She came back with a bug she picked up at the festival and I've been playing doctor looking after her. She started to perk up on Thursday. Must have been all that "Whole Earth" food at the festival, never too sure how it's being prepared, now are you? How have you been, dear Arnold?'

And then she lowered her voice:

'Have you missed me at all?'

'Of course I have. I've missed our chats ... well, amongst other things.'

He heard her give a mischievous laugh. He explained he'd been trying to find somewhere to move to the whole week and told her of his luck at finding some places to look at that afternoon.

'Oh, that is good. Now you must let me drive you there. You cannot be attempting to cycle all that way at your age. No, I positively insist. Besides, it's going to rain.'

He had no idea how on earth she knew he'd intended to cycle, but he put it down to her woman's intuition and allowed himself to be persuaded into accepting a lift.

She drove up outside the cottage and tooted her horn for him and within a few minutes they'd arrived at the address in Box. Arnold knocked on the front door as he couldn't find a bell and Hermione saw him disappear inside. Within a few minutes he reappeared but it seemed to her he'd been in there far too short a time. He got back in the car and she searched his face for some news.

'No good, I'm afraid,' he admitted. 'Just rooms within a family home. Nice enough though.'

They set off up London Road and turned left into Mill Lane, crossed the river and headed up towards Colerne. Arnold kept his eyes on the street names and as it happened the two addresses were quite close to one another. The first was in a basement which felt too damp for Arnold's liking and he could see himself getting depressed living below ground level. The other was far more suitable. The owner was a very agreeable local taxi driver who had split his house into two flats since his wife had passed away, and was looking to rent out the upper one, whilst he remained downstairs with access to his garden where he had a thriving vegetable patch. Although, Arnold thought, to call it a vegetable patch would have been an insult. The flat was bright and recently decorated and it felt like somewhere Arnold could live. It had its own entrance at the top of an outside staircase and benefited from good views south over Box Valley. Arnold got back into the car and described it to Hermione. Unfortunately someone else had shown interest that morning and the owner said he was waiting to hear back from them before he could offer it to him. As they weaved their way back towards the A4 the skies opened and the lanes filled with torrents of water.

As they approached Corsham, the rain eased up and Hermione told him,

'Lucy's gone up to London to spend the weekend with

her father. So if you like you can come over and keep me company this evening?'

He immediately accepted, knowing there was nothing he could think of that he'd rather do.

Lucy wasn't due back from London until Sunday evening and Hermione had arranged to pick her up from Chippenham station, so there was no hurry for him to leave the following morning. He had the flat owner's number safely in his pocket to call him at midday as arranged. They had a late breakfast and at noon he dialled the number. He found himself praying for good luck, or something, while he waited for an answer with Hermione stood next to him, holding his hand and squeezing it.

A voice said, 'Hello? Reverend Drive? Oh, I'm glad it's you ringing. The other chap hasn't rung back as he said he would, so I'm happy for you to take the flat, if you're still interested. You said you could move in by the end of the month, didn't you?'

Arnold confirmed the dates and said he'd pick up the keys that afternoon and pay the deposit plus a month's rent in advance. By two o'clock they were heading back up to Colerne in Hermione's car and he felt things in his life were finally sorting themselves out. As he realised this the sun came out as if to agree with him, and for the first time in thirty years he started to sense he was becoming an independent person. When he forced himself to think of his cottage it became associated with some past life, as if it was the skin of an insect that gets shed when the creature enters a new phase in its life. He thought they called it metamorphosis. How was he going to continue to find meaning in his devotion to a God who, judging by what had happened to him recently, had taken up a position on the periphery of his existence? His liaison with Hermione, and his success at finding somewhere to live, these were things he had made happen, not God. There really was no question about it.

In Colerne, Arnold wrote out his cheque to the landlord, Stan Dale, and accepted his offer of a cup of tea and a look around the garden. Stan was very proud of his vegetable growing and enjoyed the interest Hermione took in his efforts. Being the height of summer everything was growing in abundance and he said there was plenty for them to help themselves to, as there was far too much for him to eat. He insisted they take a bag full of runner beans, and two marrows which he said would just sit and rot if they didn't take them, as he wasn't partial, and Hermione promised to bring him back a jar of chutney she would make with them. Suddenly it was four o'clock and they had to leave. Stan was due to pick up a fare from Heathrow airport at six and he didn't want to be late. Arnold looked forward to packing his belongings, as he knew there would be a lot of things he would want to throw away.

He used the ten days left until the end of the month to sift through everything he'd accumulated at the cottage. There was far more than he'd imagined. He had never been one for buying a lot of clothes, preferring to have just a few things until they were worn out, at which point he would replace them, so his wardrobe didn't take long to put in order. He wasn't sure if he was expected to wear the clerical collar once he'd left the parish. He suspected not, which meant he would have to supplement his choice of normal shirts with a trip or two into Bath.

He separated his black clothes from everything else and

was surprised to discover there was very little colour in what was left. In the church he'd opted to remain in vestments rather than not, the reason being it meant that way he wouldn't have to make any choices about what to wear. Besides, whenever he had decided to go in 'civvies' to a function, people had noticed and more often than not commented on the fact, and he would always prefer not to draw attention to himself or be discussed in public, as it always made him feel uneasy. Deciding to throw out anything that was at all tired or frayed, he sorted and packed his clothes and moved on to the suitcases and boxes that were stored in the roof space above the cottage. Most of it was things he'd forgotten about and thus had managed to survive without for anything up to thirty years. In fact, he found one small case he realised hadn't been opened since he'd arrived there in 1975! Inside there was just a lot of faded documents relating to his time in Guildford and the religious college in Norfolk where he'd completed his training. He sifted through, keeping the photographs and anything else he felt was important, like qualification certificates for courses and official letters. He was just closing it when he noticed a small retaining pocket in the lid with something poking out. He reopened the case and fished out a dusty booklet with faded gold lettering on the cover. It looked vaguely familiar and he opened it to find inside a deposit account for the Halifax Building Society with his name as the account holder. The only entry was a deposit for a thousand pounds made in 1974 at the branch in Norwich. The deposit had been in the form of a cheque and attached to the page with a rusted paper clip was a letter from the auctioneers Bonhams in London. It read:

Dear Mr. Drive,

Please find enclosed a cheque for £1000, being the proceeds from the sale of a 17th century musical box, offered for sale by yourself in our recent auction of European Musical Instruments.

Yours sincerely,

Tony Nourmand

He remembered he'd inherited the musical box from a deceased relative in Hamburg he'd never met. It held no sentimental value for Arnold so he was happy for it to be disposed of by the executors of the will. At the time he had no idea what to do with the money, so he'd followed a friend's advice and deposited it somewhere and, what with his preoccupation at the time with his theological training, he'd completely forgotten about it.

CHAPTER 6

The last day of the month happened to fall on a Thursday, and Hermione helped Arnold with the move over to Colerne. Lucy was on hand and she stayed at the cottage in Corsham and supervised the loading up of Hermione's small car with Arnold's things, which he'd painstakingly packed into cardboard boxes from the local shops. He was pleased at the way he'd catalogued and arranged his possessions. His trimmed-down wardrobe fitted into three of the boxes, with footwear in a fourth. He was surprised at the number of kitchen gadgets he'd collected over the years and these filled up another. Books took up two more, then there was his old valve radio plus his bike, umbrella and the few pictures he owned, including his favourite picture of his late parents taken on their honeymoon. He took a long look at this when packing it away and studied their faces, full of joy and expectation of the years that were to come. They had married in the early years of the Second World War when happiness was to be grabbed if you stumbled upon it, as you never knew how much longer you'd be alive. Air raids were a constant threat and if you were in the wrong place at the wrong time, it could all be over.

They'd both worked in the civil service. His mother was

at the Ministry of Food in London and his father was a qualified aviation draughtsman, so too valuable to be called into the ranks as a soldier. They had met during an air raid below ground in Kentish Town Underground Station and discovered they were next-door neighbours. Several months later his father joined an aircraft design unit outside Leicester, and he'd proposed after watching the firebombing of Coventry from the top of a hill after a trip to the pub, fearing he may lose what he'd found in Kentish Town.

The move took up most of the day, with the morning spent ferrying everything over and the afternoon unpacking and organising it all. Stan had furnished the flat sparsely, which suited Arnold as he felt claustrophobic surrounded by too many things, and he moved the furniture around until he was happy. Hermione left him to it once all his boxes had been delivered but told him to call her if he needed anything. It was about five o'clock when he finally sat down in an armchair with a cup of tea in the lounge and looked over Box Valley to enjoy the view. Being early September the nights were drawing in, and within an hour he felt the light fading as the sun neared the horizon to the right of the windows. He could see flocks of crows climbing and swooping in the valley below and the drifting smoke from several autumnal bonfires curled up into the still skies. He got up and switched on a large table lamp and looked around the room. Being his first evening, he was quite happy to be alone getting used to his new surroundings. It was a novel experience for him and he took his time, acclimatising and feeling his way from room to room. The bathroom had a window, which he was pleased about, even though it had frosted glass. It looked out onto

Stan's garden and he knew he would enjoy being in there with it open in the mornings.

He sat down, picked up his book on the Inquisition, and had just started to read when he thought he heard a faint knock on his front door. He assumed it to be Stan, his landlord, and found him smiling on the doorstep.

'Hello, Arnold. Just finished for the day and wondered if everything was all right for you? Anything you need at all? No? That's good. Well ... I took the liberty of picking us both up some fish and chips from the Fat Friar in Batheaston on the way home. Do you ever indulge? I got cod for both of us, and mushy peas as well.'

Arnold didn't want to appear rude and disappoint him, so he smiled, nodding back in agreement.

'That's a relief! Well, I was going to say, why don't you come and have it with me downstairs? It's all keeping warm in the oven at the moment, whenever you likes.'

Arnold thanked him and said he'd be down in a few minutes. As he put on his shoes and slipped his cardigan on he tried to remember the last time he'd had fish and chips. It was deep down in his memory somewhere but he couldn't recall. Perplexed by this he closed his front door and walked down the stairs on the side of the building.

Stan's half of the house was very similarly decorated to Arnold's. It was as if he'd ordered two of everything and put one in each flat, and it occurred to him this was a very simple and economical way of equipping both. Stan led the way into his kitchen-diner where he'd laid out two places at the table for them.

'Just sit yourself down, Arnold, and it'll be in front of you in a jiffy.'

There was a bottle of malt vinegar, salt and pepper cellars, and a bottle of salad cream in the centre of the table. Arnold hid his dismay at the salad cream, as he much preferred the taste of mayonnaise. The layout of the flat was different from Arnold's, and he got the impression more had been done upstairs than down. Apart from the redecorating these rooms probably hadn't been altered from when Stan had lived there with his wife.

They ate in silence and the fish was surprisingly good. Stan made them both a cup of tea and they discussed Arnold's move. It was obvious Stan enjoyed some company as he was very talkative. Arnold had perfected the art of being a good listener over the years; it was a quality he thought extremely important in his line of work. It came in handy here, as Stan needed no coaxing out of his shell.

'Yes, I likes cabbing. I like the idea of being out, and driving's a favourite pastime of mine, always has been, so I might as well make some money out of it. Eh, Arnold?'

Arnold managed to stay awake through all this small talk although he was beginning to feel exhausted after all the toing and froing from Corsham. The move had been emotionally draining. Whenever there was a pause whilst Stan caught his breath Arnold filled it with a cough or a slight change of position in his chair.

'To tell you the truth I been feeling a bit lonely since Nancy's been gone. We led a quiet life up here in Colerne. Always kept ourselves to ourselves. We didn't have any, what you'd call, real friends. All the people we knew were only acquaintances, I suppose. In fact, I owe you an apology ...'

Arnold's ears pricked up at this and he shook off his blanket of fatigue.

'You see, Nancy didn't die ... She went and took off like. All of a sudden. She left me heres, and went back up North to where she'd come from originally. I felt a bit ashamed, sort of. So I prefers to tell people she passed away. It's easier for me, saying that. I hope you understand ... I'm sorry if I misled you.'

This did come as a surprise to Arnold. He could see now his arrival in Stan's life wasn't going to be as simple as he'd thought. Stan continued:

'It was all right for the first couple of year, but then I started to get lonely, like, by myself, wandering about the house. Which is where I got the idea to do the conversion and let out the upstairs bit. As soon as the work got started I began to feel better about it. And now you're here, well, I'm just so happy.'

Arnold took this as a cue to leave and tried unsuccessfully to offer some money for the fish and chips, but Stan was having none of it and insisted on making it his treat. Once upstairs alone in the quiet, Arnold started to feel sympathetic towards Stan. It must be terrible to have your partner leave you suddenly, probably similar to losing them through death, he thought. What would he feel like if Hermione were taken from him now, so soon after their relationship had begun? He guessed Stan had been married just the once and there probably weren't any children. He hadn't mentioned any and he would have done so, Arnold was certain of that.

He prepared for bed immersed in sorrow at Stan's situation, something that had been going on the whole time he'd been cocooned away in Corsham, just a few miles away. He was relieved Stan hadn't given in to depression, and he resolved to offer as much company and help as he could. He fell asleep making a mental note to buy some mayonnaise as he would definitely need it for any more shared fish and chip dinners.

CHAPTER 7

Arnold heard Stan leave early the next morning and got up slowly while he enjoyed the birdsong he could hear from the garden. He kept the window in the bathroom open so he could continue listening while he bathed, and then took a stroll outside to admire the wealth of produce that had appeared since he'd been there the first time a month before. There were runner beans hanging heavily from the neatly constructed cane wigwams, and he recognised spinach, peas, broccoli, and several large fat marrows peeking out from under their leaves on the ground. It really was a magnificent plot and Arnold couldn't compare it to any vegetable garden he'd ever seen before.

Wandering back up the stairs to his flat he made his egg and soldiers to eat in the living room with some coffee. Afterwards, he decided it was time to explore the village and headed out to cycle along every road in Colerne to get his bearings. He found a newsagent and, feeling a bit out of touch, bought the *Telegraph* to catch up on the world. When he got back he noticed a deckchair propped up against the garden shed, so he pulled it out and settled down to read the paper. After about an hour he heard a car approaching and Stan pulled up in the driveway.

Arnold got up and walked towards the car saying:

'I hope you don't mind, Stan. I borrowed your deckchair to sit out in the sun for a while?'

'You make yourself at home, Arnold. I've just popped back for a cuppa before heading up to Gatwick to pick someone up. If I can get on the motorway before two, I shall miss the crush on the M25. Can I make you one?'

Stan got another deckchair from the shed and they settled down to enjoy the afternoon sunshine.

'The garden looks wonderful, Stan. I don't think I've ever seen such a bounteous plot anywhere.'

'Well,' said Stan, 'the secret is in the treatment you gives it. You can't have too much fertiliser, I says. Come the autumn when they're all done with their growing like, I give 'em a good dressing, just like the farmers do on the fields. Then, in the spring I give it another dose, and that seems to do the trick.'

It all seemed obvious to Arnold now he'd explained.

'I was thinking,' Arnold began, 'I could help if you like. You know, with any digging, or fertilising, or anything that needs to be done. I don't know much about gardening, but I can pick things up quickly. Anyway, I just thought I'd offer.'

Stan fell silent and Arnold thought for a second or two that he'd taken offence at his suggestion. Then without looking at him Stan said,

'That's very kind of you, Arnold. And I do appreciates your offer. But the vegetables is my thing, and always has been, and I can manage very well on me own. Also it gives me some time to myself out here, so's I can think about things ... But, thank you, all the same.'

And on saying these words he slowly turned his eyes

towards Arnold and gave him a reassuring smile. Arnold nodded in an understanding way, it was another thing he'd learnt to do well at St. Tobias's.

September progressed, and autumn made its impression on the landscape. The curling smoke of bonfires became a more common feature and the air took on a mushroomy flavour as the days got shorter. Lucy left to go back to Durham in the middle of the month, and Arnold was able to stay with Hermione at her house whenever he wished. He was careful not to impose on her. He got used to spending Sunday mornings in her bed, drenched in her essence, and he stopped feeling guilty at not attending some church service somewhere. It was as if God's presence inside him was being substituted with something else, some fullness of being. He seemed to be noticing signs of life all around him and within himself, and it wasn't an unpleasant sensation.

Perhaps part of the reason for this was to do with Colerne, which was more rural than Corsham. There were no street lamps close to the house, so when the sun had gone it really was dark outside. The only lights were the security lamps that came on automatically whenever Stan's car pulled up in the driveway. He became acutely aware of when the sun set and when it came up in the mornings, and took to neglecting to pull his curtains across his bedroom windows. In Corsham he would have had trouble sleeping like that but here it was not an issue.

Stan worked long hours and was forever driving up and down to Stansted, Gatwick or Heathrow to pick people up or drop them off. This provided the bulk of his business and he was willing to leave at all hours to meet the unsociable schedules of the charter flights. Their fish and chip dinners became a regular feature over the weeks and gradually Arnold discovered more and more about Nancy, the absent wife. Neither she nor Stan had any surviving relatives anywhere, which Arnold was surprised to discover, as he'd assumed that when she'd left she had gone to join some existing part of her family in the North. Stan could furnish no clues regarding why she'd left and seemed at a loss to explain, but Arnold was careful not to press him for more information than he was willing to volunteer. He didn't want to risk making Stan morose and wished to spare him any more pain than he'd already felt.

Another aspect of life in Colerne Arnold became aware of was the remarkable stillness of the night. He started to look forward to retiring to his bed so he could lay there in the darkness and really appreciate it as a luxury. Rarely a police siren or an ambulance would invade the space and apart from Stan's comings and goings that was it for noise. Arnold came to recognise the sound of Stan's car and could tell it was different from Hermione's. As far as birds went, the odd owl was all that he heard. The pigeons didn't start up until sunrise and even they tended to be quiet if there was an owl close by.

One night, about two months after his arrival, he thought he heard some faint knocking on his front door. He thought this was strange, but nevertheless got up and went to the door to open it. There was nobody outside so he went back to bed. About fifteen minutes later he thought he heard it again and repeated the exercise of going to open the door, only to find nothing. He went back to sleep and forgot all about it until a few nights later when it happened again. After the second false alarm at the door he sat next to it in the dark this time. He must have fallen asleep because he was awakened by it for the third time. He opened the door as quickly as he could only to be confronted by the still of the night. He considered telling Stan but decided against it for the time being.

The following week his alarm clock, which was set for 8am, went off in the middle of the night and he awoke with a start. He checked to see if he'd made a mistake setting the time, but he hadn't.

He lay in bed unable to get back to sleep, confused by what had occurred. Just then, he thought he could hear someone moving across the room past the bed. He switched on the bedside lamp but the room was empty. The rest of that night he slept fitfully and tried to make sense of the increasing catalogue of strange nocturnal happenings. The next week was uneventful and the clocks went back in late October, meaning it was dark soon after four in the afternoon. Arnold began to wonder what he would experience next.

One night in bed early in November, he was trying to remember the last time he'd eaten fish and chips before arriving in Colerne, when he distinctly thought someone was trying to get into the bed with him. It reminded him of the first time he'd been in bed with Hermione, and for a brief second in the darkness he actually believed she was there with him, before the ridiculousness of the thought dawned upon him. He groped around the bed to reassure himself he was indeed alone, and had to get up and walk around for a while to steady his nerves. He'd heard of such things as poltergeists but never thought he would experience one himself, especially being a man of God.

The next day when he was sitting in his half-lit lounge

reading in the mid-afternoon, the torch he used on twilight walks came on by itself and shone its beam across the room. He got up and went over to inspect it. What made it even more curious was that the on/off button needed a good deal of pressure to operate it, meaning it wasn't being temperamental. This was the first strange thing to happen within the hours of daylight, which made him more nervous than ever, and he thought perhaps there could be a link between all these events. He was over at Hermione's the following weekend and gave her a full description of the events and, of course, she immediately had an idea for an explanation.

'It sounds to me as if it could be something unresolved to do with the house and its history. I've heard of similar things before, especially in old buildings. Why don't you ask Stan if he knows who lived there before him? It looks like it could be a couple of hundred years old, and there's a chance a tragedy or something unpleasant took place at some stage. It's worth a try. Poor Arnold, it has upset you, hasn't it?'

Arnold thought it a good idea and decided to discuss it with Stan at the next appropriate moment.

That Sunday in bed he remembered sitting in a car a long time before, eating fish and chips with his father. It all came flooding back to him, how his father would take him to Whitstable in the winter and they would buy fish and chips, and sit and eat them in the car as it was too cold or wet to be outside. There was something melancholic about seaside towns off-season, with just the locals wandering around getting on with their lives. Arnold had looked forward to these trips. It was time he could spend alone with his father and his mother would rarely join them. He realised now that she deliberately hadn't been invited, or had avoided joining them, as his father had been at work all week and he'd hardly seen Arnold. Sometimes, if they were brave enough, they would go for a long walk through the pebbles and struggle hard to move forward against the bracing wind. They would finish eating and his father would turn to him and say,

'Shall we venture out, Arnold? I'm game if you are.'

He was pleased he'd remembered this and decided to tell Stan.

Their fish and chip ritual nearly always took place on a Monday or a Tuesday, as these were the most likely evenings for Stan not to be booked for an airport trip. So, on cue, he arrived back that Monday at about seven o'clock and gave the familiar triple beep on the car horn to let Arnold know supper had arrived. Arnold gathered up his jar of mayonnaise from his fridge and trotted down the stairs to let himself in through Stan's side door.

Arnold's job was to lay the table while Stan transferred the food onto warm plates from the oven. Stan had tried Arnold's mayonnaise on his chips but had gone back to his salad cream, saying it was what he was used to. They tucked into their food and didn't speak as they ate. When they had their teas in front of them they began to talk. This time Arnold started off by telling Stan his memory of fish and chips in Whitstable with his father all those years before.

'How about that, then?' Stan said. 'Fancy that, and you's never had 'em once from then till now? Arnold, you have led a sheltered life, if you don't mind me saying so! Blimey, that must be some forty year ago, I bet!'

And then he was off, chatting about what he could remember of his own childhood down in the New Forest, where there were wild horses and gypsy camps in the remoter parts. From what Arnold could gather, he was from a large family with plenty of brothers and sisters to lark about with during the weekends and the school holidays. They would hunt and trap wild animals, like squirrels and rabbits, and trade them to the gypsies – who would eat that sort of thing apparently – for rides on their horses and home-made cakes. It sounded like another world to Arnold, who'd made do with growing up in Crouch End in North London.

'That New Forest is a remarkable place when you're growing up, Arnold. We lived right on the edge of it, outside Wimborne, and we was always in there having fun. Mind you, playing hide and seek, it wasn't a good idea to get lost in there, like. Especially when it gets dark. I remember a couple of times it happened to me and I was petrified trying to find my way out, near enough pitch black it was.'

At this moment Arnold thought he could see an opportunity to bring up the strange things he'd been experiencing upstairs:

'Funny you should talk about that, Stan. I wanted to tell you, I've been hearing things upstairs ... at night.'

'Really? What sorts of things?'

'Well, someone knocking on my front door for one thing, quite late. And when I go to answer it there's no one there. And that's not all, I'm afraid.'

'What else?'

'Well, sometimes, when I'm in bed, it feels like someone else is in the room. Even felt like they were in the bed with me once. It was most unsettling, I can tell you. Then there's my torch, you know the one I go walking with? Well, that came on, by itself, just last week.'

Stan's face went white and his jaw dropped. He was having trouble putting his cup down in the saucer and Arnold could hear the china shaking in his hands.

'Oh dear. I am sorry, Arnold,' Stan said. 'What do you think it could mean?'

Stan was finding it difficult to get the words out.

'I've no idea,' Arnold continued. 'I just wondered if you knew anything about the history of the house? As I've heard, people who believe in such things have found explanations in past events. You know, things tragic or unpleasant that have happened in the place a long time before. I suppose I should keep an open mind about such things, even though I am a man of God – or was.'

But it was clear Stan's mind was elsewhere. He got up and wandered slowly away from the table towards the door to his sitting room.

'Sorry, Arnold. Feel I've got to go and lie down. Just for a while. Please excuse me.'

Arnold heard Stan go to his bedroom and close the door behind him. He waited in the kitchen for a few minutes then cleared away and washed up the supper things. It was all rather distressing. He had no idea why what he'd told Stan should upset him so much. It was all very curious. He decided the best thing he could do was to go back upstairs, and he left some money on the kitchen table to pay for the fish and chips – as it was his turn – and quietly closed the door on his way out.

He busied himself tidying up and did some domestic chores as he couldn't focus his mind on reading anything, and it filled the time left in the evening before going to bed. After about an hour he made himself a cup of cocoa and had just sat down to browse through his Bible when there was a faint knock at his door. His immediate thought was that the unexplained knocking had returned and he pretended to ignore it. Then he heard it again, but this time it was louder so he got up and went to answer it. Stan was outside.

'Arnold ... Sorry to disturb you ... Can I come in for a moment? I need to talk to you ... to tell you something.'

Arnold opened the door and as Stan passed by he could smell the strong and distinct odour of whisky. Arnold sensed a feeling he hadn't had since the days of St. Tobias's, when he'd had to give audience to poor souls with troubled minds. Stan sat down in one of the armchairs and Arnold took the seat opposite and waited for him to speak.

'Arnold, I've gone and done a terrible, terrible thing. And I have to tell someone about it. I don't know where to start really ... where it starts ...'

'I told you about how Nancy and me lived here on our own; we never had no cause for complaints. I did my cabbing and she looked after the house, as is usual with people like us. The trouble is over the years; we cut ourselves off from everyone around us, like. Without really intending to. You probably realised by now we had no young 'uns to look after. Not for the want of trying, but it just never happened. Well, by then it was too late for us to be going off and looking for new partners. We'd grown into each other, as happens too. So we just accepted the fact we was to be just the two of us and that was that. She always did a grand job around the house and I was out all hours, as I am, up and down the motorway, but gradually dissatisfaction grew in her ... with me, like. She'd go through whole days when she wouldn't talk to me, and I'd say: "For God's sake, woman, say summat, will you?" and then she'd burst into tears and I'd try to touch her, and she'd shy away from me and not let me go near her. Sorry, Arnold, to go and use His name like that. Anyways, life went along like this for many a year and the only thing I had to keep me going was the garden, and the vegetables. I admit at times I got to talking to 'em as they were growing, like children, for want of conversation with Nancy, and I got a feeling they responded by growing better, but you'll think I'm mad for saying that.

'Then about six or seven year ago Nancy found her tongue, and she used it on me without any rest. It was as if all those years she'd stored up this hatred for me and then all of it came out. She'd surprise me suddenly by bringing up summat from years before, summat that had completely gone out of my head, like. How I'd said summat that'd upset her, and how much I'd hurt her by saying it and she'd never forgive me for it. My life became a living hell on earth, Arnold. I thought at times of searching for help in the Church, but I'd be on the point of going when I'd decide against it, as I've never been that good at expressing myself, as you can probably tell. And it made me feel uncomfortable to think of talking about these personal things to a stranger, even if it was someone like yourself, they'd still be someone I didn't know from Adam.

'Well, as time went on, I grew to hating her for all that she was throwing at me from inside of her mind. I didn't think it was fair, for her to be so cruel and unkind like that. And I started to think about ways I could get rid of her. I've never been an aggressive person, Arnold, and I've never wished bad on anyone in my life. What I believe is, what goes around comes around, always have done. But she got me thinking that way, no two ways about it. I couldn't see no other way that I could carry on living, dreading coming home after work for fear of her laying into me. I've never been a drinking man. Never normally kept it in the house, so I wasn't going to end up down at The Six Bells at night instead of coming home. Although I do admit that I had a few swigs of whisky before I came up here, like, otherwise I would never be telling you all of this. Knew I had a bottle in a cupboard from years ago. Where was I? Oh, Arnold. What must you be thinking about me?'

At this point he lay back in his armchair, silent and exhausted by the effort of recalling these unpleasant memories. Arnold had been gripping his cocoa the whole time Stan had been speaking and took a sip to see how cold it was and if it was still drinkable. A film of dried milk had formed on the surface and as he drew his mouth back from the lip of the cup the film stuck to his lips and hung down for a second or two, suspended in the air before falling onto his cardigan front. He got up and went to the kitchen to dampen a kitchen cloth at the sink and dab the stain from his front. He got most of it off but then thought it wasn't a good idea to leave Stan. He went back into the lounge and Stan was still motionless in his armchair with his eyes closed. Arnold went up and gently shook his shoulder, saying,

'Stan. Stan? Are you all right?'

Stan's eyes opened and he relaxed when he saw Arnold standing there next to him. He sat up and Arnold went back to his chair. And Stan began again.

'Then, one autumn, I was working in the garden and I started finding mushrooms growing all around the hawthorns and conifers. Over the years I've come to know the different types you get around here and I knows which are the ones you can eat and those you can't. Well, these ones in the garden were the bad kind. Amanita is the name. More common than you'd think, they be. They get mistaken for the good 'uns sometimes and people die by mistake. It made sense to me that my garden was providing me with summat I could use for Nancy. That garden has been me only friend over the years ... Until you come along, Arnold. So I collected a good few of them and mixed them in with some I bought from the shops, and she cooked them up one day for breakfast. I pushed mine around the plate while we was eating, and she wolfed the lot down and then wanted mine if I was leaving 'em! Nothing happened for a good two or three hours and it was a quiet Sunday for me, so I was going to be spending the morning in the garden anyways. I went outside to do some digging and the like, then about eleven I heard a banging and lots of noise from the kitchen and went in to take a look. I know it was about that time 'cos I heard the clock on the church up the road chiming. The kitchen was in a state, she'd been working in there, cooking Sunday lunch and there were pots and pans all over the place, as she'd gone down trying to hold on to summat, and she was a big woman, was Nancy. I took a close look at her, and got a hand mirror to hold up in front of her face, like, to see if she were still breathing. I'd seen it done on the telly, but there was no steam from her, so she'd gone. I just hoped that she hadn't had too much pain in the going; I wouldn't have wanted that for her. No.'

Arnold was having trouble believing he was hearing this correctly, and for a moment thought he may just be having a bad dream, so he pinched himself a couple of times to make sure he was awake. Then he realised he had to make sure he didn't lose Stan's coherence, before he found out what had happened next. After all, he reasoned, there's no dead person without a body to show for it.

'So what did you do, Stan?'

'Well, I covered her up with a blanket there on the kitchen floor where she was, then I found myself heading out into the garden, where I'd been digging, and carried on with what I was doing. I dug and dug, not knowing what else to do, and a few hours later I was standing in a big hole, pretty deep it was. By now it must have been close to four o'clock and the light was going, so I went back into the kitchen with me wheelbarrow and brought her out into the garden and put her in the hole. Then all I could think of was to put all the earth back on top of her, and spread the rest out around the vegetables. I just managed to finish before the last of the light went, then I started to feel tired. Exhausted, I was.'

He paused, and Arnold prompted him to continue.

'And then what?'

'I went upstairs and lay down on our bed and went to sleep. When I woke up it was the next day and what had happened seemed like it was all a dream. I looked out the window and the garden looked the same as it's always done, the only difference was Nancy was gone. I gathered up all her things, there and then, and took them down and lit a bonfire that morning, as I didn't want anything around to remind me of her or what I'd done. Later that day, it was a Monday, I got a phone call from someone asking me to do a pick up from Stansted, out of the blue, I'd been recommended like, and I just said "yes" without even thinking about it. And I'd never done Stansted before then.'

After a while Arnold realised he was staring into space, not focusing on anything, just trying to digest what Stan had told him. Stan seemed in a trance and the two of them sat there in their chairs in silence. Then an owl could be heard outside somewhere, and Arnold heard some stirring from the other chair. Stan raised himself and got down on his knees in front of Arnold with his hands clasped together as if in prayer:

'Oh, Arnold. What you been hearing and seeing upstairs … It's her, isn't it? Nancy. She's come back to haunt us, hasn't she? Your bedroom, that's our old bedroom, see, so it makes sense, don't it? She wanted you to know what I done to her and it's terrible, I know that now. The worst thing I ever done in my whole life. What should I do? Is it too late for me? Just tell me what to do!'

And with that he broke down in a slobbering mass of tears and Arnold found himself leaning over and taking Stan's shoulders to comfort him. Stan was still trying to speak through his sobbing and Arnold likened him to a child that needs human warmth and a steadying hand. Slowly Stan calmed down, and Arnold helped him to his feet and led him down the stairs outside, then in through the back door. He was silent now, and just like he would have done with a distraught child, Arnold led him to his bedroom and helped him get undressed and into bed. With a soothing voice he told him to try to sleep. He switched off the lights and quietly went back up to his flat.

He looked at the time and saw it was past one o'clock. He sat down in the same chair as before and stared in front of him at the empty chair from which Stan had delivered his confession. Without realising what he was doing, he picked up his stone cold cup of cocoa and started to drink it down in big gulps. He wasn't concentrating on what it tasted like;

his mind was far too busy dealing with the position he now found himself in. Stan had opened up his heart and was relying on him to come up with a solution. After serving God for most of his life he'd finally found himself in a position rather like God. Whatever he decided to do, or recommended Stan to do, would change both their lives entirely. Was Stan so guilty of sinning? He was full of regret and was obviously suffering terribly with the enormity of what he'd done. Perhaps there was credence in what Hermione had told him, that places hold their own identities and people's past lives spent within them. This was an enormous responsibility and Arnold felt uncomfortable with it. He didn't think Stan was in need of psychiatric help; he'd been driven to what he'd done by the inhumane way Nancy had treated him. What did the French call it? A *crime passionel*, he thought. It may have been a valid defence in France, but here in Wiltshire there would be no such understanding. Arnold decided he was too exhausted to think about it rationally any longer, and after he'd washed up his cocoa cup and brushed his teeth he went to bed.

CHAPTER 8

The sky was bright and cloudless when Arnold woke up. The first thing he did was to look out of the window at the garden wondering where Nancy was located. Presumably somewhere amongst the vegetables, according to what Stan had told him the night before. His eyes wandered over to where Stan's car was usually parked and was surprised to see it had gone. He would normally hear him leave in the morning as it woke him up, so he couldn't understand why this particular morning he hadn't. Whilst showering he was relieved Stan wasn't about as it gave him some time to think about what he was going to do. It made sense Stan had refused Arnold's help with the garden when he'd offered it that first day. He'd been there close to three months and over the period had, quite unwittingly, become very close to Stan. Rather like him, he'd had no friends to speak of and the fact they were so different and had no expectations of one another probably cleared the path for an understanding and a mutual appreciation. He had to admit he'd grown very fond of him, which made it even more difficult to decide what was the best action to take. It's all very well and good making cold and clear judgements on the actions people take when you have no connection with them, but it becomes very different when you're personally involved. That was the difference between Arnold's life at St. Tobias's, serving God, and the life he now led. When he was in the Church he was able to maintain a position of separation, without which he knew it would have been difficult to do what he did.

As a citizen, he knew he should inform the authorities of what he knew, or try to persuade Stan to go to them himself. But he was finding it difficult to assess what benefit that would have. Stan would no doubt end up in jail for the rest of his life, and Arnold had never been a big fan of jails, for the simple fact that very little good came out of them. From what he'd learnt, most prisoners spent twenty-three hours a day locked up doing nothing, and there was little attempt to rehabilitate them back into public life. They became a burden on the taxpayer and the majority of prisoners reoffended when released. No, he couldn't see Stan's going to jail being of benefit to anyone. Nancy was gone, and nothing anyone did would bring her back to life. There were no grieving relatives, if he were to believe what Stan had told him. The more he thought about it the clearer he began to see the situation. He ended up firmly believing he shouldn't do anything at all. He wondered if that conflicted with what he'd always believed being a servant of God, and had to conclude that showing compassion for one's fellow man, as Christ himself had, was of the utmost importance. God would surely accept whatever Arnold did as a manifestation of what he judged was the right thing to do, and he felt completely convinced this was correct. This filled him with a remarkable tingling sensation he likened to what he'd experienced when he was in church. He felt he was on the verge of discovering something, some new way of spreading God's love in the outside world. Was the Church itself some sort of a prison, maintaining a strict code of interpretation and obedience to the Word? If it was, it was doing itself no good at all, just like keeping all those prisoners cooped up all day long in jail. It was in the execution – and the deed – that God's will ought to be done.

Arnold felt uplifted by these thoughts, and after he'd dressed and shaved he sat down to an egg and soldiers and coffee, feeling better than he'd felt for a long time. At last he was able to do something in his life that meant something again. Now it was clear, he'd been in a sort of limbo since St. Tobias's had closed, not really connected with life. His relationship with Hermione was the one bright spark in his existence and now he thought perhaps things were going to change for the better.

He wanted to celebrate and decided to go for a bicycle ride in the crisp morning sunlight. He set off, not really sure or minding in which direction he was heading, and was soon leaving Colerne behind and plummeting down lanes with high hedges. He had to stop and get off to walk up the steep gradients on the other side of the dips. There was no traffic to speak of and he had the roads to himself. He seemed to be heading west in the general direction of Bath but had no idea where he was. He came around a bend to see a derelict building on the other side of the lane. It was quite unusual-looking and made him slow down to take a closer look. It was made entirely of corrugated iron and seemed to have what looked like a bell tower at one end that looked as if it would fall down any second. Overgrown and obviously left unoccupied and neglected for a very long time, it had all the things about it to suggest it had been a place of worship. Arnold rested his bike up against the dry stone wall opposite and stepped across the road, curious to investigate. As he walked around its perimeter he had to avoid creepers and brambles that had forced their way between the iron sheets forming the walls to pry around inside. He managed to get all the way round with difficulty and located what seemed to be a front and a back door, both secured with large rusted padlocks. He had never seen anything like it before but recalled reading about these prefabricated churches when he was studying in Guildford. They'd been supplied in the form of a kit, if he remembered correctly, and sold at the beginning of the 1900s for £200 to anyone who needed a place of worship in remote areas of the countryside. Members of a local community would each put a contribution into a fund and send off for the kit to be shipped to them. It was then just a matter of deciding where it was to be put up. He seemed to remember they'd been built on common land, and decided he would try to find out. He wandered back to where he'd left his bike and turned to look again at the derelict church and felt a sudden impulse to go inside. He wheeled his bike over the lane and let it fall within the long grass to help conceal it from any passerby. He remembered seeing a loose section of corrugated iron where a beam of light had shone through highlighting some debris inside and he made his way back round and found the spot again. Carefully lifting the sheet of iron by its loose corner he bent it back far enough to step into the gloom. At first he couldn't see anything so he kept still, and when his eyes became accustomed to the darkness he began to look around. All he could hear were the guttural noises of brooding pigeons coming from the bell tower, as he carefully stepped over several twisted metal chairs to find himself in the centre. It must have been about forty feet long by twenty feet wide, and looking up he could make out wrought cast iron frames that stretched across the width at regular intervals to hold up what was left of the roof. He wished he had his torch with him as the frames seemed to be ornately decorated, but just then there was an increase in the intensity of sunlight breaking through the clouds and the whole place suddenly revealed itself to him for just a few seconds. He had no idea these places could conjure up such a wonderful atmosphere from such meagre components. Stepping back into the daylight he knew he would have to come back another time and make a more thorough investigation.

He got back on his bike and retraced his route to Colerne, hoping he could find out from a map where this curious place was. As he arrived at the house he saw Stan's car outside. He parked his bike up and knocked on Stan's door, which was open:

'Stan ... Stan?'

He slowly walked along the hallway and stepped into the kitchen, where Stan was sitting with a cup of tea in his hands. Arnold sat down opposite him.

'How do you feel, old chap? Did you manage to sleep at all last night?'

'I'm OK, Arnold. I suppose.' He smiled weakly and paused before he spoke again:

'I imagine you've told the police, Arnold? Well, it wouldn't surprise me if that's what you done.'

'No, I haven't done anything, Stan. I've been thinking about it. What you told me. And I don't see what can be achieved by telling anyone else about this.'

Stan turned and stared disbelievingly at Arnold, saying:

'But I deserve to go to jail for what I've done, don't I?'

'I don't think twenty years in jail is going to change anything, Stan. You do feel sorry for what you've done, don't you?'

Stan nodded quickly many times, with his eyes closed.

'And you're suffering because of it, aren't you?'

Stan continued his feverish head movements.

'Well, you'll live with this for the rest of your life. It's punishment enough. But what you must promise me, Stan, is that from now on you'll spend the rest of your life in pursuit of good deeds. You'll try to bring happiness and joy to everyone you know and will meet in the future. In that will lie your redemption, not by rotting away in jail.'

Stan opened his eyes and turned to look at Arnold with obvious relief. They both got up to face one other and came together in a hug. Arnold could hear Stan breathing through his clothes and they stood there for several moments suspended in the judgement of Arnold.

Stan was in his car and away within fifteen minutes of his epiphany, after saying he felt as if he were a new man. Arnold saw him off and waved as the car rounded the bend out of sight leaving a slowly settling cloud of dust in the air. Arnold's curiosity began getting the better of him and he started to wander towards the vegetable patch. He found himself scanning the ground not sure what he was looking for. It looked like any other allotment and he soon gave up the exercise and tried to put the whole thing to the back of his mind. He climbed the stairs up to his flat and went inside to fix himself some lunch. As he opened the door he noticed an envelope on the mat and thought Stan must have popped it through the letterbox earlier and forgotten to say anything.

He picked it up and took it to the kitchen table. It had been sent to his Corsham address and forwarded on, so there had been a delay in him receiving it. Sure enough he could see the postmark originally said late September. It was from the Halifax Building Society, responding to the letter he'd sent them in the middle of August:

Dear Mr. Drive

Thank you for your letter of 20/08/2008 in which you gave details of your deposit account number 43186043059.

May I first apologise for the delay in replying to your enquiry, as the timescale involved with this account has necessitated some detailed investigations being made on your behalf. Please appreciate that as this account has been inactive for 35 years it has been difficult to locate.

I have discovered that a dormant status was allocated to it in 1980, and since then it has been administered by our investment brokers, Goldbloom & Gulbenkian, based in London. I have passed your details on to them and they will be writing to you in due course with news of your investment portfolio.

If you have any further questions please do not hesitate to contact me.

I remain,

Yours sincerely,

Carlos Buenovedad

What with his move and the unexpected turn of events in Colerne, he had completely forgotten about the letter he'd sent regarding the Halifax account book he'd found in the old suitcase. He wondered what on earth had happened to that small deposit. It had probably made a little bit of interest in the time period involved and would come in useful with Christmas coming up. He was being a bit optimistic though, as these sorts of things normally take far longer to sort out than imagined, so he revised when he would hear some news about it to sometime the following spring. Who knows, there may even be enough money to buy a little car. He'd always seen himself driving a Morris 1000 and he knew there was a centre in Bath where they renovated them and put all sorts of new technology inside to bring them up to date. He'd read an article about it in the *Evening Chronicle* just last year, he remembered. Summer would be approaching by then so perhaps he could entertain the idea of a convertible! Now that would be nice, he thought. Driving a convertible Morris 1000. Or maybe even the station wagon model, the one with the wooden framework. But they were much more expensive, he was sure. He'd just have to see what he could afford.

Arnold brought his head down from the clouds at this point and admonished himself for being so vain. All this was getting far too ahead of itself, he realised, but he had enjoyed the moment to indulge in a freedom of fancy. It was something he would never have allowed himself back in the days at Corsham. He refolded the letter, carefully putting it back in its envelope, and placed it on the mantelpiece in the lounge before the phone rang. It was Hermione:

'Hello, love. Wanted to know if you'd like to come over

for supper this evening? Lucy's due back from Durham at the end of this week. I've got a little surprise for you.'

He agreed, of course, as he knew that once Lucy was back it would be much more difficult for them to see each other. It was another reminder Christmas was approaching and he had no idea how he was going to spend it. He thought the best thing to do would be to consult Hermione as she was bound to come up with a plan for him. She insisted, as always, on coming to pick him up. He quietly hoped he could get away before Stan came home as he felt he needed a break from the house. In fact the whole idea of getting away from the place for a while over Christmas appealed to him, and he looked forward to bringing it up with Hermione.

Dead on six o'clock he heard her car in the driveway and within a minute he was downstairs. He'd been ready waiting for about half an hour, he was so desperate to see her.

'Gosh! I'll have to call you Jack In A Box soon! Off we go ...' she chortled as he climbed in. He leant across and kissed her left cheek when she offered it. He was so pleased to see her it was the first thing he said.

'And I'm pleased to see you too, pet. Now, down to business ... I assume you haven't made any plans for the Christmas period, have you?'

Arnold shook his head and was pleased to hear she'd obviously put some thought to it already.

'Well, I have an invitation for you. I intend to take Lucy on a short cruise around the Med and I want to invite you to join us. And before you say you can't afford it, it will be a little present from me. I happen to have an old school chum in the cruise business and she's managed to secure me a wonderful knockdown price for all three of us. Of course, it means we'll have to come out of the closet, so to speak, as far as Lucy is concerned, as there's no way I want to share a room with her for ten days! But I don't have a problem with that. Have you, Arnold darling?'

Arnold was positively beaming at her and shook his head again, rather like a child who knows when it's being spoilt.

'Well, that's settled then. Marvellous,' she chuckled. 'We'll have such a wonderful time.'

She spent the rest of the drive to Corsham running through the itinerary of the trip. It involved a flight to Athens where they would join the boat, then sailing down to Libya via Crete, from where they worked their way around to Tunisia. They were then to sail back via Sicily to Athens on New Year's Day from where they flew back home. It all sounded too exotic to be true to Arnold. Places like Libya, Crete, Athens and Tunisia were just vague names he'd seen in atlases when he'd been at school. He was so overawed by the whole idea he didn't pay much attention when she said Trevor Hatswell was joining them for dinner. When they arrived she explained it really was long overdue for her to invite him round, after he had so magnanimously treated them all to dinner at the Jaipur, over three months earlier.

'Ah, yes,' said Arnold, 'the last supper.'

He had just enough time to take her in his arms and kiss her before the doorbell rang.

'That'll be Trevor. I'd better let him in ...' she whispered and was off like a butterfly to the front door. Trevor followed her back into the living room like a pet dog and sat where he was told next to Arnold, and immediately started talking:

'Hello, old bean. Haven't seen you for a while. How's it going in Colerne with your taxi driver chappie? Can't remember the last time I was up in those parts. But there again, I can't remember the last time I left Corsham, actually. Time does fly by, you know. How long is it since you moved up there? Blimey, it must be all of ... nearly four months, by my estimation. Good Lord. So tell me all about it, then. Be a good chap.'

So while Hermione ran around getting them drinks and popping in and out of the kitchen to check on the food in the oven, Arnold outlined his life at Stan's house. He was intending to leave out any mention of the strange things he'd experienced during the night but unfortunately Hermione brought it up and he was forced to tell all. Trevor listened intently and said afterwards:

'That does sound spooky. Have you got to the bottom of it yet? Discovered any grisly murders there back in the Middle Ages?'

Arnold could see him taking an interest, like a terrier gnawing at a slipper. Hermione jumped to his rescue:

'Oh, do stop it, Trevor! Poor Arnold doesn't need you scaremongering. Come on, both of you. It's time to eat.'

She shepherded them into the kitchen and Arnold was glad of the interruption as it served as an opportunity for him to change the subject. Besides, he was genuinely interested in what had been going on in Corsham since he'd left and Trevor was the right person to know every tiny bit of gossip. As usual, Trevor drank too many gin and tonics and started to flirt with Hermione after they'd eaten, but Arnold was surprisingly pleased to see him after so long and didn't mind one bit. Their conversation turned to St. Tobias's, and Trevor had heard some interesting things regarding the conversion:

'Rumour has it it's all a bit iffy at the moment, what with the worries about the economy. It's the first industry to be affected, you know, the building trade. It's a lot of money to tie up, especially when you're not sure if you're going to be able to sell it on. You know, it wouldn't surprise me if it never gets started. And to tell you the truth, I won't be at all upset. Never heard of such a preposterous idea in the first place. As if you can evict God from a building! Well, it's blatantly ridiculous. Don't you agree, Arnold?'

Secretly, Arnold too was pleased that the work might be held up. But then, what could he have done about it? Until the work took place, the untouched church seemed to be testament to his contribution and the longer it remained intact the happier he would be. They managed to avoid the subject of Christmas coming up – they knew as soon as Trevor got wind of their plans, it would be common knowledge in Corsham within twenty-four hours. It was one thing for Lucy to be aware of what was going on, but they hardly wanted the whole world to know.

Finally they were able to bundle Trevor out of the door, still jabbering, and relax together on the sofa. Arnold wanted to hold on to her desperately that evening and it occurred to him how much happiness he'd missed out on for all those years and wondered what good it had done anyone.

CHAPTER 9

Lucy arrived back from Durham for the Christmas break and Arnold resigned himself to the fact he wouldn't be seeing Hermione, so he busied himself with some background reading in preparation for the cruise. First thing he did was go into Bath and spend some time at an internet cafe where he looked up the cruise company and took marvellous virtual tours through the cabins and the areas of the ship they were travelling on. He printed out maps of the ship and familiarised himself with its layout so he'd feel comfortable whilst he was on-board, as he always liked to know where he was. He also got a detailed itinerary of the places they were due to visit so he could go to the Corsham library and find out about Knossos, Leptis Magna and the other sites. The more he found out, the more excited he became, and the last two weeks flashed by. Stan seemed to be busier than ever, ferrying people up to the airports for their escapes away and Arnold realised they would need transport to whichever airport they were leaving from, and he made a note to ask Hermione. He saw Stan perhaps three times over the next ten days and their life continued uneventfully. Neither of them referred to what had happened, but Arnold did notice that the tapping on the door had stopped. Either that or he'd got used to it. Hermione rang to go over the arrangements for their departure and she had, of course, organised a pick-up from her house early on the morning before Christmas Eve. He got Stan to take him over on the way to another booking in Trowbridge. It was dark and crisp when they met downstairs at five that morning and Stan gave him a hug before they got in the car.

'You look after yourself, Arnold, in that Africa place. I don't wants nothing to happen to my patron saint, like, while you be away. Tomorrow night I'll be going to St. John's and saying a prayer for you. It'll be the first time I'll have been to church since I were a nipper and I'm looking forward to it. I got me frozen Christmas turkey dinner ready to have, so don't you worry about me. I'm looking forward to putting me feet up and watching a bit of telly, to tell you the truth. You just make sure you have a wonderful time.'

All too soon they were outside Hermione's front door and Stan was lifting Arnold's suitcase out of the car boot for him. Arnold got his purse out but Stan stopped him.

'You put that away, now. Merry Christmas to you, Arnold. I'll see you next year.'

And off he went, leaving Arnold feeling alone on the pavement, staring after the car as it disappeared at the end of the road. It was empty and still and Arnold could see his breath clouding in front of his face. He picked up his suitcase and opened Hermione's garden gate, which made a loud metallic squeak in the chill quiet of the morning. When he reached the door it magically opened and Lucy was standing in front of him smiling.

'Hello, Arnold. Seems cold out there, you'd better come

in. Mum's making us bacon sandwiches and a cuppa before our cab gets here.'

He followed her into the hallway and closed the door behind him. He liked the way she was shepherding him around rather in the way her mother always did, and he felt content and safe to be part of their family group. The smell of grilled bacon wafted from the direction of the kitchen and Hermione got them both to sit down at the table while she waited on them.

'I'm so excited, Mum. Athens is supposed to be pretty warm this time of year,' Lucy said as she poured them all cups of tea. 'Is this your first time abroad?' she asked Arnold.

'Indeed it is,' he stammered, 'I can't believe it's really happening.'

Lucy was keen to see Arnold's new passport and thought he looked very distinguished and rather handsome in the photo. He'd had it taken in the photo booth at Morrisons in Chippenham while Hermione had waited outside in her car. The photos were barely dry as he'd put them in the envelope together with the completed forms. They'd only just finished their bacon sandwiches when they heard the doorbell. Lucy jumped up, saying:

'That'll be the taxi. I'll go, Mum.'

Whilst Lucy was out of the kitchen Hermione came up behind Arnold's chair and put her arms around his shoulders and massaged his hair with her fingers. He wasn't expecting this and it gave him an immediate erection. She kissed him on the ear, then whisked his plate and cup away to the sink.

Half an hour later they were in the taxi speeding along the M4, Arnold in the front with the driver. They spent the journey talking about the trip and Arnold was surprised at how knowledgeable Lucy was of the various places they would be visiting. Part of her studies at Durham involved taking a course in Ancient History and she'd taken the opportunity to do a bit of background reading about the places they were going to. She was especially interested in Nafplio, which in the nineteenth century, with the establishment of the First Hellenic Republic, had briefly been the capital of Greece before Athens, and she told them about the 'Valley of a Million Olives' on a side road on the way to Delphi.

They arrived at Gatwick and it was the busiest place Arnold had ever been to in his life. Although it was only 7am there were thousands of people milling around in and out of the queues, trawling their luggage along behind them. He felt bewildered by it all and found the level of noise disturbing, and, not being a lover of crowded places, he was happy for the women to take control. Hermione led the way through the crowds with their bags on a trolley with Lucy in the middle holding on to her and Arnold's hands in pursuit, and gradually they edged their way towards the check-in desk for the flight to Athens. Arnold had carefully followed Hermione's instructions about packing and had made sure his hand baggage obeyed all the new security regulations. He was shocked to discover he had to take off half his clothes before passing through the security check, together with his shoes. Of course, he forgot to take off his belt and set off the metal detector. When he did take it off he had to hold up his trousers as he tiptoed through for fear of them falling down. It all seemed very pedantic, he thought, especially when he saw people could take bottles of duty free spirits that were flammable on-board the plane, and also sharp pencils and pens. There was a slight delay to the flight but finally they boarded the plane and took off. He enjoyed the sensation immensely. It was like no other experience he'd ever had, but as much as he wanted to he had difficulty looking out of the windows as they were seated in the middle section of the plane. The aircraft settled into its flight path and he realised both Lucy and Hermione had their heads resting on his shoulders as he was seated between them, and they were fast asleep, so he spent most of the flight desperately trying not to move for fear of waking them up.

He must have fallen asleep, as the next thing he knew a voice was telling everybody to fasten their seat belts in preparation for landing in Athens. He had to admit he didn't like the landing experience as much as the taking off, but then nobody likes coming back down to earth, he thought, so that sort of made sense. He looked down and noticed Lucy and Hermione each had one of his hands tightly grasped in theirs as he felt the bump of the wheels on the tarmac and heard the high pitched whine of the engines going into reverse thrust to slow the plane down. It seemed to him a far cleverer device to slow the plane down than using brakes, and avoided the possibility of skidding, although it used far more petrol of course. The first thing he noticed when he got off the plane was the heat of a warm day in Athens, and he could hardly disguise a chuckle in his voice as he turned to Hermione and said quietly to her:

'Thank you so much for this.'

Then Lucy half turned her head and smiled at him and he knew she'd heard what he'd said too, and he felt embarrassed. They both grabbed his hands again and steered him across the runway and into one of the coaches for transfer to the arrivals terminal and into line to pass through immigration. Hermione was back in charge of things and with their luggage claimed from the carousel they emerged from Customs. She spotted the sign for the cruise company being held up in the air by a smartly dressed Greek man in sunglasses. It seemed almost as busy as Gatwick to Arnold, only smellier and warmer, and soon they were being led with about fifty other people along the front of the terminal building to a waiting coach. Once fully loaded, the coach set off and he looked out of the window he was next to, and he tried to imagine what it all would have looked like when it was new. Perhaps like Milton Keynes, he thought. It puzzled him why people were fascinated by old buildings, rather than new ones. Was it because they all had imprints of past lives embedded in their fabric, like Stan's house had in Colerne? Then he wondered if Milton Keynes would ever inspire the same sort of awe in visitors there, in two thousand years ...

After about an hour's drive, they entered what looked like a port and Arnold saw a sign saying VOLOS on the side of the road. They rounded a bend past some warehouses and he saw the ship in front of them, glinting white in the afternoon sunshine. Arnold was aware that Volos was where Jason had set sail all those years ago to discover the priestess Medea, whom he brought back to Greece and married. As the coach got closer the boat grew and grew as if it had come out of *Alice in Wonderland*. They climbed from the bus onto the quay and his head spun as he looked up at the side of the boat towering next to him, and found he had to hang on to Hermione for support. He had no idea boats this big existed anywhere and the pictures he'd seen hadn't conveyed the reality of its size. It was as tall as any church spire he knew of and its smooth surface was peppered with rows and rows of tiny windows, and he was put in mind of *Moby Dick*. He started to imagine the ship as a living and breathing organism, which, indeed, it was. Their luggage was unloaded and pounced upon by an army of Asian crew members, but it had all been properly labelled by Hermione so there was no fear of any of it going missing. The passengers lined up and slowly walked up the gangway into the ship's side where, after a passport check, they were issued with a ship's identity pass. A young Indian boy called Sachin greeted the three of them and offered to escort them to their cabins. It reminded Arnold of a hotel, and of course being moored it was stationary, so there wasn't really anything to make him aware it was a ship at all. They followed Sachin along a narrow corridor and around a corner to an area with several lifts. After entering one they went up a few floors, before trooping out and down another corridor after Sachin, who finally opened two doors to adjoining rooms.

'Miss Cartwright? Please, you have room III 161. Just here. And Mr. Drive, you are here, right next door, room III 163. Please, may I have your attention for just a few minutes? I must show you the location of your life jackets. They are here. Thank you. And this is your cabin boy, Charlie. He can help you during your stay on-board with anything you may want.'

And out of thin air an even smaller, smiling Asian appeared, and Arnold was convinced he must have been standing in the wardrobe outside the bathroom door to have appeared quite so fast. And that was that. Sachin melted away followed by Charlie. Hermione closed the door to their cabin and they were instantly alone, looking out at a beautiful azure sea from the doors of a balcony at the end of their room, and at that moment Arnold was convinced he'd been transported to heaven.

CHAPTER 10

After they'd unpacked their bags and had a cup of tea, Arnold sat out on the balcony with Hermione and watched the afternoon sun slowly descending to the horizon. Their cabin was located on the starboard side of the boat and it was pointing south at its berth, so their balcony faced west away from the port. They could hear activity coming from the other side of the boat as it prepared to leave for their first overnight sail. Hermione snuggled up to him:

'Arnold, darling, is it too early for us to celebrate being here? I spotted a bottle of champers in the fridge and it seems an awful shame just to leave it there. What do you think?'

Arnold was about to answer her when there was a tapping at the door so he got up to answer it. Lucy came bounding in:

'Hey, you two, isn't it great? My room is too fab for words. Shall we have a drink, or what?'

Hermione burst out laughing so Arnold took that as a cue to fetch the bottle. Once they were out on the veranda again holding their glasses they felt a stirring in the depths of the boat and Arnold was sure he heard the engines start up, as if someone had just turned a key in the ignition of a car.

'Look, we're moving!' Lucy said.

Very slowly, the boat picked up speed and Arnold felt

it turn westwards and by looking to his right he caught the edge of Volos port coming into view from behind the boat. They advanced slowly into the Pagasitic Gulf heading south, sipping champagne, with Arnold sat in one chair and Lucy balancing on the arm of Hermione's, and everything seemed to him to be in order. They were on their way to Crete where they would dock in Heraklion the following morning and take a trip out to see Knossos.

'Do you realise if it wasn't for good old Arthur Evans, an Englishman, Knossos would never have been discovered?' Lucy proclaimed.

'Well, I don't know about that,' Arnold joined in, 'it would still exist in some form or other, I'm sure.'

'Yes, but what I mean is, the whole Minoan civilisation would be called something different. He came up with the word Minoan, didn't he? Can you imagine, nowadays, just buying up a vast, unexcavated piece of land abroad and then spending your whole fortune digging it up, just on a hunch? Apparently the word comes from the bull, which they worshipped. Very sexually oriented, they were, the ancient Cretans. That is what they were called, weren't they? I wonder if there's any link to the word "cretin"?'

'There could be a link,' Arnold answered. '"Creta" is Latin for chalk, and the landscape of Crete is very chalky, and that's part of the origin of the word "cretin", so you never know.'

'Wow, Arnold,' Lucy said, impressed, 'you are awfully clever.'

For a second he thought Hermione had said it but through the mist of the champagne he realised it had been Lucy. He looked at them both and it struck him how alike they were. They continued to chat and gazed at the changing landscape lining the gulf until the boat left the mainland of Greece and headed out into the Aegean Sea. Twilight arrived and they decided it was too cold to stay outside any longer. Lucy disappeared discreetly and they were left to themselves struggling to undo buttons and belts as they plunged into the bed to lose themselves in one another amidst the champagne. When they woke up they were incredibly hungry and Hermione got dressed and went next door to arrange a time for dinner with Lucy. They agreed to eat straight away in one of the restaurants with waiter service and they were back in their rooms by ten, ready to turn in for the early start for Knossos the next day.

Arnold was quite unprepared for all the activity the next day. Hermione had arranged for the three of them to take membership of the Club Lounge on-board, so they were able to take a quiet breakfast away from the crowds, and browse through English newspapers the boat had picked up in Athens. They made their way down to the disembarkation point and it struck Arnold there was as much security getting on and off the boat as there had been at the airports for the plane. Three coaches were waiting on the quay and they filled up very quickly. Arnold made sure he got a seat next to a window and was happy to look out and see how Crete compared to Athens. The coach ride was a lot shorter than the one they had taken to Volos so he didn't have time to observe much but it struck him there wasn't a lot of difference between them, except Crete looked a little hotter and dustier, with fewer people.

They drove through the large arrival gates at Knossos and the group was split into six. Each had its own local guide and

Hermione picked one with a clear voice so they could easily follow what she was saying, and they positioned themselves near that guide to make sure they joined her group. The site was immense so each group set off in a different direction to avoid confusion with overlapping commentaries. Arnold was spellbound as they explored some of the palace's thousand or so rooms and it became clear the extent to which it was a microcosm of a city. All the rooms seemed to be interlocking and apparently there were rooms dedicated to artists, wine manufacturers, food, prayer and even bureaucracy. He was impressed until he heard that evidence of human sacrifice had been proved, at which point he became disappointed with the whole set-up. It was also clear the labyrinthine nature of the palace meant any sacrificial victims would have trouble escaping their fate. The human mind seemed to be ingenious at devising methods for cruelty; it was something he'd also noticed from reading his book about the Inquisition. He perked up a bit when the complex sanitation arrangements were described as he had a lot of respect for cleanliness. Apparently they had baths, the first flushing toilets, and piped in spring water distributed through gravity feed systems, whose speed was controlled by zigzagging channels. Very clever, he thought. Being so big, most of the rooms had no windows, so sunlight was maximised by them being arranged around courtyards. There were frescoes everywhere featuring a lot of bulls, and in all of them the men had ruddy cheeks and the women had milky complexions, so no change there, he thought. The mystery seemed to be what had happened in the winters as there was no evidence of central heating but also no depictions of the harsh winters of Crete. Arnold emerged at the end of the tour into blinding sunlight and was left pondering this conundrum. Hermione and Lucy were chatting away next to him but he was oblivious, lost in thought, trying to work out the possibilities. Perhaps the winters in those days weren't so extreme? Or perhaps they all upped sticks and went south for the winter, like migrating birds? It seemed odd there was no evidence of winter clothing amongst all the relics they'd found. He was disturbed by Hermione shaking his arm:

'Arnold, love, are you all right? Come on, it's time for a spot of lunch.'

He was dragged by his shirt sleeves along with the rest of the group to a cafeteria where they were joined by the rest of the party from the boat. They sat down and were served the same salad, bread and a bottle of water. It tasted fine but Arnold objected to being herded about, as if they were all non-thinking bovine stock, being fed and prepared for some more sinister purpose. He tried not to let it affect him. Besides Hermione and Lucy were quite happy as they talked about what they'd seen:

'So there you go, mum, the women WERE in charge. And I'll tell you another thing I heard at uni, the Minoan women athletes used to wear sports bras! And that's at least 1500 years before Christ.'

'Well, I am impressed, sweetheart. I had no idea Christ wore one too. I just loved the frescoes, especially the ones in the throne room, with the gryphons, they were exquisite ...'

And it carried on, and drifted into the background of his thoughts.

It was true. All this had been going on two thousand years before Christ, and served to put Arnold's religious beliefs in perspective. He felt uncomfortable at the significance of this.

Did it mean God wasn't around throughout that whole time? And if he had been there, why did he wait so long to show himself to the world? With child sacrifices taking place, the very thought of which horrified Arnold, what had made him wait another two thousand years? Perhaps he was busy elsewhere in the Universe ...

'Arnold, would you like a coffee? They want to know if you want a coffee,' Hermione was asking him and he thought it might perk him up, so he said 'yes please'.

All the way back on the coach Arnold was preoccupied. The coffee had woken him up but his mind was still troubled by the possibilities the visit to Knossos had highlighted. He was sure it hadn't all been made up. A certain amount of reconstruction and embellishment had been done by Arthur Evans and his workers, but it didn't alter the basic information regarding the way the Minoans had led their lives and the facts regarding their history. Arnold started to feel very small and it reminded him of the dream he'd had when he was young, in a bed in the middle of a vast room with tall ceilings. He imagined himself going out through the roof of the coach and rising up into the air and looking down to see it speeding along the road back to the port, racing with its own shadow. Then he rose even higher and could see the boat at anchor in the harbour at Heraklion, and then he went higher still, so he could see Crete sitting in the Aegean Sea, and then the whole of Greece, and then the complete Mediterranean Sea, and then the whole world, which was just the size of a golf ball, and he realised how insignificant he was, and how insignificant everything was at that moment.

When they reached the ship, Arnold was ready for a cup of tea. He was relieved to be back in their cabin again and after his tea he just wanted to lie down in bed with Hermione to hold on to, to stop himself whizzing off into the air again. She seemed to know instinctively how he was feeling as she helped him undress and slipped his naked legs under the sheets. It reminded him of the first time they had made love the previous summer. Soon she was inside the bed too holding him close just as he'd wanted and they lay there quietly looking out of their window watching the world go by. The ship's engines started up like a little car again and the boat gently drifted out of Heraklion port heading south on Christmas Eve.

CHAPTER 11

'Merry Christmas, Arnold darling.'

This was the first thing he heard the next morning, and he felt himself growing tumescent as Hermione lightly chewed on his ear below the blankets. He still had his eyes closed but could feel the boat gently vibrating beneath him so he guessed they were still travelling. He felt the boat moving slowly in the swell and when he opened his eyes he could see a clear horizon to the west. They were heading for Tripoli in Libya and weren't due to dock there until Boxing Day morning which meant they would spend the whole of Christmas Day on-board ship. They made love in a lazy fashion and saw it was already past ten.

Hermione reached for the phone and dialled Lucy's room:

'Happy Christmas, love. Club Lounge for breakfast in half an hour? See you there.'

They got up and showered together, it was something Arnold particularly liked doing. They'd started the habit in the autumn and Arnold liked to wash her body feeling her contours in the water jets with his soapy fingers. Now whenever he showered alone it felt awkward washing his body himself rather than feeling her exploring fingers doing it. He really believed it to be a luxurious pastime and was sure he should be feeling some guilt enjoying it as much as he did.

Hermione explained she and Lucy always exchanged presents over Christmas Day breakfast, so Arnold went to his case to gather up the presents he'd brought. He was surprised to see Hermione with two small, wrapped boxes. He thought the cruise itself was her Christmas gift to both him and Lucy, but on considering her generous character he knew it wasn't enough to stop her giving them more. The Lounge was empty being so late in the morning and when they'd sat down and ordered coffee Lucy went first. She offered Arnold a neatly wrapped, thin, square packet and gave Hermione what looked like an envelope. Arnold was next and gave Lucy a packet that looked like it could have been a book and gave Hermione a box about a foot square. Finally Hermione gave Lucy a soft, square packet and Arnold a thin box about a foot long, and there was much tearing of paper and tape as they discovered what they'd received. Arnold had always enjoyed the ritual of giving presents as it struck him as a genuinely Christian act. He liked the anticipation and the unexpectedness of a present popping up out of the blue.

He'd never heard of Al Green, and there were two CDs in Lucy's packet, not one. One was called 'Still In Love With You' and the other 'Call Me'. Lucy said they were supposed to be his best albums and explained he was a soul singer who'd become a priest, even founding his own church. Arnold was curious to hear what it sounded like and asked if he could put one on in the Club Lounge, and he was pleasantly surprised at what he heard.

In the other box from Hermione there were two ties from Iran, woven from shot silk. One was in light blue with an intricate embroidered design, and the other was a patchwork of different coloured diagonal stripes. They were the most beautiful ties he'd ever seen.

'I'm so glad you like them. I found them on the internet, they've come direct from Tehran.'

Lucy gave her mother a year's subscription to the *Daily Telegraph* and Hermione bought her some clothes. Always a safe bet, she said, when they were unwrapped. Lucy carefully inspected them and gave her approval.

Arnold's choice of presents had occupied a lot of his time and as the departure date had drawn ever closer he sensed a dread of getting it wrong. Over the years he'd received presents from people in Corsham but he'd never been close enough to anyone to consider giving anything back. He'd been advised not to enter into that sort of connection with his parishioners outside of family, of which he had none, so he found himself stressing as he wandered past the shop windows in Bath looking for ideas. Then one day he was wandering by the Kitchen Shop on Quiet Street and in the window saw a pasta-making machine. Ideal, he thought, for Hermione. He couldn't recall ever seeing anything like it in her kitchen, so he'd taken a chance with it. He was relieved Lucy had taken an interest in archaeology as he'd bought her a Baedeker on Greece in Waterstones that same day. It contained detailed knowledge of the sites they were due to visit at the tail end of their trip. He breathed a sigh of relief when they both hugged him, thanking him for perfect choices. Lucy was now slightly taller than her mother and he noticed how easily her head fitted into the gap in his collar bone. When Hermione did it she had to stand on tiptoe but for Lucy it required no effort at all. He felt Lucy holding on to him a little too long and he had to think of something to say in order to break the moment, so he said:

'I've got an idea, why don't we take a stroll around the ship? We can see exactly where everything is and it could give us some ideas about what to do later. I've got a map in the cabin.'

They both thought it was a grand idea so they finished their breakfast and gathered up their presents. Once back inside their cabin Hermione gave him a generous kiss:

'Arnold, thank you so much for taking the trouble to get me something. I know you're not used to all of this.'

'Well,' he whispered, 'I hope you don't mind me saying this, but I'm beginning to feel like part of the family.'

He really enjoyed leading them around, clutching the map in his hand. He thought it would be best to start on the lower decks and that way they could end up outside on top in time for lunch. He made sure they walked along every corridor the passengers had access to and it became clear just how large the ship was. The vibrations from the engines grew louder the further down they got inside the hull and he was relieved they weren't having to sleep in any of the cabins on the lower decks. As they walked by passengers or maids would come in and out of cabins onto the narrow corridors and sometimes they would have to turn sideways in order to let a particularly large person through. As they climbed up the floors the engines got quieter and the corridors became wider, and after about an hour and a half they'd got up to their own floor. There were lifts to the front, middle and rear of the ship but they found it quicker and more fun to use the stairs. Every floor had a different scene being enacted by an ever-increasing cast list and they began to wonder just what they would find around the next corner. There was one floor that looked like the reception area of a hotel, and another that was just like a shopping mall complete with overhead, piped background music. In fact, Arnold noticed there was music everywhere, something he wasn't too pleased about. He wondered what it was about modern life that necessitated a lack of silence? He realised it was something he missed from his days at St. Tobias's. It all seemed such a long time ago ...

Another thing he noticed was the lack of animals and he was glad about that. He tolerated cats and detested noisy dogs, but was happy with most of God's other creatures. The higher decks had theatres, bars, a casino, even a health spa, and they finally emerged outside into the sunshine and gazed out at the blue sea that surrounded them on all sides, and could see there were no other ships or land in sight. There were a few seagulls flying along by the side of the ship's furrows and Arnold wondered if they lived on the boat decks, or if they came and went using boats like buses to get from one bit of land to another. There were a lot of people outside on loungers around the two swimming pools and several laughing children were holding their noses, jumping in and out of one of these, sending splashes over the side. Arnold studied the faces of the people as they read their books and drank their cocktails and thought they all looked rather exhausted. In fact, it was the weariest-looking group of people he'd ever seen. What had made them look so worn out? Could life be such hard work? He began to think perhaps in a way he'd been lucky tucked away for all those years in Corsham, sheltered and protected from the rampant chaos he was beginning to notice outside in the world. The struggles and hardships raising families, being pulled this way and that by changing economic winds and being subjected to the cupidity of vainglorious politicians playing out their personal fantasies. Here was evidence that most people actually endured their lives rather than lived them, and the realisation shocked him.

'Actually, shall we go down and get something to eat in the Lounge?' he asked the other two.

They both said they were hungry and followed Arnold back downstairs, still clutching his map, and he wondered if they'd had the same thought as him up there on the main deck, amongst the loungers.

After lunch they took a rest in their cabins and Arnold sat outside in the sunshine and read some more of his book on the Inquisition. Hermione had an appointment in the spa for some beauty treatment, a 'present to myself' as she had put it. Arnold was enjoying the time being alone when he thought he heard a faint knock at the door. He went to open the door and Lucy was standing outside:

'Hi, Arnold. Where's mum?'

'Oh, hello. She's gone to the spa. Anything I can do?'

'Oh, no, not really. I was just bored and wanted to talk to somebody. Can I come in?'

He stood aside so she could enter the cabin and they wandered onto the balcony and sat down in the two chairs to look at the passing waves. A couple of seagulls flew by quite close squawking loudly and made them both jump in surprise. They laughed and Arnold asked if she wanted a cup of tea.

'Oooh yes, that would be nice. Got any biccies?'

Arnold put the kettle on to boil and found several small packets of chocolate chip cookies. A few minutes later he emerged onto the balcony holding the tea tray and put it down on the small table between their chairs. Once they were settled and had attacked the cookies and sipped their tea, Lucy said:

'I think it's great about you and Mum. I can't remember when I last saw her looking so happy. Thanks so much.'

'Well, thank you for saying so. But I assure you, it's your mother that's been so wonderful to me. I don't know what life would've been like without her being there as she has been. I can't even imagine it.'

'You know, she'd like you to move back to Corsham into the house with her. I don't know if she's mentioned it to you, but I know that's what she wants. She asked me when I got back from Durham what I thought about it.'

'No, she hasn't mentioned it to me. What do you think?'

'I think it would be grand. I'm away most of the time anyway, so it won't affect me. But I know that's what she really, really wants. Besides, I think you're a very interesting man ...'

Arnold remained quiet, but attentive. He was curious to find out what Lucy thought of him. In the pause that followed he continued to look out to sea hoping she would say something more, but she didn't. He looked at her and caught her staring at him, which made him blush.

'Would you like some more tea?' he asked her.

'No, no thanks,' she said hurriedly, being polite and she got up, and he thought he should too. They stood for a moment facing one another, and she stepped forward to gently rest her head back inside his collar bone, as she'd done earlier that day. He awkwardly curled an arm around her and clasped her waist for a second before she moved away from him and walked back into the cabin. She left without saying another word and Arnold felt slightly confused about what had happened.

CHAPTER 12

The next morning they docked in Tripoli and Arnold was up early on deck to watch them gliding slowly into Africa. Apart from all the shipping paraphernalia and the cranes, containers and other boats, the place had a different feel and when he started noticing signs in Arabic, he knew he was a long way from home in Wiltshire. There seemed to be a lot more space than in Crete or Athens and the skyline of Tripoli was much lower and vaster than in Heraklion and Volos. He thought he saw a line of camels moving slowly along a distant road.

The boat stopped moving and he leant over the safety rail to watch the walkway being dropped down, and various crew members going down to meet with port officials on the quay. Paperwork was exchanged and studied and it seemed as if something was wrong. The Libyan officials were looking at their watches and shaking their heads, and the crew were raising their hands and pointing in the direction of the boat, and then at somewhere beyond the quay. Arnold saw the purser running down the gangplank with what looked like a plastic bag full of cartons of cigarettes and giving this to the port officials. Suddenly everything seemed to be in order and the officials signed various documents, shook hands with the purser and the other crew members and wandered off down the quay looking inside their plastic bag. Almost immediately several coaches drew up and parked next to the ship and inside their windscreens the words LEPTIS MAGNA were scrawled on bits of card. Arnold went downstairs to collect Hermione and Lucy on the way to the Club Lounge for a quick breakfast. They were looking forward to the trip along the coast eastwards to visit the site and the coach ride was a good two hours.

Libya got more desolate the further they got from Tripoli, and they saw more and more camels but fewer and fewer people. It looked to Arnold twice as dusty and dry as Crete and although the weather was beautiful it was obvious water was a priority. Lucy told them Colonel Gaddafi had constructed The Great Manmade River, a vast system of underground pipes that transported fresh water from below the desert to the coastal cities and it had allowed them to adorn their streets with luxurious palm trees.

'What I heard was that a local boy became Emperor of Rome,' Lucy said, 'and made sure the city became mega important. But then it all got silly and overstretched itself, and that was that.'

Arnold noted how succinct Lucy was. She seemed to be able to say exactly what she wanted with the minimum of effort, and he liked that.

He was very impressed with what he saw that day. The marketplace and theatre were exceptionally preserved and he particularly liked the Septeran Basilica, and sat and looked at it for a good ten minutes, so he had to run to catch up with the rest of his group, who'd moved on to look at something else.

'Arnold dear, I see I'm going to have to keep a close eye, to make sure I don't lose you,' Hermione whispered when he'd caught up. Lucy smiled at him indulgently. It was hard going scrambling around the site in the heat and they were exhausted by the time a break was called at lunchtime. The routine salad, roll and bottle of water were served up in a canteen and they managed to grab a quiet corner at one of the tables.

'I quite like the idea of archaeology,' Lucy said in between mouthfuls. 'Must be very satisfying seeing something just emerge out of the ground, that's been hidden for centuries.'

'Perhaps you might be able to volunteer for a dig next summer, love?' Hermione suggested. 'I assume you won't get paid, but it would be a lovely way to spend the summer. Abroad, somewhere hot.'

'Do you think so, Mum? Yes, I suppose you're right. I could always make some enquiries when I get back. It'd be great fun. I may even unearth some ancient relic. Maybe a 3,000-year-old empty Marmite jar.'

'Well, at least you'd get a good tan!' Hermione offered back.

Later on the coach Hermione sat by the window and Arnold sat between them. She held his hand and Lucy fell asleep resting her head on his left shoulder. Some of her hair fell on his face and he enjoyed the sensation, feeling its light touch imbued with youth. As he fell asleep he came to the conclusion it smelled like a cross between lemons and almonds.

From Tripoli they sailed overnight along the coast and up to Sousse in Tunisia where they took in El Djem, then on to Tunis to visit Carthage. They sailed through the straits of

Sicily and Arnold spent a wonderful day in Catania, where he took time out by himself to visit the many churches in the town, some of which had been buried under the lava from Mount Etna. It reawakened his spiritual beliefs and was like a breath of fresh air for him to sit again in God's spaces, pondering on the world and all its paradoxes. He began to feel he was a paradox, and within him wrestled many conflicting emotions and beliefs. He concluded that, just like the ship, he was proving to be a microcosm of everything that existed. He had enough time to go into San Placido, St. Agatha's Abbey, St. Benedict's of Nursia and the Marian Sanctuary of St. Mary, but he could quite easily have spent a week there, because of the clarity he was achieving. He would have liked to visit the grottoes of Ulysses up the coast in Acitrezza and he saw signs for boat trips going there. But as he emerged from St. Mary's he could see the sun had sunk below the roofs of the town behind him and the shadows were lengthening, so he bought an ice cream and jumped in a taxi to hurry back to the ship.

When he'd got on-board Hermione seemed in a strange mood and he asked if she was all right.

'I'm OK,' she sighed. 'Had a bit of a tiff with Lucy earlier. All rather stupid, really. Best forgotten.'

Arnold hoped she would want to share it with him, but after a bit of unsuccessful coaxing he realised she had no desire to talk about what was troubling her. He made her a cup of tea and they lay down on the bed together and had a snooze as the sun went down. Arnold woke up after a while and thought he'd heard some noise, so he carefully got up in the dark and saw something had been slipped under their door. It was a note addressed to 'Mum', and he couldn't help but read it because as he picked it up his fingers slipped between the folds and it opened of its own accord, to reveal the following:

Mum ... sorry about earlier.
Just telling the truth, as I always have done.
But don't worry about it. You're as safe as houses.
Didn't mean to upset you.
Lots of love Luce x
PS After that massive lunch I won't need any food later, so having an early night.

Arnold read it a few times and carefully put it back down on the floor by the door. He climbed back into bed and hugged Hermione's back. After a few minutes she stirred and woke up and they melted into each other as naturally as two flavours of ice cream on a hot day.

The next day they were up early as the boat glided into Katakolon harbour on the western coast of the Peloponnese, where they were due to visit the site of ancient Olympia, home of the very first Olympic games. During breakfast Arnold noticed a chill between the two women, and guessed it was connected to their disagreement the day before. He'd seen Hermione had read the note from Lucy the previous evening, but she hadn't shown any reaction to it so Arnold had put it to the back of his mind. Now it was obvious they were trying very hard with each other, something he'd never experienced before when he'd seen them together. Conversation was deliberate and strained, and lacked that spontaneity he had grown used to seeing between them. He put it down partly to the fact the cruise was drawing to an end and they would soon be heading back to the grey gloom of the English winter. Lucy was studying the ship's broadsheet, which gave details of all the trips available from the boat on a daily basis.

'You know,' she said, dropping a folded leaflet down on the table in front of Arnold, 'there's a fabulous vineyard called Mercouri on the way to Olympia, and the coach will drop you off on the way. They do a guided tour of the estate, which looks wonderful. Then they give you an open-air buffet and tasting of all the wines. Is anyone interested in that rather than any more traipsing around in the heat? I think I've had my fill of ancient ruins.'

Arnold knew Hermione was particularly looking forward to seeing Olympia as she was passionate about the Olympic Games. She'd told him she always followed the live action on television whenever they were being held. Arnold could see a possible disagreement coming up but was surprised when he heard her reply:

'Not for me, love. I've just got to see Olympia, it's the highlight of the trip for me. But you go ahead, and take Arnold with you, it'll give me a bit of time on my tod.'

Arnold didn't know what to say and was shocked at her suggestion. He was unsure what it revealed of the current situation between them. He must have looked like a startled rabbit at that moment as Hermione leaned forward and caressed his shoulder and neck at the table, by way of reassurance.

They finished breakfast and headed down towards the exit level as they had everything with them ready for the day out. Hermione got on the coach first and sat by a window with Arnold next to her and Lucy by the aisle. As they headed off down the narrow quay in the packed coach Arnold felt Hermione squeezing his hand very tightly in hers as she looked out of the window. Within twenty minutes they arrived at the gates to the Mercouri winery and the coach stopped to let passengers off. Hermione turned from the window and gave Arnold a long look, and said:

'See you later, love. And take care of my daughter.'

They kissed and Arnold was up and walking down the aisle to the front of the coach behind Lucy. Just before he reached the steps down to the door he turned quickly and thought he saw Hermione gasp, as if she were holding back a tear. He was in half a mind to go back but Lucy was at the bottom of the stairs, yelling up at him:

'C'mon Arnold. Let's go!'

So he got off the coach into the hot, dry air by the side of the road and in a cloud of dust the coach roared off.

About a dozen people had got off and he sensed the tour around the estate would be a relaxed affair. This was the first time he'd ever been anywhere with Lucy alone – apart from their cup of tea on the ship, and briefly by the mere in Corsham – and he felt awkward walking along beside her. The rest of the passengers seemed to be couples and he guessed they all probably thought he was her father. They'd been met by a young man called Dimitri who said he was one of the Mercouri family. He led them through the open metal gates and down the olive tree lined path towards the winery. Arnold heard a familiar bird voice within the groves and was surprised to see a male peacock emerge onto the track displaying his feathers to the visitors. Lucy grabbed his hand and pulled him down to whisper in his ear:

'How funny, it's like being back in Corsham!'

They were shown around the visitors centre and taken around the beautiful Italianate gardens. There was an ivy-clad stone chapel that reminded him of the one in Dyrham Park, and row upon row of vines and olive trees as far as he could see. The place was quite special, he thought, and had lovely views out over the Ichthian peninsula and towards the sea. He had no idea such beautiful places existed in the world. No wonder the guide Dimitri exuded such inner tranquility. They were seated at a long dining table under the shade of some pine trees and ate feta salad and stuffed vine leaves, with grilled halloumi cheese and freshly baked bread. Several different wine bottles were passed along the table and Arnold carefully sampled them until he found one he liked which he then accepted a full glass of. Lucy opted for the same and they chinked glasses in the bright sunshine and let the cold crisp wine relax them. As the wine took hold of their senses the rest of the table seemed to disappear from Arnold's immediate vicinity. It reminded him of the technique he'd seen in films sometimes, when a person stays in focus but the rest of the world blurs away into the distance. He started trying to explain this to Lucy but she laughed at him when he was halfway through his meticulous description:

'Arnold, you poor old thing, I do believe you're getting tipsy!'

All he could see were her laughing eyes, which reminded him of her mother's, and her lips, which were fuller than Hermione's. He guessed she'd inherited them from her father. He began to feel intimidated by her vitality and could sense he was retiring into himself, but she noticed this and tried to help him avoid this by asking:

'Oh, Arnold, isn't this fun? Thank God we didn't have to go and look at another bloody pile of old stones!'

CHAPTER 13

They finished their food and people started drifting away from the table into the grounds. Lucy stood up and offered her hand to Arnold.

'C'mon. There's about an hour before the coach is due to pick us up. Let's go for a wander.'

He got to his feet and was led by her through the sunlight into a beautiful forest, along a path between rows of pine trees that had a distinct smell in the dry heat. He could hear the gentle sound of cicadas all about him. The sheltered nature of the path meant the sounds the two of them made with their moving feet were magnified, as if they were walking somewhere inside a large building. He could feel the full effect of the wine now and all he could think of was to follow her down the path. He looked at his feet to watch where he was treading as there were exposed tree roots to trip over, sometimes hidden beneath fallen pine branches.

When he looked up she'd disappeared and he stopped to wonder what had happened to her. Then her arms materialised around his waist and he sensed the warmth of her body behind him. She pressured him to go to his left and at first he resisted, but as she continued the pressure he felt his balance go. They were slowly sliding down to the ground and he turned face up and lay there out of breath, overcome by the heady bouquet from the pinecones and branches littered around. He looked up to the tree canopy and saw slivers of the sun's warmth cutting through it. It blinded him but he was enjoying the sensation and didn't close his eyes. He felt Lucy's weight half on top of him and he lay there as if in a trance. The wine made him feel sleepy and not quite in touch with what was going on. He felt himself becoming erect and then a warmth engulfed his penis that he'd never experienced before. He pressed the palm of his left hand strongly down into the hard ground as the pleasure mounted, while his right hand groped and found Lucy's bottom curled towards him. He realised her head was in his lap and understood she must be giving him what he'd heard was called 'oral sex'.

At that moment he rushed through the foliage above and towards the gates of heaven and entered a state of bliss totally unknown to him. All around became still and they lay there for several minutes absorbing the sounds and smells, and slight gusts of warm air that wove their way through the rows of trees. Lucy moved the position of her body and lay next to him more comfortably, nestling her head in the space of his collar bone as she'd done several times before on the cruise. His left hand relaxed its grip in the dirt. He wasn't sure how long they stayed like this and it felt to him as if they were suspended in a timeless place. He heard voices to the right of where they'd come from, far off through the trees, and they both stirred to sit up and bring themselves back to the three dimensional world. Arnold was sure he must have spoiled his clothes but he felt around and was surprised to find that his trousers were dry and everything was where it should be, but he didn't understand how. They stood up awkwardly and started back in the direction of the voices, towards the winery and visitors' centre.

When they emerged from the forest they were the last members of the tour group to return and Dimitri explained it was time to head down to meet the coach on its way back from Olympia. As they walked towards the gates Arnold became more and more confused about what had happened. It hadn't been his intention to become intimate with Lucy and he was sure he hadn't encouraged her. The wine was stronger than he'd expected making him incapable of having any control over what had taken place. He'd obviously drunk far too much, but Lucy had encouraged him by continuing to fill their glasses from all the open wine bottles on the table. He noticed several of the couples were now arm in arm on their way down the drive, whispering to each other and giggling. He was sure some of them had taken the opportunity to make love in the grounds. He felt anger and frustration and he was annoyed at what Lucy had done. Had she planned this whole thing? He knew that couldn't be possible as they'd only decided to take the trip to the vineyard over breakfast. Nevertheless she'd taken advantage of him and he felt his dignity had been compromised. It should never have happened. How on earth could he face Hermione now?

At that moment he knew he'd become a victim of circumstances, another of the wretched people on earth who have no control over their lives, one of the souls he had spent most of his life trying to help. He stood despondently with the others by the gates and waited while a cloud of dust on the road slowly approached them, like some unavoidable tornado of judgement, before it became recognisable as the coach that had dropped them off earlier in the day. He now had a terrible migraine and his head was throbbing. The intense heat of the day had passed and the sun was very low in the sky and at that moment he just wanted to hide in darkness and escape from everybody.

The coach came to a halt, the doors opened and everyone trooped up the steps and along the aisle. Hermione had three seats to herself and Arnold flopped down next to her. Lucy sat down across the aisle, saying with a smirk,

'Hi, Mum. I think Arnold drank too much of the free wine.'

He rested his head on Hermione's shoulder, closed his eyes and at that moment wanted desperately to be in bed holding on to her.

After the coach built up speed she took both his hands in hers. He tried to fall asleep but the constant movement of the coach made it impossible, so he just stayed as he was hoping the whole afternoon had been a dream and any second he would wake up on-board the ship. Finally they reached the quay and Hermione gently shook him to let him know they'd arrived. In silence they got up and filed off the bus letting the conversations of the other passengers mask their own isolation. Once back in the cabin Arnold flopped onto the bed and immediately fell asleep. He dreamt he was back in the pine forest but this time he was with Hermione, not Lucy. But then in the dream he began to be unsure who he was with as the identity of his partner drifted between the two of them, so he escaped from them both and ran off into the forest.

It was the last night on the ship as it sailed from Katakolon around the Peloponnese coast and back up to

Volos where there was a hectic day of sightseeing taking in Delphi, Meteora and Itea. They were then to be taken directly to the airport where they would meet their packed luggage and fly back to Gatwick.

Arnold woke up feeling unwell the next day and excused himself from the tour, and by doing so had the whole day to himself, to try to come to terms with his confused state of mind. Hermione had packed the night before whilst he was asleep and when he got up at about eleven he noticed her suitcase sitting silently in the middle of the room. He solemnly packed his things and then paced the cabin, but her suitcase's impenetrability haunted him. He sat outside on the balcony staring down at the goings on in Volos harbour and decided to go for a walk and see if he could find his way around the ship again. He took his map with him but found he didn't need to refer to it at all. About an hour later he was up on deck in the sunshine. He went to the rail and looked out over the quay below him where several coaches were standing, ready to take the remaining passengers with everyone's luggage to the airport.

'Excuse me. It is Reverend Drive, isn't it?'

A woman was standing next to him at the rail but he didn't recognise her. She offered her hand to him which he took limply.

'Deirdre Pace. I live in Bences Lane. In Corsham. I thought it was you. How funny seeing you here. Last place I would have expected to bump into you! I was one of your parishioners at St. Tobias's. My late husband and I were regulars up until he died. A great shame it had to close. I guess it's a sign of the times, eh?'

Arnold just stood and listened to her speaking, nodding

occasionally and offering a vague smile when it seemed appropriate. He felt he was adopting a familiar character just then, like putting on an old pair of shoes or a well-worn jacket. It was an odd sensation, as if he were going back in time. She carried on talking, not really caring whether he answered or not, in that way some people can when they ask a question that has a built-in answer, obviating the need for a reply. He'd been in this situation hundreds of times before but this time it felt different, as if he were pretending to be someone he wasn't. He caught up with what she was saying:

'... funny I haven't bumped into you earlier on this trip. Still, there are so many people on-board running around doing different things every day, it's hardly surprising, is it? Are you travelling alone?'

There was silence for a few seconds and Arnold realised she was waiting for him to say something. He didn't know why, but said:

'Yes ... yes, I am travelling alone.'

And she was off again at breakneck speed as if him saying that had given her licence to continue, now that she'd stopped for a fresh intake of breath. As she went on he wondered why on earth he'd said that about travelling alone. He concluded it would have been just too tiresome to go through an explanation of who he was with on the cruise. He was sure Hermione didn't know this woman and he didn't recognise her.

She was beginning to give him a fresh headache so he excused himself and made his way down to the Club Lounge where he was able to find some peace and quiet. The coaches weren't due to leave for the airport until three, so he swallowed a couple of aspirins the staff found for him and had some lunch. He settled down in an armchair with his book and tried to read but it was difficult to concentrate. He was dreading getting to the airport and having to deal with the prospect of Hermione and Lucy together on the plane for the flight back. He realised there was no possibility now of him moving into Hermione's house after what had happened at the winery. He would stay on at Stan's for the time being, but one thing was becoming clear to him. He wanted to leave there as he had a hankering for his own space. Somewhere where he would have some genuine freedom.

CHAPTER 14

It was after two in the morning when he finally turned the key in the lock of his front door and stepped into the dark chill of his flat. He'd set the storage heaters to come on while he was away but the temperature had obviously plunged over the ten days and he shivered as he switched on the lights and picked up the few letters and mail that lay on the doormat. There was the assorted junk mail he expected, plus a couple of letters, one of which had his name scrawled across the envelope with no stamp or address, and one official looking envelope labelled as being from Goldbloom & Gulbenkian, names he didn't immediately recognise. He was exhausted after the plane journey from Athens so he decided not to bother with any of it until the morning.

It had been a trial the whole way back, sat sandwiched between the two women trying to be polite, and putting a veneer over the obvious frisson that had been generated. Finally they had both fallen asleep with their heads resting on both his shoulders and he was trapped for the duration of the flight, even though he wanted to have a pee desperately. His dire need kept him awake the whole time and he barely had enough time to make it to the first toilet when they landed at Gatwick. So it was his turn to fall asleep in the taxi waiting to take them home and it seemed as if he'd only just closed his eyes when he was being prodded awake by Hermione as they reached Stan's driveway in Colerne. He quickly said goodnight to them both as he got out, and the driver pulled his case out from the boot before speeding away into the night towards Corsham. He put an extra blanket on the bed and kept his socks on before climbing in to get warm and fall asleep. He felt like his whole body was still moving even though he was on the ground now and he began to dream he was flying through the air.

He woke up feeling refreshed but saw the time was past eleven and immediately felt guilty for sleeping so long. Funnily enough, he was pleased to be alone for a change in his bed. He let out a long, noisy gasp of wind, probably due to the airline food he'd had the day before and it made him laugh to himself. Contrary to what he'd been expecting it was a clear day outside and he got up and showered. It occurred to him he hadn't heard any sign of life yet from Stan as he would normally be woken up by his car starting up. He looked out of the window to see it still standing where it had been the night before. Making himself some tea he turned his attention to the post. He opened the letter with no stamp or address first, and inside there was a single sheet of paper covered with some scrawled handwriting:

Dear Arnold,

I hope you had a wonderful time out there in those foreign parts on that boat.

By the time you read this I'll be gone.

I've tried to come to terms with what I done to Nancy, but it's been no good. I tried to carry on and forget all about it like you said, but it still haunts me.

And I don't feel no sense in carrying on, working and everything, with only the garden as reason to live.

Thanks for your kind words of forgiveness and all your friendship, I know you always meant well for me. You are a good man, I truly believe that.

You may want to show this note to the police and tell them what I done. I'll leave it up to you.

May God treat you fairer than he's treated me.

Your friend,

Stan

Arnold read it through several times hoping he'd misunderstood it. He feared the worst with the car still parked in the driveway and realised he had to go downstairs and try to get into Stan's flat. He remembered a spare key underneath a flowerpot by the back door so he went down and looked to see if it was still there. In one respect he was alarmed when he found it as it meant he was duty bound to go inside. His hand was shaking as he turned the key in the lock and opened the door. The place was musty as if no air had been circulating and there was a strange smell everywhere. He slowly walked through the rooms calling:

'Stan ...? Hello ...?'

Then he found him in the bedroom, hanging quite still from the central beam. He immediately felt sick and rushed to the bathroom to vomit in the sink. He ran the cold tap and flushed his face in the freezing cold water and felt a little better for it. He sat down in an armchair in the living room, phoned 999 and explained what he'd found. He was told not to touch anything and wait until the police arrived. He put down the receiver and saw he was still holding Stan's note and envelope scrunched up in his right hand. He carefully folded them up and put them safely in his dressing gown pocket hoping he wouldn't be searched. He was in a quandary as to who to telephone next. His first thought was Hermione, but she would insist he come over to stay with her and he felt uncomfortable doing that, knowing Lucy was bound to be there as her holidays weren't due to finish until the middle of January. He called Trevor. His and Hermione's numbers were the only ones he knew off by heart. He heard the phone being picked up.

'Hello, Trevor? It's Arnold here.'

'Arnold! How the devil are you, old chap? Have you had a good Christmas? What can I do for you?'

He explained what had happened and Trevor immediately offered to put him up.

'Of course. You poor chap. Delighted to be of help. You just sit tight while the police wallahs do their thing. Call me back when they're done and we'll get you over here.'

Arnold felt better having spoken with him. He realised how important a familiar voice could be at such a time and was ashamed of how he'd dismissed Trevor previously. It became clear a time of crisis can crystallise things and clarify relationships and situations and he started to feel genuine affection for him. The man really was the salt of the earth. He must have been aware of the fact Arnold found him tiresome but nevertheless he'd been there when he'd needed him, which counted a lot in Arnold's book. He was having so many new life experiences, things his religious training hadn't prepared him for. A knowledge of the Bible was all well and good, but as equipment for the pitfalls and unexpected turns one encounters in real life, he began to realise it fell somewhat short.

The police arrived first, with an ambulance following behind, and Arnold took them upstairs to his flat to make a cup of tea. They all sat down in his living room and took a statement:

'So, Mr. Drive, can you tell us exactly how you came to find Mr. Dale?'

'I got back very late last night from a holiday, and went straight to bed.'

'What time would that have been?'

'About 2am.'

'And was his car parked out front when you got in?'

'Yes, it was. I didn't think anything of it as Stan was always coming and going on taxi bookings. There was never any pattern to his movements.'

'And what happened this morning?'

'I got up late, at about eleven o'clock, and I was surprised his car was still here.'

'And why would that be a surprise?'

'Well, most days he would be off very early in the morning. He had a lot of jobs ferrying people to and from the airports.'

'I see. Please carry on.'

'As the car was still there I naturally assumed he would be at home, so I went down and knocked on his door to say hello.'

'And?'

'There was no answer. Then I started to get a bit worried. And I knew where he kept a spare key, he'd shown me where it was hidden when I first moved in ...'

'Go on, please.'

'I found the key, opened the front door, and went in.'

'And that's when you found Mr. Dale?'

'Yes.'

'Did anything in his behaviour previously suggest to you he may try to take his own life?'

'No. I knew he was upset when his wife ... she left him a few years ago. He told me he'd been living alone since then.'

'And when did she leave?'

'About two years ago, I think.'

'Did he tell you where she went?'

Arnold paused and thought for a while.

'No. He told me she was from up North, so he thought she may have gone back there. That's what he told me.'

'Apart from her, do you know of any other living relatives?'

'No. He told me there were none. And they had no children.'

'I see. Well, thanks for your help, Mr. Drive. It's always regrettable to discover cases like this.'

'Yes. I'm sure. Such a waste of precious life.'

'Quite. We'll prepare a statement from what you've told us and get it ready for you to check over and sign. Would you be able to come to the station in Chippenham in a couple of days? It'll be ready by then. Here's my card. Thank you, sir.'

As they were preparing to leave Arnold asked if he had permission to stay somewhere else.

'Quite understandable, sir. Have you got somewhere to go?'

He explained he would be going to a friend's house in Corsham and gave them Trevor's number, and that was that.

He heard them leaving, followed shortly afterwards by the ambulance.

He made a fresh pot of tea to keep himself busy and phoned Trevor again, who offered to come over and give him a lift to Corsham. After he'd packed a few extra things in his case from the cruise he sat waiting with his tea. He saw the other letter sitting on the table and decided to open it to take his mind off Stan. Poor Stan. He had no intention of sharing his secret with anyone, of that he was sure. He opened the envelope and took out the folded letter inside:

Dear Mr. Drive

First may I apologise for the delay in getting back to you regarding your dormant account number #00986070059. I am now in a position to inform you of its status.

In 1980 it was received into our office for administration and investment purposes.

As it had been assigned a dormant status no permission would have been sought from the holder of the account.

It was invested in a portfolio associated with the expansion of the internet, and shares were purchased in Microsoft. In 1996 the capital accrued was reinvested in Tullow Oil, an oil exploration company, where the capital is still positioned today. These two investment decisions have led to a substantial increase in the size of the original deposit. Fortunately in this case they were the right decisions to make in a constantly fluctuating and volatile market.

I would appreciate if you would telephone me at your convenience, to discuss how these funds may now be returned to you.

I remain,

Yours faithfully,

Nigel Scott

Goldbloom & Gulbenkian

0208 943 7238

He put the letter back in its envelope and then heard Trevor's car pulling up in the driveway.

CHAPTER 15

Trevor lived in an old detached house on the corner of Pickwick Lane and the A4. Although it was on the main road
between Chippenham and Bath there was a high stone wall
surrounding the property that kept it cocooned away from
the traffic noise. Trevor had moved there in the early seventies while he was still teaching at Bristol University, when
property prices were more affordable in the countryside. Living on his own, as he'd done since his wife had died, he'd got
used to looking after himself and Arnold was surprised how
tidy the place was. The house was far too large for one person and he could now understand why Trevor had been so
effusive in offering him somewhere to stay, as he could no
doubt feel lonely in such a large place all by himself. In front
of the house was a gravel courtyard where Trevor parked his
old Rover 3000 and at the back there was a garden. Arnold
noticed how dark the house was once he got inside. The original leaded windows were small and nowhere in the house
did they let in enough light, meaning lights had to be kept on
throughout the day regardless of what the weather was like
outside. Arnold was apprehensive seeing all the leaded windows but then noticed the beautiful dark parquet flooring

everywhere and perked up. He followed Trevor up a staircase and along a corridor where he was shown into a bedroom.

'There you are, Arnold. Hope you'll be comfortable in here. I'm at the end of the corridor. There's fresh sheets on the bed for you and luckily for you the central heating's working in this room. Nice view of the garden from here, I always think. South facing. Bathroom next door. Get yourself unpacked and I'll be downstairs. I'll fix us some lunch. Pork pie and pickle any good to you? It's Bowyer's?'

Trevor left Arnold and he looked at what he could see from the window. Housing constructed in the last twenty years had destroyed what originally must have been a lovely view south to Ditteridge. After the garden and the original high perimeter wall all he could see were modern houses with small strips of garden that constituted Pickwick. He hoped Trevor had a washing machine as most of the clothes in his suitcase were dirty from the cruise. He realised he must telephone Hermione to tell her what had happened and that he was now staying with Trevor.

He went downstairs and found Trevor in the kitchen preparing lunch. Arnold discovered he was famished and was happy to accept another slice of pork pie when it was offered. After they'd eaten and were drinking some coffee Trevor asked him:

'How are you feeling, old chap? Bit of a shock, what? Last thing you expected after a holiday. How did he seem to you? The last time you saw him?'

'He seemed well enough. He dropped me off the day I left, in Corsham ...' He stopped himself then, as if he'd let slip some piece of information that he shouldn't have. He needn't have worried, though, as Trevor picked up the thread:

'And how was the cruise, may I ask? Oh, no need to worry, Arnold. I may be old and stuck-up, but I've had a pretty good idea of what's been going on between you two for a while. There's not that much happens in Corsham that escapes my knowledge. But mum's the word, old chap. I'm very glad for you. Very glad. She's a lovely woman. No doubt about that.'

So Arnold relaxed and went into some detail of the places they'd visited. Trevor was especially interested in Catania, being a church lover himself. Arnold obviously didn't divulge what had taken place at the Mercouri winery, but he was happy to have someone to share the rest with, someone who hadn't been there. He asked if he could call Hermione, and was shown into Trevor's library where an old fashioned black Bakelite telephone sat on a leather-topped desk.

It took a couple of attempts to get the number right as his fingers didn't quite fit properly in the dialling holes and slipped out several times, so at first he dialled a few wrong numbers. Then he got through:

'Hello, Hermione? It's Arnold.'

He was glad Lucy hadn't answered. If she had done he wouldn't have known what to say.

'Hello, pet. How are you?'

He told her what had happened and that he'd taken up Trevor's offer to stay. He could tell she was disappointed to hear this.

'Oh dear ... but you should have come here.'

'I don't think so, not with Lucy still there. I would have felt uncomfortable. It's fine here, it really is.'

He agreed to let her drive him to Chippenham police station when his statement was ready for signing and he said he'd call when he knew about that. They said goodbye and when he'd replaced the receiver it felt strange going back to their separate existences, after having spent the last ten days together. It struck him there were good and bad aspects to it. Like most things, he was discovering.

He spent the afternoon being shown around the house by Trevor and was relieved to discover a washing machine in a room behind the kitchen. Despite the lack of sunlight inside, the house was of decent proportions and it didn't take long for him to start feeling at home. He was surprised how easy going Trevor was. He'd always given the impression of being regimental whenever Arnold had come across him in the past. It made life brighter for Arnold to discover things can turn out better than expected. He did all his washing and found himself seeking Trevor out for some company. The sheer size of the house meant two people could quite easily live there without necessarily bumping into one another and Arnold liked that. He wandered through the rooms and found Trevor in an armchair watching cricket on television. Arnold was confused as he thought cricket was only played in the summer. Trevor burst out laughing:

'That's funny, Arnold. No, old chap, you see, they're playing in the West Indies and this is broadcast via a satellite. Live as it's happening. But they're in a time zone five hours earlier than us, so it's ten o'clock in the morning there.'

Arnold found it difficult to understand this concept fully and he offered to make some tea so that he could think about it some more. No wonder there was difficulty finding a place in people's lives for God when there was all this satellite communication going on all over the world. As he made the tea he could see it was conceivable for man to believe he was indeed God. He could quite literally make most things happen that he could imagine in his mind.

One thing he had always found hard to accept in the Bible was the concept that God created man in his own image ... didn't that mean that he himself was, in fact, God? It also followed that God was different for each individual man and woman, come to think of it. There was no logical reason why God couldn't be a woman, rather than a man. No reason at all. He noticed he'd let the tea brew for far too long. He poured out two extremely strong cups, which he weakened by pouring some away and topping up with boiling water, and wandered back in with them to sit with Trevor. Arnold didn't understand cricket very well and couldn't see much was going on, and judging by the multiple rows of empty seats surrounding the field he concluded the locals felt the same way. He remarked this to Trevor, who replied:

'Ah, but Arnold, that's the whole point. Each game takes five days to complete so the pace is much slower than most spectator sports. There's a remarkably subtle balance of power between the two teams that constantly shifts during each session, and it's truly fascinating. The fact that there's not many people at the ground is neither here nor there. There's people like me watching this all over the world.'

'Sounds a bit like chess to me, but sort of in 3D?' Arnold offered.

'Yes, it is. I like that analogy,' Trevor approved.

They whiled away a couple of hours sitting in front of the cricket and Arnold noted what a pleasant atmosphere there was in the room. They chatted about various things and he took the opportunity to confess how out of touch he felt with the modern life he'd encountered since he'd left the church.

'Well, old chap. That was bound to happen,' Trevor began, 'I can sympathise totally. I feel it the same but obviously to a lesser degree. Life is moving faster and faster, and I don't think it's just to do with me getting older. People have more and more unsolicited rubbish thrust upon them and they're ending up with no proper time to think. And no time to themselves.'

Arnold was happy to get to bed that night. There were no curtains in his bedroom and the light of a full moon fell across his bed and took the image of Stan hanging as he'd found him from his mind. He turned on his side and pulled the sheets up over his head and quickly fell asleep. The next morning he was woken by the noise of a barking dog. He checked the time in the darkness and found it to be only six thirty and tried vainly to get back to sleep by putting the pillow over his head. This failed to keep the dog out of his ears as it had been joined by others further away, so he found a tissue and made two earplugs to use, as well as the pillow. He had no idea what had set the dog off at that hour and he wondered if it had sensed a prowler, or just another animal in the area. But he had no luck in getting back to sleep and finally gave up the effort and got up at about eight. He went to the window and opened it despite the cold of the morning air, to see if he could discover where the dog was located but could see no animal in the vague direction he thought the noise was coming from. Over breakfast he raised the subject with Trevor who couldn't shed much light:

'Sorry about that, old chap. Heavy sleeper myself, so it's never bothered me. Wife used to be a heavy snorer, bless her cotton socks, so I can sleep through bloody anything these days.'

Later that day the Chippenham police telephoned to say his statement was ready for signing so he arranged to go in with Hermione the following day. Afterwards they went for a walk by the mere and discussed meeting up once Lucy left for Durham. He was relieved Hermione seemed to be approaching her old self again and she made no reference to her argument with Lucy, so he tried to forget about what had happened at the Mercouri vineyard. When he got back to Trevor's he remembered the letter from Goldbloom & Gulbenkian, and while it was fresh in his mind, he decided to call them up. He got Mr. Scott on the phone and made an appointment to go to London the following month for a meeting at their offices in Farringdon. He was asked to take his passport and his birth certificate along to substantiate his identity plus the original Halifax deposit book.

January passed uneventfully in Corsham and the odd couple got used to one another in the house. There was a small memorial service for Stan, which Arnold arranged at St. Bartholomew's, and a handful of people attended, most of them long-standing clients. Arnold spent a couple of nights away each week at Hermione's and ended up there at the weekends if Lucy wasn't down from Durham. One thing was proving an irritation, the blasted dog barking in the early mornings. It was so regular Arnold got to waking up before it had started in anticipation, and he'd just about got to the end of his tether. He managed to locate it in the garden of an adjoining house but had no idea what he could do. He made a studied observation of the owners and concluded they were the kind of people he would be unable to communicate with. He could imagine the exchange between them ...

ARNOLD: Excuse me, but your dog is barking every morning at six thirty and is preventing me from sleeping. I wondered if you were aware of this, and could you perhaps take steps to keep it inside the house until a later, more reasonable time?

OWNER: What, my dog? No, you must be mistaken. My dog never barks, especially at that time of the morning. It must be some other dog.

The trouble with people like that is they don't acknowledge the truth, even if it stares them in the face. They live in a world of denial. Perhaps because they hate their job and spend their life denying that fact? It would never occur to them to take the dog out walking for exercise, as they are always far too busy. Arnold came to the conclusion their garden must constitute a health hazard with the amount of dog litter in it.

He'd taken to riding his bike around Corsham every day for exercise, and one day he found himself entering by accident the Leafield Trading Estate and passed by the factory of Teague Precision Chokes, the shotgun manufacturers. He'd noticed Trevor had an antique gun cupboard in one of the downstairs rooms and he was sure he'd seen a shotgun inside the glass. He started to entertain the idea of putting the dog out of its misery. As he rode back to Trevor's house he realised a shotgun was something he would never be able to get the hang of. Besides, it was far too noisy. But perhaps something lighter ... like an air rifle?

CHAPTER 16

As soon as he got back he checked the cupboard again and could see what he thought was an air rifle next to the shotgun. He asked Trevor about it,

'Oh, yes. They belonged to my father. The shotgun's worth a lot of money. Bit of an antique. The other one he used to take potshots at rabbits and squirrels with. There were plenty of them around where we lived on the Somerset Flats. I suppose I should get a licence for them one of these days, but since the police station in Corsham closed down I keep forgetting to. Never fired either one of them myself. Occasionally take them out and polish them. Interested in taking a look?'

Arnold followed him down to the room and watched him unlock the cupboard with the key sitting in the lock. He handed Arnold the shotgun and he was surprised at how much it weighed. The air rifle was a lot slimmer but still seemed to weigh an awful lot.

'They're not loaded, of course. But I've got the ammo in here too, just in case we get burgled in the middle of the night. Probably serve to scare someone off, I'd have thought. Just the sight of one of them. Ever used one yourself?'

Arnold was surprised at the question and answered:

'No, never. Never even held one. Heavy, aren't they?'

'Oh, yes. Quite a recoil on the shotgun, so my father told me. Can quite strain the shoulder when it goes off. If you're not used to it.'

Now he'd been shown the guns the more he was tempted by the idea of getting rid of the barking dog. He'd never been a big fan of dogs and the beast wasn't enjoying its life as it was, cooped up in that garden the whole time, when all it wanted was a regular bit of exercise. So it really would be putting it out of its misery. As he entertained the idea, he wrestled with a terrible feeling of remorse. It was in direct contradiction of everything he'd always felt concerning the love of all forms of life. He repeatedly dismissed the thought whenever it popped into his head, but when the beast woke him up in the morning it came on like a light bulb again to torment him.

'Arnold, old chap, you've been glued to that computer recently. Come upon anything of interest?'

He'd been delighted to find Trevor had a computer rigged up in the very same room as the gun cupboard and was happy for Arnold to use it whenever he wanted. He wasn't quite sure what he could say to satisfy him:

'Nothing really, it's just such a luxury to have it there. I suppose it's probably the novelty of it.'

'Yes, I'm afraid it's quite taken over from the telly nowadays. Apart from watching the cricket I don't seem to sit in front of the box like I used to. I remember when the wife was alive we'd quite happily sit down and watch all sorts of nonsense after supper. Always ended up dozing off and never seeing the end of anything, mind you. I've tried to concentrate on the odd TV drama now and then but it all seems such drivel. And they say British telly is the best in the world! Odd that. Can't see it myself.'

Arnold tried to imagine Trevor married again but found it hard to picture. He was probably like a swan, one of those animals that mates for life, and he could see nothing wrong in that. Besides Trevor was getting old and he was too, for that matter. It looked to Arnold as if his only partner in life would turn out to have been dear old St. Tobias. He made a mental note to go past on his cycle ride that morning.

The following Wednesday was the last in the month and his appointment in London was at midday. He worked out he could get the 9:35 train from Chippenham which would give him about an hour to make his way across to the Halifax office in Farringdon. Luckily there was a tube train he could get direct from Paddington Station but he'd never travelled on one before, so Hermione patiently talked him through it. He didn't have to worry about tickets as the train ticket he'd bought included his tube journeys too, but at first he got terribly mixed up with all the different Underground lines. Trevor gave him a lift to the station that morning.

Being the first train after the rush hour it was pretty quiet but there were still types who are always on their mobile phones speaking too loudly and saying inane things such as 'I'm on the train now', or doing business deals, or giving reports about meetings they'd attended. Hearing just such a conversation going on reminded Arnold to check once again he had all the relevant paperwork with him for his meeting with Nigel Scott. He had his birth certificate, his passport, and the original account book from the Halifax together with the letter that had accompanied it detailing the deposit.

Satisfied it was all in order he settled back for a snooze as the noise of the train was making him drowsy.

He was stirred by an announcement that they were nearing Paddington, and what passengers there were started getting up and arranging their things for a swift exit. Arnold was travelling light so he headed for the door and was first off his carriage when the train pulled into the station. It was his first time at Paddington Station and as he moved along the platform following the signs he ventured a few glances upwards to take in the magnificent curved, glass panelled ceiling. Luckily for him it was a grey cloudy day. Even though it was mid-morning the place was packed but he managed to negotiate his way towards the Hammersmith & City line. He was impressed at how smoothly he was able to get over to Farringdon and once he was through the ticket barrier there he consulted a local map on the wall to pinpoint the address of the Halifax office. Out of the station, turn left, first right, and second left he memorised, and repeated it to himself as he exited into the street. He was surprised to find a cobbled street that looked as if it hadn't been touched since Victorian times. It was quite at odds with what he'd been expecting. He wasn't familiar with London at all and it wasn't until he negotiated crossing Farringdon Road that he really felt he was in some vast city. He'd completely forgotten they still had double-decker red buses in London. For some reason he thought they'd all been phased out and sold off to India but he couldn't remember who'd told him that. He noted the numbers on the doors in Paul Street, spotting the sign for Goldbloom & Gulbenkian, and pushed open the glass door to the modern reception area. There was a smart suited brunette seated at a desk who asked him who his appointment was with, asking him to sit down while she announced him. There were various investment magazines on the low glass table in front of him but he was sure he wouldn't understand a word of any of them. He picked one up and thumbed through it to look at the pictures. All the men were smartly suited, smiling, and looked very rich with red faces.

'Mr. Drive?' he heard from behind him. He guessed it must be Nigel Scott.

'Right on time, I see. Please come this way.' Scott guided him through a door and along a corridor into a private office.

'Please sit down. May I offer you some refreshment? Tea or coffee perhaps?'

Arnold accepted the offer of tea and sat down in an extremely comfortable leather armchair across the desk from Scott. It positively reeked of leather, which he liked immensely and he breathed through his nose a few times to take in the strong smell. Scott spoke, seemingly, into midair to order two teas with biscuits and then gave him a very broad smile.

'May I see the documents you've brought along to establish your identity?'

Arnold handed them over the desk and waited while Scott carefully checked them all. The tea and biscuits arrived and Arnold occupied himself munching on some ginger nuts from a plate. Then Scott got up and took photocopies of all the documents before returning them to Arnold and sitting down to pick up his cup of tea.

'It's not often I have the pleasure to let people who come in here have some good news,' he started. 'But that's the case today, Mr. Drive. I have to say your case does have a rather fairy tale-like quality to it. I have one question for you. I'm curious to know who this relative was, who bequeathed the musical box to you?'

Arnold found himself feeling unprepared as he had no idea what to say. He fidgeted a little in the leather chair which squeaked and accentuated his every movement.

'I'm afraid I can't tell you,' he answered meekly. 'But I suppose I could try and find out?'

Scott laughed:

'No, don't worry, it won't be necessary.'

Then he became serious and leaned forward:

'The fact of the matter is, Mr. Drive, you are now a man of very considerable means. That small deposit in 1974 has grown, how shall I say, substantially. In fact, today it's worth over a million pounds.'

Arnold couldn't believe his ears.

'But ... I don't understand,' was all he could manage to blurt out.

Scott went on:

'After the account became dormant it was assigned to us in 1980 and our job is to try to safeguard any unclaimed monies by investing them in what we judge to be safe bonds. After all, they may remain unclaimed as assets of the Halifax for an indefinite period. Liken it to a sophisticated deposit account at a high street bank. It just so happened 1980 coincided with the blossoming of the internet and we made substantial investments in the Microsoft company in its infancy. Well, Microsoft exploded in value and we, meaning you, made a killing by buying the shares before the boom. Then in 1996, fearing a slide in the value of the shares, we sold them and moved into Tullow Oil, an oil exploration company, which has again done phenomenally well.'

At this point he pushed a document across the table for Arnold to read.

'And as you can see from these calculations, the net worth of your account is the figure at the bottom.'

Arnold scanned the document, which showed year on year the gradual increase in the value of his £1,000.

'Of course, there have been deductions made for income tax along the way, plus an annual administration fee of thirty per cent, a standard fee, but the final figure is still very healthy indeed.'

Arnold got to the bottom of the page and read the number ... £1,089,245 and sixty-three pence.

If he'd been standing up he would have fainted and as it was his head started to spin. He took long deep breaths as he'd heard somewhere it was good for you and he slowly regained his balance. Scott smiled and said:

'Congratulations, Mr. Drive.'

CHAPTER 17

Arnold emerged onto the street in a daze and looked down to see he was still holding a half-eaten ginger nut in his left hand. For a moment he couldn't remember which way to turn to head back in the direction of the tube station, but then recalled the building had been on his left when he'd arrived so he turned right. What was it? Out of the station, turn left, first right, second left. So in reverse order it would be: up to the end of the street turn left ... second right, and then first left. Confident he'd remembered correctly he strode off down the pavement but ten minutes later he was so confused he had to ask a policeman. He was angry he'd got such a simple route wrong in his head and thought it must have been the myriad of small turnings he'd miscounted on the way back. The truth was, of course, he was still trying to come to terms with the news. Scott had asked him what he wanted to do with it all, whether he wanted the whole amount immediately or perhaps a portion of it for the time being? He'd recommended keeping part of it invested, so there would be a continuing yield. He was duty bound to add that all stocks and shares go up and down and there was no way of telling which way they may go.

Arnold stared at the large Tube map on the wall by the

ticket office and saw many names he recognised. The truth was he wanted to be somewhere out in the open with some trees around him so he could think clearly for a while. He spotted St James's Park on the same line as Farringdon was, the Circle line, and thought it sounded like the right place to go. So instead of heading back to Paddington he made his way down to catch a Circle line train heading east. The train was quite empty when he got on but as he made his way around the stops it got busier and Arnold thought it must be getting close to lunchtime. He was famished and once outside St James's Park station he looked for a cafe. He went in the first one he saw and joined a queue. He had a passionate yearn for a cheese and onion crusty roll at that moment and by the time he got to the counter this had become two, and he got a takeaway cappuccino as well. He'd never heard of cappuccino before but the picture displayed looked delicious. He liked the noise the milk frother made as it bubbled away. He walked down Queen Anne's Gate across Birdcage Walk and started to feel better. He couldn't wait to eat something and began eating his rolls as he walked along. At the bottom he crossed over the lake on the bridge and found a bench to sit on and take stock of the day.

A million pounds. Never did he think he would ever have that amount of money. He wondered if it could be some sort of elaborate hoax but it seemed unlikely someone would go to all that trouble just for him. He noticed several brazen squirrels nearby hopping about standing on two legs as they do, and he threw them some crumbs from the wrappings of the rolls. He heard some ducks quacking by the edge of the lake in front of him which made him relax, reminding him of being by the mere in Corsham. He tried his cappuccino and liked the taste of it. Knowing he had all that money made him feel different, and yet the same. It meant he could more or less live the rest of his life without worrying about the cost of anything. Also he could do whatever he wanted, and go wherever he wanted too. At the same time he was exactly the same person. He didn't feel any change in his personality and hadn't suddenly changed his opinions about anything. Perhaps gradually that would happen. He hoped it wouldn't turn him into a bad person, because he knew money had the power to do that. Just then a man with a beard and a jacket tied up with a piece of string came up and sat down on the bench next to him:

"Ere, guv. Morning. Lovely day, innit? Any chance of a few pence for a cuppa tea?"

Considering what Arnold had just been thinking about it seemed the least he could do. He fished around in his pocket and pulled out a fifty pence piece and handed it to the man who studied it:

"Cor, blimey. You're the last of the big spenders, ain't ya, Guv'nor?"

Then he was up and away like a flash, and Arnold wished he'd given him more.

Now that he'd eaten he felt much better and strolled around St James's Park looking at the emerging spring blossoms and the tourists. The cloud cover looked like it was breaking up so he decided to stay outside and perhaps make his way back to Paddington on foot. He checked on a map by the bridge and saw he could reach Hyde Park quite easily from there, and he knew Paddington was just to the North. He confidently walked along the Mall past Buckingham Palace, then headed up Constitution Hill and into Hyde

Park, by which time the sun had come out. He struck out west and tried to imagine he was heading across the meadow next to the mere. By the time he'd crossed Exhibition Road and gone past the Serpentine Gallery there was very little to remind him he was still in London, except for the sight of dog walkers picking up their dog's litter with their hand inside a plastic bag, something he'd never seen in Corsham. He imagined aliens coming to earth and thinking dogs controlled the planet and had humans to tend to their every need. He could see buildings lining the western boundary of the Park in the distance so he turned north and reached the Bayswater Road and Queensway. He asked a couple of policemen the way to Paddington and felt pleased with himself when they told him he was less than ten minutes away. He strode down Queensway looking in all the shop windows, realising he could now buy anything he saw in any of them. There were several electrical and television stores with flat screen plasma TV sets for over five hundred pounds in their windows, and a few travel agents advertising holidays abroad. Now he could indulge any whim that took hold of him, and go wherever he liked. He paused outside a store that had a camera pointing out onto the street and caught an image of himself on a display screen. At first he waved, then he saluted. He turned right as directed into Bishop's Bridge Road, and arrived at Paddington in time to board the 2:45 train.

He took a nap and woke up as his train pulled into Reading and a blind man got on with a guide dog to sit down across the aisle from him. The dog was one of those good-looking Labradors that sits with its tongue hanging out panting the whole time and it put him in mind of the barking dog outside his window. Suddenly it didn't seem that important to him. What on earth had he been thinking? His new found wealth had imbued him with a benevolence to all creatures whom he sensed had just as much right to existence as he did. With that thought in his head he bought a cup of tea and a Kit Kat from the mobile trolley and occupied himself thinking about other things. He thought about who he could tell of his good fortune ... Trevor? He felt duty bound to, but if he did the whole of Corsham would know.

Hermione was the only person he could think of who deserved to know, and he was due to see her on Friday.

His mind started to wander and settled on something Nigel Scott had brought up regarding the origin of the music box. He had to find out more about it. He could vaguely remember his parents telling him the relative who'd left it to him had lived in Germany and he was sure it was a man. Also this person was someone on his father's side. His parents had both passed away fifteen years earlier and in their effects he hadn't come across any relative they were in contact with, at home or abroad. He'd been brought up assuming nobody else in the family was left alive and got the distinct impression back then that his parents preferred not to discuss it when he'd pressed them for more details.

He noticed they'd just left Swindon so he tidied up his belongings and prepared for the next stop, Chippenham. The light was beginning to fade as he came out of the station and waited a few minutes for a taxi, but he was the only one in the queue. Seated in the back he was silent as they made their way towards Corsham. The driver spoke to him:

'Is that you, Mr. Drive? I thought's I recognised you. I vaguely knew Stan Dale from years back. Awful what happened to him. Poor lad. I heard it was you what found him, like. Tragic. Me and him fought in the war, when we wus young 'uns. As I say, tragic it was.'

It wasn't until Arnold was up in his room at Trevor's that he wondered how the relative had ended up living in Germany. Perhaps it had something to do with the war? After all, everyone's lives in those days had been affected by it in some way or another. The first thing he'd do would be to contact Bonhams in London and ask them to look into their records for the details they held regarding the sale in 1974. It may be going back too far for them but it was worth a try. There was a knock on the door and he heard Trevor outside,

'Arnold, old chap. Thought I heard you come in earlier. If you're up for some grub I'm about to poach some salmon? Ready in thirty minutes.'

He lay in bed that night discovering new implications of the windfall. One thing immediately obvious was that he wouldn't have to rely on other people's charity for much longer. He was feeling disadvantaged at imposing himself on Trevor's hospitality. However much Trevor said he was happy to have him there Arnold felt the need for some space he could call his own. He'd already tried to explain this to Hermione and at some point soon he could turn the desire into a reality. He now had the funds to perhaps make the old iron church into a home for himself. He fell asleep resolving to spend the next day compiling a list of priorities to attend to.

He was rudely awakened dead on cue at six thirty by the barking dog and felt vitriol seeping back into his consciousness. What had he been thinking of the previous day? That the dog's behaviour would suddenly change? That he would

overnight mysteriously develop the ability to sleep undisturbed? Or that he would welcome it as a joyful song of musical merit? Perhaps even think of recruiting more of the brutes
into a dawn chorus? He went to the window to see where it
was in the garden. The casement window opened outwards
to the right, which meant he had an unobstructed line of fire
down to the target. The window sill was of stone, with awkward edges, but he could use a pillow to form a soft base on
which to rest the rifle. The speed with which he formulated
this plan made him feel much better and he decided to get up
right then to begin the rest of his life.

CHAPTER 18

By the time Arnold joined Trevor for breakfast at eight thirty he had drawn up his list:

1. Phone Bonhams to request records check
2. Contact Nigel Scott and request transfer of £89,245.63
3. Contact Morris Minor Centre
4. Check internet for family tree searches
5. Cycle out to corrugated iron church
6. Book restaurant for dinner with Hermione on Friday
7. Dispose of dog.

It tidied up a lot of loose ends that had been whizzing around his head since his meeting in London. He'd spent a long time wrestling with the fate of the dog as it wasn't in his nature to kill things, but he'd justified it to himself. He'd decided it would be the first and last creature he would kill. He felt if he could do this he would have demonstrated to himself his complete independence of thought and free will. It was as if he had to defy God's word in order to prove to himself he was a free-thinking human being responsible for his own actions. It was all rather Nietzschean. He wasn't scared of prosecution for the crime. Indeed if he was caught and held culpable for it he would accept it as a natural consequence of his actions. He'd thought a lot about Stan and his crime working all this out and he saw a lot of similarity between the two situations. Stan's wife had made his life a misery and he had killed her hoping by doing so his quality of life would be improved, just as Arnold was being driven to dispose of the dog to improve his.

Having lived for a few months at some distance from the Bible, Arnold was beginning to view it in an entirely different light. Although the New Testament was concerned with appealing to man's better nature, there was still an awful lot of dogma to be followed and abided by in the Old Testament. And this was what he found so tiresome and unacceptable. What progress has been made if someone is forced to do something by their fear of the consequences of disobedience?

The same methodology had been used to formulate most laws in society, 'Do this or you will be punished'. How much better the world would be if this approach could be altered to: 'Do this, not that, because ...'

He decided to let Trevor know he'd come into a bit of money but not reveal how much. He was looking forward to telling Hermione and that's why he wanted to take her to a restaurant, to sort of celebrate. He asked Trevor if he could recommend anywhere a bit swish to take her:

'Well, there's always the Sign of the Angel in Lacock, if you want to splash out. It is pricey, mind you, but I believe it's still good. Haven't been there myself for a few years. Since the wife popped her clogs, in fact. We always went there for our anniversary.'

Arnold booked a table for the next evening and rang Hermione to let her know he was taking her out for dinner, which she was thrilled about. Trevor went off to visit some old friends in Bristol that afternoon which gave him a clear window for a few hours to get used to firing the air rifle.

He found a box of pellets in the gun cupboard and worked out how to load it. He did some target practice from the window to accustom himself to the telescopic sight. It took him a while to get used to the recoil on his shoulder when he fired, but by the time the light started to fade he felt reasonably confident he could reel off several shots into the same small area. That would be essential if he was to finish the dog off quickly. He took the rifle back down and carefully replaced it and the box of pellets in the gun cupboard. Trevor got back soon afterwards and was keen to catch up on some more cricket from the Caribbean. Arnold sat with him for a while to chat and they had a light supper before he started his search on the internet for more information about the owner of the music box. He discovered a site called Ancestry.co.uk where you could pay for a detailed search of your family tree. He thought it was well worth the £25 fee so he made the payment and supplied the relevant information. He began to feel tired and, glancing at the time, was surprised to see it was past ten o'clock so he made his way up to bed to get a decent night's sleep. He needed all his wits about him in the morning.

When he woke up the sun was streaming through his window. It was eight o'clock and he couldn't understand how on earth he'd managed to sleep through the barking. It would normally keep up its racket for over an hour until the owners let it back in and he'd never been able to sleep through it before. He got up and went to the window to see if he could catch sight of it but the house and garden next door were deserted and he began to suspect the hand of God at work. He was well rested after his uninterrupted sleep, but he felt thwarted not being able to carry out his Nietzschean plan. It struck him as an interesting conundrum. He bathed and dressed, mulling the matter over, and came to the conclusion that by some quirk of fate the dog had earned a reprieve. He had another look from his window and noticed the children's slide and other playthings were missing from the garden. He borrowed Trevor's binoculars to inspect the house close up. He had a view through the kitchen windows and it looked deserted inside, although he didn't know what to compare it with, never having looked before. He could see what he thought was a bathroom window but the glass was frosted so it was impossible to see inside. Just then he heard something behind him and looked round to find Trevor standing in his dressing gown in the doorway. He realised he'd forgotten to close the door after his bath in his hurry to spy next door.

'Morning, Arnold,' said Trevor, 'What the devil are you up to down there on your hands and knees?'

Now he'd been discovered he began to feel terrible about what he'd contemplated doing. Over breakfast he confessed and told Trevor all about his plan to shoot the dog.

'Well, old chap. I can quite understand how you felt. Would've probably thought of doing the same thing myself if I wasn't such a heavy sleeper. Unfortunately circumstances have beaten you to it. I noticed a removals van outside there yesterday morning. The bird has flown, or should I say, the dog has. Together with those awful people who owned the beast, and good riddance. Let's hope the next incumbents are more user friendly, eh?'

Arnold was relieved at Trevor's sympathetic view on the affair. He'd been so taken up the day before attending to his list he hadn't been out on his bicycle ride as usual, otherwise he would have seen the removal van for himself. He felt rather humbled by what Trevor said next:

'I have to say this is the first time I have ever heard a confession. And from a priest, I might add! Perhaps I should set up m'own church, what? There may be a demand for this sort of thing, without buying into that whole religious malarkey. What do you think, Arnold? Anything else on your mind?'

As it was such good weather Arnold decided to take an extended bicycle ride and head down the A4 west past the MOD site. He freewheeled all the way into Box and turned towards Colerne as he had a yearning to visit the corrugated iron church again. He tried to remember the route he'd taken last time but that had been unplanned, so it was more difficult to find this time. After a while all the country lanes looked alike and he was just about to give up hope when he came upon it, but from the opposite direction. He was filled with a very calming feeling when he climbed back inside the radiant space with the shafts of dazzling sunlight that seeped in and cut through the air like lasers. He came to the realisation this was the place he wanted to live.

He made sure to memorise his way back to Box this time to avoid any confusion finding it again and had the arduous task of walking his bike up most of Box Hill, as it was far too steep to cycle up. He stopped frequently to admire the views over the valley towards Colerne and Marshfield and at the top could see far into Bath and beyond to the Bristol Channel as it was such a clear day. He managed to make out the church spire at the top of Lansdown and Folly Tower beyond that, and heard a train emerge below him from Box Tunnel, watching it speed on towards Bath. He remembered he had to get himself ready for his dinner with Hermione so he climbed on his bike and cycled the rest of the way back to Trevor's.

CHAPTER 19

It was fun for Arnold to decide what they did for a change, instead of going along with what Hermione suggested. He was looking forward to telling her about his meeting in London and his plan to take over and restore the iron church. He had no idea who it belonged to but he was attracted by the idea of occupying it and slowly making it good again. He remembered someone telling him about 'squatter's rights' many years earlier. Apparently if it had fallen into disuse, and he could occupy it for long enough, it would be impossible for anyone to get him out and in essence he would become the owner. He figured it would be a fruitful way to spend the spring and would give him the opportunity to learn everything about DIY. By now he had a high regard for Trevor's opinion on things in general and thought he would ask him to take a look at it and give him some pointers.

Hermione picked him up as usual and they drove over to Lacock but they had some trouble locating the restaurant.

'This town truly is a gem,' she said peering through the windscreen, 'But all the streets look alike. I'm sure it's around here somewhere.'

Finally they came upon it. There was an old sign bearing the name swinging above the door in a strong easterly wind that had blown up. They parked and as they went in Arnold had the feeling they were moving into another time zone. The place was redolent of the Elizabethan age and when they were shown into the wooden panelled snug he promptly ordered a bottle of champagne.

'I say,' said Hermione, 'It looks like you've got something to celebrate.'

They clinked glasses and made a toast before Arnold went through the events of his day in London. He had to stop several times while they looked at the menus and ordered and he'd just got to the tramp in St James's Park when they were shown to their table. The dining room was full but they had a discreet table in one corner where they sat at right angles to one another. There was a candle burning on the table and a red rose in a small glass vase in the centre.

'But you haven't told me how much money there is for you, dear,' Hermione pointed out.

'It's a substantial amount ... about a million pounds, actually,' Arnold replied, trying not to say it too loudly, for fear of being overheard.

On hearing this Hermione dropped her spoon into her soup and sat back, placing her napkin in front of her mouth. He could see over the top of it her eyes were popping out.

'Oh, my God! Arnold! I don't know what to say,' she said, 'That's fantastic news.'

She leant forward and half whispered to him:

'You know, Arnold, you must be careful who you tell about this. Really you must, pet.'

'I know,' he said, 'But you were the one person I wanted to tell straight away.'

'Bless you, dear, bless you. Have you said anything to Trevor?'

'No, not yet. I've got to say something. But I won't specify the amount. You know what he's like.'

They finished their starters and Arnold poured them both a glass of the Gevrey Chambertin he'd ordered. It was one of the most expensive wines on the list so he thought it wouldn't be too bad with their braised lamb. He began to outline his plan for the iron church and she confirmed what he'd heard about 'squatter's rights'. She thought it sounded ambitious but she was all in favour of him giving it a go, especially as he now had the funds at his disposal to pay for it.

'I realise you prefer not to move into the house with me. I must admit I was a bit hurt at first, but ... I fully understand your craving for independence, and being a spiritual soul you need some time alone. Away from me.'

Then she put down her knife and fork and placed her left hand on his forearm and said,

'Arnold, please don't take this the wrong way, but I do love you, you know.'

He wasn't expecting her to say anything like this and was genuinely surprised. He smiled at her and squeezed her hand for a moment. They carried on with the meal and ate their lamb in silence and then he realised she'd wanted to hear him say he loved her too. He enjoyed spending time with her and he really appreciated all the ways in which she'd helped him in the last few months, but ... as much as he wanted to tell her these things he thought it was best not to. From that point onwards he felt a distinct change in the atmosphere. They chatted about various things and she brought him up to date with Lucy. Apparently she'd split up with her boyfriend in

Durham and was concentrating on her studies. She asked him what life was like at Trevor's house and he told her how much he was enjoying it. He avoided telling her about the business with the dog, as he knew she was fond of animals and he didn't want to dampen the evening further.

'I was thinking of asking Trevor for his advice. About the church. He's a mine of information and might be able to give me some useful tips.'

'Who'd have thought you and Trevor would have become such good friends?' she quipped and Arnold thought she'd said it with a slight air of irritation. She was obviously finding it hard to come to terms with. It was the first time he'd detected any hint of jealousy or vexation about her during their friendship and it began to trouble him. The rest of the meal was uneventful but by the time the bill came and Arnold paid he felt he'd been on a long journey that evening. On their way back to Corsham he admitted feeling tired from the wine and Hermione said she was too. That night was the first he'd spent in her bed when they didn't make love.

The next day Hermione seemed back to her normal self and said she was keen to take a look at the iron church. She suggested they drive over that afternoon as the bright weather was holding up and Arnold was pleased at her interest. When they reached Colerne he gave her directions and once parked up he proudly guided her around to the back and held open the loose iron sheeting so she could step inside. He was noticing more and more each time he went there and this time he had a good look at the bell tower, to find there was no bell. Perhaps it would be a good home for the bells of St. Tobias if he could just get hold of them.

'Arnold, it's wonderful. How on earth did you find it?'

He explained how he'd discovered it cycle riding from Stan's one day.

'I wonder who it belongs to? You'll have to do a bit of research on Trevor's computer to find out. Do you think it was built on common land?' she mused.

He knew that meant the land belonged to everyone who lived in the parish but to no individual in particular. Hermione immediately felt the urge to tidy up and started gathering up the aluminium chairs littered across the floor. Arnold joined in and the bright sun in the west gave ample light for them to see what they were doing. Most of the chairs were twisted and broken but they salvaged a good few that still folded up properly and leant them against the back wall. This commotion stirred up a lot of debris and dust from the floor and they had to make a swift exit to avoid breathing it in. The noise also disturbed the pigeons inhabiting the place and they found themselves shielding their faces as these made a bid for freedom too. Looking at themselves outside, they laughed when they saw how dishevelled they'd become.

'Come on, Arnold, I think it's time we got back and cleaned ourselves up,' she suggested.

He liked the sound of this as it probably meant they would shower together again.

At around seven the phone rang at Hermione's and he heard her voice yelling for him to get it. He picked up the receiver and heard Lucy's voice again:

'Hello, Mum? ... Mum? It's me.'

'Oh, hello, Lucy. It's Arnold here.'

There was a pause and he heard the line go dead on him.

He stood looking at the receiver for a few seconds and had just put it down when Hermione appeared.

'Who was it, pet?'

'Lucy, but I think there was a bad connection. She asked for you. I'm sure she'll ring back.'

'She's probably calling from her mobile. I wish she would use a proper line as it costs me a fortune.'

The phone rang again and Arnold picked it up and immediately passed it to her saying loudly:

'Here she is!' so that Lucy could hear him. This time it wasn't Lucy but a cold caller, as he heard Hermione saying

'No, thank you ... No, I don't ... Thank you, but no ... goodbye,' and he felt foolish at his mistake.

He had to admit it had upset him Lucy wouldn't speak to him. It was two months since they'd returned from the cruise and he'd deliberately kept her out of his thoughts. He'd purposefully tried to forget what had or hadn't happened at the Mercouri winery, as all it did was confuse him when he tried to remember. How he wished he could move into the iron church at that moment.

CHAPTER 20

He walked back to Trevor's on Sunday afternoon and got an early night, leaving Trevor up watching some cricket from New Zealand. When he woke at about eight, he wondered how he would have felt if he had indeed shot the dog. At the time he was convinced he would feel no remorse but now he wasn't so sure. He'd only been out of the church for six months but had already been on a roller coaster ride, running through a plethora of emotions and experiences. More than he'd had the rest of his life up until then, he was sure. How controlled his little sphere of activity had been in the cottage. How sheltered he was beginning to see he'd been there. No wonder the people on the cruise ship looked so terribly tired, if what he'd seen in six months was any indication of the normal lives they had to navigate their way through. He had a few things left on his 'to do' list he wanted to deal with that day and after his egg and soldiers he made himself comfortable by the phone. First of all he called Nigel Scott to tell him what he'd decided.

'Hello, Mr. Drive. That's all fine, but I'll need a written authorisation from you to that effect before I can action anything. Why don't you put it all down on paper with your bank details and put it in the post today Recorded Delivery? I should get it tomorrow.'

Next he found an address and number for Bonhams and realised he'd been just a few blocks away when he'd walked towards Paddington the week before. He called and spoke to several people before he was put through to their Records Department. He quoted all the information he had and was told it would probably take a couple of days to access the information he was looking for, so he left Trevor's phone number to call him back on.

Finally he telephoned the Morris Minor Centre in Bath and made an appointment to go in that afternoon to discuss his needs and see what was available. He saw no reason why he couldn't now afford a station wagon complete with wooden trim around the back. Or maybe a convertible? It struck him that if he wanted he could afford both.

He decided to get the bus from Pickwick into Bath. It was something he hadn't done for a long time and the idea appealed to him. He picked out his smartest jacket and trousers for the trip and was just ironing a shirt when Trevor appeared in his dressing gown:

'Morning, Arnold. Excuse the attire. Got drawn into the cricket last night. Fascinating passage of play after lunch. Couldn't tear myself away. Ended up staying up far too late and drinking far too much brandy. Still, what's life for, eh? Off out?'

'Yes, I'm going into Bath to the Morris Minor Centre. I was thinking of buying a car.'

'Very nice,' Trevor replied. 'You seem to be splashing the cash around at the moment. Had a bit of luck at the bookies? I never took you to be a gambling man.'

'I'm not. But I came into a bit of money recently from a deceased relative and thought it might be nice to have one. I've never owned a car before. What do you think of them?' he asked, knowing Trevor would set him straight.

'Morris Minor? An English classic. Can't go wrong with 'em. The place in Bath is supposed to be the business, right enough. Shall I give you a ride in? I wouldn't mind taking a look m'self.'

Arnold preferred going in alone and said:

'I was going to take the bus in. You're welcome to join me?'

He knew all too well Trevor would never take a bus into Bath under any circumstances.

Later on, as he waited outside The Two Pigs for the bus, he thought he'd explained the windfall adequately enough. Trevor seemed to have accepted it without asking any difficult questions. The bus was on time and he got on making sure he had the exact money ready for the driver. He knew how irritating it was to be on a bus and have to wait while people fumbled in their pockets and purses for the right change. There were very few passengers on-board so he had difficulty deciding where he wanted to sit, especially when a couple of people recognised him and wished him 'Good morning, Vicar', obviously unaware he was no longer in the church. He loitered close to the driver and ended up sitting at the front so as to avoid any conversation with the two women who'd recognised him. Once seated with a good view ahead, he relaxed and enjoyed the ride into Bath, which took them down the B3109 and across the Five Ways junction, and then up past the Kingsdown golf course to hurtle gloriously down the hill into Batheaston. They inevitably got stuck in lunchtime traffic on the London Road, and the going was so slow Arnold decided to get off and walk the rest of the way. It took him a good half an hour but he was able to take the footpath down by the river, which he'd never done before, saving him some time and making pleasant surroundings to walk along in. He'd forgotten what an attractive town Bath was and felt lucky to be so close to it. While he'd been immersed in Corsham he'd hardly visited the place and it struck him how easy it is to become blind to what's right under your nose.

They were extremely helpful at the Morris Minor Centre and showed him three different models. He just couldn't make up his mind which one to go for, the convertible or the station wagon, and then he had an idea:

'Would it be possible to fit a sunroof in the station wagon? An electronic one?' he asked the salesman boldly.

'Yes, I suppose so,' he replied. 'Could run a bit expensive, mind you. Let me find out.'

He went into an office and returned with an engineer who had a pencil behind his ear and overalls on. Arnold hoped he wasn't going to get too technical and say it wasn't possible. But he surprised him by saying:

'Yes, I don't see why not. The dimensions for the roof are the same as for the saloon, and we fit them in those easily enough.'

He led Arnold over to the green station wagon they'd been inspecting and got out a tape measure.

'You're limited as to how big it can be, 'cos it's got to slide away under the roof behind, see. But ... how about that? Big enough?'

He held his extended tape measure against the roof panel. It looked large enough and Arnold said it would be fine.

They told him it would add a few hundred pounds to the cost, but what did he care? He had enough money to buy a fleet of Morris Minors, with or without electric sunroofs. They said it would take a few days to fit but Arnold told them not to worry as he had to arrange the finance. He'd never bought anything so expensive before, so he asked them:

'How would you like me to pay the money? Cash?'

They both looked at him, and at each other, and smiled, and the salesman said:

'A cheque or banker's draft will do. Just bring it with you when the car's ready.'

Arnold still had one more errand to run whilst he was in Bath. He had with him the letter for Nigel Scott requesting the bank transfer he'd written before leaving Corsham and he wanted to go by a post office to send it off. By chance, he'd noticed one on the Lower Bristol Road on his way into town so he followed the river back the way he'd come to go past it. He decided to continue along as far as Batheaston before catching the bus the rest of the way, so he was able to avoid the fumes of the rush hour traffic. As he walked along he thought he'd done very well that afternoon, ordering the right car and then getting a sunroof fitted. It was by far the best option. The sun was so unpredictable the amount of time a convertible's roof would be down would be minimal, and he had the safety factor to consider as well. Funnily enough, the same two women who'd recognised him on the bus ride in earlier were on the bus back. They smiled and said 'Good afternoon, Vicar' again politely to him so he stayed down at the front with the driver.

'Well, old chap, that's awfully decent of you. I gladly accept!' said Trevor, when he invited him out to dinner that evening. Arnold had caught him completely by surprise when he got back to the house.

'It's the least I can do to thank you for putting me up since January. I'll leave you to decide where to go.'

Trevor picked The Inn at Rode, just a short drive from Corsham and a place he'd heard good reports about. Arnold was happy with the suggestion. It gave him the opportunity to find out about more places he could take Hermione to. They booked a table for eight o'clock, that way they could tuck in and Trevor would be back in time for the start of the cricket in New Zealand. Arnold wanted to tell him about the iron church and what he wanted to do with it.

The dining room at The Inn wasn't busy, being a Monday, and they were able to choose where to sit. Arnold didn't recognise many of the dishes on the menu and asked Trevor for help. The confit duck sounded delicious according to Trevor and they both ordered soup to start followed by that, washing it down with a bottle of Châteauneuf du Pape, again on Trevor's advice. Once they'd got a glass of wine in front of them Arnold raised his and said,

'Thank you so much for all you've done. I had nowhere to go and you took me in.'

'Rather like the Nativity, eh?' Trevor replied with a laugh and they clinked glasses.

'But you could have gone to Hermione's,' he continued, 'It wouldn't have been the worst place to end up ... in her bed, eh?'

Arnold then tried to explain how he felt about her:

'She's a wonderful person, there's no doubt about that.

But I feel it's important to try to create a place of my own somewhere.'

'Well, now you've got a bit of dosh, you'll be able to do that, won't you? Not that I'm in any way trying to throw you out. Lord, no! Wouldn't think of it. Nice to have you aboard. Just wondered if you had any ideas. That's all.'

Sensing an opportunity to tell him about what he'd found, Arnold said:

'I have actually. I stumbled across an old iron church. Just outside Bath. It's completely derelict at the moment. I feel an inexplicable desire to live there. Does that sound odd?'

'Mmm, sounds interesting. Where did you say it was?'

Arnold tried to give him a more precise location and Trevor suddenly recognised it:

'You know what, I think I know where you mean. I used to drive up that way to go into Bristol every morning and I do believe I remember passing it. It looked pretty dilapidated back then. It must be ready to fall down now.'

'It is. But I want to restore it. Would you mind coming up there with me and taking a look? I'd appreciate your opinion about what needs to be done.'

'Delighted to, old chap. When shall we go? Tomorrow?'

CHAPTER 21

The next day they motored over to the iron church and Trevor had a good nose around inside. Overall, he thought it was possible to renovate and offered Arnold his help. He said they'd been called 'tin tabernacles' back in the day, and confirmed that they were built on common land or land donated to the parish by landowners. Trevor thought it could get expensive and wondered if Arnold had adequate funds to see it through. On Wednesday, Arnold spent all morning looking for his driving licence and discovered it in pristine condition in a plastic folder from his days in Norfolk. It had expired, of course, so he had to go to the post office and fill out some forms and pay for a new one, which he learnt would take about ten days to arrive. Nigel Scott received his letter and was making the transfer using a chaps' payment, but he didn't say who they were. Trevor gave him some help organising his car insurance and that evening he went to Hermione's for supper. On Thursday, he rang his bank to confirm the £89,245.63 had arrived, and he got a call from Bonhams telling him they'd searched their records and would be writing to him with information regarding the origin of the music box. He didn't sleep well that night, as he was due to pick up his Morris Minor the next day and he was excited. This time he accepted Trevor's offer of a ride into Bath. He realised he hadn't driven for about thirty-five years and could be a bit rusty. They parked Trevor's Rover on the forecourt at the Morris Minor Centre and once Arnold had dealt with the money side of things they gingerly set off for a test drive, with Trevor sitting beside him in the passenger seat. They slowly went up to Bear Flat and on to the Wells Road where there was less traffic. They circled right the way round the top of Bath and came in again down Bathwick Hill, by which time Arnold felt pretty confident he'd rediscovered his driving skills. When the sun came out, Trevor took it as a cue to press the button for the sunroof, which quietly slid open with a luxurious purr above their heads. They picked up the Rover and Trevor followed Arnold back to Corsham. On Saturday he picked up Hermione and they motored down to the coast, where they managed to find a place to have lunch by the sea at West Beach. It was sunny and crisp so they took a walk under the red Jurassic cliffs afterwards to look for fossils in the rocks. With Hermione's arm tucked in his and breathing in the fresh sea air he felt a bit less like a fossil himself.

On Monday morning, the letter from Bonhams arrived:

Dear Mr. Drive

Following your enquiry we have investigated our records and can inform you that the following lot was sold at the Mechanical Music Auction in Hamburg on March 3rd 1974:Musical box circa 1786 manufactured by Jacquet Droz & Leschott in Lucerne, Switzerland.

Price attained by lot: £1,100 (including sales commission)

Lot supplied by Krebs & Koenig, Hamburg.

Bought by Frau Rosa Hoeppell nee Dreuber.

We hope this information is of use to you.

Yours sincerely,

Ella Rheingold

Bonhams Archives.

He was pleased as it gave him the name of the buyer, but disappointed it hadn't revealed any information regarding the origin of the piece. Krebs & Koenig were presumably the executors of the will of the relative and he would have to get on to them to search their records for the name of the deceased. He felt there was no time like the present and rang international directory enquiries to get a number for the firm in Hamburg. The operator could find no trace of them so he hung up and went on the internet to search there. He drew a blank, went to the online telephone directory for Hamburg, but still had no luck. There were hundreds of Krebs & Koenig's but no companies listed under their combined names and he began to feel he hadn't made any progress at all. He took a break at lunchtime and after meticulously making and eating a toasted cheese, tomato and Marmite sandwich (one of his favourites) he took a drive over to the iron church. He was beginning to thoroughly enjoy driving again as he found it strangely relaxing and it allowed him to concentrate on his thoughts.

Once inside, he carefully set out one of the aluminium chairs he and Hermione had salvaged in the middle of the floor and sat quietly to look around. It was the first time he'd been motionless there and he tried to imagine what it must have been like with a congregation. It certainly had the same feel as a stone church to him. Perhaps it was because of the intense amount of praying that must have taken place there over the years. It served to reinforce his theory that God didn't have to be confined within the walls of a conventional church and could be found anywhere if one just had the eyes to look for Him. He noticed there were five cast iron frames supporting the roof and, although they were rusty, they looked solid enough. He got up and walked along underneath them and on tiptoe gave each a hefty tug and a push to find them all still securely in place. He was especially glad of this as they were holding the roof up. As he stepped outside again through his improvised back door, he noticed there was renewed vigour in the ground cover surrounding the building. Brambles had begun to wake up from their winter dormancy and were beginning to quickly sprout and invade. The first thing he would have to do would be to buy a strimmer to secure the perimeter of the building against them.

Back at Trevor's, he checked how his family tree search was progressing. He'd filled in his personal details and those of his parents when he'd opened an account at Ancestry.co.uk the week before and was expecting some results. He wasn't disappointed. Next to his father's name a brother called Reginald Edward had appeared who Arnold had never heard of before. He wondered if this was the relative who'd left him the musical box. Who was this mysterious uncle and why had his parents never mentioned him?

His date of birth was shown as 1897 and there was a question mark where the year of his death should have been. This

Reginald Edward was an elder brother of his father's, with seven years between them. Reginald Edward would have been seventeen years old when the Great War had begun in 1914 and therefore old enough to enlist. If that had been the case what had happened to him?

He'd noticed that part of the service on Ancestry.co.uk was access to records of military personnel from the two wars, so he went to the right page on the site and put in a search for his uncle. All he had was his full name and year of birth, but he guessed his place of birth to be London, the same as his father's. He punched 'enter' and immediately got a match. His uncle had enlisted on 17th April 1914, been put into the 19th Light Infantry Brigade, and been sent to fight in Mons in northern France. There were no details of his death or his demob, so Arnold began to entertain the possibility that he'd been captured and perhaps sent to a POW camp in Germany. He didn't know where to go from there. It seemed the records from German POW camps were very sketchy in the Great War, so he tried to think of something else he could do. The only other bit of information he had was the name of the buyer at the auction so, while he was at the computer, he got access to the online Hamburg telephone directory again and looked up the name. He was surprised to find there was indeed a Rosa Hoeppell listed, at Milchstrasse 17, Hamburg. Perhaps it could be the same one, although he couldn't quite see how she would be able to help him discover anything about his uncle. He'd recently discovered Google Maps during his computer browsing, and not knowing what to do next, he entered the address in Hamburg. A street map appeared on the screen with a red circle pinpointing the location. He pressed the lower magnification button several times and got an idea of where Milchstrasse was in Hamburg. There seemed to be a large lake just a few streets away and surprisingly enough it was almost in the centre of the city. Just then Trevor stuck his head around the doorway:

'Arnold. Any chance of getting on there myself soon? Sorry if you're in the middle of something.'

The following morning he drove out to the large B&Q outside Chippenham and bought a strimmer, a petrol can, secateurs, a pair of heavy duty gardening gloves, some black plastic sacks, and an aluminium ladder you could adjust for use on sloping ground. He drove out to the iron church and spent a few hours going round the outside, clearing all the brambles and low-hanging branches from the surrounding trees. The brambles were particularly awkward to deal with, and the secateurs came in handy to cut them up into manageable pieces he could pack away into the bags, but he had to be careful not to puncture the gloves doing this. He ended up with half a dozen full sacks that he put in the back of the station wagon. Once he'd loaded his tools in as well, the car was rammed full and he realised he didn't know what he was going to do with the debris, but as he drove along he decided the best thing was to ask Trevor if he could have a bonfire in the back garden.

The rest of the week he spent either in B&Q or at the iron church. The inside had to be cleared out first of all, so he bought overalls and some masks to stop him breathing in the dust he would stir up while he was sweeping with the industrial broom he'd bought. Once he'd done this, it became clearer what was needed inside the building. If he was indeed to live there he would need a water supply, a source of electricity, some sort of a loo and bathroom, and a kitchen, as he was determined to master the art of cookery. It was part and parcel of his desire to become independent. He bought himself a laptop computer and a printer in the Comet next door to B&Q, as he felt he was spending far too long on Trevor's and he didn't want it to become an issue between them. The evenings were spent devouring online guides to renovation, plumbing, carpentry, electrical systems and any other skill that came into his mind as something he would need. Trevor suggested he go out to the church with Arnold at the start of each week and discuss a work schedule for him. His advice proved invaluable as he was forever suggesting short cuts and savings that could be made. He saw Hermione every weekend and kept her up to date with developments with 'Arnold Keep' as she'd chosen to call the place. She said it reflected his intention to 'seize it from under the noses of the authorities' and stay there as long as he could, and he agreed with that. She pointed out that, until he became the legal squatter there, he would be unable to connect to any water supply or electrical network. He'd already assumed that and had started to investigate generators, solar panels and rainwater collection systems, as these would have to be used once he'd moved in.

Every night he fell asleep soundly at Trevor's after a hard day's work and found it more and more difficult to leave at the end of each day. As soon as he'd left he wanted to go back and could hardly wait until he was on his way there again in the morning. The walls had been completed and their fastenings replaced with weatherproof versions, and by the beginning of May he'd started on the roof panels. There had been some rotten timber in the roof, which had needed replacing and he allowed Trevor to bring in a builder friend of his:

'Completely trustworthy. Never tell a soul. Salt of the earth. An old pal of mine.'

Arnold was glad he had as he'd never have been able to do it all by himself. He already had a generator installed and could power the whole place up with a 240 volt supply. Just as soon as the roofing was completed he could install his rainwater collection system, but he had a large polyurethane water tank raised up in a cradle out back that would make do until then. By the end of June he was lying in bed at Trevor's house contemplating moving in.

CHAPTER 22

Trevor's builder friend installed a bathroom for Arnold (as plumbing was the only aspect of DIY Arnold was unsure about) and the builder had already answered lots of technical questions for him. He seemed genuinely bemused at Arnold's little project and was more than happy to drop by and check something for him. Together they constructed a small kitchenette hidden behind a stud partition wall in one corner of the building. His sleeping area consisted of a raised gallery running along the rear wall away from the road and accessed via several wide, wooden steps set in a half spiral curving up from floor level. The builder complimented Arnold on the carpentry involved and was genuinely impressed at his skills. To simplify the plumbing, the bathroom was put next to the kitchenette and the only thing Arnold was unhappy about was the lack of a window looking out from it. The builder jovially agreed to help him reconstruct the bell tower so he could finally provide a home for the St. Tobias bells, but as he had no idea when, or if, he could secure them they thought it best to wait with that. The powering up of the electric system proved a major landmark as it meant Arnold could linger on much later in the evenings attending to the myriad of jobs that still remained.

Finally, in mid-July, he was able to spend his first night there and being by the side of a country lane he thought it would be as quiet as it had been at Stan's house. But the serene stillness was often punctuated by the sounds of night creatures, a new experience for him, and in fact it wasn't a peaceful night's sleep at all. He was woken up repeatedly by animal cries, bird shrieks and what sounded like things falling onto the roof and he realised the countryside is far from the quiet place people who live in towns presume it to be.

He was up early the next morning and set to work after showering and eating his egg and soldiers with coffee. He'd noticed a drop in the water pressure in the bathroom taps and was sure there was a blockage somewhere in the feed line from the tank outside.

At about nine thirty he heard a car pull up outside and recognised it as Trevor's, who stuck his head inside the open front door:

'Morning! Anybody at home?'

Arnold emerged from the bathroom and greeted him warmly before putting the kettle on.

'So, how was the first night? Did you repel any unwelcome guests? And were there any early morning arias performed by local dogs?'

Arnold sighed:

'I didn't sleep at all well. There seemed to be constant noise throughout the night. But I'm sure I'll get used to it. It's just a matter of time.'

They sat down with some tea and Trevor looked around the place, which at that moment was enjoying several shafts of brilliant sunshine streaming in through the south facing windows:

'Well, old chap. Who'd have thought a few months ago, you'd be here? An ecclesiastical squatter, no less. By the way, got a little something for you. You could call it a house warming present.'

He produced a plastic bag, which he handed over to Arnold. Inside was a wooden board with the words ARNOLD'S KEEP formed from thin branches deftly carved and nailed in place. A woven border of similar thin twigs neatly surrounded the name.

'Got the name from Hermione. She said that's what the two of you have been referring to the place as. Rather pleased with it. Do you approve?'

Arnold loved it and they went outside to prop it up against the wall. After admiring it for a while they went back in and Trevor asked him:

'Speaking of the dear girl, when did you last speak to her?'

Arnold thought for a moment and realised he hadn't seen her for several weeks but remembered she'd gone off to visit some friends in Truro in June:

'Not for a while. Is she back from Cornwall yet?'

'God, yes. Word has it she's going back to Tony. Apparently he's split up with the secretary bird and has been making overtures to her. Undying love. Can't live without you sort of thing. Thought I should prepare you. I'm sure she'll be telling you what's what when it's been settled. You see, they never divorced. And she idolised him. We used to see them a lot in Corsham, the wife and I, when it was all hunky-dory before they split up. Sorry to be the bearer of bad news, old chap.'

It wasn't something he'd been expecting at all. Tony never came up in any of his conversations with Hermione. In fact, Arnold had quite forgotten she was still married to him. He'd been preoccupied with the Keep while she'd been away in Cornwall and he'd assumed she would have contacted him on her return. The fact she hadn't done so told him a lot. His mind raced back to their dinner at The Sign of the Angel, when he'd admitted to her he yearned for somewhere of his own, where he could attempt to find himself. She must have taken that as a signal that their future together was far from certain. No wonder she had begun to seriously entertain the possibility of returning to Tony. If it was true, he wondered if she would stay on in Corsham, or decide to move up to London where Tony lived. He couldn't remember where she'd said it was ...

Trevor could see Arnold was lost in his thoughts and decided it was time to leave;

'Got to dash. On my way into Bath. Pesky dentist's appointment at 11. Been putting it off for months. You'll have to get a phone line in, or a mobile, or something.'

He was right, of course. Arnold had no form of communication out there. He felt like calling Hermione at that very moment, but knew it was impossible. So he tidied up the tea and breakfast things and drove off into Bath determined not to leave until he had some sort of a phone working in his hand.

He had difficulty punching in the right numbers on the tiny keyboard of the Blackberry he ended up buying, but, after a few abortive attempts, started to get the hang of it and sat in his car in Victoria Park waiting whilst Hermione's phone rang in Corsham. He imagined what it sounded like in her hallway, ringing as he'd heard it countless times when he'd been staying there. His heart quickened in pace as he waited. But this time it wasn't answered and she hadn't switched on her answering machine. He tried it several more times, but no one was at home so he reluctantly gave up. He didn't know what he would have said by way of a message, even if he'd had the chance to leave one, and he felt he'd avoided an awkward moment. It made him feel completely uneasy and listless, just sitting there in his car, and he didn't know quite what to do next. It was, of course, the effect of what had or hadn't happened at the Mercouri vineyard. After that he'd felt awkward around her, knowing he was keeping the events that afternoon with Lucy a secret. Fastening his seat belt he started the engine and moved off through the park with no destination in mind. He followed the road to the exit and turned left to go down the hill and join the A4 on the west side of Bath. He found himself on the dual carriageway heading out towards somewhere called Corston and turned left at a roundabout to join the A37 going south. After about an hour he saw a sign to a place called Stourhead, which sounded vaguely familiar, and he decided to follow the signs. He parked up in the car park and walked over to the entrance gate to pay an admission fee. There was a large house on his left but he preferred to stay outside in the open air. He ignored the arrowed signs to the house and followed the paths down over a hillside, emerging onto a winding walkway that led down to a beautiful lake. There were tall, mature conifers interspersed with herbaceous shrubs and it was obvious it had been planted meticulously at some point. Whenever he stopped, he was rewarded with a lovely view, and he could see there were various mausoleum-like stone buildings positioned on the hillsides surrounding the lake. Arnold was compelled to visit each one in turn, sitting quietly to enjoy the different views on offer. The whole place was enthralling and felt as if it had escaped the frenetic progressions of the world, remaining cocooned away, protected in a special dimension of its own. Arnold lost track of how long he'd been there and sat for a long time in the sunken grotto, whose walls were festooned with thousands of shells that twinkled in the dark as he moved his head slightly one way or the other. He finally sat down to rest on the steps leading up to the final building, the Temple of Apollo, drinking in the vista as if it were a three dimensional painting. He watched the sun sinking slowly towards the horizon on his left. It had such a calming effect on him he ceased to fret about Hermione and the fact she might be going back to Tony. If it were meant to be, he would accept it. Besides, he'd just commenced what he felt was a new chapter in his life moving into the Keep. He sensed there were many things left waiting to happen and for him to discover. His life was far from over. Just then, the sun finally touched the silhouette of land on the horizon below and he decided it was time to leave.

The next few weeks were hot and sultry and he preferred to spend them alone out at the Keep. He'd gradually been moving his things over whilst the renovations were in progress so there was nothing much left at Trevor's. He made a habit of trying Hermione's number every day but didn't get to speak to her. There never seemed to be anyone in and her answering machine was never on. All around the iron church everything grew in profusion and he was constantly trimming tree foliage and clearing away brambles as they sent their exploratory tentacles out to probe and try to gain new ground. He'd noticed there was an abundance of rabbits in the area and had taken to rising early and observing them through the telescopic sight of the air rifle he'd borrowed from Trevor. He found himself beginning to take pleasure in sharply focusing on one and watching it go about its business, oblivious to the fact it was being watched. There was an excitement about it that was intoxicating. The iron church was surrounded behind by higher ground that had been excavated to provide the flat piece of land on which it sat and the fields above were occasionally filled with grazing sheep. He knew in advance which days the sheep would appear as he could hear them bleating first thing from within his bed and he would sleep in a little later those days. Occasionally a car would speed past down the lane or he would hear a group of hikers amble by, but no one knocked at his door. Trevor always spent that time each year motoring around the country visiting old friends, and so Arnold settled into a period of solitude punctuated by long walks, bicycle rides, home beautification and some reading.

One morning he found an envelope pushed under his door. He recognised the extravagant handwriting as Hermione's and took it up carefully as if it were a delicate flower, ready to disintegrate in his hands. He sat down at his kitchen table and opened it to find a handwritten letter inside.

My dear Arnold,

It seems ages since we last spoke and I have to admit I've been avoiding us meeting. I've been spending time in London with Tony, my husband. Perhaps it will be a mistake but I've decided to go back to him.

I've realised he still loves me dearly, and that I'm still in love with him, after all this time, and water under the bridge as they say ...

He wants me to live in London with him and I've agreed to give it a go.

I'm going to keep the house in Corsham for the time being, just in case it doesn't work out.

You know how fond I am of you, and always will be.

I'm so glad you've finally found somewhere of your own where you can be yourself.

I'm sorry if this isn't what you wanted to hear, but I'd be relieved if you can try to understand.

Yours ever,

Hermione

It didn't come as a surprise after what Trevor had told him a few weeks earlier. In fact, it came as a relief to know the truth. He wasn't even sure if he was unhappy with what she'd said in the letter. It became clear to him how important it is to know the truth whatever it turns out to be, even if it is unpleasant. It was uncertainty that was the difficult thing to endure, not the facts themselves. With this in mind, he resolved to try his best to unravel the mystery of the music box that his uncle had bequeathed to him, that had led to his current comfortable situation. Whatever lay in wait for him to discover, he was sure it would be better to know the truth than to remain in the dark. His situation reminded him of what he'd experienced when he'd tried to make his way across the living room of his cottage in Corsham, when the bars of shadows from the sun's rays had imprisoned him. He felt foolish now, remembering how he'd attempted to get around with his eyes closed, feeling the empty air in front of him with outstretched hands, bumping into furniture and very nearly falling over.

He found the letter from Bonham's with the address of the buyer of the music box, Frau Rosa Hoeppell, and decided he would go and visit her in Hamburg to see if he could, at the very least, take a look at it. He'd been unable to find any more information about his uncle and he thought perhaps the music box would reveal something more. His Blackberry provided him with internet access but until that moment he'd not had the need to use it. He fumbled with the central wheel to navigate through the various pages and booked himself a flight on easyJet from Bristol to Hamburg the following weekend. He spent a tense half hour looking for his passport, which he hadn't used since he'd returned from the cruise seven months earlier. He discovered it still in the breast pocket of his linen jacket he'd worn on the journey back from Athens, together with the leaflet about the Mercouri vineyard. The boarding pass for the flight home to Gatwick fell out when he opened up his passport to double check it was still valid.

He carefully wrote out his flight details and Frau Hoeppell's address in Hamburg in block capitals so he could show it to a taxi driver when he arrived.

CHAPTER 23

It felt strange to close and lock the door behind him when he left for the airport on Saturday morning. It had just gone five o'clock and the outside world hadn't yet woken up. He felt the corrugated iron walls reverberate and echo as he threaded the padlock through the tabs he'd fitted on the door and heard it click shut. Arnold really did live there and inside was his new life. He was sad to be driving away towards Bristol airport and every mile registered on the milometer made him feel a little less secure. He wasn't looking forward to arriving at the airport and having to find somewhere to leave his car, but following the signs to the long term car park he found a free spot immediately he turned in the gates. It was only a short walk to the terminal building and within fifteen minutes he'd cleared customs and security and was sitting waiting for his flight by the departure gate. It couldn't have been easier. The airport was very quiet; apart from some piped music coming from an opening clothes shop there was very little to disturb him.

He hadn't bothered with his egg and soldiers, and feeling peckish unwrapped the egg and cress sandwich he'd prepared the night before, with added Hellman's mayonnaise and a generous sprinkling of fresh ground pepper and sea salt. He bought a cappuccino from the cafe and noticed an equivalent sandwich to the one he'd made on sale there for a whopping £3.49. He was glad he'd thought ahead to make his own. He spent time calculating how many egg and cress sandwiches he could make for the same price. A half dozen eggs from the local farm cost about £1 (free range), a loaf of bread about the same and 50p would buy you two tubs of cress, so £2.50 would be enough for six sandwiches, making the unit cost about 42p. He added a few pence for butter, mayonnaise, ground pepper and sea salt, plus the cost of hard boiling the egg, say 4p, making a unit cost of 49p. Subtracting that from the £3.49 left £3. He thought he'd work out how much an egg and cress sandwich maker made by the hour, if that's all they did all day. He pictured himself making an egg and cress sandwich and timed the whole process. Once the egg had been hard boiled it would have to be cooled down (or rinsed in cold water) before it could be peeled and sliced, but it would be possible to hard boil six eggs at the same time, bringing the cost of the electricity per sandwich down. In fact, it would be easier to make six sandwiches simultaneously. He worked out in his head six eggs could be boiled and cooled down in ten minutes. Each sandwich would then take two minutes to make, giving a final time of twenty-two minutes to make six sandwiches, so in an hour you could make 16.3636 sandwiches. Therefore the egg and cress sandwich maker made £49 an hour, assuming he got the whole £3.49. It struck him it was more than he'd been making at St. Tobias's.

As his flight departure approached the seats in the lounge began to fill up and by the time boarding finished the plane was nearly full. They roared into the air and he was reminded of the exhilaration he'd felt the first time on the plane to Athens. Having arrived at the airport so early he'd been one of the first onto the plane and had got a seat for himself at the front, next to a window. He looked out at the receding landscape around Bristol as they gained altitude and when the view disappeared, it left blue skies outside above the clouds. He looked to see who was sitting next to him. There was a man in a suit, Arnold imagined him to be a German businessman, probably on his way home for the weekend. Next to the aisle was what looked like a tourist, a middle-aged woman with curly, fading blonde hair, dressed in a fleece with a hood. She wore a pair of stretch blue jeans and had on what looked like hiking shoes. He guessed she was going to Hamburg on a walking trip. It occurred to him he hadn't bothered to investigate the cultural heritage of the city at all. There were bound to be many things worth visiting, but in his hurry to leave he'd left no time to even consider using the trip to explore the place. No matter, he thought, he could always return at a later date if he wanted to. He noticed the woman was studying a guidebook of the city and after about an hour she yawned and put the book in her bag, so he took the opportunity to ask her if he could take a look. She offered it with a smile and he spent the last part of the flight discovering Hamburg was one of the top sex destinations in the world, and the Beatles had spent years there before they'd become successful. It was a large port city close to the North Sea and subsequently extremely wealthy, as all ships arriving there had to pay a toll. The vast dock area had become more or less redundant as unloading now took place closer to the coast, and the largest redevelopment in Europe was taking place along the waterfront. There were apparently two main railway stations and one had curiously been built to accommodate the arrival of their erstwhile king, who had refused to arrive in the city at the same station as his subjects. Arnold had no idea such hierarchy and inequality had existed in German society. He studied a map and confirmed the address he was going to was located close to the large lake, Allße-nalster, in the town centre. Just then the plane intercom announced they were preparing to land so he closed the book, returned it and fastened his seat belt.

Outside the terminal in the Hamburg air, he was glad to be on the ground again. He got in a taxi, showed the address to the driver and they set off in the sunshine. Arnold was surprised how close the airport was to the city. After about ten minutes they were driving through leafy suburbs. It was very pleasant – much greener than he was expecting and with a calming, tranquil air about it.

'Are you visiting for long, sir?' the driver asked in perfect English.

He could see a pair of cold, blue eyes studying him in the rear view mirror.

'No, just overnight,' he replied, and added a smile for good measure.

'Ah, that is a shame. We have a very nice city here. Plenty to see. You want to see some sex clubs?'

Arnold was surprised at how forward the driver was being, but then he remembered the sex trade was a major tourist attraction.

'Ah ...no ... thank you. Not just yet.'

The driver chuckled:

'Aha. Maybe later? I will give you my card.'

'Ah. Thank you. Yes. Very good,' he managed, and took the card, not wanting to appear rude.

The roads began to get wider, the trees larger as they progressed into the centre and it struck Arnold as being rather odd. They drove past Stadt Park, which was surrounded by very grand houses, and into Eppendorf, then through Harvesterhude and into Poseldorf.

Arnold asked if the Bahnhof Dammtor, the railway station built for the king, was far away and the driver was impressed he knew of it:

'Ah, so! You have done some research, I see. Yah, it is very near. You would like to drive past it?'

Arnold thought it a good idea and a few minutes later they rounded a bend in the road and the handsome building loomed into view. The driver told him:

'We have the main station, Hauptbahnhof, in the centre of town, but this one is called a "haltepunkt" station. It means in German that no journeys start or end here, or change direction.'

Milchstrasse proved to be just a few minutes' drive from the station and the suburb of Poseldorf in which it was located was extremely grand. Most of the white houses looked like they could be foreign embassies, with elegant stairways up to large double doors, and flagpoles outside many of them, though he didn't recognise any of the flags flying. There was no wind, and most of them were limp; draped around their poles as if they were asleep. They passed a hotel called the Garden on Magdalenstrasse which looked very proper and Arnold realised he hadn't taken the trouble to book a room for his one night's stay in the city. Never mind, he thought, perhaps he could get a room there later on. Most of the walled grounds had luxurious gardens with rhodo-dendron bushes and magnolias peering over the tops of high walls. As they pulled into Milchstrasse, Arnold noticed it was less grand than adjoining streets, rather like a mews street he had seen on his trip to London. He guessed it could have originally been where the carriages and horses were kept for the larger houses. There were cobblestones that made the wheels of the taxi purr. They came to a halt outside number 17. Arnold paid and got out, holding his small overnight bag. He pocketed the card his driver had given him, walked up to the door and rang the bell. After a while he heard some noise and the door opened on a security chain. A pair of small brown eyes looked up at him through the crack. There was a slight, aged lady with long grey hair, wearing glasses at the end of her nose, with a startled look on her face:

'*Ja? Guten morgen.*'

Arnold couldn't speak a word of German so he spoke slowly in English and hoped for the best:

'Hello. Mrs. Rosa Hoeppell?'

She looked at him curiously and replied:

'*Ja?*'

'I'm so sorry to disturb you. I do not speak German. My name is Arnold Drive. I have come from England today. I am looking for a music box that I think you bought at an auction many years ago. I was the person who sold it. It was left to me by a relative ...'

At that moment the woman interrupted him:

'You say your name is Drive?'

'Yes, that's right. Arnold Drive. I used to be a priest.'

Arnold didn't quite know why he'd added that bit of

information. Maybe he thought it would reassure her. She fumbled with the security chain, opened the door and said:

'But, *mein Gott*. It cannot be possible. You cannot be ... Is it true? Please, come in. Please. Please.'

He went inside and she gently pushed him from behind along a corridor into a shaded living room with comfortable button-down chairs and several shiny pieces of antique mahogany furniture, including an elegant grand piano. There was a beautiful Turkish carpet on the floor and net curtains at the windows. She forced him down into one of the chairs and looked at him, smiling kindly over her glasses:

'Now, we will take some tea. *Ja?*'

CHAPTER 24

Frau Hoeppell reappeared carrying a tray of tea things with two china cups and saucers. Whilst she served him she kept stopping and staring at him as if he were an exhibit at a museum, and he began to fidget in his chair. She apologised:

'*Entschuldigen*. Please forgive me. But you must have no idea, *ja*? That we are related.'

On saying this she sat down opposite him and watched as his face filled with confusion. She continued:

'You are my nephew. I was married to your Uncle Red.'

'What ... you mean Reginald Edward?'

'Yes, that's right. But we always called him Red. You know, from his initials. And his red hair.'

Arnold began to sense the world falling about his ears and exclaimed:

'But I thought you were the buyer of the music box at the auction?'

'Yes! That too. Let me explain. This is *ein* big surprise for me too. But I can tell you everything.'

She took a sip or two of her tea – which he noticed she took the 'Russian' way, black with a squeeze of lemon juice – then carefully placed it back on its saucer on the table between them and settled into her chair to begin:

'Did you know that your uncle became a prisoner of war in Germany? He was captured at Le Cateau after Mons in September 1914 and kept in a camp in northern Germany near Gottingen. It was one of the first to be established in the Great War. His bright red hair meant he was very noticeable, and the commandant of the camp, Klaus Borringer, discovered he was a keen chess player, like himself. So they started to play chess together and got to liking one another. You know, Red was a charming man, and Borringer could speak fluent English. He was from a wealthy family that owned several factories around Germany that made *knopf* ... how do you call them, buttons? Red learnt a lot of German from Borringer, and at the end of the war Borringer offered Red a job as his chauffeur. Well, Red had no wife or children to go back to in England, so he decided to take the job and stay in Germany. It was a simple formality for such a well-connected man as Borringer to arrange this for his English friend.'

She stopped to take another sip of her tea before continuing:

'Borringer was married but with no children at the time, and the family lived outside Gottingen in a large fine house. Red became Borringer's valet, and, when he wasn't driving him to and from the factories, he would cook, wash the clothes and generally help in the house. This was when I met him. Borringer's wife had twins in 1926 and needed immediate help and I applied for the job. My family lived close by in a village called Klein Lengden. I was barely fourteen and, how do you say, never been kissed? I got the job and moved in to be the assistant of Red. He taught me how to cook and grow vegetables and everything to do with the house, except for the baby things, which came naturally to me. Of course, we fell in love. We got married in 1930 and although there was a dark mood over Germany then, we had the happiest of times. We stayed with the Borringers. They treated us as their friends, and we were content to carry on running the house for them. Borringer's business became very successful and the build-up of the armed forces in the thirties brought him large government contracts for buttons, for the uniforms. There were big dinners at the house and I remember one summer night when Adolf Hitler came. He drank a lot of wine. Borringer now had five factories running, and Red would be away with him every week for several nights. Borringer's father had died and he had become the chief of the business. Then one night in 1937 when they were away on one of their trips the Gestapo came to the house and arrested me. My family was Jewish and there was a national – how do you say in English, purge? – growing. The Jews were blamed for everything. The villages were where it was the strongest, of course, and when my family was investigated, they found out where I was working. Red came home the next day and discovered I had been taken away. Borringer tried to find out where I was but Red's status was also in danger because he was an Englishman. They took me to Lichtenburg castle, close to the Polish border, it was one of the first concentration camps. In 1939 I was transferred to the women's camp in Ravensbruck, north of Berlin, where I stayed until 1945. It wasn't a death camp, but it was still a very bad place. The officers raped the women and medical staff performed grotesque abortions. I was lucky I did not fall pregnant when I was there. Women died all the time and there was a constant supply of new victims. Some of them I am sure were not even Jewish. Some did not speak German. I was liberated and it took me three months to make my way back to Gottingen. The Borringer house had been destroyed, by bombs I think, and I started to look for Red. I walked to the nearest factory, which was on the other side of Gottingen. But it was closed up and deserted. I did not know what to do next so I just began to walk. I did not know in which direction I was going. When I got tired or hungry, I stopped at a house and the people would give me something to eat or somewhere to sleep. At one house the man said he had worked at a Borringer factory and told me he thought the Borringers had gone to live in Hamburg. So I started to walk to Hamburg. I walked for weeks and then I came to Hamburg. I asked everybody, in every shop and post office and station. I asked every person I met if they knew where I could find the Borringers and a man with red hair. Then I was walking through Blankenese and saw a car coming along the road. I thought I recognised it as the Borringer's car. I went into the middle of the road and stood in the way. It stopped and Red jumped out of the car and found me there. It was a coincidence that you find in life, that he was driving with Borringer along the road on that day.'

Frau Hoeppell seemed relieved to have reached this point in her story, and sat back in her chair to sip some more tea. Then she began again:

'It was as if I had been born again when he took me in his arms. I did not think I would ever see him again. He thought I had died in a camp somewhere. He looked a lot older than his forty-nine years, but what did I look like? He said he had spent the whole time blaming himself for not being at home when I was taken away. I suppose this was what had troubled him and made him so saddened all this time. We cried like children for a long time there in the street, hanging on to each other, and we decided not to spend one minute apart from that day forward. Borringer and his family had moved to Hamburg when the factories had closed in 1943, when Germany sensed they were losing the war. No new uniforms were made but they had stockpiled in the earlier times. Borringer had wisely kept money in the good years and collected dollars since Pearl Harbor happened in 1941. He was able to set up a new house with his wife and children, and Red also, in Blankenese, outside Hamburg. Slowly, I readapted to normal life again, and Red and I grew vegetables and lived in a small cottage next to the Borringers' house. Their twin sons had been drafted in 1944 and both had died in the fall of Berlin. Borringer and his wife did very little apart from live through each day. All their family had perished in the war and in a strange way Red and I became a family for them. We still kept the house and cooked their meals, and made sure the fire was always lit in the winter times. On warm days, we would drive them down to the Elbe. We would sit in the sun and have a picnic and watch the ships glide up and down the river to the docks, and Red and Borringer would play chess again. When Borringer died in 1964 he left a music box to Red. It was something he had owned since the Great War and Red knew it well. He remembered it being in Borringer's office at the camp when they had first become friends. It was, of course, of great sentimental value to Red. He would open it and listen to the tune when dusk came every night.

'Red told me about his brother – your father. He had lost contact with him since the Great War ended. Your father had never forgiven him for not returning to England. He had become like a traitor – or how do you say in English, a pariah? – to all who knew him back home. Your nationalism at the time would not allow such unpatriotic behaviour. Not that we Germans would have been any different, perhaps we could be worse. Red sent him letters but never got back any reply. But he found out his brother had a son called Arnold, and he made me promise that when he died I would make sure the music box went to you. When he died in 1974, you were sent a letter about the music box but I was surprised to learn you wanted it to be auctioned. Well, I thought, if you did not care to own it, I would like to. Lotte, Borringer's wife, died soon after Red and left me the remains of their house. It was falling down, but I still have the piano over there and a few pieces of the furniture. Would you like to see the music box?'

It took Arnold a few seconds to realise she was asking him this, and of course he wanted to see it:

'Yes, please. I would like to see it very much. Is it here?'

Frau Hoeppell nodded and got up from her chair. She went across the room to one of the antique pieces by the windows and came back holding a warm, brown, wooden box in her hands, which she carefully passed to him. Arnold delicately opened the lid and a simple tune began to play from inside. At first it was gay and spritely, but as the mechanism unwound it slowed down and stopped while he held it, before the end of the musical measure was completed.

She smiled and said:

'It is very old now. Almost worn out. Like me. It reminds me so much of Red.'

She sat down in her chair.

'So I was very glad that you did not want to keep it. It

was the one thing that had everything of our lives connected together. There are words to the tune.'

And she began to sing:

Die Gedanken sind frei, wer kann sie erraten,
sie fliegen vorbei wie nachtliche Schatten,
Kein Mensch kann sie wissen, kein Jäger erschießen
mit Pulver und Blei, Die Gedanken sind frei!

Und sperrt man mich ein im finsteren Kerker,
das alles sind rein vergebliche Werke,
Denn mein Gedanken zerreißen die Schranken
und Mauern entzwei, die Gedanken sind frei!

'It is about free thought and expression.'

Arnold felt he needed to explain to her why he'd auctioned the music box:

'I was very young at the time. I had just started at college to become a priest. My parents never told me I had an uncle ... Red, I mean. So it had no significance for me. I'm sorry. My parents pretended he did not exist. It was a terrible thing to do.'

'Yes. He was very sad about it. Especially in the last years, when we were not busy working and had more time to think about what had happened in our lives. I am so glad you have come to see me today. How long are you staying in Hamburg?'

'Only until tomorrow. But I have no other plans. I came to visit you.'

She insisted on making fresh tea and began to show him

all the photos she had in her scrapbooks. Arnold was curious to see what his uncle looked like. The older photos from when she had joined the Borringer household were black and white, so his red hair was not evident, and by the time colour photos started to be used his hair colour had all but gone. But Arnold could see how lively his uncle had been in the thirties. He was good looking, with a mischievous look in his eye and all the photos were of happy, smiling faces. Klaus Borringer looked distinguished and his wife had been very beautiful. The house in Gottingen was grand with extensive gardens as no other buildings were evident in the photos. Frau Hoeppell looked extremely young and Arnold calculated she must now be in her nineties. He was astounded at how bright she was for her age.

'But you must be hungry now,' she said and was gone before he could say anything. She came back with a tray laden with cheese and paté, pumpernickel bread and German chutney. The sight of the tray did make him feel extremely hungry, and he didn't wait to be invited to help himself. As he ate, she looked on approvingly like a mother hen watches her brood satisfying an appetite.

After a while Arnold sat back satisfied. The cheeses had been delicious and he especially took a liking to a smoked Bavarian one. A third round of tea appeared and he looked at his watch to see it was nearly 2.30pm. He mentioned this to Frau Hoeppell, who replied:

'I think you will find it is 3.30. We are an hour ahead here in Germany.'

He remembered he had arranged nowhere to stay for the night but told her he was staying at the Garden Hotel around the corner as he didn't want her worrying unduly. She invited him to meet her the following day for an early lunch at Cafe Bodo's Bootssteg, next to the Allßenalster lake. She wrote down the name of the place for him, saying she went there every Sunday at 11am.

He thanked her for her hospitality and left, and in Milch-strasse he heard his footsteps across the cobblestones accompany his galloping thoughts as he tried to digest everything.

CHAPTER 25

Arnold had memorised the way to the Garden Hotel from Milchstrasse and within five minutes he was checking in at the front desk. He deposited his overnight bag in his room and went downstairs to ask for a map of the area. He checked whereabouts he was in relation to the Allßenalster lake and then promptly set off towards it. He felt like walking round it to stretch his legs and he thought he would keep his eyes open for the Café Bodo's Bootssteg, where he had agreed to meet his aunt the next day. It was a very pleasant temperature outside and with the map in his hand he navigated his way to the lake's edge and began to trace a clockwise circuit of it. There were yachts and rowing boats scattered across the surface and he was surprised at how different Hamburg had turned out to be from what he'd imagined. His image of a grey, soulless, industrial town would have to be discarded in favour of this verdant, warm, friendly place, full of trees and gardens and open space. Ducks, swans and geese floated by as he made his way along and he found the tune from the music box going around in his head. It sounded very familiar to him, but then, that's what good tunes are supposed to do. He likened it to a good hymn, like 'Oh come, all ye faithful', which had such a good rousing tune it was impossible not to remember it. He hadn't understood any of the words his aunt had sung but she could certainly carry a tune. He wondered in amazement at her longevity. Just then a restaurant came into view in front of him and he checked to see if it was Café Bodo's Bootssteg, but it wasn't.

The perimeter of the lake began to meander a little and he found himself crossing a couple of bridges. At one point, he couldn't stay next to the lake and was directed up to a road which he didn't enjoy much, but he was soon back down by the water again. He passed various courting couples who had located discreet places for themselves, and had to cough loudly upon approaching, so as not to make them feel uncomfortable – as well as sparing himself any embarrass-ment. He passed several more eating places but not the one he was looking for, and emerged onto a stretch of the lake adjacent to a major road on a higher level where the greenery became sparser. There were weeping willows placed at inter-vals along the bank but he'd preferred the stretch where he'd started out. He had to climb up to the road to cross a bridge full of noisy traffic, where the lake spilled down to a lower level on the south end, rather like a waterfall. Then he was back on the side closest to his hotel and Milchstrasse, and he came upon Café Bodo's Bootssteg by the lakeside, in a nice spot with a jetty and some small boats moored.

As he walked towards the hotel he wondered where his Uncle Red had been buried and if it was somewhere he could consider getting to while he was in Hamburg. His flight didn't take off until eight the following evening, so there was plenty of time as long as it wasn't too far away. He felt in his pocket and found the card the taxi driver had given him. Not quite a sex club, but he was sure the driver Boris wouldn't mind. He made a note to ask Aunt Rosa the location of the grave when he saw her for lunch.

The long walk had tired him, so he decided to take a shower and order some food up to his room rather than bother going down to the restaurant. By the time ten o'clock came he was in bed reading his book on the Inquisition, but he'd only read a few paragraphs when he found his eyelids drooping. He closed the cover of the book and switched off the lights, and fell asleep with the melody of '*Die Gedanken sind frei*' going round in his head.

When he arrived at the cafe the next morning it was busy and his aunt was already sitting at a table outside sipping what looked like an orange juice. She greeted him with:

'Good morning, Arnold. I trust that you slept well? I am having – what do you call it – a "Buck's Fizz", I think? Would you join me, please?'

She immediately got a waiter's attention and ordered one for him before he could say no.

He sat to her right and as they chatted looking at the lake she fondly touched his forearm:

'You know, you are my only surviving relative. And what of you? Do you have family now? Are you perhaps married?'

'No. Until last year I was the vicar at a church, in a village in the English countryside. But the number of people who came was getting smaller so the church was sold. I was given a pension.'

'I am sorry. And what has happened to the church?'

'Well, the idea was to turn it into some apartments. But I think the building work has stopped now because of the bad economy.'

'But that is so sad. And what are you doing now?'

He explained how the money from the sale of the music box had grown by investment and that he was now living in the iron church.

'But, Arnold, that is a fairy tale! I am so glad that the music box has brought you some luck. Now we are both happy. I have the music box and you have some money to do what you want. Let us drink a toast!'

And she raised her Buck's Fizz and clinked her glass against his.

They ordered lunch and after they had eaten Arnold asked where his uncle was buried. She told him in Nienstedtener cemetery close to Blankenese, near where they had lived next to the Elbe. She said she liked to go there as often as she could, and it would be a nice way to spend the afternoon. Arnold found Boris's card and would have called him on his Blackberry but he'd left it in England, so they asked a waiter to make the call and arranged to be picked up. They continued to chat over coffee while they waited and Arnold asked her if she knew what the words to the music box tune were in English:

'Yes, I do ...*Die Gedanken sind frei, wer kann sie erraten*
Thoughts are free, who can guess them?
sie fliegen vorbei wie nachtliche Schatten
They fly by like nocturnal shadows
Kein Mensch kann sie wissen, kein Jäger erschießen
No man can know them, no hunter can shoot them
mit Pulver und Blei, Die Gedanken sind frei!
with powder and lead, thoughts are free!
And then it goes on:
Und sperrt man mich ein im finsteren Kerker,
And if I am thrown into the darkest dungeon,

das alles sind rein vergebliche Werke,
all this would be futile work,
Denn meine Gedanken zerreißen die Schranken
because my thoughts tear all the gates ...
und Mauern entzwei, die Gedanken sind frei!
and walls apart. Thoughts are free!

'It was never far from my mind when I was locked up. It reminded me of Red and the Borringers' house where I had been so happy before I was arrested. Every time I sang it in my head I thought that perhaps there was some hope, that something good could happen, maybe.'

Her words touched Arnold and he sat lost in thought for a while, mindful of the power music can have over people. He knew how much people had enjoyed singing the hymns at his services and he was aware that music plays a central role in all religion.

Just then, the waiter came to tell them their taxi had arrived and they gathered up their things to leave. Arnold asked about the bill but his aunt said it had all been taken care of, although he had no idea how that could have happened as neither of them had left the table. He visited the bathroom and through the half open window he could see Boris waiting outside by the door of his car smoking a cigarette. He emerged from the restaurant and they waited for Rosa to appear:

'Hello again, sir. Nice to see you today. No sex clubs open at this hour, I'm afraid.'

'No. I'm here with my aunt. We want to go somewhere called ... Blank something?'

'Ah, you must mean Blankenese. Very nice place. Near the river. Somewhere in particular?'

'My aunt knows where. A cemetery.'

'Very good. About forty minutes to get there.'

Rosa came out, and they helped her into the back of the car.

Arnold realised how much he was enjoying himself as they drove out to the cemetery. There were endless tree-lined roads with beautiful houses and gardens and what seemed like forests on both sides of the road. The sun burst through the foliage again and again and the only thing that marred the journey was several traffic queues they got stuck in. It was a Sunday afternoon and Blankenese was a popular weekend destination. Boris wasn't sure where the cemetery was but Rosa, in her indefatigable way, gave him clipped directions in German which he answered with '*Ja, wohl!*' and '*Klar!*'. About an hour later, they drove in through the gates of a large cemetery on the Elbchaussee and pulled up on a gravel driveway next to a few other cars. They helped Rosa out of the car and gathered up a bouquet of flowers that Arnold had insisted they buy on the way. Boris said he would wait by the car and smoke while they visited the grave and placed the flowers. He walked along the aisles of graves in silence, with Rosa's arm firmly gripping his. There were very few people around. She guided him first left, then right and then a couple more turns before they came to the spot where his uncle's grave was, next to that of Klaus Borringer and his wife Lotte. On his headstone, under his full name, which had been changed to 'Dreuber', and the dates of his birth and death, was the following inscription:

Man kann ja im Herzen stets lachen und scherzen und denken dabei.

Rosa sensed Arnold would want to know what it meant:

'"In one's heart one can always laugh and joke, and think at the same time." It's another line of the song from the music box.'

Arnold slowly knelt down and left the bouquet of flowers on the grave. He stayed there kneeling for several minutes in prayer.

They walked slowly back to the car and Arnold would have got lost without Rosa's directions. The cemetery seemed vast and reinforced the fact that so many people had lived, been busy and died in just this one town. It was the biggest one he'd ever been in.

Boris suggested they show Arnold the Elbe, so they drove further along the Elbchaussee into Blankenese and followed a side road that took them down to a good vantage point. Arnold got out of the car and leant on the balustrade to take a look down. It was a huge river and he was just trying to imagine what size of boat would be using it, when he heard a loud ship's horn which made him jump, and a tanker crept into view round a bend from the direction of the docks. It was a good hundred yards long, black and rusty, and took a full five minutes to silently disappear from view, heading for the North Sea. He began to notice people below him walking along the bank. They were smaller than he was expecting, suddenly making the river and the tanker seem even larger. Two small boys were running along as if to catch up with the escaping tanker. He heard an angry parent shouting after them:

'*Kommen sie hier!*'

He felt a nudge at his shoulder. Boris was standing next to him holding out an ice cream:

'There you go. Who's been a good boy?' he said with a smile and started to laugh.

Arnold smiled back and took it from him. Rosa had stayed in the car and Boris said something in German to her through the open window and she laughed too. Arnold was suddenly very glad he'd taken the snap decision to visit Hamburg.

CHAPTER 26

They dropped Rosa off at Milchstrasse before stopping at the hotel to pick up Arnold's things. She made him wait in the hallway while she fetched something for him, which turned out to be a framed picture of her and Red in the garden of the Borringers' house outside Gottingen. They were standing in front of a fallen log arm in arm and he had a pipe in his mouth and looked very dashing. She had a blanket draped around her shoulders and seemed very happy. At first he declined to take it but Rosa insisted, saying she had many more inside. He thanked her and promised to keep in touch and visit again. The roads were almost empty on the way to the airport and he thanked Boris for giving them so much of his time.

'It was my pleasure ... is it Mr. Arnold? You have quite an auntie there. She is a real lady. One of the old school, is that what you say? She reminds me of my grandmother. Still alive, still enjoying life. We will be happy to be like that one day, yes?'

It made Arnold inquisitive and he asked:

'Are you from Hamburg?'

'Hanover, actually. I came here in the late seventies, when I was seventeen. To get work at the docks. But when it all closed down in the nineties, I had to find another job. My parents are still in Hanover and my grandmother lives with them. Hamburg in the seventies. Let me tell you something. It was *fantastisch*. Girls. Drugs. Music. Massive party time! And what do you do, Mr. Arnold?'

'I used to be a priest. Until last year.'

Boris evidently began to think he'd been too frank with his description of the Hamburg scene in the late seventies and started to apologise but Arnold stopped him with:

'No, it's quite all right. I'm not offended.'

There was a few minutes silence before Boris asked:

'And what do you do now, sir?'

Arnold felt Boris's blue eyes staring at him again in the rear view mirror:

'I ... er ... I'm not too sure. Just living, I suppose.'

On the plane, Arnold realised that he wasn't really sure how to describe his life now. 'Exploring' was the best word he could find. That weekend certainly felt like an exploration. It was as if part of his life had been revealed from behind a curtain he hadn't noticed was there before. He felt enriched by what he'd learned and it explained much of his parents' behaviour. No wonder they'd denied him any knowledge of his uncle. He recalled Rosa telling him Red had written letters to his father but had received no replies. Arnold still had a box of his father's papers he'd only cursorily looked over, but now he thought perhaps he might find a letter from his uncle somewhere there. He tried to remember where the box was located and decided it would be the first thing he would attend to when he got home. He dozed off and was woken up by the announcement the plane was preparing to land in Bristol.

The sun was setting when he left the airport on his drive back towards Bath. He threaded his way east through Chew Magna and navigated several narrow country lanes to emerge just west of Corston and the A4. It was much more direct than using the major roads and he felt a sense of achievement as he saw the outline of Bath on the horizon. As he drew up outside the Keep he could see a full moon emerging towards the south and it looked immense. Everything looked the same as he'd left it the day before, but he felt he'd been away a lot longer. As he opened the door he saw there was a folded note on his doormat. It was a sheet of lined paper from a ring-bound pad and he could see in the moonlight the words 'The Occupier' scribbled untidily on the uppermost half in a mix of lower case letters and capitals. He switched on the lights and sat down to read it:

Dear Sir,

My name is Pete. I have recently arrived in the area from Hull and am looking for work. If there is some job (large or small), that you need doing I am your man.

I will call back presently.

Yours faithfully,

PETE

Short and to the point, Arnold noted. He started to prepare for bed and found himself listing in his mind the unfinished tasks left to do as he settled down. He still had a problem with the water supply to the shower, and he'd noticed a lot of rattling whenever a strong wind blew up. Then there was the flat area of ground in front, which he fancied would make a good vegetable patch, as it faced due south ...

Tap. Tap, tap ... Tap, tap, tap, tap ...

Knock ... Knock... Knock, knock, knock ...

This is what Arnold heard early the next morning.

KNOCK. KNOCK. KNOCK!

Someone was banging on his front door.

He got up, put on his dressing gown and went to see who it was.

On the doorstep, he found a man, shorter than himself, with shoulder length brown hair and a moustache. Arnold judged he was in his thirties and dressed in a finely striped red and white shirt, which hung down outside a pair of faded well-worn denim jeans.

'Good morning, sir. I hope I'm not disturbing you today. Did you get my note? My name's Pete. I'm from Hull and I'm looking for work.'

Having just woken up, Arnold didn't quite know what to say without being rude, so he just asked him:

'Can you come back a bit later on?'

The man looked unsure what to say next, but then brightened up and said:

'Righty-o!'

He then turned on his heels and walked off down to the road.

Arnold closed the door and went to look at what time it was. Five minutes past eight. This fellow Pete certainly was keen, he thought. He had no desire to sleep any longer, so he showered, noting the inconsistent flow of water from the nozzle. He got dressed and made himself an egg and soldiers with a cup of coffee.

It was about ten o'clock when he heard the same tap, tapping on the front door and he guessed it was his visitor returning. This time Arnold felt more prepared to receive him. He opened the door and said:

'Good morning. So you're Pete?'

'I'm sorry about calling on you so early before. I don't have a watch and it gets so light in the mornings this time of year.'

Arnold appreciated his apologetic tone and warmed to his soft sounding voice:

'Not to worry. Would you like to come in for a cup of tea?' he found himself saying.

'Oh, that would be nice. Ta,' said Pete and trotted in past him and stood in the middle of the Keep, saying, 'What a lovely place. Right lovely. Where shall I sit down?'

'Oh, anywhere will do. Tea or coffee?' asked Arnold.

'I'm not fussed. I'll have what you're having,' said Pete, sitting down in Arnold's favourite chair.

'So you're from Hull?' Arnold asked, putting the kettle on to boil.

'That's right. Do you know it? Mind you, it's been a while since I were there, like.'

'No. I don't. And you're looking for work?'

'I am. Anything will do. I'm pretty good with me hands. Done all sorts of things since I left school. Me dad's a fish-monger so I started out helping him and since then I been travelling. I done all sorts. You name it. Thank you.' He took the cup Arnold offered him.

'Tea or coffee?' he asked Arnold, who looked at him not knowing what he meant.

'Is it tea or coffee?' Pete asked again, "Cos if it's coffee, I takes milk ... if you've got some, that is.'

They sat talking for a good hour and Arnold decided Pete was completely harmless and very good company. He'd been travelling around the country for some time knocking on people's doors asking for work. He avoided towns as he found town folk 'not so down to earth' with 'no time to chat'. He hadn't gone hungry the whole time. It put Arnold in mind of his Aunt Rosa who'd walked through Germany looking for Red after the War, relying on human kindness. Arnold showed Pete around the Keep and explained what he'd done to make it habitable. Pete was extremely interested in all the aspects and it seemed he'd had experience in most of the skills it takes to construct a house. Arnold could see how with Pete's help he could very easily finish off all those jobs that inevitably get forgotten when one moves in somewhere. He even toyed with the possibility that they could install the bells from St. Tobias's, if he could just get hold of them. They agreed a daily wage and Pete said he was able to start the next day, which was a Tuesday, but promised he wouldn't arrive until 9am.

The week raced by and Arnold began to look forward to Pete's arrival each day. The drill would be the same. Pete asking what was 'next to do on the list', and Arnold consulting a scheme he'd drawn up that first day. They would discuss the job in hand over a cup of tea and then set to work. Arnold provided Pete with tea or coffee, and prepared sandwiches for lunch for them both, and Pete heaped praise on the quality of these:

'Mr. Arnold, I've never in my life ever tasted a bacon sandwich quite as good as that one!'

Arnold explained in great detail the intricacies of making his favourite sandwiches, with the various dos and don'ts of each one.

It got to Friday and it occurred to Arnold he had no idea where Pete was staying whilst working for him. He guessed it must be close by and probably within walking distance. He decided to ask him:

'I hope you don't mind me asking, but where are you sleeping?'

'Well, I'm camping, as it happens. I've got me tent pitched in a corner of the field up behind. It's quite comfortable, actually.'

Arnold was shocked to hear this. Although on thinking about it, many people camped during the summer months, and several hundred thousand did just that at the large music festival they held every June down in Glastonbury, Hermione had told him. But it didn't appeal to him:

'What about when winter comes? I mean, not this winter, but in general. What do you do then?'

'Well, I keep me socks on for one thing. It depends how cold it gets. I've got a couple of sleeping bags, and several times last January I had to get inside both of them, when there were snow on the ground.'

Arnold could hardly believe what he was hearing.

Pete was happy to work at the weekend too. Probably because he had nothing else to do and he was enjoying putting his skills to use. Arnold explained how he'd happened to discover the place quite by chance one day while on a bike ride, and been seized by the desire to live there. Pete could identify with this feeling:

'Aye. I know just how you would have felt. To suddenly sense something so strongly, that you know you just got to go and do it. It was like what I felt when I first went on the road. I woke up one morning at me dad's house and knew I just had to get away. That day. And you feel so good inside after you done it.'

'Where did you go first?' Arnold was curious to hear about Pete's journey. It sounded like some sort of a personal quest but without knowing what you were looking for.

'First of all I went north, up the coast. I'd heard of Whitby but never been there, so thought I'd make for there. It were spring, so the weather changed from one day to the next. I got a good few soakings, mind, but it were all right. After there I got as far as Durham – nice place, Durham. A town, mind you, but not very big. And then I went west that summer, across Northumberland. Followed Hadrian's Wall, I did. Did you know that the Roman guards, on the wall, they used to rub salt in their wounds to keep them awake at night? It were lovely up there. Then I got to Lancaster and went south and spent last winter in North Wales.'

'So you haven't been back to Hull for over a year?' Arnold calculated.

'You know, I hadn't really added it up.' Pete thought for a second, 'But you're right, I haven't.'

'Don't you worry about your father?' Arnold asked him.

He'd told him his father lived alone in Hull and had no friends to speak of. His mother had died a few years before.

'Now you mention it ... aye, I does. Mostly when I'm trying to get to sleep nights.'

The rest of Saturday, Pete worked well but more silently than before and Arnold was concerned that he'd made Pete feel guilty about leaving his father alone. On the Sunday when they were having their lunch break, Pete asked him:

'Do you see's much more work here for me? I'm only asking, Mr. Arnold, as I were thinking ...'

Arnold looked at his list and said:

'There seems to be quite a lot left down here.'

'In that case,' Pete continued, 'I thought I might well take a trip up to see me dad. In Hull. What you said made me think. With what you been paying me I can afford to take a bus or a train, and go see him. Just for a bit. A few days like. And then come back. What do you think?'

'I think that's a splendid idea, Pete. I'm sure he'd be very pleased to see you.'

CHAPTER 27

Arnold was surprised how much he missed Pete the next day. He'd grown used to hearing his characteristic 'tap tap' on the front door in the mornings, and as he made his egg and soldiers in the silence he realised he didn't want to spend the day alone. Pete had left his tent neatly packed up outside long before Arnold was awake and he found himself studying it as it sat obediently by the front door like a dog, waiting to be allowed inside the house. He moved it into the living room, as if its very presence was serving as a substitute for Pete, and after breakfast he tried to imagine the journey to Hull. There was an early morning National Express coach leaving from Bath and Pete had politely refused to take up Arnold's offer of a ride in to the bus station. Arnold supposed he would take a local bus in or try to hitch a ride, or perhaps even walk. He thought the journey would probably take up the whole day, getting Pete into Hull that evening. He found himself listless and unable to concentrate on anything in particular. Pottering around, he inspected the jobs they'd completed and was pleased with what he saw. He remembered he wanted to look through his father's papers in the hope he may discover a letter from his Uncle Red somewhere, but first he had to remember where he'd stored them and spent the next few hours searching fruitlessly. He tried all the obvious places and despondently sank down into his favourite chair to rack his brains. Staring round the room he began to question his memory and wondered if there was a possibility he'd lost them. It was also possible they could still be at Trevor's house. He'd put the folder under his bed there and couldn't remember retrieving it during his extended move over to the Keep. The more he considered it the more he became sure that was where they were. He rang and asked Trevor if he could go over and pick them up. Trevor was pleased to hear from him:

'Of course, old chap. Any time you like. Here all day, more or less.'

Arnold was glad to get out of the house and realised he hadn't been anywhere since Pete had arrived. He took the opportunity to pick up some supplies in Corsham before he stopped off and found Trevor unsurprisingly glued to his TV again, watching some cricket match:

'Fourth test. England, South Africa. Riveting stuff.'

First thing he did was secure the folder, which as he'd thought, was still under the bed upstairs. The windows were open and he could hear children's voices and a barking dog floating up from the houses below. He took a quick look outside and noted it was coming from the very same house as before, but this time with a different breed of dog and a different batch of children. He was happy to leave the room and closed the door behind him, knowing he wouldn't have to live through it all again.

He made coffee and served them both pork pies he'd picked up at the supermarket. He knew that was one of

Trevor's favourites. They chatted through the cricket and Arnold told him about his newly found helper:

'I've acquired a ...' and here he faltered, as he wasn't sure how Pete should be described. 'A ... companion ... sort of. He just knocked on the door a week ago. Very skilled. He's helping me with all the odd jobs. Very skilled. And a very nice bloke. From Hull. Bit of a traveller. Called Pete.'

'That must be nice for you,' Trevor responded. 'A bit of company, out there in the wild. Be careful, though, Arnold. You don't know him from Adam. And these days, there isn't much sincerity about, I'm afraid.'

He ended up staying all afternoon, and as he drove back, Trevor's words remained with him. He wondered if he'd misplaced his faith in Pete and realised he knew very little about him. He looked back over the brief time he'd been away from Corsham and no one had disillusioned him yet. He concluded he must be a pretty good judge of character. Either that or he'd been extremely lucky. He ended up thinking it was probably a mixture of the two.

Once back in his favourite chair, he carefully looked through the folder's contents and came across a large stiff manila envelope in which there were several smaller envelopes of differing colours and sizes. They seemed quite old due to their unusual weight and the address was scrawled in the same spidery handwriting across each one. Arnold studied the stamps and reckoned them to be German. They'd all been opened and he pulled out a very flimsy sheet from inside the first one and spread it out on the table. It was very difficult to decipher the handwriting, which was the same as on the envelope. It read as follows:

My dear brother,

I've heard no news back from you. I do hope illness hasn't struck you down? It's very difficult to determine if my letters have been getting through to you or not.

Here in Germany things carry on as they do everywhere.

We have a new girl who started working in the house recently, called Rosa. Very nice, she is. But quite young. Eager to learn, and I'm enjoying showing her the ropes.

It's hard to imagine you over there, involved in a similar existence, but in Blighty.

Perhaps you've chosen not to reply to my letters. This I would be saddened by.

Hoping to hear some news from you soon.

Your ever loving brother,

Reg

Arnold carefully replaced the sheet in its envelope and took up another. The paper inside was more substantial than the first and he concluded that it was, in fact, older. This was confirmed when he read:

Dear Nathan,

You're most probably wondering what happened to me, your brother Reg. Well, I'm alive!

I was captured and got put in a camp for the remainder of the war, but it wasn't all bad.

I ended up becoming good friends with the German CO, and he turned out to be a nice chap.

When the war finished he offered me a job as his chauffeur!! So here I am, living in Germany.

He runs a few factories that make buttons.

The Germans aren't that different from us, as it turns out.

Whatever they tell you over there, don't believe it. It's all propaganda.

I hope you can understand and forgive me for not coming back.

Not sure if you should tell Mum and Dad. They probably wouldn't like it and I don't want to upset them.

Better off they think I died in the war?

Looking forward to hearing from you.

Your loving brother,

Reg

There were three other letters, making five in all. Arnold read them again in chronological order and was saddened by the change in tone of them as it slowly dawned upon his uncle that his brother wasn't going to reply to him. It had obviously been too much for his father to accept. His own brother had become a traitor and deserted his country. Arnold assumed patriotism had been much stronger in Britain in those days between the two world wars. No wonder his uncle had ceased to exist within the family. Rather than tell him his uncle had died in the war, his parents had decided to completely erase his very existence. His father and mother had finished their lives with this skeleton in the cupboard that he'd had no inkling of. They were tarnished with deep shame. Probably thinking if anyone knew of it they too would be looked upon disapprovingly.

It struck Arnold how different Britain was then and how much it had changed. There seemed to be good and bad aspects to both eras. Back then the family unit was strong, but society was rife with pride, inequality, and hypocrisy. Now there was a breakdown of the family unit, but a sense of freedom, openness and opportunity unheard of before. Oh dear, he thought, if only there could be a readjustment to incorporate all the good points of the two ... He concluded this was implausible and a naïve view of the world. He noticed the light fading outside and began to feel extremely weary and went to take a nap, hoping that the world would be a better place when he woke up.

CHAPTER 28

The sun was blazing through the windows when he woke up the next day. He felt ravenously hungry and realised the pork pie at Trevor's was the last thing he'd eaten. He quickly showered and on his way to the kitchen noticed the letters he'd found from his uncle still on the table where he'd been reading them. It immediately brought Red's sadness seeping back into his mind and he determined to write to his aunt in Hamburg that day telling her he'd found them.

It was so hot he took his coffee, boiled eggs and soldiers outside to eat in the sunshine. He'd doubled his ration of eggs that day being so hungry and added a slice or two of cheddar to go with an extra piece of toast. He'd just finished eating when he heard a noise below and a bicycle came into view carrying what looked like a postman. He pulled up by the side of the road and fished out a bunch of letters from his shoulder bag, saying:

'Good morning, there. Are you Arnold Drive? And is this Arnold's Keep?'

Arnold went down to meet him and was handed several letters, one of which had Trevor's Corsham address crossed out and his new address boldly written across it in what looked like Trevor's handwriting. Arnold was wary of receiving anything that looked too official as he guessed it meant the local authorities knew what he was up to living there and would be planning to oust him.

He recognised the insignia of Goldbloom & Gulbenkian in the top corner of one envelope and found a statement of his funds inside together with a short note from Nigel Scott. He recognised Hermione's handwriting on a second and on the final one he read his name and address typed inside a clear plastic window, and noted the address of the Bath District Council in the top left hand corner. He sat back down in the wicker chair on his porch and opened it. Inside was a demand for Council Tax. No eviction notice, no court summons, just an invoice for £845.35, together with a covering letter explaining that if he preferred to pay by direct debit annually he could save £68. He felt relieved and smiled to himself as he opened Hermione's letter. At the top was an address in London:

Dearest Arnold,

No word from you since I dropped my note through your letterbox a few weeks ago. Now I'm worried about you.

Please let me know all is OK at the Keep?

Haven't been able to check with Trevor, he never answers his phone these days. Must be that blasted cricket he's glued to the whole time.

Things are progressing in London. Tony seems to be behaving himself, so far. Being rather sweet, dare I say it!

Fondest thoughts

Hermione xx

Arnold saw that he was treating Hermione rather in the way his father had treated Red all those years before. He was beginning to realise just how important communication was between human beings. The lack of it could have unaccountable consequences. His life within the church had been about communion with God, neglecting the fact that communication between individual people was vastly significant to their lives and feelings, perhaps more so than with God. He began to gain a sense of how isolated he'd become at St. Tobias's. He knew now that he had been out of touch with the needs of most of his parishioners. He resolved to write to her at the same time as his aunt and within the hour he was driving down to Batheaston post office carrying his two letters ready for stamping. In his hurry he left without his mobile phone and he was about to find out just how useful it could be.

It was turning into a glorious day's weather and he had the sunroof fully open. He felt the sun's heat on the top of his head as he went in and out of the shade of the overhanging trees on the country lanes and at that moment he was glad to be alive. He seemed in a dream as he queued up at the post office and bought the stamps for his letters to Germany and London. They were the new type you don't have to lick and he missed the taste of the glue on his tongue that he'd always associated with posting letters. He asked how long this type had been in use and was surprised to be told it had been a few years.

Various thoughts came into his wandering mind as he drove and he realised he wasn't fully paying attention when a large, dark-coloured Land Rover emerged from around a bend ahead of him. The road was narrow at that point and he was sure the other vehicle was travelling much too fast. He swerved to avoid running into it and felt his car lurch to the left and go down a bank. He'd forgotten to put on his safety belt and rose from his seat into the air and headed out through the sunroof. Darkness engulfed him as he passed through foliage and he lost consciousness. He awoke unable to move his head or neck, although his arms responded slightly when he tested for any feeling in his hands. He couldn't see anything at all but discovered he could move all his fingers. Discounting the awkward position he was in he thought he had the use of both his arms. With difficulty, he moved them around his hips to search for his phone in his trousers but realised he'd left it at home. He started to feel weak and wanted desperately to sleep so he decided there was nothing he could do except stay still and wait to be discovered. He remembered reading somewhere that when in doubt, an injured person should not be moved. As he tried to remember where he'd read that, he drifted into the waves of a comforting sea that engulfed him lovingly and at that moment there was nowhere else he wanted to be.

He seemed to float just under the surface of the sea for an age, only occasionally breaking through the surface when he saw his car upside down next to the road and his shoes sticking out from some dense undergrowth. He knew it was the sea as he could feel the force of the tide pulling him in different directions. Then he was back under the surface again and when he looked down it was as if he were looking up into the sky instead of down into the water. Of course there were no vapour trails of jet planes, and instead he could discern shapes at varying distances from him and he began to see they could be other people. He began to get used to his weightlessness but his clothes were irritating him, and seemed to hamper his movements. He really wished he could take them off and get rid of them but he knew that was impossible. He broke through the surface a few times and caught glimpses of activity around his car, but he wasn't very interested in any of this and just wanted to get back below the surface again. He wanted to see if he could get any closer to any of the people he'd glimpsed and see if he recognised any of them. He assumed he must be quite far down as it wasn't very bright and was getting darker by the second. It was all rather odd. He wasn't a strong swimmer and had never been able to hold his breath for very long but neither of these things seemed to be a problem. He decided not to worry and just 'go with the flow', as Hermione used to say to him.

After a while he thought he saw someone else way off to his right so he tried to make his way in that direction to catch up with them. As he got closer he thought they looked vaguely familiar and when he drew level the man turned and looked sideways at him in half recognition. Arnold was surprised to see the man's hair turning red in front of his eyes and knew it was his Uncle Red, even though he'd never met him. What was even stranger was that his uncle seemed to recognise him and there in the sea they shook hands. Arnold said:

'Uncle Red! I knew it was you. Rosa told me all about your time in Germany. I'm so sorry my father never replied to any of your letters.'

His uncle looked wistful and replied:

'Well, I sort of expected him to react that way. I did come over once to Blighty, to visit him and your mother in the fifties. That's how I knew about you. I asked around and managed to find out where they were living. I guessed they weren't going to stray far from where the fruit fell. Your grandparents had already passed away by then. Nathan wasn't very happy to see me but he did invite me in for a cup of tea. Your mother was out at the park with you at the time so I didn't manage to meet either one of you. You may bump into your father down here. I've seen him periodically but he never stops for a chat.'

And with that his Uncle Red turned and swam away, and within a few seconds had disappeared into the dark waters.

Arnold carried on and wondered who he was going to bump into next. He didn't seem to be near the surface but it didn't concern him. He was beginning to manoeuvre his way around quite effectively despite his wet clothes, and was enjoying being pulled this way and that by the vagaries of the current. Instead of fighting against its force he was learning to give in and be drawn along by some fateful thread. Just then, he could see he was being taken towards a vortex and felt an increase in his speed as he approached it. He seemed to be sucked in and spun around many times, as if he were in a washing machine, and was surprised to find he was getting giddy. Unexpectedly he emerged from this central eddy and was spun out in a bundle into some still waters where he was able to clear his head and look about. He felt the current lifting him up and carrying him back down into the darker waters again.

He couldn't tell if the water was warm or cold and he had no trouble with his vision although at times it grew pitch black around him. He could see deep below him various things growing, presumably on the sea floor, but it didn't seem that interesting. It was rather like looking out of a window of a tall building onto a busy thoroughfare and feeling unconnected with any of it. He was more interested in who he was going to bump into next and was convinced he'd see someone he knew sooner or later. Just then a school of fish passed by and he was surprised to notice them all speaking to one another in some foreign language. Several of them stared at him as they glided by but none of them found him that interesting. Then he saw a shape come towards him from the dark and he recognised Stan:

'Hello, Stan. Very nice to see you again,' he offered when they got close.

'My dear Arnold. Fancy seeing you down here. How are you these days?' he heard, although Stan's mouth wasn't moving.

'Oh, mustn't grumble. Spent some time in Corsham after what happened. Now I'm in my own place, just outside Bath. You know, I never said anything. To the police. It just didn't seem right.'

'Thank you, Arnold. It wouldn't really have mattered if you had done. I was gone and away, so it wouldn't have affected me, like. In fact, me and the wife reacquainted ourselves down here. She don't go on like she used to up there. Not at all. In fact, you'd think 'twas a different person, if you'd a' known her like. Back then. Funny how things turns out, innut?'

He was glad Stan was feeling happier than before and after he'd drifted off Arnold felt a pleasant warmth spreading through his body. It made him feel energised. He couldn't think of any other way to describe it. Now he positively raced along and looked up to see rays of light penetrating the surface of the water. He could see the beautiful azure tones of the sea coming to life. But it was short lived and once again he descended into deeper water where he drifted with the currents, like a piece of seaweed at the mercy of the sea.

His body started to feel heavy and he began dropping through the water, which got darker the lower he got. Then he stopped falling and seemed to be at rest on a platform, presumably the sea floor. He looked about but there was no sign of life, just an undulating surface, rather like what he remembered of the desert in Libya when he'd been on the cruise. He didn't know what to do so he just sat down. He lost track of how long he was sitting there and there was no way for him to measure the length of time as nothing about him changed at all. Then he felt sure someone was watching him and turned to see somebody he didn't recognise sitting quite close by. The man was older and looked sad and frail. When he noticed Arnold looking at him he managed a slight smile and said:

'Hello. I know who you are. You're Arnold, aren't you?'

This surprised Arnold, but before he could say anything in reply the man continued:

'Pete's told me about you. You look like a nice man. I was a bit worried about him up till now. But now I've seen you I won't worry no more. He said you were a good 'un.'

Arnold could vaguely see a likeness in the worn face, and realising it was Pete's father said:

'Oh. I'm pleased to meet you. How is Pete? Will he be coming back to Bath soon?'

'Oh, yes. That he will. Soon enough. He tells me you used to be a man of the cloth?'

'Yes, that's right.'

'And why did you stop doing that? Did you lose the faith?'

'No, not really. Although I must say I've become a bit disillusioned with the whole thing since.'

Pete's father raised his eyebrows when Arnold said this, so he tried to explain what he meant:

'You see, my church was sold. There weren't enough people coming.'

'Oh, really. And why was that? Weren't you communicating with them?'

Arnold felt a little under pressure now, but he didn't mind. In a funny way he felt it was giving him the opportunity to explain himself. Something he hadn't felt the necessity to do since he'd left St. Tobias's. He thought hard for a while and then said:

'I can see now that I wasn't. When we were being taught how to be a priest no one talked about how important communication was. The accent was on communion. With God. I've learnt all this a little late in the day, I'm afraid.'

'Oh, dear,' Pete's father said. Now he looked a little more consolingly at Arnold:

'Oh, well. Don't worry about it. We can't get it all right. Nobody can. Nobody's perfect.'

Then he stopped and looked down below him for a moment before raising his head and saying:

'Very nice to meet you, Arnold. You take care.'

And he turned and floated off into the darkness.

CHAPTER 29

Arnold sat for a while on the seabed and thought about what Pete's father had said. Several large jellyfish pumped their way past him, looking like animated chandeliers, he thought. They were beautiful and Arnold wondered how on earth they managed to get through life in the ocean without damaging themselves. He noticed light was increasing above and he was curious as to what was going on, so he made his way up to investigate. Although he hadn't missed the light earlier he was pleased to see some now and could feel his spirits improve as he ascended and the light intensity increased. He thought he could feel heat but he was wary of getting too close to the surface, as he felt safer in the water. He sensed some activity above and manoeuvred himself so that he was horizontal and could keep an eye on what was happening. Then what looked like a large face became discernible above the surface and when it broke through the water he saw it was Hermione. She started speaking and her voice began to reverberate through the water, so much so that he could hardly tell what she was saying:

'Arnold. Can you hear me? Arnold?'

Then she was gone. It had scared him a little as her face had seemed so large. She obviously knew he was down there, or perhaps she wasn't sure. He wanted to let her know he was but had no idea how to make this happen. He tried to get as close to the surface as he could without actually breaking through, as he sensed that would be unsafe. He thought he could make out her face and several times she came closer, as if she were looking into a goldfish bowl. Yes, that was what it was like. Arnold realised he could be inside a goldfish bowl and Hermione was studying him through the glass. But if that were so, how was she managing to break through the surface? He couldn't work out how it was possible. It would have to be a very large bowl if she was able to stick her whole head below the surface. Perhaps it was a fish tank. As he was trying to make sense of all this, another shape came close to the surface and suddenly broke through. It was Trevor and his voice was even louder than Hermione's:

'Arnold? Hello? Anybody there? Arnold? HELLO!'

This last 'hello' was delivered at such an ear shattering volume Arnold was knocked back deeper down into the water by the shock wave it generated. He managed to escape the frightful noise and thankfully Trevor's face left the water. It was all rather bewildering. He decided being at the surface didn't agree with him and he decided to stay away from it for the time being. It was much more comfortable in the quieter, darker water depths lower down and perhaps he would run into some more people he knew there. Besides he didn't quite feel like going out into the bright light just yet.

One thing he couldn't understand was why he wasn't feeling hungry. He hadn't eaten anything the whole time he'd been down there and it struck him how much easier it was not to have to think about such things. It also meant he didn't need the loo, but then if he did want to pee he could just as easily do it right where he was. No one would know and he was sure that's what fish did. In fact, the entire ocean was probably made of fish poo, but it doesn't stop people from bathing in it. Ever. Anywhere. He started to wonder if fish poo contained something beneficial to humans, as everyone always comes back from bathing in the sea feeling much better. Or was it because of the sea air, and all the salt? Just then he felt a shift in the current and he was turned in another direction, and came face to face with his father. Curiously, he didn't think it was that strange, and his father didn't look that surprised to see him, he could tell. He just looked at Arnold with that same expression he'd always worn, showing neither approval nor disapproval, and he was the first to speak:

'So, Arnold. Still dissatisfied with life, I see?'

How on earth he'd come to that conclusion Arnold didn't have the faintest idea, but his father had always had fixed ideas and opinions about him since his childhood.

'What makes you think I'm dissatisfied?' Arnold challenged him.

'You always are. It's easy to see that,' his father replied without really explaining.

Arnold thought it was time to ask about his uncle:

'Why didn't you ever reply to Uncle Red's letters? It made him very unhappy.'

'It's always about Red, isn't it? First it's your mother, going on about it. Now you. Will everyone just stop going on about bloody Red!'

Arnold couldn't understand where his father's resentment was coming from.

'It was always the same. When we were growing up. Why

can't you be more like Red? Red would never do that. It just was never enough, what I came up with.'

Arnold saw his father was envious of Red and the attention he'd obviously got being a redhead and the elder of the two brothers. By not replying to the letters his father had finally been granted the upper hand in their lifelong competitive relationship. Arnold could see now how, unwittingly, he'd become a substitute for Red in his father's eyes. Through Arnold he was able to continue the competition with his brother. It would explain why his father always distrusted him and up until now, Arnold had never been able to understand his strange behaviour. He remembered asking his mother several times about it and she'd replied:

'You know what your father's like.'

But that was the whole point. He never had.

Now this was clear he began to look at his father differently. He felt sorry for him and realised his upbringing with his brother explained everything. It was a classic case of sibling rivalry.

It was unfortunate his relationship with his father had suffered as a result. He was discovering a lot about families. Perhaps some aspects of people's behaviour could be explained by looking back a generation or two to help in trying to make sense of it all. Not that it would change anything, it would just make life a little easier and simpler. That's what Arnold thought he wanted, a simple life. No complications, or complicated people to try to understand. That's what takes the energy, he decided, trying to fathom them out and the reasons why they do what they do.

He'd been so wrapped up in his own thoughts he hadn't noticed his father had gone, without even saying 'goodbye'.

Well, that was in character, he thought. Just then he heard a voice behind him, saying:

'Now, let me guess. You must be Arnold, Red's nephew.'

He turned round and was presented with someone he didn't know but looked vaguely familiar. The new arrival could see the puzzled look on his face and introduced himself:

'Klaus Borringer. At your service. It is a pleasure to meet you. I can see a likeness between your features and Red's. You are his brother's son, no? But what a man your uncle is. So much charm. And good humour. Of course, he's a bit lonely here without his Rosa.'

Arnold wanted to tell him about Rosa:

'I went to visit her in Hamburg recently. She looked very well for her age. She said she was very happy when she worked at your house.'

'Ah, yes,' Klaus remembered, 'The day we stopped in the road and found her there. It was nothing but a miracle. I will never forget when Red saw her. And then he jumped out and took her up in his arms. My God, it was such a moment! I will never forget. Yes, we had good times together, although it was hard after the war in Germany. But we had each other. Red had Rosa, and I had my Lotte. It did not seem to matter, when at night we could hold each other close.'

He lost himself in this thought and Arnold wondered if he should say something, but decided to wait politely for Klaus to collect himself. When he did, he added:

'Such times. Such times. We were the lucky ones. So, will we be seeing more of you? Will you be staying long?'

Arnold wasn't sure what to say:

'To tell you the truth, I really have no idea. I just suddenly found myself here.'

Klaus smiled:

'Yes, we all do! But if you don't know if you are staying ... perhaps you are not going to?'

That sounded logical to Arnold, in a funny sort of way. Klaus held out his hand to him:

'Very nice to make your acquaintance, Arnold. If you want to know about buttons, I am your man.'

And at that Klaus floated away on the current.

For the first time since he'd been in the water, Arnold was sleepy and felt his eyelids drooping. Everything about him was fading to black, so rather than resist it he let himself drift away into the void.

CHAPTER 30

When he woke up he knew he wasn't in the sea any longer. He didn't know where he was, or if in fact he was still alive. It seemed to him then as if the episode in the ocean had been a dream, although at the time it had felt very real to him. But where he was now didn't make him think it was any more, or less, real than what had come before. Having never died before he had no idea what it was supposed to be like. He certainly didn't feel as mobile as he'd been under the water and now he couldn't see anything. But he could hear things. He began to distinguish little sounds coming at him from all directions and he began to recognise them as familiar sounds, slight as they were. There was the faint sound of a distant bird singing somewhere and he thought he heard a click or two, the sound of something electrical working like a refrigerator, and this seemed much closer than the sound of the bird. He tried to carefully move his fingers and his toes. He'd heard it said somewhere that they are the best things to test if you want to determine if you are alive, and he felt them responding to his commands. He wanted to test other parts of his body to see if they moved as well but found it impossible to locate them. It was all rather bewildering and he began to think he had, indeed, died. At that moment he wished he could be back in the water again. At least it was more interesting than where he was now.

Then he heard a creaking, as of someone moving slightly in a chair, and it made him say:

'Is there anybody there?' but all he heard was:

'Unnnngghhhhh.' Then there was a pause, followed by:

'Arnold? Did you say something?'

He thought he recognised Pete's voice reaching him from somewhere in the darkness. He tried to say it again but louder this time:

'I said, is there anybody out there?' which came out as:

'Unnnng, unnnnghhhhha.'

The voice spoke again:

'You did! Well, how about that then? I better go and tell someone.'

He heard a chair being moved across what he thought was a smooth, polished floor and the sound of someone getting up and walking across a room. There was a change in the atmosphere as if a door had opened, and a busier, noisier world entered. Arnold listened intently and could hear human traffic outside going past. It was as if he were in, yes, a hospital! That was it! He'd either woken up in a hospital room, or he was dreaming he had, or he was dead and the afterlife was a hospital. Just then he recognised the sound of the turning wheels on a bed or something going past the open door and several voices in conversation, only a glimpse of which he caught as they went past. This combination of noises receded as it travelled down what he assumed was a hospital corridor and left him in silence. In a short while he heard people coming back into the room and felt someone come up close to where he was. He could smell a rather nice scent on them as they got closer and he heard a man's voice he didn't recognise saying:

'Hello, Arnold. Are you awake? If you are, try to say something.'

He didn't like the way in which he was being spoken to, as if he were a helpless little schoolboy, but he put that aside and spoke again:

'Yes, I am awake. Who are you?' ('Hnnn. Hggghnnnnhgh. Hnggghhnnnnggg?')

'Now listen carefully, Arnold. You've had a nasty accident, and you've been asleep for a while. But you're going to be all right. Don't try to move suddenly. I'm Dr. Seagrove. You've got a brace on your jaw, so you won't be able to speak properly until you've healed some more. You actually broke your neck but we've managed to patch you up and we're hoping you'll make a full recovery. But a lot will depend on you and your patience. You've lost your vision but we are expecting it to return little by little. But it's going to be a long process.'

So he hadn't died. Now he remembered his accident. He'd been to the post office in Batheaston to post his letters to Aunt Rosa and Hermione, and was on the way home. He hadn't put his seat belt on which was probably why he'd injured himself so badly. He guessed his car was a write-off. Oh dear, what a mess he'd got himself into. He concentrated on the voice again:

'... important thing is you're still alive. You're a very lucky man. Many people would have died after sustaining your injuries. Now just lay quiet for a while. I'll be back to see you later.'

The scent faded away and he heard the doctor leave the

room after speaking quietly to someone. After he'd gone there was a silence. He heard Pete speak again:

'Arnold ... Arnold? If you're awake make a noise, will you? Just so's I know.'

'Hnnnn.'

'We'd better work out a way of communicating with each other, don't you think?'

'Hnnn.'

'I been thinking. I seen you moving your fingers just now, so why don't we try using those?'

'Hnnnggnn.'

'What I thought was ... if we start with your thumbs. Move your right thumb for "Yes", and your left thumb for "No".'

Arnold wiggled both his thumbs for Pete to see:

'That's right. Well done! So, do you understand you're in hospital?'

Arnold wiggled his right thumb.

'OK. That's a start. Do you want me to leave you?'

He wiggled his left thumb.

'Good! OK. Let's get going, shall we?'

Arnold had to admit he was very glad Pete had shown up. They spent the next few hours putting together a rough vocabulary he could use until his jaw got better. The right hand was used for active, positive things. If, for instance, he wanted something he would grasp at the air. The left hand was used for more passive things, such as if he wanted to know more he could waft the air towards him. Once this was in place, he wanted to know what had happened since the accident and how long he'd been in hospital, but Pete had already guessed this and began to tell him:

'You've been in here for nigh on five weeks. Asleep the whole time till today. I was held up back in Hull. I got there and me father were poorly. He always did drink a fair bit but being on his own made it worse. I'm the only one he had. He'd lost his job at the fishmongers because of the drink a while before I got there. I went to his place and he could hardly open the door he was so drunk. He hadn't been eating properly and looked like a skelington. I gave him a bath and found he had huge bed sores. Well, then I realised I couldn't look after him meself so I called for an ambulance and they took him to the hospital. They did as much as they could but it was as if he'd given up. He picked up an infection in there, then it got worse and after about a week he passed away. That's why I didn't come back. I couldn't. I had to organise his funeral an' all. When I did make it back down to yours there were a note for me pinned on your door ... from Trevor? I phoned him up and we been taking turns to sit here with you in case you woke up and didn't know where you was. He's been terribly nice to me, Arnold. I been staying at his place in Corsham as me tent's still at yours. Well, I hope it is? Either that or it was nicked from where I left it outside, the morning I left.'

Arnold was quick to reassure him his tent was safe inside the Keep. Good old Trevor. He'd made sure Pete hadn't got lost in the chaos of the accident.

'Well, Arnold,' Pete continued, 'I really think we made some progress today. But it's getting late now, past six, and the doctor told me not to tire you out. I've let Trevor know you're awake and he's coming in tomorrow to see you. If you want I can come in as well?'

Arnold let him know he liked that idea and waved goodbye as Pete left the room. Then he was alone in his dark space, but it didn't feel so bad now he knew he was alive. And Pete and Trevor were there for him. He experienced a genuine swell of feeling for them both and he was glad they were his friends. As he lay there in the company of his machines and electrical gadgets purring along, keeping him nourished and monitored, he thought back to what Pete had told him about his father's death. Should he tell him about his encounter in the ocean? He may think he'd lost his marbles. But it was strange how he'd been made aware of his death while he was in his coma. He decided it was best to confide in Trevor first, and ask his advice about whether it was appropriate to tell Pete or not. And after he'd settled this in his mind he drifted off into a peaceful and untroubled sleep. There was so much he needed to find out.

CHAPTER 31

It wasn't so much being in hospital that bothered Arnold, it was the fact that it was so boring. He felt totally helpless in the dark without any company. He woke up early the next day and waited patiently for Trevor and Pete to arrive. He spent the hours going through the Keep trying to make up a new list in his mind of things that still needed to be done. He was sure he could convince Pete to stay on once he was out of hospital. There was the idea of a vegetable patch around the perimeter. He reckoned it to be close to the end of September, so it would need to be started on pretty soon. What with winter coming on he had no idea how cold the place would get. In his original renovation he'd fitted insulation panels within the walls but they were yet to be tested. He thought he may be able to fit in a wood burning stove somewhere and use that to generate extra heat. Come the spring they may be able to install the bells from St. Tobias's if he could just find out where they were being stored. At that moment there was a tentative knock on the door and he heard a voice enquiring:

'Hello ...? Mr. Drive?'

Slowly someone entered the room.

'They told me you'd woken up. That is good news. I

understand it's difficult to speak but no worries, you're on the mend and that's what counts. My wife will be pleased. You may remember me, Mark Cubitt, from the architect's office? You came in last year to see the plans for the conversion ... to St. Tobias's? Well, I've brought the scale model with me. I did promise to get it to you. I thought it might perk you up to have it.'

And Arnold heard him put something down next to his bed, and then some wrappings being removed:

'I was careful not to damage it on the way over in the car. It's been safe at the office until now. There you are!'

Arnold could imagine him standing back and proudly presenting it to him, unaware that he couldn't see a thing. He didn't want to make Cubitt feel uncomfortable so he pretended he could see it and waggled his fingers around excitedly, saying:

'Urrrnnnggghhhhh. Rrrrrrhhhhhhuuuuuunngggh!' ('It's splendid. It really was kind of you to bring it over.')

On hearing what he sounded like, Arnold was reminded of the early Frankenstein films with Boris Karloff's monster. He was surprised when Cubitt said, as if he'd understood him:

'I'm so glad you like it. I was my wife's idea, actually, to bring it in for you. Did I tell you she's from Corsham, and was baptised at St. Tobias's? She'll be over the moon to hear you're getting better. I suppose you heard the news about the development? Nothing much we could do about it, I'm afraid. Once we presented the plans and they were accepted and paid for, that's when our involvement ended. Great shame, though, I must say. I hear there's a petition being organised to try to stop it, so we'll have to hope somebody somewhere listens. But I do have some good news regarding the bells. I told the developers of your interest and they've had them brought down from the tower. They said that after all your involvement with the parish they'd be happy to pass them on to you. Well, I must be off now. So glad you're recovering. Goodbye, Mr. Drive.'

And Cubitt was gone, leaving Arnold wondering what he'd meant concerning 'the development'. Now he was even more anxious for Trevor and Pete to arrive. Trevor would know the full story, being the eyes and ears of Corsham. Arnold was aware of the recession and the stalling of the building works at St. Tobias's, but he'd heard nothing new. He realised he hadn't been in Corsham for well over three months, apart from when he'd dropped by Trevor's to pick up his father's papers, just before the accident. Trevor hadn't mentioned anything then, so something must have happened recently. In fact, since he'd been out of action in his coma. It was very good news about the bells though. Then he heard a couple of nurses come in and his bed was changed, and by the time he was settled again Trevor and Pete arrived:

'Hello, old bean,' Arnold was pleased to hear Trevor's familiar voice once again:

'Glad you've decided to hang on for a bit longer, with us mere mortals.'

It felt like old times again.

'Pete here tells me we can communicate with you.'

Arnold wiggled his right thumb, and then wafted the air towards him with his left hand:

'What can I tell you? Well, your car's a write-off for starters. I suppose it must have been a "hit and run", or, more precisely, a "non-hit and run". The police guessed you must have been forced off the road by some crazy lunatic. They want to speak to you about that at some stage. Pete here is happy to stay on for as long as you want him to, to help out. He's shown himself to be more than capable of that. Oh, I telephoned Hermione and told her you've come round and she says she'll be down to see you tomorrow. It's the weekend. It's not the first time she's been in. She rallied round, when you were first admitted, the good sort that she is.'

Arnold wanted to hear something about St. Tobias's and again wafted the air with his left hand but more vigorously this time. Trevor must have noticed the scale model sitting on the table as he added:

'I say, isn't that St. Tobias's? You won't be happy to hear what's going on over there, old chap. Blasted developers have decided they can't afford to convert it into flats after all. Plans are afoot to turn it into another bloody supermarket. They'll get a grant to do that, of course. Corsham's up in arms about it. Petition. Letters to MPs. The lot. Don't quite know what will happen. Only just heard. Hot through the grapevine.'

Oh dear. That was bad news. He doubted if the petitions and letters would amount to anything. He remembered the great effort to try to get the railway station reopened and that idea had fizzled out. He recalled they wanted to build a supermarket there too. Such is the march of progress in the modern world. Homogeneity of human taste and choice, and the destruction of social frameworks. The two seemed to go hand in hand these days. And people wondered why society was breaking down. Why on earth couldn't they create a park instead of a supermarket? He supposed they would argue that the old and infirm citizens needed as many shopping facilities as could be provided within the town. That old chestnut. And they'd probably included plans to build a doctor's surgery at the same time, as a contribution to the community. We are all, how did Trevor describe it earlier, 'mere mortals'? Just about summed it up, really. As individuals a community seems pretty powerless to have any say in matters of planning. Just look what had happened to Bath in the fifties and sixties. Atrocious building, which had only just been knocked down and put right. He'd heard the number of pubs in Bath had halved after they'd completed the 'development' in the city centre after the war.

He'd just gathered his thoughts when he heard Pete's voice:

'What I was thinking, Arnold, was, if you like, I could go to the library and get some books, so I can read to you. It would pass the time. You could pick out what you wanted me to get.'

Arnold thought that a superb idea and wiggled his right thumb frantically.

Trevor added:

'That's the ticket. Turn the situation on its head. Find succour in adversity, as they say. I think I've got a list somewhere, from the *Telegraph*, a few years ago; the best books written in the twentieth century. I thought it might come in handy one day. I'll hunt it out. It'll be a good start. I can also recommend Trollope. Can't go wrong with some Trollope. I've got most of 'em at home.'

This was enjoyable. Having his friends around helped Arnold enormously and he couldn't see how he'd survived for all those years in solitude in Corsham. He supposed never having experienced true friendship meant he had no idea what he was missing. It would be easy to get by with very little if you had no idea of what having plenty was like. Once you've experienced something, it's hard to forget. It's easy to assume poor people are unhappy but he sensed that was simplistic, and not the case at all. Making an assumption like that served the purpose of justifying our consumer-driven way of life. What really takes place, he was sure, was that people with very little make do, and have to spend more time being industrious, most often leading to more fulfilling lives. He'd seen affluence lead to idleness, and idleness can often be destructive. He was reminded of what he'd seen on the cruise ship, all those unhappy people ...

Pete and Trevor's voices carried on in the background as the two of them talked about various books they'd read which they could recommend. Some of them he'd read before and some he wouldn't mind revisiting, especially as he would be read to, which he was sure would be a completely different experience. All because of his stupid accident. He wondered how long he would have to remain in hospital. Months probably. He hoped his jaw mended soon as he really missed being able to talk. He decided he actually missed it more than being able to see. He thought the ability to speak should be regarded as the sixth sense, as it was so important. It was the only sense that enabled man to engage with his fellows whereas the other five were primarily concerned with survival. Thank God his remaining four were still working. Well, sort of. He had no idea when he'd be able to feel the rest of his body.

'Any chance of getting a cuppa char around here?' Trevor asked loudly, 'I'm parched.'

Arnold slept for a while when they left to start their book garnering. Later on Pete returned with the list Trevor had found at home. He began to read the titles out to Arnold who picked those he fancied hearing, together with a few he'd read before. Pete had brought a Trollope with him Trevor had selected, *The Way We Live Now* and Pete began to read it to him. He'd never heard of Anthony Trollope before but he had to admit it was rather good. Such an unfortunate name, he decided. Perhaps it was a 'nom de plume'. But why on earth would someone adopt such a strange name to become a writer? His real name must have been even worse. After a few hours Pete stopped, presumably at the end of a chapter, and put the book down to say:

'Excuse me, Arnold, but I'm knackered. I'm going to have to stop now. It's getting late. But I'll be back tomorrow. I think your friend Hermione is coming to see you in the morning, so I'll leaves you until after lunch, and we can continue then. Is that OK?'

Arnold wiggled his right thumb. He heard Pete put the book down and leave the room, saying:

'I'll see you tomorrow then. Sleep well. Nighty night.'

'Uuuuunnnnnngggghhhh,' Arnold replied.

He experienced his eyelids drooping even though he couldn't see anything and he thought this was probably a good sign. At least it meant his eyelids were working. It wasn't any darker with his eyes closed but it did help him to relax. Now he'd been out of his coma for a day or so he could see how strange his underwater dreaming had been. He realised all the people he'd met had been dead, including Pete's father, whereas Hermione and Trevor had only appeared at the surface, and they were still alive. He remembered his revelations concerning the relationship between his father Nathan and Uncle Red, and wondered if that had been manufactured by his brain, or if there was any truth to it.

When he woke up the next morning he wondered what time it was and guessed it to be early as there wasn't much noise. He heard the nurses going up and down the corridor and occasionally one would stick her head in to check on him and his machines. He carried on compiling his list of jobs until Hermione arrived:

'Darling Arnold. Good morning. Am I late? I got an early train down. I brought you some flowers. At least you'll be able to smell them.'

He listened as she unwrapped some cellophane around a bouquet and held them close to his face for him to smell. They did smell intoxicating and he was left bathed in their fragrance after she'd moved them away, saying:

'Now, where's that vase I brought with me last time? Ah yes, here it is.'

He heard her pick something up and move across the room to a sink, where she removed what was in the vase and replaced them with the new arrivals, saying:

'There!'

She then walked back across to reposition the vase and sat down next to his bed. He felt her grasp his fingers saying:

'Oh, Arnold. I'm so happy you're awake. We were so worried about you. All those weeks. I could hardly sleep. You could have died. So silly not to wear your seat belt. Has Trevor told you what happened?'

He shook both his hands, which were still holding hers, and thankfully she interpreted this as meaning he didn't know, so she continued:

'They found you that night, by the side of the road, in a

sloe hedge. A local farmer had come by on his tractor and seen your car upside down in the ditch. Apparently that stretch of lane is notorious for accidents. He called for an ambulance and they got you out. You'd broken your neck, but it was a clean break and thankfully most of the nerves were still intact, just a little displaced. You're in a cast down to your waist, as you had rib injuries too. They don't think you'll be out of it for a good few months, but perhaps if the ribs heal quickly the cast can be made smaller. The really good news is that you've woken up and can hear and smell, and wiggle your fingers and toes. It means the signals are getting down the spinal column. Dearest Arnold. What more can I tell you?'

He squeezed her hands and moved them backwards and forwards, and to and from her, as if to ask for news about her, and she understood, saying:

'Me? I'm fine. By the way, I did get your sweet letter. Tony is still behaving himself. It is strange living in London again but we're up near Hampstead Heath, so it's a bit like living in the countryside. Lucy's doing well in Durham. She's been there most of the summer making candles and selling them in local markets. She began a course in Archaeology and is really enjoying it, so she says. And she passed her exams at the end of the year too. She's only got one more year left. It's all gone so quickly ...'

At the mention of Lucy, Arnold's attention began to drift.

CHAPTER 32

He was just getting used to Hermione's company again when she declared it was time for her to leave:

'Gosh, Arnold. Just look at the time! It's nearly four o'clock. I must go. I have to go in to Corsham on the way back and pick up some things from the house. I promised Tony I'd be back in time for supper.'

And then she was gone, leaving him feeling helpless again. He'd completely forgotten how much he enjoyed being with her, what with moving into the iron church, his trip to Hamburg, and the arrival of Pete. She promised to come back down again the following weekend and bring a few books she was sure he would enjoy. His lack of speech had accentuated how removed he'd grown from her and he realised he hadn't spoken with her properly since she'd gone back to Tony. Oh, dear. He did hope she was happy living in London. He judged it must be vastly different to Corsham. All those people living on top of one another. But it hadn't dented her enthusiasm for life and he was glad about that. Just then Pete made his entrance and saved him from any further melancholic self-pity. He picked up reading the Trollope where they'd left off the day before, but after a few minutes Arnold found he couldn't concentrate and he gesticulated wildly for Pete to stop.

'Oh, sorry, Arnold. I just assumed you wanted me to carry on from yesterday,' Pete offered.

Arnold shook his hands and pointed at Pete, as he wanted him to talk:

'Oh, OK, then ... Well, now, what shall I tell you? I could tell you about my trip to Hull, if you like?'

Arnold clapped his hands together and gave Pete the thumbs up.

'Right. Well. After I left me tent outside yours I walked down to the main road and got a bus into Bath. The Hull coach was fuller than I expected, but I managed to get a row of seats to meself at the back. I was sitting there alone for a while when I became aware of an awful smell coming from somewhere. As I said, the coach were quite full, and when we stopped at Swindon some more people got on-board, but no one came to sit next to me. Then I suddenly thought, maybe that smell is coming from me! I worked out I hadn't had a shower for three or four days, since you'd let me use yours in the middle of the week. I'd been outside most of the time and hadn't been in a confined space, apart from me tent, for ages. It made me feel terrible. So I went in the toilet at the back and had a good wash at the sink they got there. It was quite difficult what with the movements of the coach and the sink being so small. I did the best I could, there were some liquid soap, and I knew it had been me, 'cos at the next stop, a young girl got on and sat down in the row I was in, and smiled at me. I think it were Birmingham where she got on. Then I was right tired and went to sleep. When I woke up we was pulling into Manchester, so she must have got off somewhere in between. I got something to eat at the coach station in Manchester, as by now I were famished. But the sandwiches weren't a patch on yours, Arnold. And right expensive they were too. We stopped there for about half an hour which was good, as it meant I could stretch me legs and walk about for a bit.

'When I got back on I went to where me things were and there were a black bloke sitting on the back seat, but there were enough room for the two of us, so I sat down. And then, after we set off, after about fifteen minutes, I thought I could smell another awful smell close by, and I realised it were 'im, the black bloke! It were a terrible smell, and suddenly I thought, that's probably how I smelt a few hours ago! Well, I couldn't say anything to him. It's not what you do. And I thought, ain't it terrible how people can go about the world, without washing properly, and sitting next to clean people and not caring about it at all. It's just not right. Then I thought, well, it must be hard to tell if it's you yourself that's smelling bad, and not somebody else. I started to breathe through me mouth, so as not to smell the smell, and that were the longest part of the journey for me. There were no more stops before Hull, so I had to sit there next to the black bloke, for the rest of the journey, breathing through me mouth. I caught his eye a few times, and he smiled at me. Seemed nice enough. Do you think I should have said something? About the smell? I were so grateful to get off in Hull and get some fresh air into me lungs, I can tell you.

'It must have been about nine o'clock when we got to Hull, and as I was beginning to get hungry again I thought I'd get some fish and chips on me way to me dad's. He lives close by the best one in Hull, just a few minutes' walk away. It were the place he used to work in, and they got a chippy in the front. So I went in and asked if they'd seen him lately, which is when I got a bit worried. No one had seen him for weeks, like, so I went straight round to where he lived, to check if he were all right. And that's when I found him.'

Pete fell silent for a while before continuing:

'Come to think of it, I never did get any fish and chips while I were up there. You can get some of the best in the country in Hull, you know.'

After Pete had left for the day, Arnold thought back to when he'd met Pete's father while he'd been in his coma. He wondered if he would recognise him if he ever saw a photograph. Now that would be odd indeed. He also wondered if and when he'd be able to see again. The doctor had told him they expected him to regain his vision, but he knew they always said that sort of thing to patients, just to make sure they don't give up hope. Ultimately recovery depends on the will of the person involved. He'd seen many people in hospital giving up the will to live and passing on soon afterwards. It happened to many people when they lost their partner and life ceased to hold any attraction. He started weighing up which sense he would least like to lose of the five, not counting the power of communication, which he'd decided was the sixth. Well, he knew now what it was like not to be able to see, but it wasn't all that bad, and there are so many things he knew he wouldn't miss seeing. And if he could see, but he couldn't hear, what would that be like? He guessed it would probably make you very withdrawn and cut off, in a much more profound way than he was feeling then. Probably to do with the fact we use our hearing much more than our sight to communicate and get a sense of our surroundings. Losing one's sense of taste would be odd, he thought. Now that would isolate you. He tried to imagine eating his egg and soldiers without being able to taste the flavours. The same with touch, he concluded. Smell he was sure he could do without, especially after what Pete had told him of his experiences on the coach.

For the next few days, Pete read to him from the Trollope and Arnold listened patiently, but he found it far more absorbing to listen to Pete when he was just talking in general. The next subject he spoke about was litter, when he came in the following day:

'You wouldn't believe what I just seen on the way over today! There were a man, walking his dog along the road outside the hospital. An Alsatian. And when the dog did its business he got out a plastic bag and picked it all up with it. Then he tied a knot in the bag and instead of putting it in a waste-bin, he left it in the bloody road! Now where's the logic in that, Arnold? As if there's not enough garbage on the streets as it is. I seen a lot of roads in this country over the last couple of year, what with me travelling, and there's more and more of it every day. The trouble is it's not going away, and most of it's made of plastic, that won't break down. You know what I discovered? There's two types of degradable plastic apparently. There's the one kind that does break down into simple atoms, like. But there's the other kind, that just breaks down into tiny, tiny bits of plastic, which get everywhere and end up being more dangerous than it were before! It's quite frightening, actually.

'I had an idea the other day. You know there's all these prisons full of people not doing anything all day long, all over the country? Well, why don't they get them all out, in chain gangs, picking up the litter? They'd probably enjoy doing something useful for a change. It might even give them a sense of community; that they're contributing in some way. Do you think that's a good idea, Arnold?'

Arnold gave him the 'thumbs up' sign and clapped his hands together in applause. The idea did make a lot of sense. Pete continued, obviously on a roll now:

'I'd also make it illegal to use plastic for packaging. And also that white polystyrene they use to pack up stereos and fridges and the like. That breaks down into loads of small bits that go everywhere. What on earth are we doing letting this stuff get used? I seen it on the coastline when I was up north from Whitby, there's an awful lot of it about. What was wrong with using glass bottles? And paper bags? I'm all for progress, but this is going backwards, as far as I can see. Apparently, in the middle of the Pacific Ocean, there's a huge island the size of a European country, made up of human rubbish. Just imagine that, Arnold. It's out there now, floating about. Getting bigger. All the currents must be gathering it all together like that. Another thing I thought of was, you know all this radioactive waste that's accumulating around the world and no one knows what to do with it? Well, why don't they just put it in a rocket and blast it into outer space? Seems obvious to me.'

At that moment Trevor entered the room.

'Hello, everyone. All good? How's the patient?'

Arnold acknowledged the enquiry by half turning his hands over, as if to say 'about the same'.

'Good, good. That's the spirit, old chap.'

He turned towards Pete to ask him:

'And how's the Trollope going?'

'Oh, not so bad,' Pete replied, 'Actually we were just talking. Well, I have been, of course. I was telling Arnold what I been noticing about the world. All around me.'

'Is that so? None of those confounded conspiracy theories you keep going on about, I hope? That's the last thing dear old Arnold needs to speed up his recovery.'

'Oh, no. None of that. No, just like, you know, about … things. That go on. Like garbage. And nuclear waste. Stuff like that.'

Arnold could tell Pete had felt slightly put out by Trevor's brash tone with him, and had decided to keep quiet. Trevor could now hold the floor:

'Hermione dropped by on her way back to London. Seems intent on making a go of it with Tony. I insisted on giving her a lift to Chippenham station. She had an awful lot of stuff with her. Can't be much left in the house by now, apart from a few bits of furniture. It must be in her mind to get rid of it at some stage. By the way, she's awfully relieved you're on the mend. Now, exactly how far have you two got with the Trollope?'

CHAPTER 33

Autumn progressed and by late November Arnold's jaw had mended sufficiently for the brace to be removed. He found it difficult to eat properly as his cheek muscles had been out of use for so long, and he got cramp when he exercised them too vigorously. It was wonderful to be able to speak again and he gradually reacquainted his tongue with the marvels of the English language. Little by little, his vision returned and he and Pete began to take turns reading the books out loud to each other, which gave his mouth and tongue – and his eyes – the exercise they needed. He was careful not to read too much, on Dr. Seagrove's orders, lest he disturb the slow restoration process taking place in his optic nerves. The ribs healed well and by Christmas the cast had shrunk down to the size of a large, white cummerbund around his waist.

It snowed in the week before Christmas and he marvelled at the brilliance of it outside his window. He found he had to squint to look directly at it. Once he'd started eating properly his visitors spoiled him with various treats, like Bakewell tart, and he was overjoyed to be tasting food again. He'd completely taken it for granted previously and thought it was a shame to have to be deprived of something to fully appreciate its value. A universal inbuilt fault of the human condition, he was forced to admit. He began to leave his bed and slowly exercise his legs with the help of a walking frame and looked forward to getting outside, even though the temperature was freezing.

Pete was wonderful, always on hand every day making sure he wanted for nothing, encouraging him to walk those few extra steps. The extensive reading they'd done over the months had awakened Pete's curiosity and he enrolled in some local educational classes, one in English and one in Literature. Arnold was sure he wouldn't have recovered so well or so quickly without him and began to entertain the thought perhaps he would be allowed to return home at some point. He brought it up several times with Dr. Seagrove, who would reply:

'Now, now, Arnold. All in good time. Let's not get ahead of ourselves. There's not much difference between being stuck indoors here and at home, you know.'

Arnold knew he was right. Once spring arrived, and any threat of ice or snow had disappeared, that would be the time to enjoy the Keep and its surroundings.

One afternoon Trevor came by for tea and Arnold thought it a good moment to bring up his underwater dreaming.

'Where's Pete today?' he asked.

'Preparing for some test or exam, I believe. What was it on? He did tell me ... Oh, yes. Something about the "contribution of Victorian values to melodrama in the contemporary English novel".'

They sat sipping their teas for a while, then Arnold began,

'I've never told you this, Trevor, but when I was in the coma I had a strange dream.'

He was hoping for an inquisitive reaction and got it when Trevor replied,

'Really? What about?'

'Well, I was below the sea. Meeting people.'

'How very interesting. They do say the sea represents life in dreams. So that's no bad sign.'

'But the odd thing was, I knew who all the people were. But some of them I'd never met before. Like Pete's dad. My father was there too. In fact, all the people I met were dead. What's strange is that at the time I didn't know Pete's dad had died. What do you make of that?'

'That's extraordinary, Arnold. Almost as if you were having some sort of, what do they call it? Pre-cognitive experience? Is there any way of telling if Pete's dad were still alive at the moment you dreamt of him? I suppose not. It would mean you had predicted his death, so to speak.'

'I've no way of telling when it happened. But I had the feeling he was already dead, when I met him. I mean he looked dead.'

Arnold thought this sounded very odd, but it was unusual to meet someone who'd died, even in a dream.

'What I mean is, as I was talking to him I assumed he was dead, rather than alive. Do you follow me? Oh dear, it's so difficult to explain. What I wanted to ask you was, do you think I should mention it to Pete?'

'Mmm, probably not, old chap. Not if I were you. You know, some things we should keep to ourselves. Sounds fascinating though. You were probably on the border between life and death at that moment. Sounds like something straight out of a Powell and Pressburger film. Do you know them at all? *Colonel Blimp? A Matter of Life and Death?* David Niven?'

'Can't say I do,' Arnold replied. 'Also, I have to tell you this ... you and Hermione were there as well, in my coma. Well, not exactly IN the sea, but poking your head through the surface of the water, you were both calling out to me.'

'Extraordinary stuff. I'm glad to hear we were still alive. Tell you what, I could bring you in a DVD player and some films. Better than watching the rubbish they put on the telly over Christmas these days.'

He could tell he hadn't described his dream very well. It was so difficult to describe what it was like. He remembered meeting Klaus Borringer just before he came out of the coma and it put him in mind of his aunt. It dawned upon him he hadn't received a reply to the letter he'd posted just before the accident. He had no idea if there was any unopened post out at the Keep but he assumed Pete or Trevor would be checking on it. He brought it up with Trevor:

'By the way, have either of you been checking if any post has arrived for me? At home?'

'Of course, old bean. Pete and I have taken it in turns to go by there every week. Didn't think there was much point in bringing any of it in to you, mind, until you could actually read it yourself. I never have been one for opening other people's mail. There's quite a bit we've collected in a shoebox at my place. I'll bring it in tomorrow.'

Arnold sorted through it and first separated the junk mail. There were a couple of letters from Nigel Scott, regarding his investments, and a lilac envelope with what looked like German stamps on it. He opened it and found a letter from Rosa, dated September 30th:

My dearest Arnold,

What a pleasure it was to receive your letter! I must apologise for not having replied sooner, but I have been ill. Many years ago, in the camp, I picked up a strain of hepatitis that occasionally comes back to remind me of those dreadful times. I become very tired and have fever that can last during several days. This time it stayed far too long, and after two weeks I have only just been able to get about again. It is a reminder that the candle of life cannot burn forever.

How are you? And how is your iron church? It was wonderful to meet with you and I hope it will not be too long before you can come to see me again. Have you made plans for the Christmas period? I will be here and you are most welcome to share a glass or two of Ratsepulser with me then.

Your ever loving,

Aunt Rosa

As he read the letter her voice came back into his mind and he could imagine her reading the words to him herself. He wanted to call her immediately and hear her voice so he asked Pete if he could bring his Blackberry into the hospital. He would dearly love to have spent Christmas with her, but being stuck in the hospital would make that impossible. He would just have to wait until he got out in the spring. The hospital was beginning to feel like a prison, he had been there so long.

'Pete?' he asked.
'Yes, Arnold?'

'Can you do me a great favour?'

'OK, if I can.'

'Take me outside. Now. I don't care what the doctors or anyone says. I just need to be outside. In some moving air. I don't mind how cold it is.'

Pete exhaled noisily, then said:

'All right. But not for long. You're going to get me into a load of trouble. I'm not kidding.'

Pete helped him up from his bed, wrapped his dressing gown around him, and draped his duvet over his shoulders. With the aid of the walking frame and Pete, Arnold slowly ambled along the corridor to the lift and made it down to the ground floor. They headed for the two large, plate glass doors, which glided open silently as they approached them. A nurse behind the reception desk was busy on the phone with her back to them as they passed, but stared open-mouthed as she turned and caught a glimpse of them disappearing through the doors into the night.

It felt wonderful to escape from the hospital. The air was much colder than he'd imagined but it felt good. It made him feel alive again, and he could feel his blood moving around his body, attempting to come to terms with the cold. Of course, his newfound freedom wasn't going to last long and after a couple of minutes they heard the sound of several nurses running out after them. But he didn't mind their anger. It was worth it just to remind himself there was indeed a world beyond the double-glazed windows. As he was led back inside, he heard a police siren sounding somewhere from within the city of Bath, and then the double doors shut tight and he was again hermetically sealed within the building.

Christmas was festive around the hospital. There was constant activity and coming and going. The staff were wonderfully helpful and did everything they could to lighten the mood of the place. He tried calling Rosa in Hamburg every day but hadn't managed to get to speak with her, and on Christmas morning he tried again, but the sober ringing tone was all that came through the earpiece of his Blackberry. Pete and Trevor came by in the afternoon and brought in some presents. Trevor had splashed out on a personal DVD player with a set of noise-cancelling headphones and they spent some time looking through a collection of films they'd picked out for him. Hermione had dropped in on Christmas Eve with an interesting invitation for him:

'Arnold, would you like to come up and spend New Year's Eve with Tony and me? There's plenty of room at the house and Tony is dying to meet you. I could come and collect you and drive you up in comfort. I've already spoken with Dr. Seagrove and he thinks it will do you some good. He's still a bit cross with you after the shenanigans last week, what with your walkabout, but he does realise a little break would be beneficial. You could stay a couple of nights. We'll have a nice meal with some of Tony's friends. What do you think?'

How could he say no? It was as if she had read his mind, as always, and he immediately accepted.

CHAPTER 34

Arnold waited impatiently the several days before Hermione came to pick him up on New Year's Eve. He watched several of the films Trevor and Pete had given him to while away the time and especially liked *Citizen Kane* and *The Producers*. Hermione had driven down the previous night and stayed at the house in Corsham, and by ten o'clock they were on the road. He was keen to find out more about London life. She'd obviously come to terms with the change in pace and recognised the advantages and disadvantages of living there:

'London's all about what you put in,' she explained. 'It's so vast, with such a variety of people. You can be quite anonymous if you want to be. What I like about it is, you have to make an effort to keep in touch with people, whereas in Corsham that's not necessary. All you have to do is walk down the High Street and you're bound to bump into somebody you know. In London you really do appreciate it when someone has taken the trouble to meet up. And there's lots to do, of course.'

'Does it disturb you?' Arnold asked. 'All those people living on top of one another? I've always thought it would make one feel insignificant. And lost.'

'Arnold, one can feel lost anywhere. Even somewhere one knows really well.'

They fell silent and he thought for a while about what she'd said. He supposed it would help if you were inquisitive and thirsty for knowledge. An ignorant man wouldn't know if he was missing something. But as soon as he became aware of the possibilities available, he couldn't help himself wanting to know more. Arnold wasn't sure which was the more attractive situation to be in. At times he would love to be the man who knew nothing. Knowledge itself seemed an evil force, the robber of innocence and spreader of avarice. He'd reluctantly come to realise that man was his own worst enemy, the very abilities his brain gave him were the things he had to guard against. They always seemed to be the reasons for his undoing.

It was a novelty to enter London by car. Not having to concentrate on the driving meant he could look around as they sped along and he noticed the people and the buildings they passed. Hermione said it wasn't all that busy being New Year's Eve, but it looked awfully crowded to him. She didn't go directly to where she and Tony lived, instead taking a detour to show him Buckingham Palace and Trafalgar Square. As they passed the palace, he remembered when he'd walked past it on his trip to London the previous spring. In some way the buildings seemed grander and more austere now, but perhaps that was because all the trees were without their leaves this time and looked as if they were standing to attention. They drove down the Mall and went through Admiralty Arch, and Hermione pointed out Nelson on his column. The square was thronged with tourists and London didn't seem quite such an alien place to him as he shared their enthusiasm. They threaded their way up to Highgate through Regent's Park and he liked what he saw of that. It did seem to be a park fit for a king. He'd had no idea parts of London could be so beautiful and he was put in mind of his first reaction to Hamburg, when he'd visited Rosa the summer before. Oh dear, he thought. He longed to discover the reason for her silence.

Finally the car came to rest outside a red-bricked, detached house on a leafy quiet street. Hermione helped him out and he negotiated his way up a gravel driveway with the aid of his walking frame. She opened up a shiny black door with some keys and he shuffled into the hallway. His small brown suitcase appeared next to him on the carpet.

'You must be feeling tired, pet. How about having a lie down?' she offered.

'Yes. Good idea. Where's Tony?'

'Oh, he's off playing golf but he'll be back in time for supper. We've invited a couple of friends to join us. I've put you in a room down here. It's got its own bathroom and will save you having to worry about stairs.'

She picked up his case and led him into a small bedroom with casement windows that looked out to the front of the house. She helped him out of his coat and shoes and onto the bed and left him to rest. Within a few minutes he was drifting into a welcome sleep.

It was dark when he awoke, and as if by magic there was a soft tapping on his door. Hermione opened it, saying:

'Wakey wakey. Arnold? It's five o'clock. I thought you may want to have time to freshen up. I've brought you a cup of tea.'

She came in and switched on a bedside lamp, and placed the cup and saucer next to it, saying:

'There you are.'

Sitting on the bed she placed the palm of her hand on his forehead and he saw her smiling down at him, the picture of concern:

'How was your little sleep? Feeling better, I hope. Tony's just got in. He's looking forward to meeting you. You've plenty of time to get ready. There's a towel in the bathroom. Just shout if you need any help. Drinks are at seven.'

She leant forward, kissed him on the tip of his nose and got up to leave the room. As she was at the doorway Arnold said:

'Thank you, Hermione. You really do know how to look after me.'

He felt much better for his sleep. The hospital had sealed the edges of his cast with some waterproof plasters and he carefully undressed and washed himself, determined to do it without calling Hermione. It was the first time he'd managed unaided and he felt a sense of achievement as he slowly got dressed. He opened the door to the hallway and shuffled out on his frame.

The end of the corridor opened up into a large kitchen, and Hermione and someone he assumed to be Tony were sitting at a table with glasses of wine. They got up when he entered the room and Hermione introduced them:

'Arnold. This is Tony.' Tony got up and shook his hand:

'So pleased to meet you, Arnold. How about a small cele-bratory drink? I don't think we ever met when I was in Cor-sham. I was back and forth on the train to London all the time, and I'm afraid Sundays ended up being spent at home with a large gin and tonic at about noon. Red wine?'

Arnold accepted the glass Tony poured and was relieved how easygoing he seemed.

'Should be good fun this evening,' Tony continued, 'Got a food writer and his wife coming over, so Hermione's a bit beside herself, thinking they're going to find fault with everything. Absolute rubbish, of course. They're secretly bloody pleased someone's invited them out for dinner! That's the trouble being one of their sort. Never get invited anywhere! Cheers.'

They chinked glasses. Arnold took a sip of his wine, and asked:

'So what exactly do you do? Hermione told me it's something in television.'

'Yes. Production. Behind the scenes. Very boring most of the time. Endless meetings trying to squeeze infinitesimal amounts of money out of accountants from television channels. Started out wanting to be a cameraman, but that became so dull. Like most things. They always seem more glamorous until you're actually doing them. Did you find that in your game? In the church, I mean?'

Arnold liked Tony's directness, and the conversation made him liven up. He had to admit once he was in the church full time his perception of it did change, so he attempted to explain:

'I suppose the idea of being in the pulpit ... with a congregation, listening to what I had to say was exciting to start with. I used to look forward to it ... But after a while, the thought of having to come up with something new, week after week, I suppose it did seem... to become a chore ... to a degree.'

He was relieved he'd managed to finish his train of thought.

'There you are! My point entirely!' Tony congratulated him, 'Cheers!'

Just then the doorbell rang and Tony was off to answer it:

'That'll be Charles and Veronica.'

Arnold looked to Hermione, who winked at him mischievously. She moved over to where he stood, and said:

'I'm so glad you two are getting along. Thank you for coming, Arnold. It's lovely to have you here.'

Tony's voice approached them down the corridor, mixed with two others. Charles and Veronica still had their coats on, and were holding several bottles of wine in their arms.

'Here, Hermione. Where do you want these?' Veronica asked.

'Well,' Tony said emphatically, 'that bottle of Krug's going nowhere!'

'Tony, no! Hands off!' exclaimed Veronica, holding the bottle close to her. 'It's for twelve o'clock. Midnight toast. It's got to go in the fridge, of course.'

She caught a glimpse of Arnold and said:

'Ooh! Who's this? Sorry. The name's Veronica. What's yours?' And she regally stretched out her hand to him. Tony jumped in before Arnold could speak:

'This is Arnold. Late of the church. Well, what I mean is ... used to be our vicar down in Corsham. Up visiting for a few days. Recovering from a nasty car accident.'

'I am sorry to hear that. Very pleased to meet you, Arnold,' Veronica said.

'What, the accident? Or having left the church?' quipped Tony, following it with a laugh.

Charles stepped forward and also offered his hand.

'I'm Charles. Hi, there.'

Arnold heard the pop of a champagne cork and accepted a glass from Hermione whilst Tony took coats out to the hallway. Arnold realised he was trying to hold two glasses as well as his walking frame, so he put the one holding the red wine down on the table and they all raised their glasses to announce loudly,

'Cheers!'

'Here's to us!' Tony added.

They stayed in the kitchen drinking for a while before Hermione insisted they leave her to get dinner ready. Tony herded them into the living room where an elegant dining table was set. Tony and Charles stepped out to smoke cigarettes leaving Arnold alone with Veronica, who wanted to know all about his accident. After he'd briefly explained what had happened she said:

'But, Arnold, that sounds simply horrendous. You're lucky to be alive. No wonder you had to leave the church. Isn't there some sort of insurance in place? You know, for loss of earnings, job, etcetera?'

Arnold was quick to correct her:

'Oh, no. I left the church before the accident. Last year, in fact.'

'That is bad luck. I'm sure you would have been covered if you were still with them. Employers are liable for that sort of thing, you know. It's the law.'

It was obvious he wasn't getting through to her, so he explained that he'd been made redundant.

'Sounds like you've had a bumpy ride. Do tell me, what was it like being a priest? Is there really all that hanky-panky going on with the choirboys, that they would have us believe?'

At that moment, Tony and Charles came back from their smoking, laughing, and Arnold was spared from having to answer her.

The evening continued and Hermione served up spaghetti bolognese she said she'd prepared several days earlier. Everyone drank copious glasses of wine, except Arnold who sipped cautiously at his, and as a result he noticed how merry everyone else was getting. At one point, when Tony and Charles were smoking outside and Hermione was busy clearing plates away, Veronica started flirting with him. They were sitting next to one another at the table and she leant towards him and started nibbling on his ear, whispering:

'Oh, Arnold. You're such a darling.'

He had to admit it was a surprisingly pleasant sensation, but he was careful not to encourage her and waited patiently until the others returned. None of whom noticed.

After cheeses, Hermione brought out a pudding and over coffee and a brandy he accepted a cigar from Tony and they stepped outside to smoke. It was a crisp, still night but the wine had fortified them against the chill. Tony lit both their cigars and stood back to look up into the black sky.

'What a fantastic night. Quite clear. We're lucky in this part of London. You get to see the stars when it's clear like this.'

Arnold looked up and could see a few, twinkling above their heads.

'Very good of you to come, Arnold. Are you having fun?'

'Very much so. It's good to get out of the hospital. I've been stuck in there for so long. Hermione's been so good to me.'

As he said this, Arnold wondered if she'd told Tony about their liaison in Corsham, and their cruise together, but the haze of the moment and the well-being generated by the brandy enabled him to drop the thought. Tony took up the subject of Hermione:

'She's an absolute gem, isn't she? Can't believe I persuaded her to give me another chance. I made a complete bloody mess of it first time around. Didn't know what I had, basically. It's only when you lose it you realise what a fool you've been. Don't deserve her, I really don't.'

They stood in silence and continued to gaze up into the night and Tony continued:

'The one good thing to come from our first time round the block was Lucy, of course. Completely grown up now. Came by on Christmas Day, but it was a fleeting visit. Wanted some money, naturally. To do a cookery course in Goa. In India.'

'Oh. Is Lucy still at Durham?' Arnold asked, and felt odd mentioning her name.

'It's her last year, I think. Lose track of the time, to tell the truth. Doesn't seem that long ago she was tiny, running around Corsham, wearing her butterfly wings. Down by the mere, that was her favourite spot.'

Arnold remembered her there, after the last supper at the Jaipur, before he'd left his cottage. That didn't seem so long ago, although it was, in fact, nearly eighteen months earlier. He found himself silently agreeing with Tony. Time slipped by, whether you liked it or not.

They heard some screeching voices from inside the house and Charles stuck his head out of the front door:

'According to Hermione, you've got precisely a minute and a half to get yourselves back inside. Come on!'

They left their cigars in an ashtray outside the front door and hurried back to the living room where Hermione was ready with the open bottle of Krug and five full glasses on a tray. The radio was on and when the chimes of Big Ben started Tony turned up the volume. As the voice announced it was midnight they all raised their glasses and toasted. Arnold found himself quite caught up in the exhilaration as they all hugged and wished each other 'Happy New Year'. Suddenly he heard the strains of Tamla Motown music fill the room and Tony and Hermione began dancing, whilst Charles clapped and sang along. Veronica tried to pull Arnold out into the corridor but he resisted her efforts and almost fell over in the process, losing hold of his walking frame, which went over. This curbed her enthusiasm as it attracted the attention of Hermione, who rushed over to pick it up, saying:

'Do keep an eye on him, will you, Veronica?'

The doorbell rang and Charles went to answer it.

'That'll be Frank and Liz from next door,' Tony said. 'I told them to drop by.'

Charles returned with four or five people, all dressed as if they'd been out somewhere.

The first man after Charles, Frank, came bounding forward to hug Tony, saying:

'Tony, you old bugger. Happy New Year. Just got back from a really boring party in Maida Vale. I brought a couple of friends along. Hope you don't mind? Liz … what are their names again?'

Liz stepped forward and introduced a couple, and Arnold thought she said they were German. There was also a much younger pair, probably in their early twenties. He guessed they were part of Frank's family.

What with all the noise and the loud music, Arnold couldn't hear what everyone's names were, but he smiled politely and shook their hands. He suddenly felt light-headed and managed to navigate his way over to a large sofa to sit down. He closed his eyes and absorbed the music. He remembered he'd been fond of Tamla Motown music when he'd been a student in Guildford. It took him back to a pub he used to go to on Friday nights down by the river where they would play it on a jukebox. He tried to remember the name of the pub. He was brought out of this by a soft voice asking him:

'I say, are you feeling all right?'

He opened his eyes and looked to his left, where the young woman who had come with the neighbours was crouching down and looking at him earnestly. He smiled and nodded reassuringly, taking and squeezing the hand she'd held out to him. She proceeded to sit down next to him, still holding his hand, saying:

'Thank God for that. For a moment I thought you'd passed out. My name's Caroline. What's yours?'

He paused for a few seconds to get his bearings and replied:

'Arnold. It's Arnold. I think I'm all right. Thank you.'

'Mmm, you look a bit pasty to me. C'mon, let's get you outside for some fresh air.'

At that she helped him up and onto his frame and they made their way down the corridor to the front door, leaving the party in full swing.

Once out in the cool air Arnold started feeling better. He inhaled and exhaled a few times, seeing the mist of his breath floating away, and felt her hand on his back gently stroking him.

His head started to clear and he began to wonder who this girl was. As if she'd read his mind, she immediately spoke:

'I'm Zach's girlfriend. Zach is Frank's son. Frank lives next door.'

'... Caroline?' Arnold said, to check he'd remembered her name.

'Yes, that's right! And you're Arnold, aren't you?' She continued, 'Zach used to go out with Lucy, up in Durham. They split up in the summer. After he'd graduated he came down to live in London.'

'Did you know Lucy at all?' he found himself asking.

'Not really. Don't mention the "ex" and all that. I saw her briefly a few days ago when she came by to see her folks.'

'Did she leave him?'

As soon as he'd said it he wondered why he'd asked the question.

'I'm not really sure. It was probably to do with the fact that he was leaving Durham. It's hard to keep things going when you're living in two different places.'

He could see she was happy to talk about it, and hadn't noticed what an odd thing it was for him to ask.

'Shall we go back inside now?' she asked. 'Let me give you a hand.'

CHAPTER 35

The party went on past two o'clock but Arnold was exhausted and went to bed not long after getting back in the house. Before retiring, he shuffled around the party on his frame, making sure he said goodnight to Hermione and Tony and their guests. In his room he started to undress but ran out of steam after getting his trousers and shoes off, and got into bed with the rest of his clothes on. He was certain Hermione wouldn't mind. He could still hear the music playing but it didn't stop him drifting into a deep sleep whilst he tried to take stock of how much he'd drank.

The next morning, he was woken up by the sound of Hermione tapping at his door and quietly coming in to leave a cup of tea on the bedside table. He pretended to be asleep, as he didn't feel well enough to have a conversation. She softly kissed his forehead and said 'Good morning' before leaving again. He lay there with his eyes closed and thought back to the events of the previous day. So much had happened since he'd left the hospital. He kept remembering little things out of sequence, and having to rewind in order to fit them in. It started to get a bit hazy when he got to around midnight, but one thing clear in his mind was when Caroline had helped him after his funny turn.

When they'd got back to the living room, she'd introduced him to her boyfriend Zach, the neighbour's son. Arnold noticed how youthful and good looking the boy was. While Zach was explaining what he was doing in London he'd tried to imagine him with Lucy.

'I was at uni in Newcastle on a film course. It's only a ten-minute train ride from Durham. I met Lucy through some friends there. We realised my parents lived next door to her dad! What a coincidence! He's helped me get into film production in London. Well, I'm a runner, actually. But that's how everyone starts.'

'Tell me, how was Lucy? Have you seen her over Christmas?' Arnold had asked.

'She dropped by last week. Seemed very excited about going to India.'

The German couple had been very pleasant. They were from Berlin and were interested that Arnold had an aunt in Hamburg. They were friends of Frank's wife, Liz, and Liz worked with Agata, the woman, and she had family in Hamburg. Frank and Liz were extremely friendly and seemed to know an awful lot about him. So much so he'd started to feel uncomfortable, and that's when he'd excused himself in order to get away.

He began to regain consciousness and thought he could sense the unfamiliar pains of a hangover lurking in his head. The last time he'd had one of those was the day after the Mercouri vineyard visit and as soon as he recognised it, it kicked in, as if it had been waiting patiently in the wings for a cue. His head started to throb and he began to feel dehydrated, so he gingerly stretched out some fingers to reach the cup of tea Hermione had brought. Unfortunately his spatial awareness wasn't working properly and he knocked the cup off its saucer and onto the floor, spilling the contents. He didn't know what to do next, but the noise in the silent house must have alerted Hermione. She came in, saw what had happened and returned with a tray and sponge to clear up the mess, saying:

'Arnold. I do believe you must be hung-over! Don't worry, pet. I'll bring you another cup. And perhaps an Alka Seltzer for that head of yours. Won't be a tick.'

Arnold couldn't remember the last time he'd heard anyone mentioning Alka Seltzer. It was a brand name from his childhood. He had no idea they still made the things.

Once he'd drunk his tea and enjoyed the fizzing Alka Seltzer he started feeling a lot better. There was no hurry, according to Hermione:

'Tony's still in bed. In a much worse state than you are! Better you lie low whilst I finish tidying up. I'll make us some brunch when you're both up and about.'

She left him propped up in bed, as he would have been if back at the hospital. But how infinitely more comfortable he felt where he was. He realised he was in London, somewhere he'd always thought of as an unfriendly place, and just look at him, totally relaxed and feeling quite well. Apart from the hangover, of course. He wondered what 'brunch' was, and if it would be something nice to eat.

Within half an hour he was washed and dressed, and pulled open the blinds to see a clear blue sky outside the casement windows. There was a robin sitting on the branch of a holly bush right outside, which he took as a good sign for the day ahead and the year that was just beginning. He opened the door to his bedroom and shuffled along the hallway towards the kitchen, where he found Hermione pottering, putting things away.

'Happy New Year,' he wished her with a smile, adding, 'Sorry about the tea.'

'Happy New Year to you too, pet. Have you made any resolutions? Apart from, I presume, not mixing your drinks! That's what causes the hangovers, you know. Let me make you another tea.'

He sat down and enjoyed sitting there, chatting with her. Everything seemed to be in order when Hermione was around.

He considered her question about making resolutions:

'I haven't given it much thought. It's only just hitting me what a year the last one was. I do believe more has happened to me in the last twelve months than in the rest of my life.'

He was surprised once he'd said it how frank he'd been. She put a fresh cup of tea in front of him and sat down.

'Dear Arnold. It has been a bit of a roller coaster year for you, hasn't it? Now Agata ... Liz's friend? She told me last night you have an aunt in Hamburg. Do tell me about her. When did you discover that? And she said you've been over to visit her!'

So he related the whole story, of how he'd researched what had happened to the music box at the auction all those years ago, and of managing to trace Rosa, about his trip to Hamburg, and how he'd visited his Uncle Red's grave. Hermione seemed genuinely surprised at what he told her, saying:

'But, Arnold, that's remarkable news. I had no idea you'd been to Hamburg! How adventurous of you! And your aunt, still alive. When did you last speak to her?'

'I got a letter from her when I was in hospital saying she's been ill. She invited me over for Christmas. Of course, I couldn't go. I've tried calling her but no one answers.'

'Come on. Get the number off your phone and we can try it now, using the landline here. You can wish her Happy New Year.'

Arnold found her enthusiasm infectious and got his phone to read out the number. She dialled it and waited expectantly in silence, saying:

'It's ringing.'

They continued to wait for a minute or two, but there was no answer.

'Now it's stopped ringing, and there's a continuous tone. Oh dear,' she said. 'I don't know what that means. Never mind. Let's try again later. Do you like scrambled eggs and smoked salmon?'

Tony appeared dressed in a stripy, blue towelling dressing gown and a pair of slippers, roused by the smell of cooking.

'Morning, Arnold. Cor blimey, my head feels like a steam-roller's gone over it. All my own stupid fault, of course. Happy New Year, anyway. I thought I could detect the unmistakeable smell of scrambled eggs and toast down here. Bless you, love.'

Hermione put a plate of food in front of him and he noticed the smoked salmon:

'Wonderful. Just the job. Don't mind if I start, do you? Ravenous.'

Arnold watched in amazement as Tony dropped his head down and attacked the food. It was as if he had no real need for the knife and fork he was using. He could just as easily have eaten straight from the plate.

Hermione reprimanded him:

'Tony, please! Do you have to be so uncouth? We have guests.'

He immediately straightened up and apologised, like a schoolboy being scolded, then slowed his eating down in pace with the others. It was plain to see how mindful he was of Hermione's humour, and Arnold hoped their reconciliation continued to be the success it deserved to be.

After brunch, Hermione suggested they take Arnold for a look at Kenwood House, part of the 'real London', as she described it. They drove there in a few minutes and managed to park right behind the large house. He hobbled along on his frame and they sat for a while on a bench in front to admire the Constable-like view of the meadow sweeping down to the lake, which was populated by a few swans and what looked like ducks to Arnold.

'Reminds me of the mere in Corsham,' remarked Tony, 'but much grander, of course.'

They sat in silence, drinking in the beauty of the view. Arnold said:

'I had no idea London was like this. I can see why you don't miss Corsham.'

'Can you see yourself ever leaving the countryside, Arnold?' Tony asked. 'Do you think London could be a place for you?'

He thought about this carefully before answering.

'I don't think it really matters where you end up, just so long as you know where you are.'

It was beginning to get dark so they got up to leave. It had been a perfect time to be there as hardly any other people were about. Which was odd, Arnold thought, in a city of fifteen million people. By the time they got back it was twilight and Hermione suggested a cup of tea. They sat in the kitchen and discussed getting him back to Bath the next day. Frank and Liz had invited them over that evening and Tony suggested dropping by.

'Seems a shame not to pop in. It's only next door. Just a few yards.'

Hermione was having none of it:

'Not for me. I need my beauty sleep. Besides I'm driving tomorrow, don't forget.'

Tony couldn't resist the temptation of some more fun and said:

'All right, love. You don't mind if I go, do you? Won't be long.'

Arnold and Hermione ended up sitting together watching a black and white film called *All About Eve*, with a bowl of chicken soup and crackers she conjured up out of nowhere. By the time the film finished he was ready for bed, and he found himself not really caring what the time was. Hermione helped him along the corridor and came to tuck him in. As he lay there in the dark it struck him it had been the first day he hadn't had his egg and soldiers since he'd been in Hamburg, visiting Rosa. They'd forgotten to call her again and he fell asleep determined to remember to try in the morning.

CHAPTER 36

Arnold felt saddened to leave the house in the morning, having experienced such friendship and warmth there. London had turned out to be completely different to what he'd been expecting and he realised it was futile to presuppose things about places, or even people. As they wove their way through the sleepy suburbs, it struck him he'd been disappointed not to catch a glimpse of Lucy during his visit. She'd barely crossed his mind since his accident, but the mention of her name several times on New Year's Eve had brought her streaming back into his consciousness.

'Penny for them?' Hermione enquired, having noticed how pensive he was. 'You look miles away, pet.'

'Sorry. It's just I've had such a wonderful time. And London, well, London isn't what I expected.'

'There. You see. What did I tell you? It's full of surprises, isn't it?'

They sat in silence and Hermione concentrated on her driving for a while. As they approached Hammersmith he wanted to try calling Rosa again and asked if they could stop. Hermione pulled into the forecourt of the first garage they came to and while Arnold tried calling she took the opportunity to buy petrol.

'Any luck?' she asked, as she got back in the car.

'No. Nothing,' Arnold replied, with the phone still at his ear. 'I'm beginning to get a little worried.'

They pulled off from the pumps and rejoined the carriageway.

'Could she be visiting anyone over Christmas?' Hermione asked.

'I got the impression she had no friends who were still alive. And she told me I was her only relative.'

She pulled a face and said, 'Oh, dear. It doesn't sound too promising. I do hope everything's all right.'

But Arnold had an idea and started busily studying the screen on his phone while he pressed some buttons.

'I've just remembered someone I can ring in Hamburg,' he said. 'Perhaps they can call round and check on her if I ask them.'

He found the number for the taxi driver, Boris, as he'd called him several times whilst he'd been in Hamburg. He rang it and a message came on in German. Arnold guessed it was asking the caller to leave a message, so he said:

'Hello, Boris. This is Arnold, Arnold Drive. We met last year when I visited my aunt. You drove us to the cemetery and took me to the airport? I hope you remember. Can you call me as soon as possible, please? Thank you. And Happy New Year.'

He left his phone number twice, reading it out carefully. Hermione smiled as she understood what his plan was.

'Arnold, that's awfully clever of you. I'm sure he'll call you. Boris, was it?'

Arnold took most of the drive explaining how he'd met Boris. He hadn't mentioned him when he'd recounted his

Hamburg trip the day before. He'd just got to the part where they'd had ice creams by the Elbe when they neared junction eighteen. Hermione steered the car down the slip road onto the A46.

Arnold's phone rang. He'd been holding it tightly the whole journey, just in case. He thought the noise of the car would mask it ringing if he put it down anywhere, and he didn't want to miss Boris if he rang back:

'Hello? Boris! You got the message! Yes, I'm well ...'

He decided to avoid saying anything about his car accident.

'And you? Good, good. I want to ask you, you remember my aunt, and where she lives? Yes, that's right, Milchstrasse. Can you do something for me? She's been sick and I am worried. Can you go and check if she is home? She doesn't answer the telephone ... No, I've tried many times. I got a letter before Christmas. She said she was not well ... Yes. Thank you so much. Thank you. Yes. Please call me with any news. Goodbye.'

Hermione took his free hand and squeezed it.

'There you are. You'll soon know what's going on. He'll find out, I have a good feeling about him.'

They drove past Dyrham Park and saw the hills of Bath coming in and out of view as the road zigzagged its way down from the high ground. It was a clear, dry afternoon and Arnold felt he'd been away far longer than just two nights. It was the same when he'd returned from Hamburg. He was pleased to catch sight of the familiar landmarks: the church on Lansdowne Hill, the spire of the Abbey below, and the bold lines of Camden Crescent looking peerlessly over the town. As they approached the hospital, reality began to jolt

him awake. It would be quite a change from the last two days
and he readied himself for the cold plunge in. At least he had
Boris's phone call to look forward to.

Hermione helped him back to his room and stayed for a
cup of tea before heading back. The nurses were pleased to
see him and were relieved he was in good spirits for a change.
Since his short walkabout before Christmas he'd been irri-
table and realised now there was no reason to take out his
frustrations on them. As they sat having their tea, Hermione
asked what he thought of Tony.

'I thought he was a thoroughly decent fellow to tell you
the truth,' he replied. 'I wasn't expecting to like him at all.
But he went out of his way to be friendly.'

'Yes. I'm so glad!' Hermione said. 'It was the one thing I
was worried about. It would have been awful if you two had
taken a dislike to one another. Darling Tony. Yes, he was trying so hard. And I could tell he liked you, pet. He really did.
He told me so. Thought you were ... one of the good guys, I
think he said.'

One of the good guys. Arnold liked that expression. He'd
never heard it before. It sounded American, but he liked the
way it sounded. He thought back to the party.

'I had a brief chat with Zach, Lucy's ex-boyfriend? Seems
a nice boy.'

'Yes, he is. I'm quite sad they split up, actually. While she
was with him I didn't used to worry. Now I hardly know what
she gets up to. When she swept through at Christmas she
didn't look settled at all. I asked her what her plans were and
she said she was heading to Goa for the New Year. Apparently there's a gang of them going from college. I do hope

she's all right. I told her to make sure she had all the right jabs. But she's pretty organised in those things, generally.'

They finished their tea and she decided to leave.

'I'll come down next week, perhaps even bring Tony if it happens to be the weekend,' she promised.

'I'd like that,' he said.

As the sun went down outside his window, he settled into his armchair and felt lucky to still have Hermione's friendship. Thankfully it had survived romantic entanglement and he was pleased she'd got back together with Tony. He suddenly thought of the scale model Mr. Cubitt had dropped off for him and turned his neck to look at it sitting on the small table. His vision was improving as he could see it was getting dusty. He'd been unable to move his neck without any pain until then and he chuckled to himself.

The light faded and he dozed off, knowing there was time for a nap before they came round with the evening meal. He was woken up by his Blackberry, which he'd put close by, ringing on the tray attached to his armchair. He picked it up feverishly and pushed the green button:

'Hello? Hello?' There was a pause:

'Hello. Mr. Drive? Ja, it is Boris here calling you. From Hamburg.'

'Boris! Thank you for calling. Is there any news of my aunt?'

'Yes. I was visiting to her address just now. So I ring the bell. No answer. Then I knock on the door. Still no answer. So I knock some more. And then a neighbour comes from another apartment and tells me she is no more there.'

Arnold was scared when he heard this. Boris continued:

'Ja. She is gone. To the hospital.'

'Did they tell you when, and where?' he asked.

'Before Christmas, it was. They tell me where they take her. So I go there now and ask for you. OK?'

His heart relaxed and he replied:

'Thank you, Boris. Thank you for checking.'

'Don't worry. It's no problem for me. I like this lady. She is very nice. And grand. How do you say, proper? OK. I will call when I have news of her. Bye bye.'

And then he was gone.

Arnold's mind raced back to when he'd visited his aunt in Milchstrasse. He presumed the neighbour lived in one of the adjoining buildings. All he could recall was the street's cobblestones and a few shops, like the kind you find in central Bath, around Sally Lunn's Tea Shop behind the Abbey.

His phone rang again. This time it was Trevor:

'Hello, old bean. Hermione just called to say she's dropped you off at the hospital. Happy New Year! All tickety-boo? Did you have a nice time? How was Tony?'

Arnold briefly told him about his trip, the drive through London, the dinner, the party, and the visit to Kenwood. He told him how affable Tony had been.

'Well, that's a relief. I didn't want to say anything before you left, but I have to tell you, I wasn't too sure you'd get on. Sounds like you had a whale of a time. Knocking back the old champers, what? Oh, called to let you know Pete is back at the Keep. He was keen to start on the veg patch, as the weather's been so mild. You know, dig it up in preparation for planting. I thought it made sense, so I gave him my blessing. Does that sit comfortably with you?'

CHAPTER 37

The weeks drifted by, and Arnold continued to recuperate. Boris had discovered Rosa sitting up in a hospital bed. She'd smiled when he'd approached, remembering him from when they'd met in the autumn. She'd been there since the week before Christmas and looked set to remain there for some time. Arnold instructed Boris to visit regularly with flowers and to keep him up to date on her condition. Arnold was desperate to visit her but had to be patient with his own recovery.

He passed the time reading books and watching films Trevor brought in. It was interesting to see what Trevor thought he might be keen to watch, as he never asked him for any guidance, but most of the time he found them worthwhile. Pete used Arnold's trusted bicycle to come and see him but he was busy out at the Keep most of the time and his visits became infrequent. When he did appear it was with extremely detailed descriptions of progress with the vegetable patch, and Arnold looked forward to seeing it. He worked out between the winter and summer solstices there were a set number of ten-day periods, and after each there was a distinct change, by about ten minutes, in the time the sun set and came up. If he could think of a job to be done around the house he would jot it down somewhere to pass on to Pete. But he began to notice a change in Pete's behaviour. It was as if Pete were a child growing up and Arnold was a relative, who didn't see the child that often, so was able to notice things the parents were oblivious to.

First of all, Pete had started to gain weight. He'd never been that large to begin with so it wasn't something Arnold was unduly worried about. Secondly, he seemed increasingly withdrawn and uncomfortable conversing with the nurses at the hospital. Early in February, Pete said he wanted to borrow Trevor's air rifle, to 'scare off them bloody vermin rabbits'. Apparently they were threatening to decimate the vegetable patch, just when the seedlings were starting to poke their heads out of the ground. Of course Trevor agreed.

Boris kept in touch and occasionally would call him from Rosa's bedside and give her the phone so they could speak. Her condition stabilised but hearing her frail voice just made him want to visit her all the more, and he resolved to go to Hamburg immediately he was discharged from hospital. Hermione came down most weekends, but Tony never came with her. She announced she was going to Los Angeles, where Tony would be working throughout the summer on a new TV series:

'It's ages since I've been,' she enthused. 'I wonder if it's changed at all. Last time I was there a police car pulled up and asked me what I was doing. Well, I didn't know quite what to say to them. All I was doing was going for a stroll. Apparently people don't do that sort of thing there, so to them it appeared suspicious. How ridiculous!'

The day arrived when Dr. Seagrove gave him the 'all clear'. It was 9am to be precise:

'Arnold, you're an extremely lucky fellow to have survived. You seem to have made a complete recovery. But you'd better avoid any extreme physical activity. Football, that sort of thing. Fall in the wrong way and I can't guarantee that spine of yours won't buckle. Swimming would be good though. You're free to go.'

Arnold rang Trevor to tell him the good news and asked him not to tell Hermione he was going immediately to Germany, knowing she would worry and try to stop him going. Trevor was happy to be part of the subterfuge:

'That's splendid news, old chap! Totally understand. You've got to do what you've got to do. I can book you a flight over the internet right now. I've still got your keys, so I'll pop out to the Keep, get some clothes for you, come and pick you up, and drop you at Bristol airport. All part of the service. And don't worry, mum's the word as far as Hermione's concerned. Now where's your passport?'

He managed to get him a flight to Hamburg later that same day with an open return. On the drive to the airport Trevor mentioned he hadn't seen Pete out at the Keep.

'It did look a trifle scruffy, I must say. Smelt a bit, too. Of animals. Cats and dogs. Didn't see any around the place, though. Rather odd, I thought.'

Arnold couldn't understand this. Perhaps Pete had got himself a pet, and not said anything. But that wouldn't be right, not to tell him. He decided it would have to wait until he got back.

Trevor had picked out a sober suit from Arnold's scant collection of clothes, and a few changes of shirts and underwear:

'Wasn't sure how long you were planning to stay, as you never said. This little lot should see you OK for a week or so.'

They sped along the country lanes and Arnold tried to dial Boris's number as he wanted to ask him to meet him, but the signal kept disappearing as they wove up and down the dipping hills. They were held up by a traffic jam going through Chew Magna as the schools were coming out for the day, but within a few minutes they were turning off for the airport. Trevor walked him inside the terminal building:

'Good luck, old chap. Wish I still had a relative or two I could go and see. Speaking of which, I may be away when you get back. I'm heading up to the Scottish Highlands for a while to do some trout fishing. An old buddy of mine from Bristol's based up there. I've been meaning to visit him for a while. Haven't picked up a rod for years. Quite looking forward to it, actually.'

It was the middle of March, and the sun was still above the horizon when they took off. Being the middle of the week there was plenty of room on the flight. He noticed the emergency exit row was empty so he asked if he could sit there. The stewardess had no objection, assuming he was able-bodied, and he was pleased he was no longer considered an invalid. He sat by the window to the left of the plane, stretched out his legs and gazed through the glass at the sun setting in the west.

He'd managed to get hold of Boris before boarding and was looking forward to seeing him. He remembered what he looked like, but would Boris recognise him? His hair had grown a good three or four inches while he'd been at the hospital. Every time he'd considered having it cut the urge had disappeared as soon as he'd shaved. He checked his wallet to make sure he had euros, and found several hundred euro notes still there from his last trip. He ate a sandwich and drank a bottle of water, and when he went to the toilet he looked at himself in the mirror. It was the first time he'd done this since the accident and he looked quite different. His trousers felt tighter and he guessed he'd put on about a stone. He was wearing normal clothes, and was standing properly, and his hair was longer, but there was something in his facial expression new and unfamiliar. He didn't look as timid as before. Taking out his passport he studied the photograph, which had been taken eighteen months earlier, prior to the cruise with Hermione and Lucy. He hardly recognised himself and wondered if he'd have problems entering Germany. He returned to his seat and began to think perhaps now, finally, he'd become just another man in the street. That was it; he didn't look like a clergyman any longer. The dawning of this left him feeling adrift, rather like a boat come loose from its moorings. He wasn't sure if it was a pleasant feeling. He took another look at the photo and it was as if he were looking at someone else. He watched the sun finally disappear below the horizon and closed his eyes, hoping he could just relax and let the current take him where it would.

They landed in Hamburg in darkness and once through immigration he hurried through customs. Being such a small airport, it was easy to spot Boris. He looked the same as Arnold remembered and they embraced warmly.

'But you look different,' Boris said. 'That hair! And you are, how do you say, fatter? Yes. Of this I am sure. Come. We can talk in the car.'

He took Arnold's small case from him and led the way out to where he'd parked.

Once in the cab and driving, Boris must have read Arnold's mind:

'OK. We take you to check in, *ja*? The Garden Hotel? And your Aunt Rosa. I was there this afternoon; after you told me you were coming, to give her the good news. This she was very happy to hear. She is in good spirits. Still very, how do you say, fragile? But she can smile. And what a smile! Boy oh boy, I bet she was something when she was a youngster. *Ja*. No problem!'

Arnold was relieved to hear this.

'Can you take me to see her tomorrow morning?'

'Of course. No problem!'

They arranged to meet at 10.30am, and Arnold had enough time to get some boiled eggs and toast at the buffet breakfast before he arrived. They had a wide selection of teas but he wanted a cup of that strong coffee they make in Germany, which he thought went well with the eggs. He carefully sliced his toast up into fingers to dip in his eggs, but found to his dismay they were all hard-boiled. He didn't have enough time to ask for some to be cooked to order, so he ate the eggs as they were, with a bit of salt and pepper, and found some delicious fruit jam to spread over his soldiers.

The hospital was fifteen minutes' drive from the hotel, but the traffic was slow moving and Arnold calculated he could probably walk it in less than half an hour. Once inside he noticed how clean it was and how perfect all the staff's uniforms were:

'Boris, is this a private hospital?'

'No, just an ordinary one. Called UKE. For the people,' Boris answered.

'But it looks brand new,' Arnold enthused.

'That's because it is!'

They rounded a corner and entered a ward, and Arnold saw Rosa in the far corner of the room in her bed, looking tiny amongst all the white pillows and duvets. She had what looked like some tubes attached to her left wrist, and some machines close by were obviously monitoring her various functions. Boris leaned over and whispered in Arnold's ear:

'I'll get a coffee. Leave you with her for a while, *ja?*'

She had her eyes closed, but sensing someone approaching her bed they opened, as Arnold came up and smiled down at her.

'Arnold! You are here! That is *wunderbar!*'

She made to raise her head from the pillows but Arnold stopped her, saying:

'It's all right, Rosa. Please lie still.'

She obeyed and relaxed, and her eyes wandered over his face and noticed his hair.

'Your hair. But it has grown so long!'

He realised neither she nor Boris knew of his car accident or his own long stay in hospital, and he decided there was no reason to tell them.

'Do you like it, Aunt Rosa? I thought it was time for a change,' he said.

'It makes you look more handsome. More manly. Dear Arnold.'

He felt he should explain why he hadn't come any sooner but, as if by telepathy, she slowly said:

'It doesn't matter. You are here now. I have been here a long time. I lose count of the days. I feel my candle is almost burned down. Sometimes I wake up and think I am already dead, and heaven is a hospital. Dear Arnold.'

He stroked her right hand and she closed her eyes. It was plain to see she was very weak, and not wanting to exhaust her he pulled a chair up and sat down in silence, continuing to stroke her hand.

They remained like this for several minutes and after a while Arnold felt a tap on his shoulder. It was Boris.

'I just met with the doctor. He would like to speak with you.'

Arnold carefully released her hand and put it under the covers, but her eyes opened.

'Back in a moment,' he said, and stood up.

Boris took him across the ward to a desk where a doctor was waiting for him.

'You must be Herr Drive. Thank you for coming. I understand you are her only living relative?'

'Yes, that's right. And she is mine,' Arnold confirmed.

'*Ja*. As that is the case I have to tell you that we may reach a point where a decision must be made. About her ability to survive this illness.'

'What do you mean?' asked Arnold, surprised.

'I am so sorry for my English. It is hard for me to explain. You must forgive me. Your aunt is very weak, and to some extent we are relying upon the machines by her bed to sustain her. If her natural ability to keep her organs working gets weaker, she will in essence remain alive only because of the machines. The family must decide then whether to continue the treatment or not. I am sorry, but this I have to explain to you. It is the law.'

Arnold didn't like what he was hearing. How could he make a decision about whether or not Rosa should live?

'Doctor, thank you for explaining the situation. Perhaps

I can give you my telephone number, and if this moment arrives you can call me and I can let you know what to do?'

The doctor made as if to stand to attention in agreement and found a pen and paper. He continued:

'Herr Drive. It may seem a terrible thing to have to decide, I know. But be aware that the machines will always be used wherever they can be the most effective. Our work here is to save as many lives as possible. Good day.'

He clicked his heels, smiled briefly at Arnold, and turned to stride off down the corridor.

Arnold began to feel light-headed and put a hand down on the desktop to steady himself. He had no idea this sort of thing went on in hospitals, but it did make complete sense. It was not an attractive vision. There were only so many machines, and only so many beds.

He let go of the desktop and slowly walked back to Rosa's bedside where Boris was sitting. His eyes met Boris's and he raised his eyebrows slightly in order to convey his troubled state of mind. Boris sensed something was amiss.

'Perhaps it is time for us to go?'

Arnold nodded in agreement and bent down to whisper 'Goodbye' to his aunt, adding:

'See you later.'

She was obviously tired; her eyelids moved faintly and she made a tiny noise to acknowledge what he'd said.

Outside the hospital's glass doors they stopped and Arnold described the conversation he'd had with the doctor.

'Hmmm,' murmured Boris. 'That is very hard for you. I am sorry. What say we get some early lunch?'

He let Boris decide where they should go and as they drove in the cab he thought he sensed they were heading back towards the lake, and sure enough it came into view. They pulled up outside the Café Bodo's Bootssteg and Arnold remembered it from his lunch with Rosa the previous September. Being early, it wasn't full and they were able to get a table looking out over the lake. They ordered and sat quietly for a moment, enjoying the view from the windows.

Arnold spoke first:

'She is very weak. You were right. Fragile. I'm so glad I came when I did. If I'd left it any longer ...'

Boris interrupted him.

'There's no need to speak like that. Things will be as they are. It is nice to see you with her. Before I went to get coffee I watched for a while. She was so happy to see you again. It is *fantastich* that you arrived at this time. It is, how you say in English, determined? Now let's have a beer.'

CHAPTER 38

It was easy for Arnold to settle into a routine during his stay in Hamburg, built around the hospital visiting hours. Boris would sometimes drive him over after breakfast but most days he would walk there, as Boris would be busy working. He enjoyed seeing him but he preferred to walk as it gave him a chance to familiarise himself with the town. He would see Rosa for an hour or so and get a bus back, to take lunch in one of the restaurants dotted around the lake. After a brisk walk around the edge, he'd catch the bus back to the hospital and walk home to his hotel in the evening. Her condition didn't change and she remained weak and unable to speak for very long without closing her eyes, but she was always pleased to see him. Herr Koertze, the doctor who spoke with him, nodded whenever he saw him and would sometimes ask for his opinion about Rosa's state of mind. Arnold wasn't able to comment as she wasn't speaking much, but he asked if there was any news concerning her medical condition.

'Frau Hoeppell is suffering from an acute condition caused by a long standing virus in her body,' Koertze told him. 'As she gets older the virus takes a stronger grip, and I'm afraid it is only a matter of time before it overcomes her. There is only so much we can do in cases like these.'

Arnold concluded all he could do was remain in Hamburg, hoping perhaps his presence was helping her combat the virus in some way.

He'd been there close to two weeks when he got a call one afternoon. He was just returning to his hotel from his second look in on Rosa when his Blackberry rang and he recognised Boris's voice.

'Arnold? Hello. How are you today? I wonder, would you like to meet up this evening? We can relax and take some supper together?'

Arnold thought this a grand idea. He hadn't seen Boris for nearly a week and felt he could do with some company. Boris was the only person he knew in Hamburg and he'd be a good sounding board for any concerns about his aunt, so he immediately agreed.

'Good. I will pick you up at about 7.30? It suits you? OK. See you then.'

They headed off in Boris' cab and took a direction Arnold wasn't familiar with.

'Where are we going?' he asked.

'Tonight, I take you to a *fantastich* Italian restaurant. One of the oldest in Hamburg. In St. Pauli. I booked a table for us.'

They turned down a main street and Arnold sensed this was the area in Hamburg he'd read about, known around the world for its sexual establishments. He peered through the windows as they drove down the wide dual carriageway of the Gorch-Foch-Wall and noticed large neon signs outside what he guessed were nightclubs. It was a bright, early spring evening and they weren't flashing their messages just yet. They passed the Laeiszhalle on the left and the street narrowed to become Holstenwall. After a couple of junctions they were on the Reeperbahn and Arnold wasn't ready for the full frontal assault of the entertainment displayed there.

'Don't worry, Arnold. It won't bite you. You are safe with me!'

He saw Boris watching him in the rear view mirror, laughing.

He turned off the Reeperbahn into Davidstrasse and parked where he could, next to the entrance of Herbertstrasse. As Arnold got out he noticed high boards erected at the entrance to this street and read a sign saying 'Entry for men under 18 and women prohibited'. He turned to ask Boris about it:

'What does this mean? It looks a bit like a ghetto of some sort.'

Boris laughed:

'Ah, so! I understand. No, it's not a ghetto. Just a place for men. That's all.'

He laughed again and then continued, taking Arnold's arm:

'We are going just up here, to Cuneo. This place has been in Hamburg for many years, nearly one hundred, I think. We will have a good meal.'

They entered a shabby doorway and were transported into another world. He could hear what he guessed to be Italian being spoken by various waiters running this way and that carrying dishes, and at several of the tables by the diners. It felt as if it could have been at any time during the night rather than only eight o'clock. They were shown to a table, given menus, and Boris pointed out a large oil painting that hung on a small wall close by:

'Do you see that painting? It has been here many years.

In it you can see the family members. And the young man and woman standing behind the seated man? They still work here. He is their father, he started the place.'

As if by magic the woman in the picture, advanced several decades, came to their table to ask what they wanted to drink.

Boris turned to Arnold and said:

'The house wine is very good. Shall we take a carafe?'

After a sip or two of the wine, Arnold felt relaxed. He was happy Boris had suggested they go out together. It made him say:

'Thank you, Boris. For being so helpful. I really appreciate your kindness toward me and my aunt.'

'Not at all,' he replied. 'It has been my pleasure. Here's a toast to my good friend Mr. Arnold Drive,' and they clinked their wine glasses together.

Boris knew the menu pretty well and suggested they start with some home-made pumpkin ravioli pasta and follow it with something called saltimbocca. Once they'd given their order, Arnold was keen to find some other subject than his aunt to talk about, so he asked:

'How's work? Have you been busy? I was sure you were because I haven't seen you for almost a week.'

Boris sat back, passed his hands through his hair and answered:

'Oh, *ja*. There will always be work for cabs. No matter what happens there will always be people who want to travel in a taxi. Especially if it is raining.'

Arnold was keen to for more information:

'What about the airport? Do you go there? I mean, that's where I met you.'

'*Ja*, but only if it's quiet in the town. You can be sure there will be fares from there, but the trouble is, you don't know where you will end up. I was lucky with you. You wanted to go to the centre. It's not always the case. But you would be surprised, there are many tourists who come to Hamburg just to come to this area, St. Pauli. It's very famous, you know. For the "men only" places.'

'Oh, yes, I'm sure,' Arnold said, feeling slightly uncomfortable at the thought.

Boris continued:

'You know, Arnold, you mustn't be too judgmental about these activities.'

Arnold fidgeted in his chair.

'I'm not. Not at all. I just don't know much about it. There's not much of that sort of thing where I live.'

'Ah, I see,' Boris indulged him, continuing:

'You know, it's the oldest job in the world. There were women for sale before there were taxis, and probably even before religion was invented. Here in Europe we understand the necessity for this kind of work. How important it is to the community ...'

Arnold saw an opportunity to comment:

'Oh, so you see them as, some sort of ... community workers?'

'Exactly! That is the point. A healthy community must allow for such things, such ... services.'

At this point, he refilled their glasses and ordered another carafe of wine, just as the pasta arrived. Boris told him all the prostitutes in Germany were regulated. They paid taxes, took compulsory health tests and were issued with health certificates to show if any client wanted verification. It was obviously completely accepted. What a shame opinions were still so bigoted in the UK, Arnold thought.

As the meal continued they drank more wine, probably more than Arnold was used to, but he was having such a good time he didn't worry. Boris was right, the restaurant was exceptional, and the atmosphere was just right. The saltim-bocca was very tasty and Arnold guessed it was some sort of meat wrapped in ham and cheese. He'd never had anything like it before and thought it may be something he could try to prepare himself when he got home. Boris was keen to discover Arnold's sexual history, and was surprised to learn he'd only recently made love for the first time. He found this hard to believe.

'But that is amazing. You are quite a new boy, still. So here's to the new boy.'

And he raised his glass for another toast. He began to tell Arnold about the various girlfriends he'd had over the years. Boris admitted he had slept with customers in his cab:

'Well, why not? If a beautiful woman comes your way, does it matter how it happens? You must take the chances life presents to you. If you don't, you never know what could have been. One time I was taking a lovely lady to the airport and she wanted to make love in the back! How could I refuse? Of course, I always carry protection, how do you call them in English, "johnnies?"'

Arnold was fascinated by Boris's stories, and they tucked into some tiramisu while he divulged ever more remarkable tales:

'I remember once, there were two girls, quite young, hitching to the airport. It was a few years ago. They told me they were on their way to a rock concert of their favourite band, I cannot remember what the name was. They told me they didn't have enough money to buy the plane ticket. It wasn't very much, perhaps two hundred euros together for the two of them.'

Then Boris stopped and just looked at him, with a devilish grin on his face.

'And?' Arnold wanted to find out what had happened next.

'Well, what do you think? I had them both! I took a slight detour to the Stadtpark and we parked up and went into the bushes. Oh, no problem, it was the summer, so very warm outside.'

'And you gave them the money for their plane tickets?' Arnold was incredulous.

'Of course. Why not? I tell you, they were *fantastich* girls. Both of them.'

Suddenly a coffee and a glass containing a clear liquid were put in front of him, and before he knew what was happening he was downing the contents of the glass. It was like fire, but it felt good.

'Ah!' said Boris. 'I see you like the grappa! Very good for you.'

He drained his glass and then turned to get a waiter to bring them another.

After the second grappa, Boris asked for the bill and looked conspiratorially at Arnold:

'Now, we will go for a small nightcap. Not far. Just two minutes' walk from here. Very nice place. Some pretty girls there for us. *Ja?*'

Arnold's weak protestations were brushed aside and he found himself following Boris out of the restaurant and left along Davidstrasse, towards the Reeperbahn. The street was busier and groups of garish people loomed past. There were women heavily made up, some looking as if they would be at home in a circus. Snippets of different languages entered his ears as he strode purposefully after Boris through the people. He wasn't quite sure what on earth he was doing, but he didn't care at that moment. The grappa had taken hold of his senses and he felt strong enough to do anything. He was aware of a wide road with heavy traffic. They crossed the Reeperbahn, turned down a small side street and reached a doorway. Boris pushed open the door, pulling Arnold in after him, saying:

'Here we are.'

They moved along a dark corridor opening onto a dimly lit room with a bar along one wall. There were several girls, some sitting, and some standing by the bar, talking and smoking cigarettes. They immediately noticed Boris and Arnold and two moved towards them. Boris seemed to know them:

'Cindy. How are you? Gabriella. So nice to see you. Now this' – he pointed to Arnold, – 'is my good friend Arnold, from England. He does not speak German, but that's OK, *ja? Alles ist klar!* Now, let's just sit down somewhere and we can all have a little drink together.'

He selected a booth with dark velvet covered seating and sat down next to Cindy, a blonde, while Gabriella, a brunette, made Arnold sit down with her. She seemed to be sitting extremely close to him even though she didn't know him at all. She spoke softly in his ear:

'So, your name is Arnold? That should be Arnie. With your sexy long hair, and big muscles.'

He could feel her touching his arm and squeezing it rhythmically through his jacket. Normally he would have objected but it was enjoyable, so he sat passively and smiled at her.

A bottle of Jack Daniels appeared on the table with four tumblers and a jug of ice. Boris put ice in the glasses and poured four large measures. He passed them around and proceeded to nestle his head in between Cindy's shoulder and her hair, and she responded by using her free hand to massage his thigh. They giggled and carried on as if they were by themselves. Arnold looked at Gabrielle and could see she was a pretty girl, probably in her twenties, not much older than Lucy or Caroline, the girl he'd met on New Year's Eve. He took a swig from one of the tumblers. It tasted very sour, very cold, but strangely warming, though in a different way to the clear liquid he'd had at the restaurant. He felt Gabriella's tongue slowly licking his left ear and began to feel aroused. She was pressing her breasts up against his arm now and he took another swig of the icy, dark liquid and began to stroke the space between her thighs, exposed below her short dress, through the nylon of her stockings. Her thighs felt warm and soft and parted immediately as if to encourage him.

Some energetic music started up and Boris and Cindy got up to dance. Arnold could hear them singing along to the words of the song.

'Yes, sir, I can boogie ... all night long. YES SIR, I CAN BOOGIE ... ALL NIGHT LONG.'

He discovered Gabriella to be kissing his face and could feel her taking his jaw in both her hands and biting his lips and tongue.

Suddenly Boris was over where they were sitting, shouting:

'Come on, Arnold. Fuck later on. Time to dance!' And he grabbed his arm and pulled him up from the booth and Gabrielle went with them, laughing. They began swaying to the music, and the tune changed without a break.

'It's a' raining men. Hallelujah. It's a' raining men. Amen. IT'S RAINING MEN. HALLELUJAH. IT'S RAINING MEN. AMEN ...'

Arnold had never danced like this before and had no idea how to move properly, so he just followed his instincts and closed his eyes, and didn't care how it would seem to anyone watching. The music coursed through his body and he lost himself within the deafening sound. He could feel himself moving as if in a vacuum and was almost taken back down below the ocean, where he'd been in his coma. He opened his eyes briefly but much preferred dancing with them closed, so he entered the darkness again and very soon was flying through the air without any weight at all.

CHAPTER 39

His first sensation when he awoke was of an intensely dry mouth, followed by a throbbing pain behind his eyes. It resembled what he'd experienced in London on New Year's Day, but ten times worse. He yearned for an Alka Seltzer and lay with his eyes closed, half expecting Hermione to materialise with the fizzing potion in a glass. Slowly opening his eyes he recognised he was back in his hotel room in Hamburg. He pinched his eyelids together and felt a searing pain above his right eye, so he scrambled out of bed to look in the bathroom mirror. He was partially clothed in his underwear and shirt, and had a bruise over his eye. He unwrapped a plastic glass in the bathroom, filled it with cold water and drank with an unquenchable thirst. He drank three glasses very quickly and wondered what the time was. His Blackberry was in his neatly folded trousers on a chair by the bed but was out of power. He found the charger in his suitcase, plugged it in and saw the time was 11.15. There was a signal saying he'd missed a call. He didn't recognise the number as Boris's, but could see the +49 denoting Germany in front of it. Wondering who could have called, he took a shower and changed his clothes, then went down to reception to see if he could find some coffee. It was far too late for breakfast of course, and too early for lunch, so he headed down to Bodo's Bootssteg by the lake to get some air. The short walk did him some good and he noticed there were still two croissants sitting in a pastry case on the bar. He ordered them with some coffee and as he ate he felt his spirits lifting. The sugar allowed him to think more clearly and he remembered the meal with Boris and the two girls in the bar. After that his mind was a blank. He had no recollection of what had happened next or how he'd got back to the hotel. He looked again at his Blackberry and thought about the missed call. He remembered Dr. Kreutze had taken his number down in case there was a need to contact him urgently about Rosa. Rushing out he ran back up Alte Rabenstrasse looking desperately for a taxi. He'd almost gone the whole way up to Rothenbaumchausee before he found one, and was so out of breath he couldn't say where he was going when he got in. He finally blurted out 'UKE' and the taxi driver recognised the word, saying:

'Oh, ja. Universitat Hospitalen. UKE.'

He spent the whole ride getting his breath back and it was the longest taxi ride he'd ever taken. He kept checking the time, as if just by doing so he could speed up the journey. After what seemed like an eternity they pulled up outside the hospital and Arnold thrust a fifty euro note through the driver's window and dashed inside. He reached the ward to find an empty bed where Rosa had been the day before. He felt terrible. His dedication to visiting her every day had in the end amounted to very little. He hadn't been there when it mattered. He sank down in the chair he'd sat in the day before and stared at the freshly made bed. After some time a voice behind him called, 'Herr Drive?' and he recognised it to be Dr. Kreutze's.

He felt a hand on his shoulder and the doctor continued:

'I am sorry. We tried to call your number last night. But there was nothing to be done. Your aunt had an extreme heart seizure at 11.30pm. She died instantly. I am so sorry to tell you this. When you are ready there are some formalities we have to complete. Please take your time. Just ask at the desk for me when you are ready.'

He continued sitting there. He'd hardly known his aunt and yet her loss was extreme. Through her, he'd discovered the existence of his Uncle Red and so many things about his family. She'd been his one link to them all. Since they'd met, her impact on his life had been immense. The sounds of the hospital began to filter back into his consciousness and realising he would have to find the doctor again, he stood up listlessly and trudged back to the desk, where Kruetze was busy over some paperwork.

'Doctor?' he said sheepishly. Kreutze raised his head.

'Ah, so. Herr Drive. Yes. As you were the only surviving relative you must sign the death certificate and identify the body. When do you want to do this?'

Arnold saw no reason to delay, so he followed Dr. Kreutze down a corridor and into a lift. The lift descended below ground level and they emerged onto a silent corridor where the air was still and had a strong smell of formaldehyde. Arnold breathed through his mouth to avoid smelling it. The doctor held open the frosted glass door of the morgue for him and checked the names on the large metal drawers until he found the right one. He pulled it open, raised the sheet, and Arnold saw Rosa for the last time. But she didn't look anguished. Her face wasn't fixed in a terrible grimace. The last time he'd seen a dead person was Stan, and it all came seeping back to him, when he'd discovered him in Colerne. He half expected her to open her eyes and begin a conversation with him, as if she were still in bed upstairs in the ward. He wasn't frightened or shocked, just reminded of life's impermanence. She looked as she'd always done, just a little greyer and perhaps he noticed a sense of peace in her facial expression. He turned to Dr. Kreutze and nodded, and Kreutze replaced the sheet over her head and closed the drawer. They left the morgue and went back up in the lift.

Arnold had to sign some papers and Kreutze told him he should go down to registration and reclaim Rosa's personal things. There wasn't much, just the clothes she'd been wearing when she'd been admitted. And her purse, which contained a few euro notes, some coins and a set of keys Arnold presumed were to the apartment. He checked the things against the list, signed for them and they were given to him in a new mint green plastic bag. He wandered towards the foyer of the building with the bag clasped to his chest and went outside into sunshine. He didn't know what to do or where to go so he began walking. He wandered up Martinisstrasse and followed it through Eppendorf. He could see some trees in the distance. Heading in their direction, he found himself in a park bordering the river and took a straight path towards the water. He could see what looked like a cafe by the water's edge and thought it would be a good idea to sit down for a while. It had a pretty garden with tables and umbrellas open giving shade. It was empty, which suited him, and he sat down at one of the tables out of the sun. The umbrellas were green and had 'Perrier' written on them and he noticed the green was the same as that of the plastic bag containing Rosa's things. He ordered a coffee and opened the bag to look through them. There was a slight scent to the clothes and he wondered why there wasn't a way to make dead bodies smell better than of formaldehyde. Just then his phone rang:

'Arnold? How are you today? How is the big drinker? Ha ha! You were a handful last night, I have to say.'

'Boris. I've had some terrible news. Rosa died last night. A heart attack. It was very sudden.'

'Are you there? Now? At the hospital?'

'No. Now I am by the river. In a park. At a place called' – he looked down at a coaster on the table – 'Boothaus Silwar.'

'I know it. Stay there. I will come now.'

His coffee came and he sipped it, enjoying the tranquillity of the garden. He looked down at the plastic bag, thinking it was all that was left of Rosa.

He ordered another coffee and drank it, and Boris arrived.

'I am so sorry. Tell me what happened,' he said, as he sat down.

'There's not much to say,' Arnold began. 'I woke up very late and checked my phone. They'd tried to call me last night, but the battery was flat. I went out to find a coffee and realised it was the hospital who had called. I went there and found her empty bed.'

'I am sorry. What did they tell you?' Boris asked.

'She had a massive heart attack just before midnight and died instantly. I feel so terrible ... I wasn't there. When it mattered.'

'But you could not have changed anything. Yes? If you had been there?'

'Probably not. But, I don't know, for some reason it makes sense I should have been there for her. Instead of getting drunk. In a bar.'

They both fell silent and the sound of a woodpecker reached them from somewhere high up in the trees. Boris stood up and turned to him, saying, 'Come on,' and strode off through the cafe towards the river. Arnold picked up the green plastic bag and followed him without thinking. He noticed Boris talking to a man in a kiosk. He emerged saying:

'We are going on the lake. Follow me.'

He led the way to where some boats were moored and climbed into one, holding it steady while Arnold stepped on. He loosened the mooring rope and with the aid of an oar pushed the boat away from the jetty. Suddenly they were in the middle of the river. Arnold grabbed the other oar and asked, 'What do I do?'

Boris was sitting in front of him facing forward and said:

'Paddle like hell. Do exactly what I do. With the paddle.'

He watched Boris move the oar through the water, alternating it on each side of the boat to strike a rhythm, which he mimicked as best he could. It was something else he'd never done before, canoeing. He was surprised how fast they began to move and realised they were going downstream towards the Ausenalster. They went under several bridges with traffic flowing over them and then approached the vast body of the lake. He decided the main thing to do was to keep his head down and paddle, and try to keep everything else out of his mind.

'By the way,' Boris shouted, 'last night. You collapsed on the floor in the bar. Cindy and Gabby had to help to drag you out. I took you back to the hotel in a cab. But don't worry, I wasn't driving!'

Arnold shouted back, 'I never usually drink like that. I'm sorry I spoilt the evening.'

'It's OK. After I put you in your bed I went back to them. They are both good girls, I can tell you. Is everything OK back there?'

They paddled and paddled, and Arnold was happy to be doing something other than thinking about Rosa, admonishing himself. A few other canoes were out on the lake and one came close, and the occupants hailed them and waved. Boris exchanged some words with them in German and they all laughed. After about an hour they stopped paddling and allowed the boat to get carried along by the current. Boris cleverly used his oar to steer and Arnold realised he was taking the boat towards Bodo's Bootssteg, which he saw coming up on the right hand side. They glided into the jetty there and Boris secured the boat, saying:

'I think we better take some lunch, *ja*?'

They took their usual table looking out over the lake and ordered some weinerschnitzel and two beers.

Boris spoke first:

'So, Arnold. I have to tell you when my grandmother died. We spent many hours, many days, the whole family, at the hospital. Wanting to be with her until the last moment came. After a week or so, we were all exhausted, and one by one had to rest and leave the hospital. And then, when we were all gone away, she decided it was time for her to go. We all thought perhaps she was waiting for us to leave, so she could go when no one was watching. Perhaps it was better like that. For your aunt too, maybe.' He sipped his beer and paused, looking out at the lake.

'Perhaps you're right,' Arnold said with resignation.

'So, I guess you will be going back to England?' Boris asked him.

'Eventually. But first I must sort out Rosa's affairs. There's the apartment. I suppose I'll have to go through her things and see what's what.'

'She will probably have a will. Somewhere. With an *anwalt*, probably,' Boris added.

'What's that?' Arnold asked.

'What do you call it in English ... a lawyer, *ja*?'

'Yes, perhaps. Hopefully I'll find some papers somewhere and it will all make sense.'

'But she will have left everything to you, no? There was nobody else. That's what you said.'

Arnold realised Boris was right. After lunch he decided to wait until the following day to start, as all the paddling had tired him out. The thought of an early night with a fresh start in the morning allowed him to relax.

CHAPTER 40

Arnold strode out purposefully from the hotel in the morning sunshine in the direction of Milchstrasse and was there in less than ten minutes. He matched the three keys with the locks on the front door and slowly pushed it open. There was a mustiness in the corridor but he did recognise Rosa's scent from the last time he'd been there and from her things he'd been given at the hospital. He could still feel her presence as he took some steps forward and went to the living room where they'd taken tea the previous autumn. It looked undisturbed and surprisingly ordered, considering she'd been taken to the hospital in a hurry. He noticed the windows were closed and pulling the net curtains aside, opened both of them wide to let in some fresh air. Looking around he saw the button-back chairs where they'd sat and the shiny grand piano.

One of the pieces of mahogany furniture was a bureau, which he thought would be the best place to start looking for relevant papers. He turned a small brass key in the lid and it opened on its creaking hinges. Inside there were many neatly-filed papers in wooden stalls, in what seemed to be alphabetical order. He looked under 'A' and found papers with the printed name of an *anwalt* embossed along the top and he could see the address was in Hamburg. He gathered up the papers and envelopes from inside the stalls and took them over to the table by the window where the light was better. He found what he guessed was Rosa's will in a foolscap envelope and although he didn't understand German he recognised his name written on the first page and repeated throughout the document. It didn't differ much from his father's will.

At that moment he was startled by a noise and he turned in his seat to find a woman of similar age to himself standing in the doorway, looking surprised.

'*Entschuldigen Sie bitte. Aber was ist das? Wem sind Sie?*'

He guessed he was being asked who he was. He got up and took several steps towards her but she promptly moved backwards away from him. Without thinking he started to speak in English:

'Excuse me. My name is Arnold Drive. I am Rosa's nephew ...' he stuttered.

'*Aber wer zum Teufel sind Sie! Ich habe Sie noch wie zuvor gesehen.*'

('But who the devil are you! I haven't seen you before.')

He held up the keys to the flat:

'I was given the keys at the hospital. I'm sorry if I scared you. I was beginning to sort through her things ...' he continued to explain.

'*Aber was machen Sie hier? Wo haben Sie diese Schlussel her?*'

(But what are you doing in here? Where did you get those keys from?')

He repeated his name and, again, how he had come to be inside the flat, but the woman became increasingly agitated and turned to run from the room along the corridor.

He could only assume she hadn't understood what he'd been saying. He feared the worst and thought the best thing he could do was to call Boris. She reappeared with a man, probably her husband, just as Boris answered. The man was dressed in green pyjamas and had presumably been aroused from his bed. He began to bark in guttural German at Arnold, who could only offer his Blackberry to the man, with the voice of Boris issuing from the tiny speaker, saying:

'*Allo ...? Allo ...? Ja ...? Arnold?*'

The man looked curiously at the phone, then accepted it from him and carefully raised it to his ear to listen. He could see the woman, armed with a brass poker and an umbrella, taking shelter behind her husband. Without thinking, he knelt down to pray in front of them. The husband angrily shouted down the phone at Boris, but a conversation finally began between them and Arnold could hear the man slowly calming down as he realised who Arnold was and why he'd suddenly appeared in Rosa's flat. His wife then grabbed the phone from him and started talking with Boris and she began to laugh:

'*Ja. Gute. All ist klar. Ja. Ja.*'

Her husband gently helped Arnold up from his knees and his wife passed the phone back to him smiling. He heard Boris's voice:

'Arnold? The woman is the neighbour I met when I came to check on your aunt. She thought you were a thief! Now she understands everything. It's all OK!'

Now the neighbour couldn't do enough to help him. She insisted on making him a pot of tea, whilst her husband scratched his head, bowed and excused himself to go back to bed with a yawn. Arnold recognised some of the same pumpernickel bread, chutney and cheeses arriving on a tray with the tea, and thanked the neighbour, who decided to leave him to drink his tea and continue with the paperwork.

He had no idea how long he'd been sitting there when he finished and sat back from the table. His second (or was it his third?) cup of tea had gone cold when he took a sip from it. He'd found various things apart from the lawyer's papers: a lease agreement for her apartment; what looked like authenticity documents concerning some of the furniture; and two small booklets which reminded him of saving account books from building societies, with small deposits in both. He went back to the bureau and in one of the drawers found the scrapbooks they'd sat and looked through together. There were also many old letters arranged in bundles, which he guessed related to different correspondents. He found the letter he'd written to Rosa before his accident and opened it up to read. He looked around the living room but couldn't see the music box anywhere. He was keen to hold it again and listen to its tune. It was the thing that had brought them together. He double-checked, looking behind all the furniture, but could see no sign of it. He thought perhaps she'd moved it from its place near the window. He went through to her bedroom and found it on a small table by the bed. He carefully picked it up and opened the lid, but the mechanism remained still. He re-closed it and tried to give the small key in its side a turn, but it didn't seem to want to move, so he stopped for fear of doing any damage. She'd probably been right when she'd told him it was almost worn Fout. He thought it may be possible to get it repaired somewhere in Bath when he got back home. He inspected the cupboards in her bedroom and, apart from her clothes, he found some jewellery in the drawer of a dressing table. There were several rings and earrings, and one striking black jade necklace, which he could imagine her wearing.

Suddenly feeling very weary, he decided to call an end to the day and solemnly took the tea tray back to the kitchen, where he washed up and dried the things and put them back in their places on the shelves. Gathering up the music box and the jade necklace, he put them in a bag with all the correspondence and the scrapbooks of photographs, and closed the windows. Within the walls and the bag was all that was left of his aunt's existence.

As he walked back to his hotel he noticed the passersby wrapped up in their lives, entirely ignorant of Rosa and the things she had experienced in her life. He wanted to stop them and show them the scrapbooks, and explain who the people were on the pages. He wondered how people managed to find the capacity to be joyful when faced with death. He'd conducted countless burials and been present at many wakes, but had never enjoyed delivering the funeral liturgy. His sense of loss was always too great for him to feel mortality as something positive. It was the one thing he'd never quite accepted, the concept that death was a renewal mechanism for life; that the departing soul was returning home to God. He realised now the immense void left by someone's death meant that he'd never been completely convinced of an afterlife. It was one of the central tenets of his faith, and yet, Arnold suddenly understood, it had never felt real to him.

When he reached the hotel steps he didn't turn to climb them but continued walking and wandered down to the edge of the lake. He found a bench and sat quietly to clear his head of the mustiness of the flat. Opening the bag, he took out the jade necklace and sat there feeling the pieces with his fingers, rather like an Arab playing with some memory beads. A pair of mandarin ducks chose that moment to walk in front of him, followed obediently by a line of small ducklings. They were barely more than a few weeks old. The parents took to the water and the babies did the same and they swam off in a troupe, soon becoming tiny dots on the surface. He was mindful of closing a chapter in Hamburg and had an over-powering desire to return to the Keep and immerse himself in his own life.

CHAPTER 41

It took Arnold several more days to tidy up Rosa's affairs. Boris was of immense help ferrying him around Hamburg, to and from the lawyer's office, where he signed various paperwork and had the will read out to him. He was able to arrange for her to be buried next to Uncle Red and the Borringers in Nienstedtener cemetery, and he ordered a headstone for her grave. He asked for an inscription and after much thought decided a quote from the music box song *Gedanken sind frei* would be appropriate, and go well with the inscription on his uncle's stone:

Und sperrt man mich ein im finsteren Kerker,
Meine Gedanken zerreißen die Schranken und Mauern
entzwei
And if I am thrown into the darkest dungeon,
My thoughts tear all the gates and walls apart.

It wasn't ready in time for the funeral, but Boris promised to make sure it was delivered and installed correctly after Arnold had left. Boris borrowed a black limousine from the cab company in which they drove to the cemetery in Elbechausee, and Rosa's neighbours, the Schonherrs, came with them to pay their last respects. Mrs. Schonherr was tearful as the coffin was laid to rest and cried into his shoulder as her husband looked on with his eyebrows raised. On their way back to the car he whispered in Arnold's ear:

'*Entschuldigen Sie meine frau. Sie ist uberreizt, die Arme.*'

('Excuse my wife. She's overwrought, poor dear.')

He assumed it was an apology for his wife's display of emotion, although it didn't bother him in the slightest. They were delighted when he suggested, through Boris' translation, that they accept the various pieces of furniture in Rosa's flat. They had no room for the grand piano, but Boris had a sister who played and was happy to accept it. The landlord of the flat was very understanding and ended Rosa's tenancy agreement, and all that was left was to arrange for a local charity to come and take away her clothing. And that was that. In less than a week he was checking out of the Garden Hotel and on his way to Hamburg airport in the back of Boris's taxi. They hugged each other tenderly outside the terminal and Arnold promised to come back to visit the grave when the headstone was in place. He wrote his address down and invited Boris to visit him in the coming summer, to which he replied:

'My dear friend, I would love to. I have never been to England. You never know, perhaps they will tidy up the Reeperbahn one day and I will open my own sex club in Bath. *Ja?*'

He really was incorrigible, thought Arnold. But with a heart of gold.

During the flight he found his thoughts occupied by the difference between Good and Evil. It wasn't as cut and dried as Arnold had always assumed. Was Boris an evil person? He didn't think so. And yet his mind was impure. He was an opportunist, capable of debauchery, fornication, and he'd admitted to all manner of sexual perversions, and yet his heart was in the right place. He'd proved that. The year before at St. Tobias's, Arnold wouldn't have spared the time to even consider if someone like Boris had a place next to God. But now he was convinced Boris was a good person, in spite of himself and all his faults. He looked forward to seeing him again in Bath and showing him around.

He was so glad he'd left the church. If he hadn't he wouldn't have experienced this ... this ... enlightenment. It was the only word he could find that adequately described what he felt. Yes, that was it! Enlightenment. He'd experienced so much recently, he felt he'd turned a corner and was starting to see things differently. It was as if he'd been observing life in only two dimensions previously and now he was noticing the depth of human frailty and complexity as well. That was the point, seeing all the different vagaries of a person, all at the same time – their faults, their virtues – and trying not to judge them. Perhaps even feeling love for them. He fell asleep with a smile on his face.

They touched down in Bristol in the late afternoon and he found a taxi to take him home. He was relieved to see the English country lanes again, and was glad he wasn't driving in the failing light and falling rain. The driver seemed to be going much too fast for his liking and he asked him to slow down as they emerged from the Chew Magna traffic and weaved their way up past Corston. He could see the lights of Bath emerging from the valley ahead through the wet windscreen. They skirted Bath and soon afterwards he was being set down in front of the Keep.

Arnold watched the taxi pull off and disappear around

the bend, then picked up his suitcase and climbed the wet steps up to the front door. There were lights on but no sound came from within. He knocked purposefully several times on the front door, calling out:

'Hello? Pete? Hello?'

He waited a while, knocked and called a few more times, but then thought it ludicrous he should be waiting outside his own front door, so he lifted the unsecured latch and pushed open the door. Stepping inside, he was aware of a pungent smell attacking his nostrils, of what he thought to be animal flesh. He felt sick and began to breathe through his mouth to avoid it. He looked around, hardly recognising the interior as the one he'd left all those months before. He switched on the main light to get a better look and realised why there was such a stench. All over the walls were animal pelts and what looked like squirrel tails, on strings and in various stages of drying, or decomposition, he wasn't sure which word described them more accurately. There were literally hundreds, giving the impression the walls were made up of them. He carefully moved around the space not quite believing what he was seeing. In addition, there was something else that felt different. He worked it out; the table where he ate was in a different position. It had been moved up onto the platform where his bed had been, and his bed was now on the floor, in a far corner away from the door. Why, the whole place had been rearranged! This upset him as much as the animal pelts on the walls. He couldn't understand why Pete had done this. It was as if he'd taken over the Keep as his own home. Hearing a noise he turned to see Pete standing inside the front door.

'Arnold. Bloody 'eck! What are you doing here? Why

aren't you in the hospital? Well, what a surprise. So they've finally let you out.'

All Arnold could do was voice his own questions, rather than answer any of Pete's.

'But, Pete, what's been happening here? Why have you moved all the furniture around? And what are all these dead animals, these skins, doing over the walls?'

They both stood staring at one another, taking in what they saw. Arnold, at the transformation his beloved iron church had undergone, and Pete surprised to see Arnold apparently recovered, and out of hospital.

Pete was dressed in a coat of pelts, a Davy Crockett hat, and was carrying Trevor's air rifle slung over his shoulder. He propped it up against the wall and walked across the room to where Arnold was standing. He seemed much bigger to Arnold, than when he'd last seen him.

'Well, then, Arnold. You better give me a hug. Why didn't you let me know you were coming home?'

As he was being bear hugged, Arnold was aware of the full extent of the odour coming from the coat Pete was wearing. He found it overpowering and had to hang on to Pete, for fear of collapsing in the fumes. Pete noticed his sudden weight in his arms and misinterpreted it:

'There, there, Arnold. You must sit down. I'm surprised they've allowed you out. You don't seem well at all. Let me get you a chair.'

Effortlessly holding Arnold up with one hand, he swivelled round and picked up a chair with his other, and placed it firmly behind Arnold's knees for him to sit in. He'd obviously gained strength since Arnold had last seen him, which was at least two months earlier. He hadn't seen Pete at all during the last month or so he'd been in hospital. He sat back in the chair and looked around him. Pete stood looking him up and down, with his hands on his hips.

'Pete, I don't know how to say this ...' he started to say. 'But I'm distressed to see what you've done. It all looks so ... so different. And these pelts, they ...'

But before he could continue, Pete interrupted him, saying:

'Arnold, you wouldn't believe those pesky rabbits. There's an army of them right outside the door. I've been trying to keep the numbers down. But they just multiply, as soon as your back's turned. They've got into the vegetable patch. Then there's the grey squirrels. They're almost as bad. I borrowed Trevor's gun. I've had to restock with ammo twice. Are you hungry?'

Without waiting for an answer, he turned and went to the kitchen area, still talking:

'Got some lovely rabbit stew here. That'll set you up nice. Let me get you some. It just needs warming up.'

Arnold tried to pick up the thread of what he was trying to say:

'The point is, Pete, I'm finding all this quite unacceptable. And as far as the furniture goes ...'

Pete interrupted him again:

'Oh, yes, I knew you'd prefer it like this. It feels much better to be eating higher up above the ground. More formal. The bed being up there was claustrophobic. And dark in the mornings, as well. Where it is now, the light comes through the windows from the east in the mornings and wakes me up.'

He fell silent at the stove preparing a bowl of stew for

Arnold. He brought it over on a tray with some roughly cut bread and a spoon:

'There you go, Arnold. You get that down you. You'll feel much better after. You'll see.'

Arnold did as he was told. Meanwhile Pete got another chair and sat down beside him, watching him eat with a broad smile.

Arnold was surprised how good rabbit meat tasted. He couldn't recall ever having tried it before and when he'd finished he put the bowl down on the tray and took a long look at Pete. He thought he looked ridiculous in his fur hat and coat, but felt it wasn't the moment to say anything.

'It's good to see you, Arnold. I wasn't expecting you back until late in the summer. Well, I'll just have to squash up a bit in here, so there's room for you.'

Arnold didn't like the sound of this. He was never expecting to 'share' his home with Pete. It just wasn't big enough. So he said:

'But, Pete, there just isn't enough room in here for the two...'

'No, Arnold, I insist. I'll make up a bed for you next to mine. All snug like. No need for you to go anywhere else.'

Arnold was becoming increasingly worried. It was clear Pete had spent far too long by himself and had lost grip on reality. He decided to try to reason with him:

'Now, Pete, I really am pleased to see you. And the place is looking very smart. But I did prefer where the bed was before, and the table ...'

Pete stood up and took the tray from Arnold's lap, and strode back to the kitchen, deliberately making lots of noise while Arnold carried on speaking. Arnold raised his voice to hear himself above the racket:

'And the table too. I'm sorry, but it's going to have to be... PUT BACK THE WAY IT WAS. AND THERE REALLY ISN'T ENOUGH SPACE IN HERE FOR THE TWO OF US TO SLEEP. SO YOU'LL HAVE TO GO BACK TO SLEEPING IN YOUR TENT AGAIN!'

The racket in the kitchen suddenly stopped as Arnold was speaking:

'LIKE BE ... fore.'

There was a silence from the sink, and Arnold began to feel scared.

CHAPTER 42

He could see Pete's silhouette by the sink, like a big, brooding bear. He didn't know what to say, so thought it best to remain quiet. After several minutes, Pete emerged from the darkness with another bowl of stew and slowly stepped up to the table to sit and eat it. The platform stood a good four feet above the ground and Arnold was put in mind of a tribal chief as he studied Pete's large pelted shape hunched over the table. He felt belittled. No words were spoken between them and all Arnold could hear was the noise of Pete's spoon hitting the side of the china bowl as he slowly ate. When he'd finished he sat back and pushed his chair away from the table with his feet and Arnold saw him rolling a cigarette. This came as a surprise and he said:

'I didn't know you smoked.'

'There's a lot of things you don't know about me, Arnold. I been doing a lot of thinking while you been lying in that hospital bed.'

He sat back and lit his cigarette.

'I found out all sorts of things. What's been going on. All around us. Things we have no idea are going on. Controlling us. Keeping everyone in line.'

The more Arnold heard, the more he could see Pete had disengaged from the world.

'Modern life, it's a total distraction. Television. The internet. They're using it to control us. Most people don't get it. But I do. There's so much lying going on. Keep everyone busy, wrapped up in details. Little things please little minds.'

Arnold started to notice the smoke from Pete's cigarette. It smelt sweeter and more aromatic than usual tobacco smoke and he started to watch it drift slowly around the room.

'They got us all dependent on oil. For no reason. There've been plenty of new inventions, alternatives, but they've all been bought up by the oil companies. Kept secret. Locked away. And Global Warming. There's another lie. Anyone with any intelligence can see the climate's being changed by the activity on the surface of the sun. Always has been. You've just got to go back in history to see that. They're called solar flares. The Sahara desert used to be a jungle, on Ancient Earth.

'If they really want to sort out a supply of energy, all they've got to do is look at the ocean. The planet's two thirds covered with water, constantly moving, and nobody's twigged it. It's a natural dynamo, the ocean is. Dead easy to build generators all along the coast, and use the tides to get power. YOU CAN'T TELL ME, WITH ALL THE BRAINS WE GOT, ALL THE EINSTEINS IN THE WORLD, NOBODY'S THOUGHT OF THAT? IT BEGGARS BELIEF!'

Pete was shouting and Arnold was afraid he might get violent. He kept quiet, and after a pause was relieved to hear him continue in a calmer tone:

'So, it's all a con. Keep the little people in line. Like me and you. But I know what's going on. We may think we've come on in the world, but we're all bloody stupid. Nothing's changed within the human brain since we were living in caves. Darwin's evolution? It's rubbish. Anyone with half a brain can see there's no connection between us, and animals. We're just an experiment. Put here by alien intelligence. They've been supervising us, the whole time. Seeing what we get up to, with our superior minds. Our superior intelligence. You want to see some intelligence? All you've got to do is watch them squirrels for a while. Smartest creatures you'll ever see. Aye, they are that. Even smarter than your mate, Clever Trevor ... YOU'LL ALL REALISE WHAT'S GOING ON, WHEN IT'S TOO LATE!'

It was as if he were talking not just to Arnold, but to a large group of people, or the world in general. The room fell so silent Arnold could hear the sound of Pete's chair, which creaked as he rocked slowly backwards and forwards, on its back legs, as he puffed his cigarette. The smoke curled lazily around the room, hanging heavily in the still air and Arnold started to see it forming shapes, like clouds. Pete stood up and said:

'Let's have a cuppa tea, shall we?'

He went back to the kitchen into the shadows again. Arnold was exhausted and remembered he'd only just arrived back from Hamburg. He wondered what the time was and took his Blackberry out from his pocket, but all he saw was a blank screen. The battery was flat. He guessed it to be somewhere between eight and nine o'clock. He was drained of energy and couldn't figure out what he was going to do. He felt his eyelids droop and heard Pete rummaging around, gathering up blankets and what looked like a blow-up mattress, presumably meant for him. But he didn't care any more and without any argument collapsed on it when Pete had it inflated, allowing himself to be covered up. It was the last thing he was aware of before falling into a deep sleep.

When he awoke the next day he was alone and noticed the air rifle had gone from next to the front door. He went to check but it was locked, and remembered Trevor still had his set of keys. So for the time being he was to be a prisoner in his own house. He found some ground coffee in the kitchen and made some toast, but the only trace of eggs was an empty tray he recognised from the time of his accident. He made do dipping his buttered toast into the coffee as he couldn't find any marmalade or jam. He found some mail addressed to him by the front door but had no idea when it had been delivered. There was a letter from the bank, and one from the hospital, asking him to attend an appointment in two months' time for a check-up. Just then, he heard a key turn in the lock and Pete opened the door, with several rabbit carcasses hanging from a string around his neck.

'Morning, Arnold. Did you sleep OK?'

He seemed placid enough so Arnold saw no reason not to be civil and replied:

'Yes. Thank you. Been busy today?'

'Aye. Got a few more of the buggers this morning. No squirrels about. It's more fun trying to nail them. More of a moving target, y' see. Any of that coffee left? I could smell it coming up the steps.'

Arnold heated up the coffee and poured him a cup. Pete said:

'It's going to take some getting used to. Having you back here.'

Arnold didn't know how to interpret this and asked:

'I wondered, can I have a shower?'

'Of course you can. Be my guest.'

Showering made him feel better and he found some clean clothes. They were all where he expected them to be, folded away in their proper drawers. He recalled he'd done a clothes wash just before the accident. He found Pete at the raised dining table, cleaning the fresh pelts from the morning's cull. The strong smell of animal flesh was renewed in the air and Arnold desperately wanted to get out, into some clean air, so he asked:

'May I see the vegetable patch? I've been looking forward to seeing it.'

Pete looked up from his work.

'Really? OK, then. Just a moment.'

He stopped his work and washed his hands before leading Arnold out through the front door and round the left perimeter of the Keep, to where he'd been planting.

Arnold had to admit it was impressive. There were ordered rows of perpetual spinach, carrots, lettuces, radishes, plus canes supporting runner beans and tomatoes, even a bed of potatoes. There was a row of plants he didn't recognise, with large, thin, star-shaped leaves. And no sign of any slugs or weeds anywhere. It put him in mind of Stan's plot, but on a smaller scale.

'But, Pete, I had no idea it would be so ... thriving!'

'It's totally organic. I wanted it to be a success. There were a bit of a crisis when the rabbits got in. In March. But I soon put paid to their little game. At night is when they try it on. Then there are the squirrels. Partial to young radishes, they are.'

Pete allowed him to inspect the plants but seemed keen to stay close, as if he feared Arnold may bolt suddenly and make a dash for freedom. But Arnold had no such thought in his mind. He'd only just got home and despite Pete's strange behaviour he was still very much enjoying it.

Later that day, when Pete was busying himself outside, Arnold searched through his suitcase and his pockets and realised he'd left his phone charger in Hamburg. This rein-forced his predicament. He was virtually cut off from the outside world and totally dependent on Pete for the time being. He would have to deal with his foibles and strange beliefs as best he could, and wait for an opportunity to get away. He desperately hoped Trevor or Hermione would try to get in touch with him, but remembered Hermione was in Los Angeles with Tony, and Trevor was in the Highlands of Scotland fishing. They would think he was still in Hamburg tending his sick aunt and would never suspect he could be back home under 'house arrest'. He began to panic.

However wrapped up Pete was in his conspiracy theories and distrust of the world, Arnold discovered his day-to-day existence was remarkably ordered. He would be up and out very early hunting rabbits and squirrels until about nine. Meanwhile, the postman's visits were erratic. His approach to the front door was silent so Arnold never seemed to be at the door exactly when he arrived. He would listlessly wan-der round the Keep waiting for Pete to return in the hope of some relief from the small space and the smell. Pete would spend the morning gutting and preparing the meat and pelts from his hunting trips, which meant the place reeked like a butcher's shop most of the time. Arnold spent the time breathing through his mouth to avoid being violently sick.

Occasionally Pete would roll one of his cigarettes and the sweet smoke would give some respite from the awful stench. Thankfully, the afternoon was spent in the vegetable patch and Arnold began to look forward to it. He found the work therapeutic and they worked side by side until the sun was low in the sky. He began to anticipate the progress a crop would make overnight and was surprised at how fast some of the plants were growing. It was a constant battle against the wild vegetation surrounding the plot. Cow parsley, ground elder and blackberry runners were the boldest intruders, together with the constant arrival of dandelions. They would spend the evenings having rabbit stew and Arnold would be forced to listen to Pete's views on the world. It was clear he'd done a vast amount of reading when Arnold had been in hospital and had an amazing ability to remember snippets of information that served to reinforce his bizarre theories. Once Pete had smoked a cigarette after dinner Arnold would start to feel incredibly tired and fall asleep.

Pete was convinced man hadn't been to the moon at all and the whole thing had been staged in a film studio somewhere in America. Arnold had difficulty trying to think of a good reason why that should be, but Pete had the answer:

'It's all to do with the armaments industry. The business of making weapons. All that research into space exploration, the outcome of it all is amazing technology that they can use for weaponry. Night vision, for one thing. Basically, space research is a legitimate way to find better ways to kill people. It's as simple as that. So let the population think we got to the moon, and the funds'll keep flowing. IT'S A GLOBAL BUSINESS, WEAPONS!'

He was also convinced man's destiny was to make a mess of the world, and civilisation was a vague attempt to keep a lid on things:

'Man behaves like an animal most of the time. We're all just a step away from complete bestiality. And I don't mean no shagging goats neither. Just look at what happened in the Second World War. Those Nazis, they took some beating, in that respect. And the Japanese. Mind you, the Serbs weren't that far behind, and THAT WERE JUST A FEW YEAR AGO!'

Arnold spoke about his aunt and her terrible experiences in the concentration camp. Pete listened attentively and when Arnold described how he and Rosa had got to know about one another through the music box Pete was keen to see it. Arnold explained that it needed to be repaired. Pete held it in his hands and admired the fine marquetry. He opened the lid and Arnold was surprised to hear it start playing its tune again:

Die Gedanken sind frei, wer kann sie erraten,
sie fliegen vorbei wie nachtliche Schatten,
Kein Mensch kann sie wissen, kein Jäger erschießen
mit Pulver und Blei, Die Gedanken sind frei!

Und sperrt man mich ein im finsteren Kerker,
das alles ...

It stopped abruptly. Pete carefully handed it back to him.

'How very odd,' Arnold said, 'it's started working again.'

'Not odd really,' Pete said, matter-of-factly. 'If you think of the changes that've gone on in its circumstances. All the things it's been a witness to over the years. And you just took it up in an aeroplane. There's different pressures going on up there. Probably unblocked its energy patterns. You've owned it twice now and it's got confused. Probably thinks you're going to get rid of it again.'

CHAPTER 43

Arnold thought it only right he should tell Pete about meeting his father during his hospital coma. He got the chance when they were working in the vegetable patch one afternoon. They'd been talking about their families and Pete presented his theory that children spend their lives trying to satisfy their parents' expectations of them. Arnold could see some truth in this, but he could see no way out of the dilemma. He decided to tell him about his dream:

'I had a very strange experience when I was in hospital, before I woke up. I dreamt I was under the sea. I met several people there that were already dead. Like my mother and father. But also your father.'

'That's right weird,' Pete answered. 'I wonder if when it happened – I mean, the dream – he were already dead? But I suppose there's no way of telling that.'

'Do you have any pictures of him?' Arnold asked. 'I'd like to see what he looked like.'

'I've got a couple with me somewhere. I'll go and find them,' Pete said, getting up.

His father turned out to be larger than when he'd appeared to Arnold, but as Pete pointed out he'd lost weight towards the end, and was a shadow of his former self. There were two pictures, one with his wife, standing proudly with Pete as a baby in her arms. The other was from much later, a faded colour print of him standing in his fishmonger's apron next to a table covered with fish. He looked happy and was smiling in both of them. Arnold mentioned this to Pete.

'Aye,' he replied. 'They were happy days in Hull, back then, before me mother went and died. He hadn't taken to the drink then. They was both workin' while I were a nipper. There were always a plate of food on the table when I got home from school. Funny how people are happiest when they're busy with the simple things, just getting on with it. You know, the basics.'

Arnold recognised a universal truth and it made him remember something:

'I got home from school once and found it strange my father was in the house. I wondered why he wasn't at work and found out later he was in between jobs, but I had no way of grasping that, being so young. When you're a child you've no idea of the effort involved in providing those basic things you take for granted.'

'Did you get on with your dad?' Pete asked.

'Not really,' Arnold admitted, 'I never had the faintest idea what was going through his mind. He was inscrutable. I found my mother more approachable.'

Pete thought for a second:

'Inscrutable. That's a good word. My dad were like that. Didn't give anything away. Until the end. When he was in pain.'

'I think they're all the same,' Arnold added. 'They don't think it's the done thing to show any feelings but strength. I suppose I'd feel the same. Shall I make us a cup of tea?'

'That's a grand idea, Arnold,' Pete sat back in the earth and started to roll one of his cigarettes.

Arnold put down his trowel and got up. He dusted off the dirt from the knees of his trousers and walked round to the front door. As he was filling the kettle and putting the teabags into the cups it struck him he was out of sight of Pete, and the front door was open. Without engineering it, here was an opportunity for him to get away. He thought about what he would do, where he would go, whilst the kettle boiled. He absent-mindedly poured the boiling water into the two cups and replaced the kettle on its stand, then quietly went through the front door and turned right, away from the vegetable patch. He got to the back of the building and scrambled up the steep slope where there were hazel trees growing, not really knowing in which direction he was heading. He pulled himself up the bank grabbing at any branches that came within reach, trying to make as little noise as possible.

In a few minutes, he was clear of the plot and walking along the edge of the field above, where sheep were grazing. At first he found it difficult moving over the uneven ground and his knees hurt – he hadn't walked any distance since he'd got back from Hamburg. The sheep made noises as he walked through them and they hurriedly cleared a path for him, clumsily bumping into one another. He headed up the field towards a copse at the summit and saw the sun wasn't far from the horizon. They'd been working in the vegetable patch for several hours and he decided to find somewhere he could lie low and hide overnight, then at first light he could make a move. He found a sheltered hollow at the base of an old oak tree inside the copse and managed to get comfortable. He sat and listened to the moving foliage as the light wind pushed and pulled the branches above his head. Minutes passed, which became an hour, and the light began to fade. He felt the temperature slowly drop and pulled some loose branches over himself to keep warm. Luckily he had on his thick tweed jacket, so he felt confident he could survive the night without freezing. Feeling tired, he closed his eyes and began to hear noises around him. Several birds hopped by and a lone owl above his head announced itself with an extremely close cry that made him start.

There had been no rain the previous couple of weeks, so the ground was thankfully dry and he soon dozed off. When he woke up it was pitch black and very cold. He heard some noise close by, as of a large animal carefully treading through the undergrowth, and he wondered if one of the sheep had wandered into the copse by accident. He also realised it could be Pete. He concentrated on keeping still, but the cold was making his teeth chatter, and he grimaced to keep his lips sealed and hide the noise. Suddenly, he was blinded by a light shining in his face and he heard a voice saying:

'There you are, Arnold, you bloody bugger. I had a feeling you wouldn't go far tonight.'

It was Pete, of course, and he could hear irritation in his voice. He felt himself being grabbed by both arms and lifted up off the ground as if he were just a light rag doll. Pete pulled him along, saying:

'Now, what on earth did you want to go and try that for? I thought we were getting on. I know these bits like the back of me hand, what with the rabbits and all. You left a right mess on that bank round the back. Anyone could see what direction you took off in. I'M REALLY DISAPPOINTED IN YOU! I REALLY AM.'

Pete shook Arnold roughly as he hung limply in the air shivering from the cold. He had no idea in which direction they were heading, or what Pete would do to him. He was fearful of the man's strength, which was much greater than his own. They went through some bushes, down an incline and suddenly they were back at the vegetable patch. Once inside the Keep, Arnold's body warmed up and his teeth stopped chattering. He sat still where Pete had put him down, scared to move, and accepted a bowl of rabbit stew, which he ate ravenously.

'What time is it?' he dared ask, but got no answer, as Pete was rummaging around in the kitchen.

After a while, he reappeared and clamped what looked like a bracelet on Arnold's left wrist. It was made of rusted metal and was attached to a long chain, which he threw over one of the main iron joists, running across the ceiling. He secured it with a padlock to itself, and said grimly:

'You've left me with no alternative.'

He came over to inspect the manacle, saying:

'There you go, that'll stop you running off again. I found it when I was digging in the plot, outside. I thought it may come in handy one day.'

Arnold felt wretched. There was just enough slack on the chain for him to lie down on the blow-up mattress, so he curled up into a ball and fell asleep.

In the morning, he was woken up by the sound of two letters dropping on the mat by the front door. He crawled over to where they were and managed to reach them with his free right hand. One was from the local council with a clear plastic window and was a breakdown of his council tax payment due for the coming year. The other had a Hamburg postmark and he didn't recognise the handwriting. It was from Boris.

My dear Arnold!

I hope this letter finds you well and in good spirits. Your aunt's headstone is now in place and looks very grand. I enclose a photo for you. I have decided to visit you in Bath soon. Business is quiet in the summer so it's a good time to come. I think I told you, it will be my first trip to the UK.

I am looking forward to it.

I will fly to London and have a look around, then I will telephone you.

Your friend,

Boris

He realised he missed Boris. In fact, he missed Trevor. And Hermione. He couldn't help but feel depressed. This isolated life with Pete was getting to him, and he could see no way out. It must be the way monks used to live before the Reformation, when they grew vegetables, embellished texts and spent the rest of their time praying or in silent contemplation. But that was then. Arnold had travelled a bit now, and he could no longer imagine life rooted in one place. He'd got used to some of the luxuries life had to offer. He could see the slope mankind was destined to fall down, getting used to those luxuries and ending up restless and dissatisfied. Did that mean the loss of independence and the power of independent thought? It was the conundrum of modern life. Arnold contemplated his situation as a prisoner, deprived of every liberty and freedom, and it began to sink in.

He was put on the chain when he was alone and at night. There wasn't enough of it to allow him to move around the room and make his breakfast, so he had to wait until Pete returned from his early morning hunting. When alone, he frequently took out the photo of Rosa's headstone Boris had sent. It started to acquire cracks and bent corners, being taken in and out of the envelope so many times. As the days went by and turned into weeks, he calculated he'd been back from Hamburg well over a month. He hadn't mentioned Boris to Pete at all, and saw no reason to reveal any information about him. He was angry with himself for leaving his phone charger in Hamburg and the significance of not having it grew, now he knew Boris was on his way over. Boris would try calling his Blackberry and, getting no reply, would run out of time before catching his flight back to Hamburg.

After showering one morning an idea occurred to him, so he politely asked Pete:

'I wonder, can I sleep in your tent? Outside? I really would appreciate a change of air. It's warm enough now.'

Pete stopped working on his pelts and thought for a while. He slowly got up from his chair and stepped down from the platform to approach Arnold. He crouched down and placed his face very close to Arnold's and stared into his eyes suspiciously:

'Now, Arnold. This isn't some new plan of yours to try to get away, is it?'

'No, it's not, Pete. I just can't get used to this smell. Of the pelts. Now it's getting warmer they seem to whiff a lot more, especially at night. I'm finding it hard to get to sleep.'

'Hmm,' Pete stood up, walked back to the table, prevaricated for a while and looked down at the pelts he was working on, obviously thinking it over. Arnold waited in silence for an answer.

'Well … I'll have to find a way to secure you outside, overnight. I can't have you running away again. You'll get me locked up.' On saying this Pete turned and stared at him.

'No, no. I totally understand that,' Arnold agreed.

'Let me go and have a look outside.'

He went outside and Arnold heard the key turn in the front door, then heard him at the back of the building. After about ten minutes Pete came back, saying:

'All right. You can go outside. I can put me tent up at the back there for you and fix your chain up. It will have to come through the letter box, mind, so you won't be able to close the tent entrance all the way. It might mean you get some of those rabbits visiting you while you're asleep. Nibbling at your ear holes. As long as you don't mind that?'

'No. I won't mind that, I'm sure. Thanks, Pete,' he agreed. Pete was quick to continue:

'But come the morning it will have to come down and you'll come back inside. I don't want Clever Trevor coming back again, snooping around.'

Arnold was surprised to hear this, and couldn't stop himself asking:

'What do you mean, coming back again? Has he been?'

'Aye, it were a few weeks ago. Very early. With your girlfriend, he was. I was just coming back meself. Caught them down by the road, luckily, just before they came up the steps.'

'What did you tell them?' Arnold was desperate to know.

'I told 'em you was still away. That I didn't even know you'd left the hospital. We don't want them muscling in up 'ere. They'd want to lock me away, too. It's nice the way it is. Just you and me, Arnold. WE DON'T NEED ANYONE ELSE. They're the dangerous lot.'

This news further demoralised Arnold. So they were back. He realised there was only one other person who knew where he was. The taxi driver who'd brought him from Bristol airport that first night.

Knowing Trevor and Hermione were close by depressed him terribly, more so, it seemed, than if they'd been far away. So he concentrated instead on the thought of sleeping outside for the first time, and it brightened him up. After working on the vegetables that afternoon, Pete put up his tent. They ate supper in silence and Arnold was led out on the chain. He'd never slept in a tent before but it meant he could sleep alone. It was something he'd missed. Pete snored heavily and once he'd been woken up Arnold found it hard to get back to sleep. He had a small torch he could use and once settled under the covers he began to feel a bit better. It felt luxurious being alone at night for once, and comfortable too, and he thought how valuable simple things can turn out to be. He tested the torch but after a few minutes decided he would prefer to lie in the dark instead and listen to the sounds of the night around him.

CHAPTER 44

As the days passed, Arnold's life became more intertwined with Pete's. They got on well enough. Arnold found it difficult to admonish Pete for the way he was treating him, but he was constantly wary and afraid for his safety. Pete's sudden outbursts of temper had shown Arnold how strong he'd become and he was fearful of what this strength might be used for. He'd never spent time around someone like this before and it was mentally draining. He put Pete's behaviour down to some condition he had no control over. He plainly wasn't aware of the reality of what was going on.

Arnold did enjoy their afternoons in the vegetable patch though. It was always stimulating and yielded discussions about far-reaching subjects, some of which Arnold had knowledge of, and others that were new to him. It seemed to be the one time Pete was at ease. Although he was a good listener, Arnold preferred when they talked about something he was familiar with, so he could make a contribution. They discussed religion regularly. Pete was adamant it had been brought into existence by necessity. He was convinced man had been placed on earth by some alien intelligence, and religion was man's way of reconciling this:

'Stands to reason, Arnold. The massive leap from animals

to humans is too big to be explained just by science, and that clever bloke Darwin. There's too many missing links. The idea we could be a scientific experiment, guinea pigs if you like, for something more intelligent than us? Well, it's unacceptable, to our brains. So we made up this "pseudo-explanation", called it RELIGION, and everyone's accepted it. You got to admit the theory there's some other intelligent force out there, is just as plausible as most religions' assumption that there's some bloke who looks like us, with ultimate wisdom, who we'll all join in some other dimension one day, if we behave ourselves while we're down here. Bloody ridiculous. And we'll all live happily ever after, Amen.'

'Look in the Old Testament. There's loads of references to "fire chariots in the sky" and "seraphims" and the like. What are they supposed to be, then? Down in South America, there's ancient drawings showing men in what look like spacesuits, crouched down in spaceships. We've got such a conceited view of ourselves. Well, to admit there's some other form of life, more intelligent than us? It's just not on, is it? For thousands of years we been telling ourselves we know what's what, and what's best, and we own the planet, and such like, fuelling our egos. Beating our chests like bloody cavemen. Saying what a superior form of life we are. To be told we're insignificant, just an experiment, and not "IN CONTROL". That's the main point. CONTROL. A species fooling itself it's tamed the elements, the planet, even space. Whereas, in fact, we know BUGGER ALL!'

When Arnold thought about it, he could see there wasn't much difference between the two views. The idea of God existing was just a bit more romantic. What if man, using his imagination and his aptitude for embellishment, had transformed Pete's spacemen into celestial beings, with the ultimate purpose of doing good? It would make it more palatable to the masses. It explained why man strived to reach oneness with his maker, via acts of selfless generosity. He pointed this out to Pete, who was quick to jump in:

'That's all well and good. But what's happened is, it's been hijacked by the opportunists. Man's avarice and greed have come into play. Some people used the basic idea for their own gain, and built palaces for themselves. You've got to admit it's been going on since religion were invented. Someone sees an opportunity to exploit and principles go out the bloody window. What's this new idea called, Religion? 'Ere, we can make money out of that. And do you know what, Arnold? RELIGION is TAX FREE!'

Arnold didn't understand this. Pete explained:

'They're all registered as flippin' CHARITIES. It's the same all over the world. Now you can't tell me that's not a con!'

Arnold couldn't believe people were capable of such subterfuge in the name of God. The Diocese, who'd employed him at St. Tobias's, was registered as a charity, and of course they owned valuable assets, like the land their churches were built on. Pete had followed his train of thought:

'Didn't they close your office down? When turnover was poor? Didn't they sell off the church and the land it was on to a developer? And you got pensioned off. Sounds just like a business to me.'

Arnold was shocked at how cynical Pete was and pointed out:

'You don't seem to be recognising any of the good work the Church does.'

'Granted,' Pete conceded, 'there are individuals who serve the community. Like you. And hats off to you, and people like you. But that's not my point. It's all camouflage, getting in the way of the truth. Religion's a business. Always has been. Making money out of people's fear of the unknown. I was brought up a "God fearing" person. Now what's all that about, then? Why the FUCK should I be "FEARFUL OF GOD"? Shouldn't "LOVE" – rather than "FEAR" – be the message? OR HAVE I GOT IT WRONG? EXCUSE ME. I DON'T LIKE BEING THREATENED. NOT EVEN BY BLOODY GOD!'

Pete stabbed a tomato with his trowel and made Arnold jump. They worked on in silence for a while and Arnold pulled out a dandelion that had managed to hide between two spinach plants.

He had to admit that perhaps Pete had a point. It had struck him before how, strangely, sometimes the fear of God was the reasoning behind behaving correctly and morally. Pete collected himself and continued:

'It's the way society instils decency within the population. By waving a stick at them. And why do they do it? Because it's always worked. The threat of going to prison keeps crime down. Just look at America. In New York and California you're given three chances, "Three strikes and you're out". It scares people and it's cleaned up crime. These strawberries look ready to eat. Shall we have them for supper tonight?'

Arnold would lie in bed in the tent thinking over what they'd discussed earlier. A lot of what Pete believed made sense, and this fact depressed him even more. All the years he'd been in Corsham he had never questioned or analysed his faith. He'd bathed himself in it and been satisfied offering help and guidance whenever he could. He saw how simple life had been then, and how much more complicated life was outside, in the harsh reality beyond the stained glass windows.

At that moment he heard some noise at the tent entrance and switched on the torch. He could see the zipper was being slowly opened, to reveal Boris standing with a finger up to his lips in the darkness. He came in and carefully squatted down beside him, whispering:

'Arnold. I've found you! Thank God. Are you all right?'

Arnold was dumbstruck. He nodded and held up his right hand, bearing the rusty metal bracelet.

Boris inspected it and the chain looping down above them from outside the tent:

'Hmm. I'll have to come back with some sort of tool to break this.'

'What are you doing here? I mean, I'm so pleased to see you,' Arnold spluttered, trying to keep his voice down.

'I came down yesterday by car from London. I kept on trying your phone, but it did not respond. Didn't you get my letter?'

'Yes. But I left my phone charger at the hotel in Hamburg, so it's not been working ...'

Boris interrupted him to continue:

'It took me a long time to find this place. You are really out in the wilds here. It was very late and dark when I found it so I came back this morning. I knocked at the door to ask for you. A strange dressed man came to the door and said you'd moved away, and he didn't know how to get in touch with you. This, I thought, was very strange.'

Arnold couldn't understand why he didn't know Boris had called:

'What time did you come by today?'

'At 8.45 this morning.'

'That's when I was taking a shower,' he realised. Boris carried on:

'So I went away, but kept an eye on the place, from a distance. Then I saw you come out with that man ... Who is he? And why is he keeping you locked up?'

Arnold found himself stuck for words and couldn't find a simple explanation, so he just said:

'That's Pete.'

'Anyway,' Boris said, 'I have to get you out of this pickle. I will come back tomorrow, in the night. I will bring some bolt cutters with me for the chain. Goodnight. See you tomorrow.'

Arnold found it hard to get to sleep after Boris left and in the morning had difficulty not thinking he'd dreamt the whole episode. After all, there was no evidence of Boris's visit. He'd even re-zipped the tent as far as he could, so as not to arouse Pete's suspicions. The whole of the next day Arnold found it difficult. He didn't want to give Pete any idea of what was going on. He assumed Pete hadn't realised who Boris was when he'd called, as Arnold had taken care never to mention him. All day long, the minutes dragged by and he hoped Pete didn't notice his agitation.

'Are you sure you want to keep sleeping outside?' Pete asked him. 'There's plenty of room here inside with me.'

'Thank you for the offer, Pete, but I want to stay outside in the tent.'

'Had any night visitors? The Holy Ghost?' Pete joked. 'Or

creepy crawlies? This time of the summer, that's when you get 'em.'

Arnold made to laugh nervously at this, saying:

'No. None yet. Fingers crossed.'

After supper he lay awake in the tent waiting for Boris, fearful of making any sound that may attract Pete's attention, just a few feet away from him inside. There was no way he could fall asleep so he watched the clear dark sky through the gap left by the slightly open zipper, where the chain came through. As the sky got blacker, he spotted a few stars coming out. He found it remarkable they were there the whole time, throughout the day, shielded from view by the brightness of the sun. He thought it was rather like his belief in God. He had a feeling it was always there but sometimes it was obscured by the intensity of what was going on.

He hadn't undressed or taken his shoes off, in the hope that when Boris arrived he could be cut free and they'd be able to slip away quickly. The minutes passed and he was beginning to wonder if it had, after all, been a figment of his imagination playing tricks on him the night before. The minutes stretched to hours and he wrapped himself up in his sleeping bag, as the night was growing cold. He dozed off to sleep thinking about his cottage in Corsham, somewhere he hadn't thought about for a long time. He'd enjoyed living there even though he'd spent all that time worrying about stepping on the shadows of the window frames ...

'Arnold? ... Arnold?'

It was Boris in the tent entrance again. He looked rather like a Coptic priest, Arnold thought, with his face framed by the edges of the tent zipper. Scrambling in he sat down, switched on his torch and had what looked like a pair of bolt cutters with him.

'Everything all right?' he whispered, and Arnold nodded back.

'Now, let me see what I can do with these.'

Arnold held the torch so that Boris could use both his hands to position the chain between the blades of the cutters.

'Here we go,' he said quietly, and with an emphatic movement of both his arms the blades sliced neatly through the chain, the two ends of which were suddenly in free fall. The shorter length, a few links long, was attached to Arnold's bracelet, and fell with a clink onto his sleeping bag. The longer one whipped back and hit the side of the tent. Being heavier and travelling further it made a loud thud which alarmed Boris:

'Come on. We must leave now.'

He grabbed Arnold's hand and they climbed out of the tent, fearful they had woken Pete up. Boris led the way as they stumbled downhill away from the Keep towards the road. They reached the hard tarmac and ran to where a BMW was parked up on a verge. Suddenly in the stillness of the night they heard a single bell chiming behind them. Arnold couldn't understand where it could be coming from. He thought it sounded familiar, like one of the bells of St. Tobias's, alone, without its companion. They jumped in the car and as the engine roared into life it obscured the sound of the bell, and they sped off into the darkness of the country lanes.

CHAPTER 45

It had been a long time since Arnold had driven in the area and it was difficult to direct Boris. The only place he could think of to head for was Trevor's house. At night all the lanes looked the same and they spent a long time exploring the maze of tunnel-like roads, and at one point he was sure they drove past the Keep again. Finally they reached a crossroads he was familiar with. Arnold saw a white sign for Corsham in one direction and North Wraxall in the other, so they followed the sign to Corsham. He began to see the faint orange glow of street lamps in the sky ahead and sure enough, pulling up at a junction, they found themselves at the A4 just west of Chippenham. Turning right Arnold saw Trevor's house just after Pickwick Lane and they pulled into the driveway. There were no lights on, understandably, as it was after three in the morning. They got out of the car and Arnold pulled the old metal door bell a few times and heard it sounding familiarly inside the depths of the house. After several minutes a light came on upstairs. He heard Trevor shuffling down the stairs and approaching the door. It opened and Trevor stood there, bleary eyed in his pyjamas with his nightcap on. When he saw Arnold he exclaimed irritably:

'Arnold, good God! What brings you here at this hour? And who the devil's this?'

He ushered them inside the living room where they sat down. Trevor continued:

'Have you only just got back from Hamburg? My word, you were there a while. Why isn't your blasted phone working? I've been ringing it for the past few weeks. The damn thing isn't responding at all. Never did get on with them, mobiles. Can't see what all the fuss is about. People don't answer when you do ring them. And I thought the point was, to be able to reach people, what?'

Arnold introduced Boris and explained as best he could what had happened since he'd gone to Hamburg. After he'd described Pete's state of mind and the conditions at the Keep, Trevor offered them both a brandy and said:

'Of course, it doesn't surprise me. The chap's been going off the rails for months. Ever since he began staying out there, around March time, when you were in hospital. I noticed him looking at me strangely whenever I bumped into him. You want to be careful it doesn't happen to you. Living in the middle of nowhere has its disadvantages, you know.'

He noticed the metal bracelet on Arnold's wrist:

'And what's that? A manacle? Don't tell me he's been keeping you chained up out there?'

'That's exactly right. He's been a prisoner in his own house,' affirmed Boris.

'Boris snapped it off with some bolt cutters,' added Arnold. 'That's why we're here. I'm sorry it's so late ...' finished Arnold, and he took a large sip of his brandy.

A moment's silence followed and they all began to speak at once. Arnold said:

'I don't want to call the police.'

Boris said:

'I think we should call the police.'

And Trevor said:

'What the devil is the time?' But he caught the word 'police' being mentioned by the other two, and offered:

'Do you think he's dangerous? Pete, I mean? He's obviously as mad as a brush.'

'Probably not,' said Arnold, 'he's only got an air rifle.'

'That's mine!' exclaimed Trevor. 'Bloody lunatic asked me if he could borrow it for a while. Had a rabbit problem. At the time I couldn't see why not.'

'I saw several knives there,' Arnold added. 'But I don't believe he'd harm anyone. He's not like that.'

'Oh, come on, Arnold,' Trevor disagreed. 'You're not suffering from that Stockholm thingy, syndrome, are you? Defending your captor. It's a well-known phenomenon, I've read about it. Happens all the time to hostages.'

'No. I'm not,' protested Arnold. 'I'm just sure it's not in his nature to be violent.'

'And how do you know that's all he's got up there? Weapons-wise?' continued Trevor. 'That's all you saw. Doesn't mean he hasn't got an arsenal stashed away, out of sight. Machine guns, grenades, and the like.'

Boris agreed with this:

'He's right, Arnold. You cannot be too sure. It's definitely a matter for the police.'

'No, no. I don't want them involved. Not yet anyway.'

He had visions of Pete being dragged off in a police van and put somewhere in a cell to be assessed and sent to jail, or hospital. He added:

'Look, he's had plenty of opportunity to harm me if he'd wanted to. And he hasn't.'

'Oh, I see,' quipped Trevor, 'all he's done is kept you prisoner for a while. Locked up in chains. Nothing really.'

There was a pause as they all sipped their brandies. He wanted to ask Trevor about the bell he thought he'd heard when they were getting away:

'Just now, as we were running towards the car, I heard the sound of a bell, coming from the Keep? It sounded like one of the St. Tobias's bells.'

'Really?' Trevor looked mystified for a moment, then said:

'You know what? He could have managed to get one of them installed in the tower. I do remember my builder friend taking them out there one day, months ago. I knew you wanted them so I asked him to pick them up once the Diocese got in touch. Pete must have talked him into helping him install it. Clever blighter. No room for both bells, of course. Way too small.'

Arnold gathered his thoughts and with as much conviction as he could muster, said:

'At the moment I just need to sleep. I'm feeling very tired. Perhaps we can discuss it in the morning?'

He looked at Boris and then at Trevor, and they both acquiesced. Trevor said:

'If that's what you want, old chap. No problem-o. Leave it till the 'morrow. You can have your old room back. Still made up. And Boris? Follow me, please.'

Trevor led the way as they trooped up the stairs. He took Boris down the corridor past the bathroom to another of his bedrooms. Arnold crawled into his old bed and realised he still had the manacle and chain on his left wrist, but it was far too late to do anything about it. The brandy had made his head swim and he allowed himself to be swallowed up in its warmth and flushed towards a vortex where the bell was still chiming.

They gathered in the morning for some breakfast and after removing Arnold's bracelet and chain using a hacksaw, some pliers and a good deal of effort, they discussed what should be done. Trevor began:

'Now look, Arnold, I totally understand your aversion to the police. I realise Pete's been a great help while you were in hospital and all that. But the fact remains; he's been keeping you locked up. Against your will. And you can't do that. It's a criminal offence.'

Arnold was quick to respond:

'But I came to no harm. And I'm sure he meant me none. I've no idea why he's behaving like this, but going to the police is wrong. I think it would be a mistake.'

Boris suggested:

'OK. So why don't we all go there now and have a look? If there's a problem, I can easily call the police on my *handy* ... my cell phone.'

They agreed this was a good idea and went in convoy, so Trevor led the way in his old Rover with Boris and Arnold following in the BMW. They parked a little way down the road and approached the Keep on foot. As they climbed the steps to the front door Arnold thought he noticed something different about the place. He realised the tent was gone and could see the remains of the chain he'd been attached to hanging down outside from the letterbox. He noticed Boris had a stout piece of wood in one hand, presumably to be used as a weapon if need be. He reached the front door and knocked loudly. They waited for something to happen but in the silence all that could be heard was the gentle chattering of birds and the breeze moving branches in the trees. He knocked again. Still there was no sound from within. The door was locked but Trevor had brought Arnold's keys with him. He stepped back and Boris opened the door slowly. It creaked noisily on its hinges. The place seemed to be empty apart from the pelts hanging on the walls. Arnold noticed Trevor's air rifle lying on the table. They carefully looked around but there was no sign of Pete.

'Well, old chap,' said Trevor, 'looks like the bird has flown.'

Arnold suggested they have a cup of tea and put the kettle on, saying:

'I must say I'm relieved.'

'He's obviously smarter than I gave him credit for,' added Trevor.

While they were drinking their tea, Arnold recalled the last conversation he'd had with Pete:

'I've just remembered something. Yesterday evening I told him I hadn't slept well and he asked me if I'd had any visitors. In the night. I wonder if he'd heard you come by the night before?'

'It makes sense,' Boris agreed. 'He was very suspicious when I met him.'

'That would explain why he's taken off,' Trevor added. 'Probably heard you two leaving last night. Started ringing the bell, then scarpered. Didn't want to be around when you came back with the law.'

Arnold was glad Pete had gone. He really didn't want him to be subjected to any imprisonment or psychological assessments. He'd heard about people being sectioned because their way of thinking didn't fall into line with that of the status quo. The reasoning was they could then be looked after and wouldn't pose a threat to society. The only threat Pete represented to society was that he suggested an alternative way of looking at things, and Arnold understood some people would see that as dangerous and threatening. He hoped Pete was all right, wherever he was.

After finishing their tea, they made a thorough search of the place and concluded Pete had indeed left for good as he'd taken all his things. As the reality of this settled in his mind, Arnold couldn't help feeling sad. Over the previous year he'd grown very fond of Pete. He couldn't help feeling an empty space had opened up in his life. Perhaps Trevor had been right, and he was displaying the Stockholm syndrome. Trevor and Boris offered to help him tidy the place and restore it to the way he'd had it before his accident. Boris was in no hurry to return to Hamburg and Trevor offered to put them both up.

Arnold was relieved to be staying in Corsham again. Over the next few days the three of them took the pelts down and slowly the smell began to leave the Keep. About a week later, he thought it was time he got a new car. Boris ferried him in and out of Bath and within two weeks his life bore a resemblance to how it had been before. He took Boris on the open top bus tour round Bath, which he'd never done before. Boris said he couldn't really see a sex club being tolerated there. After spending a few days looking round the Roman Baths and the Abbey, he said he needed to get back to Hamburg. Arnold wanted to see Rosa's headstone so went with him. It looked perfect when he saw it. It made him realise he'd reached closure there, and he saw no reason to linger. Once again, he found himself at Hamburg airport giving Boris a hug, saying goodbye.

'Dear, dear Boris. Thank you for everything. All your help. And your friendship, I've really appreciated it,' he said.

'Ach, it was a pleasure. And an honour to have known your auntie. Please keep in touch. And come back to Hamburg soon.'

As Arnold walked through to the departure gate he had real tears in his eyes, and he hoped no fresh dramas awaited him at home.

CHAPTER 46

Arnold became very industrious on returning from Hamburg, but kept in mind what Trevor had said. He took to visiting Corsham regularly and spent time at the library improving his knowledge. He kept a notebook in which to write down anything significant he could check on later. He could have done all this on his laptop at home, but judged the necessity of driving into Corsham was part of the process of avoiding isolation. He rediscovered the mere and enjoyed sitting back in his favourite spot watching the comings and goings of the ducks, and took to eating at the Jaipur regularly. Sometimes he would go there with Trevor and sometimes alone, but he enjoyed both experiences equally. His afternoons were dedicated to the vegetable patch where he would think over everything and nothing in silence. August came and went, as did September, and in the middle of October a letter dropped through his letterbox with a familiar handwriting mixing capitals and lower case on the envelope. He opened it with curiosity and found a letter from Pete inside:

Hello Arnold,

I thought it was about time I wrote to you. I saw you leave that night with the foreigner who came to the door looking for you and the only thing I could think of was to ring the bell. (I forgot to tell you I put it in while you were poorly. I knew you always wanted one of those from the church?) I thought it was better for me if I slipped away. The last thing I wanted was to be locked up somewhere. They'd want to rehabilitate me, even though I don't think I'm in need of it meself. I realise now it weren't right what I did to you with the manacle and chain and all. First I went to London. I thought as you'd probably put the police on to me it would be easier to avoid being caught in a big place with loads of people about. I walked up to the motorway that night and hitched a ride with a lorry heading east. The driver were a kind man and he bought me a big breakfast in a services we stopped at. He were heading right through London and I got dropped off slap bang in the centre at a place called Marble Arch, do you know of it? There were a big park, called Hyde Park, right next door and I fancied sitting for a while and getting some rest. I slept all day in the sunshine under a big tree and no one bothered me at all. I walked to the edge of the park and found a right nice area with loads of foreigners, tourists and Arabs and the like. It were called Queensway, have you been there? People seemed friendly enough and I sat in a caff and watched them going by for a good few hour. There were lots of foreign food there, and it were good and cheap too so I was happy enough. After the sun went down I thought to go back to the park to sleep but all the gates were closed and I had to look around for somewhere to kip down. Well, I found a perfect little spot on a side street *opposite the park. There were a recess in a garden wall just the right size for me to put down my sleeping bag. I stayed round there for a couple of weeks in the end. What with the park right across the road it were like being on holiday. The man who had the caff I went to gave me some shifts washing up when he were busy, which were mostly at the weekends. I have to say though, after a while I started to get bored. As you know I like to do things with me hands, and I felt idle just washing up there in London. It were very busy with people all the time, in fact Queensway hardly ever shuts down except for a few hours at night, but I missed having time to meself. So one day I got it in me head to go to Wales and that's where I am now.*

I want to tell you how grateful I am for everything you done for me. You showed me just how kind a person you are and you started me wanting to know about things. Up till I met you I was happy accepting what happened to me as if it were already written down and couldn't be changed at all. Now I know life's different to that. If you've half a mind you can get stuck in and make some decisions for yourself. Like you've done, Arnold. It were great living out at the Keep with you. So I'm sorry for what happened in the end and I hope you can forgive me.

I'm keeping a low profile in Wales. I don't understand why the English give the Welsh people such a hard time as they seem OK to me. They're very kind and quiet, and to a person polite and respectful. First of all I went to the Gower peninsula and camped on the beach for a bit. Do you know it? There were loads of fishermen about so it were easy enough to live. I could keep clean, what with the sea, and if I was lucky I could help out in the local campsites for a few bob as well. Towards the end of August I went further west and found a lovely spot, an island off Tenby, with a monastery on it with monks and all, and I stayed there a few days till the monks noticed me tent and turfed me off. Now I'm in Pembrokeshire and it's great here. Nobody bothers me and I don't bother them. I'm camped in the dunes in a dip so I'm sheltered from the wind. The nearest town is a good five mile away, which is close enough for me. There's a whole bit of the beach covered in shells and when I walk through them I sometimes see one that's interesting and pick it up to have a look. Although a lot of them look the same they're all different up close, rather like human beings, I suppose. If you put them up to your ear they all make a different sound, like words do, and it makes me wonder if I could write a book one day, made of shells. Perhaps I'll write a book about you. I been thinking a lot about you Arnold, and I think what you need is a lady companion. I hope you don't mind me saying that.

Have you ever thought how long it takes to make sand? I knows it's made from rocks and shells and the like, that have been broken down by the weather, but how long must it take to do that? And what about before there were any sand? What was there then? I like to walk along the beach first thing in the mornings and at the end of the day. In the morning the sea looks fresh and clean. And when the sun's going down over the *sea it shines through the waves as they rise up, coming in, and I play 'spot the fish' with meself. You'd be surprised at how many you can see if you concentrate.*

I often wonder what it must be like the first time you see the sea. If you suddenly came to it and you didn't know it were there like. You'd probably think it was some big boiling load of hot water, and you'd be scared to go anywhere near it. What with the noise and all.

I got terrible toothache about two weeks ago and walked into town to find a dentist. It were a few mile, but not too far. There were just the one there, and he was so kind to me. He prodded about a bit to find out where it hurt, and told me I still had me wisdom teeth! (I thought I'd had them all out when I were a nipper.) Apparently they're still under the gums and they don't like to disturb them unless they get infected as there's the nerves for the lips and the tongue down there. I told him I had no money and he said not to worry. He gave me some pills for free, antibiotic I think they were, and told me to come back to see him if the pain didn't go away, which it has done. I can't get over how kind he was. The towns here are just like everywhere else. Fences and walls everywhere, and signs saying Private. Keep out. What they don't realise, the people what puts the signs up, is that the walls and fences are making little prisons for them all, keeping them confined inside. Maybe that's what everyone normal wants to be, confined. And safe. Safe as houses.

You'd like it here, Arnold. There's no litter anywhere.

Love from Pete

He put Pete's letter down and was compelled to find and hold Rosa's music box again. He collected it from next to his bed and went to sit with it outside his front door. Carefully winding the key several turns he opened it up to hear the tune gaily issuing from it. He was relieved it was still working and hadn't needed to be repaired. Somehow he interpreted it as a sign of approval from Rosa, that all was in order. That the box was in its rightful place. He realised if he hadn't been forced to leave St. Tobias's he would never have discovered the existence of his Uncle Red, and would never have met Rosa. Or Boris. Or Pete. It made him aware of the significance of all the small things he'd done, that they all had consequences, some good and some bad.

He felt happier now he knew Pete was well and repentant about what he'd done. Of course Arnold had forgiven him. It felt good to be vindicated in his assessment of character. Pete was a gentle soul with no mind to cause anyone trouble. The tone in his letter put Arnold in mind of the way Pete had been when they'd first met, which he thought was encouraging. Sadly he just didn't fit in with modern life. And Arnold realised in many ways he didn't fit in either.

The letter made him consider all that had happened in the two years since he'd left the church. He'd been totally unprepared for civilisation when he'd moved from his cottage. Having been confined within the church all those years he'd been protected from the chaos he'd experienced since leaving it behind. Pete, with his naïve oddball philosophy, was right. You could make things happen without God's help. Arnold began to see life was like a turbulent sea, turning and twisting, with no apparent pattern or logic to its movement. You just had to try to stay above the surface and make sense of it all if possible. Sometimes you would experience some good feeling about something you did, or someone you met, and these moments were to be cherished. But they were never meant to last. Arnold was convinced of that. It made those moments all the more special, and valuable. And human. He thought it was probably why sadness had become such a large part of people's lives. As they got older they were made more and more aware of the frailty and transience of happiness, and the inevitability of change and destruction. The tune slowed down and stopped in mid stanza, and at that moment, Arnold felt he was in touch with everyone dear to him, and continued to sit cradling the box in his lap, staring out over the valley.

Trevor taught Arnold how to play chess. They took to playing regularly at Trevor's house but it had to be dovetailed into the cricket schedule on television. There always seemed to be a match going on somewhere in the world, starting either in the middle of the night or in the late afternoon. And of course, Trevor had to watch all of it. England experienced an Indian summer that year and Arnold began to smell once again the pine oil of the original panelling within the Keep, and realised the acrid smell of the rabbit pelts had completely disappeared. There were severe thunderstorms too, waking him up in the night with the ferocious and deafening sound of rain hitting the metal walls. He liked the way the noise gradually disappeared as the storm passed by and he would fall back to sleep.

Throughout the autumn he constructed a balanced life for himself, carefully mixing human contact with solitude. He took out Rosa's music box in the evenings and sat by his open front door listening to the tune play and tried to empty his mind of everything while the sun went down. Hermione came by for tea on a trip to Corsham and was keen to find out everything that had happened that year, and after he'd finished telling her she said:

'My dear Arnold, you have such an intriguing life. Things just seem to happen to you, don't they?'

Christmas approached and he accepted Trevor's invitation to spend it in Corsham. Trevor made him stay several days and he learnt how to stuff and roast a turkey. He watched most of a five day Test match and it dawned on him what a thoroughly engrossing game cricket was, once you understood what was going on. The Jaipur was open throughout Christmas and he started methodically working his way through their menu. The staff began to recognise him as he would go there so often, sometimes several times a week. They told him about their new chef, who was keen on feedback from the diners, and he prided himself in making notes about every dish he ordered, and the waiters would take these notes back for the chef to read. He was always honest about the food but there were few things he didn't like. The waiters paid him special attention and took to giving him the same table when he came in. He would sit facing the wall even when alone, partly to concentrate on the tastes which he would close his eyes to appreciate, as if he were blind, and partly to avoid being recognised and disturbed by any of the other diners, who may have been former members of his congregation. It took him about six weeks to work through the menu and when he'd finished the final meal and paid his bill he pointed this out to the waiters, who said:

'Chef says please to tell us when you can come back next time. Chef has extra special dishes for you to try. Just for you. Not on menu.'

Arnold was excited and readily accepted an invitation to come back as their guest the following weekend. He spent the next few days looking forward to what the meal would be and did some research into Indian food and curries at the library. His favourite combination had become Chicken Tikka Masala, with Palak Badami and white rice. Not only was it very tasty but he liked the way the colours sat together on the plate.

The evening arrived for the special invitation dinner and something made him put on his best jacket and shirt as if it were a celebration of some kind. He was thinking of inviting Trevor along but thought better of it, as he was their guest and decorum didn't permit him bringing someone else. He thought he might finally get to meet the chef. Perhaps he'd come out from the kitchen and eat with him at his table.

Arnold drove into Corsham and impulsively made a point of passing St. Tobias's to see if he could detect any recent activity, but it looked the same as always. He hadn't been past for several months and no one had yet got round to developing it. The way the economy was headed he couldn't see how that was likely to change in the foreseeable future. He parked up outside the Jaipur and went inside to be shown to his usual table. It was early, soon after six, and he was the only customer. His thoughts were now filled with St. Tobias's, wondering if it was to remain an empty shell where religion had once been practised, a relic of an earlier time when God's presence had made more of an impact on life.

The waiters fussed over him as they prepared the table, placing metal trays with candles in them to keep the dishes warm, and fetched him a glass of Cobra beer and some poppadoms, which he always liked with some lime pickle before his meal. One by one they appeared and hovered like moths, saying:

'Good evening, sir.'

'Very good to see you, sir.'

'Special meal tonight. Just for you.'

'Chef's special. Very good.'

He seemed to have the entire staff attending to him that evening, putting their heads over his shoulder one by one to welcome him. Then the dishes appeared and he was astounded by their variety. There were traces and suggestions of flavours he couldn't put names to, but were instantly familiar. He'd never had an Indian meal quite like this one. Every plate of food was just the right size, big enough to get used to the taste but not big enough to become overpowering. He had no time to ask what was what, as the procession was constant, and he lost count of the number of different dishes he tried. After about an hour he had to stop eating due to a lack of any more space in his tummy and he sat back in his chair completely full up. One of the waiters came up and said:

'Now chef come out, sir. Want to meet you. One moment please.'

He was just entering that phase after a meal when contentment and relaxation blend together, keeping each other company, when he felt someone standing behind him, and two hands gently covered his eyes. A faint perfume reached him, a mixture of lemons and almonds, stirring feelings that had lain dormant for a long time, which he thought he remembered from the Mercouri vineyard.

'Hello, Arnold. Long time no see.'

Lucy Cartwright came around the table and sat opposite him wearing dungarees and a chef's apron, saying softly with a chuckle:

'Bet you didn't think there'd ever be a white female chef at the Jaipur, now did you? Ha ha ha!'

He experienced a whole gamut of emotions just then and all he could think of to say was:

'Lucy ... it's you. Lucy.'

Looking into her laughing green eyes once again he became lost and found at the same time, and sensed he'd come home, and maybe everything would finally slot into place.

SUBSCRIBERS

Unbound is a new kind of publishing house. Our books are funded directly by readers. This was a very popular idea during the late eighteenth and early nineteenth centuries. Now we have revived it for the internet age. It allows authors to write the books they really want to write and readers to support the writing they would most like to see published.

The names listed below are of readers who have pledged their support and made this book happen. If you'd like to join them, visit: www.unbound.co.uk.

Geoff Adams
Jackie Akehurst
Rich Bailey
Helen Bates
Valéry Blue
William Bonwitt
Anatoly Boshkin
David Boyd
Robert Branick
Christian Brett
Adam Broadway
Xander Cansell
Vicki & Alan Cattermoul

Belinda Cauwood
Steven Chapman
Juan Christian
John Cochrane
Richard Collett
Allister Combe
Grant Curley
Martyn Davies
Paul Davies
Colin Davis
Nick Davis
David Deeson
Jim Dorman

Scott Douglas
Lawrence T Doyle
Robert Eardley
John Lewis Eaton
Andreas W. Eisenberger
Nigel Evans
Isobel Frankish
Fred
Mark Gamble
Alex Glanville
Salena Godden
Andrew (Bug) Gregory
John A Groat
Rotem Hakim
Geoff Hampson
Paul Harbour
Roshone Harmon
Robert Hermsen
Loraine Heywood
Bryan Hopson
Christopher Hornby
Marc Hughes
Nick Hughes
Jane Hunt
Jon Hunt
Darran Hurst
Jonathan Jackson
Monika Jatautaite
David Jolley
Gail Jones
Kev Jones

Arthur Kalkbrenner
Theresa Kavanagh
Rachael Kerr
David Kidd
Richard Lacey
Phil Laferla
Andrew Lay
Jimmy Leach
Barry Leedham
The Luncheon Club Quo
    Vadis
Shaun Lunnon
G. J. Lutz
Stewart Mcallister
Alex McCulloch
Ian Macdonald
Donald MacKay
Val MacLeish
Karen Mcleod
John Macmenemey
Alan McNiven
Paul Madden
Roger Miles
John Mitchinson
Gary Morris
David Morton
Jochen Mosthaf
Steve Munro
Geoffrey Newcomb
Michael O'Cain
Mark Oliff

Tsuyoshi Oyama
Christopher Painter
Dave Parker
Matthew Parry
Gordon Pollard
Justin Pollard
David Pope
Christina Puplett
Marc Quataert
James Radley
Jill Richards
Frank Roper
Gavin Russell
Roy Russell
Mark Seton
Stephen Shaw
Howard Silverstone

Lisa Skeggs
Mo Skeggs
Simon Skeggs
Annetta Slade
Richard Stephens
Richard Stubbs
Tony Stubley
Andy Swallow
Dave Taylor
Marc Thorner
Frederic Tourlouse
Paul Van Acker
Gill Walker
Steve Walker
Claire Whelan
Andy Wray

A NOTE ABOUT THE TYPEFACE

The body of this book is set in the Sorts Mill Goudy typeface, created by designer Barry Schwartz (b. 1961).

It is a revival of the Goudy Old Style typeface, originally created by Frederic W. Goudy (1865–1947) in 1915 for American Type Founders, the dominant American manufacturer of metal type from the late nineteenth century up until the middle of the twentieth.

Goudy himself did not train as a designer of type until he reached his forties, when he decided to quit his job keeping the books of a Chicago estate agent and retrain. Over the following 36 years, Goudy would become feverishly prolific, creating 113 fonts – more usable typefaces than some of the world's most revered type creators and punch cutters.

The 'ou' of Goudy is pronounced in the same way as the 'ou' in *out*, *pout* and *gout*.